Robert Silverberg was born in Ne͏ [...]
first novel while still a student a [...]
has been a full-time writer since g͏ [...]
more than fifty novels, as well as [...]
archaeology, and has been nomina͏ [...]
fiction than any other science-fiction writer. He recently won
the 1990 Hugo Award for Best Short Story. He and his wife
live in the San Francisco area.

By the same author (in Grafton)

Face of the Waters

The Collected Stories of Robert Silverberg

Volume One: Pluto in the Morning Light

Grafton
An Imprint of HarperCollins*Publishers*

Grafton
An Imprint of HarperCollins*Publishers*
77–85 Fulham Palace Road,
Hammersmith, London W6 8JB

This edition published by Grafton 1992
9 8 7 6 5 4 3 2 1

A catalogue record for this book
is available from the British Library

ISBN 0 586 21369 4

Set in Times

Printed in Great Britain by
HarperCollinsManufacturing Glasgow

For *Ellen Datlow*
Byron Preiss
Shawna McCarthy
Don Myrus
Marta Randall
Jessica Amanda Salmonson
George Scithers
and – especially – *Alice K. Turner*

Acknowledgements

'Blindsight', 'Symbiont', 'Snake and Ocean, Ocean and Snake' and 'Tourist Trade' first appeared in *Playboy*.

'Amanda and the Alien', 'Hannibal's Elephants', 'Multiples', 'Against Babylon' and 'Hardware' first appeared in *Omni*.

'Basileus' first appeared in *The Best of Omni*.

'Homefaring' was first published as a limited-edition volume by Phantasia Press.

'Sailing to Byzantium' was first published as limited-edition volumes by Underwood-Miller.

'Gate of Horn, Gate of Ivory' first appeared in *Universe*.

'Sunrise on Pluto' first appeared in *The Planets*.

'Dancers in the Time-flux' first appeared in *Heroic Visions*.

Contents

Introduction

Since the beginning of my writing career, almost forty years ago, I've always written both novels and short stories. My first professional sale was a short story and the second was a novel, or perhaps it was the other way around. The rhythm of my writing life was established right at the beginning: a few short stories, then a novel, then some more short stories, and then another book. I never thought twice, or even once, about whether I was primarily a short-story writer or a novelist. I was a writer, period. I've always written at whatever length seemed appropriate to the story at hand; and, because I have always been a writer by trade rather than one who follows the ebb and flow of inspiration, I've also written according to the needs of the marketplace. When it was novel-writing time, I wrote novels. When editors wanted short stories from me, I wrote short stories.

It isn't that way with all writers. Some are distinctly novelists, and some are not. Ray Bradbury has written a couple of novels, but he's basically a short-story writer. The same is true of Harlan Ellison. On the other hand, John le Carré and John Fowles may have written short stories at some time in their lives, but I haven't seen them, if they exist. (Fowles occasionally writes novellas, at least.) Robert A. Heinlein wrote few, if any, short stories after the first dozen years of his career. Hemingway's lifetime output of short stories was enough to fill one good-sized volume, but he too wrote most of them in his first dozen years.

I could make long lists of writers who are basically one thing or the other, but not both. On one hand are the novelists for whom short stories, after their early years of writing, are rare or non-existent events. In science fiction and fantasy the names of Frank Herbert, E.E. Smith, Jack Vance, Stephen Donaldson, and Andre Norton come quickly to mind; outside it, those

9

of Graham Greene, Evelyn Waugh, William Golding, John Steinbeck, Norman Mailer. And then there are the short-story writers whose ventures into longer lengths are just as uncommon: Theodore Sturgeon, Clark Ashton Smith, William Tenn, and Damon Knight; Edgar Allan Poe, John Collier, William Trevor, and Mavis Gallant.

Certainly temperament has something to do with this. Some writers feel impossibly cramped within the rigid confines of the short story: they need hundreds of thousands of words to move around in. Others see the novel as a vast and interminable journey that they would rather not undertake, and prefer the quick, incisive thrust of the short story. But then there are those who are masters of both forms and choose in the second half of their careers to work in only one, usually the novel, like Hemingway or Heinlein; surely the author of 'The Snows of Kilimanjaro' and 'Capital of the World' still knew how to write short stories after 1940, and the author of 'Requiem' and 'The Green Hills of Earth' did not mysteriously lose his ability at the short lengths around 1949; but *For Whom the Bell Tolls* and *Stranger in a Strange Land* were matters of higher priority and the short stories ceased. It's harder to cite writers who gave up novels after an early start to concentrate only on the short story: Paul Bowles, perhaps, or Truman Capote.

In today's science-fiction field, very few of the well-established writers bother much about short fiction, and even the newcomers tend to move on as quickly as they can to immense trilogies. There's a simple economic reason for this. Checking the most recent volume – 1988 – of the encyclopedic yearbook of science fiction and fantasy compiled by Charles N. Brown and William G. Contento, I discover that 317 original s-f novels and 264 fantasy novels were published in the United States in 1988, up from 298 and 256, respectively, the previous year. The five professional science-fiction magazines in 1988 managed to put out a total of just forty-nine issues. If they averaged six short stories an issue, that would be a grand total of 294 published during the entire year. (Plus, let's say, 150 more in the various book-format anthologies devoted to original s-f stories, and in the slick magazines like *Playboy* and *Omni*.)

That means that for each short science-fiction story published in 1988 (for which the author might have received anywhere from $150 or so up to a maximum of $5,000 in a very few cases), there were 1.3 s-f or fantasy novels published (and for novels the pay begins at about $2,500 and goes up into the stratosphere). The arithmetic, for the professional writer, is unanswerable. Writing short stories doesn't make much sense financially. If you write them today you have to want to write them for their own sake. The pay is almost incidental: you do them for love.

Or, in my case, because you really can't stop yourself.

When I was starting as a writer in the 1950s things worked the other way around. Unless your name was Heinlein or Asimov, you didn't think much about getting books published. If you wrote for a living, you wrote short stories and novelettes for the magazines, just as quickly as you could. The magazines would pay you anywhere from one to three cents a word: a 5,000-word story therefore would bring you $50 to $150, before such things as your agent's commission and the exactions of the Internal Revenue Service were figured in. It wasn't much, but at least the market was big – fifteen or twenty different magazines, most years, many of them published every month – and if you worked fast enough, under a variety of pseudonyms so that the readers didn't weary of your name, you might hope to earn $15,000 a year or so, not a bad livelihood back then, when rent on a fine apartment in New York City was $150 a month and dinner for two at a de-luxe restaurant cost no more than $25, wine included.

To do that, though, you had to write and sell a short story to some magazine or other a couple of times a week, every week of the year – a constant, unending stream of publishable material. You needed not only to be capable of generating story concepts at will but to be cognizant at all times of each magazine's buying status – which one was in desperate need of copy, which one was currently overstocked, which one was overstocked on *your* stuff and didn't want to look at any more just now. It was an insane way to live and an almost impossible thing to succeed at; but those of us who chose to live that way and who did actually succeed at it usually didn't realize it couldn't be done, and so we just went ahead and did it.

Coming up with two or three worthwhile story ideas a week – especially in a field like science fiction, where you invented some new world or even a universe every time out – was a formidable proposition. Now and then you might be able to stretch an idea to 15,000 or 20,000 words and sell it for $500 or so, which gave you a little time to breathe between manuscripts. A rejection, of course, was a catastrophe. (But there were so many magazines that a capable writer could usually count on selling his stories *somewhere*, possibly on the fifth or sixth attempt.) Writing books, for which one major idea would suffice if you could devise enough subsidiary themes to keep the story going for 60,000 words or thereabouts, was one way off the treadmill. But the market for novels was an extremely slender one – just three publishers, as of the late 1950s, buying perhaps fifty or sixty books a year, most of them from old-line writers recycling their magazine serials of the 1940s. If he could break into the charmed circle a beginner might actually be able to sell a book or two a year, at $1,000 or $1,500 each, but it took weeks to write one and there was always the ghastly possibility that none of the three markets would want to buy it.

It was, in other words, a tough time to be a science-fiction writer. You had to be very stubborn, very resilient, and very prolific in order to survive. It helped also if you were young, young enough to stay up all night if necessary to knock out a story to meet some editor's sudden request for help, and I was the youngest one in the business those days, not much past twenty, full of crazed vitality and drive of a sort that was already beginning to diminish among the old guys in their thirties who were my rivals for those few places on the contents pages of the magazines, guys like Fred Pohl, Ted Sturgeon, Phil Dick, Bob Sheckley. So I earned a fair living and always paid the rent on time and eventually things got a lot easier for us all. But I never had the luxury of being able to think of myself as a 'novelist' or a 'short-story writer' or any other kind of specialist. I wrote what seemed to make the most sense to write. If Don Wollheim over at Ace Books said he was having trouble that summer finding novels to publish, I wrote a novel for him. If John Campbell at *Astounding Science Fiction* let it slip that he was running short of stories in the 7,500-word range, I would have one for him the following Monday. One doesn't necessarily produce a lot of undying masterpieces that way, but one does, at least, hone one's versatility and command of technique.

Introduction

Today, of course, everything is different. I haven't had to worry about paying next month's rent for a long time, and my novels are contracted for three and four years in advance at prices that would have been beyond all belief when I was starting out. My annual income isn't up there with the earnings of the phenomenal Messrs X, Y and Z, whose books spend weeks at a time at the top of the best-seller lists, but it's lofty enough to seem startling to someone like me who remembers writing stories at a cent a word as fast as he could type. My economic situation is secure, as such things go for writers, and my future earnings are assured for years to come – all from novels. And yet I continue to write two, three, even four short stories a year, and the occasional novella of 25,000 words or so. Why? Certainly not for the money. Even though a magazine like *Omni* or *Playboy* will pay me considerably more for a short story than I used to earn from a novel thirty years ago, I'd still be better off putting in the time on a book. Short stories are bothersome things to write, at least for me. They can't be turned out in joyous breathless bursts. Instead I have to carve them out of recalcitrant rock, chipping away constantly at extraneous material that conceals or deforms the ideal shape of the material. Usually I need to do two or three drafts before submission to get them properly into focus and sometimes (as you'll see from the introductions to some of the stories in this book) I have to do another couple of rounds of revision after the editor has had a chance to read it. Even at today's elevated story prices I'm earning a very routine wage indeed by the time the job is done.

But sometimes, even for the professional, more than just the money is involved.

This discussion so far has concentrated almost entirely on the production side of writing. I haven't said a word about art; I might just as well have been talking about manufacturing bookcases, or raising potatoes, or some other useful and straightforward activity in which the muses aren't generally considered to be involved. I've made it more than clear that writing is my business: that I am in the profession of producing verbal objects which I place on sale to the highest bidder. I chose from the outset to make writing my sole means of support, and so I have always worked hard, produced my verbal objects at a steady pace, and taken care to be paid, and well, for my labour.

Well, I know Samuel Johnson's famous line, 'No man but a blockhead ever wrote except for money,' and I can certainly see the point of it, especially on the days when there's blood on the computer keys after I've finished working. All the same, writing fiction *is* different from manufacturing bookcases or raising potatoes. The muses *are* involved, however much the writer wants to think of himself as nothing more than a hard-nosed businessman. And a lifetime devoted exclusively to maximizing one's income per word seems to me like a pretty stultifying affair. Money's a useful thing and you won't hear me say a word against it. But a writer who's totally money-oriented – who writes the same thing over and over, for example, or who writes things that he despises, or who writes with only a fraction of his skill because he thinks his readers are simple-minded, or who writes about things that don't interest him because that's where the money is – is a writer who over the years will dry out from within, whose spirit will corrode and decay, who will sooner or later find himself embittered and hollow, trapped in an anger he can barely understand.

I've done my share of writing purely for money, when circumstances made that necessary. And I'm not one to write purely for the love of the art – sonnet sequences, let's say, that I stash away in the secret recesses of my desk. I write for publication and for pay, not for private pleasure. But I try to guard myself against the death of the soul that comes from making money the be-all and end-all of my days.

Novels are more lucrative to write than short stories, and, for me at least, they're easier to do, page for page. Nevertheless, although novel-writing is my main line of work and my chief source of income (and a considerable source of pride and pleasure, when things go the right way) I do continue to do short stories, however much sweat and pain they may cost me, because of the challenge that they represent and because I don't care to exempt myself from the harsh discipline of creating something that's complete in twenty or thirty pages. (Or sometimes eighty or ninety, in the case of novellas like 'Sailing to Byzantium'.) I never lose sight of my professionalism even then, and you will see again and again that this story or that in this book was written at the request or suggestion of some editor, rather than out of dire internal compulsion. But a dire internal compulsion is there none the less: the compulsion each year to test myself against the rigorous demands of the shorter forms. It's an exhausting kind of mental exercise that gets harder all the time. I'd just as soon allow myself to give it up altogether – which is why I don't dare stop.

I did in fact stop writing short stories once, in 1973 – the prelude to a total withdrawal from writing, the first and only one of my life, that was to last the next five years. As I noted in the introduction to my previous collection of short stories, *The Conglomeroid Cocktail Party* (1984), my life had taken a troubled turn then and I had grown weary, disheartened, generally sick of everything – especially writing. Putting even more words on paper, concocting still more stories of imaginary and remote times and places, had begun to seem pointless to me. So I gave it up. I thought I was quitting it for ever. As things turned out, 'for ever' lasted until the autumn of 1978, when I began to write the novel *Lord Valentine's Castle*, and by January of 1980 I had begun writing short stories again too. The first products of that return to my métier were assembled in *The Conglomeroid Cocktail Party*. Here is the next instalment: stories written between November 1981 and July 1985.

I've written other short stories since, of course. Some of them will be included in another book like this one that I'll be assembling before long, and the rest too will be collected some day, I hope, along with ones yet to be written or even conceived. If all goes well, I'll be starting on a new story next week. Not because I need to, or even because I especially want to, but because – it sounds very romantic, I guess, though I'm not a very romantic person – because I *have* to. There are plenty of other things I'd rather be doing, I have to admit – tidying up the garden, perhaps, or taking a trip up the coast, or just sitting in the sunshine and giggling quietly to myself. But story first, sunshine afterwards. I won't allow it to be any other way. I can't.

Somehow, for all my pretence of cold-eyed professionalism, all my insistence that writing is simply a job like any other, I've discovered to my surprise and chagrin that there's more than that going on around here, that I write as much out of karmic necessity and some dire inner need constantly to rededicate my own skills to my – what? My craft? My art? My profession? All three, I suspect. The short stories collected here testify to that. I wrote them for money, Dr Johnson. But I could very likely have made even more money if I had spent the time in other ways. Mainly I wrote these stories because I couldn't *not* write them. Does that make me a blockhead, Dr Johnson? Perhaps it does. Perhaps choosing to be a writer in the first place, for whatever reason, is a blockheaded thing to do. Well, so be it. Here is a book of stories. They involved me in a lot of hard work, but for me, at least, the results justify the toil. I'm glad I wrote them, however big a headache some of them caused me at the time. Writing them, it turns out, was important for me, and even pleasurable, in a curiously complex *ex post facto* way. May they give you pleasure now too, of a less complicated kind.

Robert Silverberg
Oakland, California
June, 1990

Homefaring

I had always had a sneaking desire to write the definitive giant-lobster story. Earlier science-fiction writers had pre-empted most of the other appealing monstrosities — including giant aunts (*sic!*), dealt with by Isaac Asimov in his classic story 'Dreamworld', which I have just ruined for ever for you by giving away its punchline — but giant lobsters remained fair game. And when George Scithers, the new editor of the venerable science-fiction magazine *Amazing Stories*, asked me to do a lengthy story for him, I decided that it was time at last for me to give lobsters their due.

The obvious giant-lobster story, in which horrendous pincer-wielding monsters twenty feet long come ashore at Malibu and set about the conquest of Los Angeles by terrorizing the surfers, might work well enough in a cheap Hollywood sci-fi epic but wouldn't stand much chance of delighting a sophisticated science-fiction reader like Scithers. Nor did it have a lot of appeal for me as writer. Therefore, following the advice of one of my early mentors, the brilliant, cantankerous editor Horace Gold, I searched for my story idea by turning the obvious upside-down. Lobsters are pretty nasty things, after all. They're tough, surly, dangerous and ugly — surely the ugliest food-objects ever to be prized by mankind. A creature so disagreeable in so many ways must have some redeeming feature. (Other than the flavour of its meat.) Lobsters are quite intelligent, as crustaceans go. And so, instead of depicting them as the savage and hideous-looking critters they really are, what about putting them through a few hundred million years of evolution and turning them into wise and thoughtful civilized beings — the dominant life-form, in fact, of a vastly altered Earth?

A challenging task, yes. And made even more challenging for me, back there in the otherwise sunny and pleasant November of 1982, by the fact that I had just made the great leap from typewriter to computer. 'Homefaring' marked my initiation into the world of floppy disks and soft hyphens, of back-up copies and automatic pagination. It's all second nature to me by now, of course, but in 1982 it was a brave new world, and a very strange one. Each day's work was an adventure in terror. My words appeared in white letters on a black screen, frighteningly impermanent: one electronic sneeze, I thought, and a whole day's brilliant prose could vanish like a time traveller who has just retroactively defenestrated his own grandfather. The mere making of back-ups didn't lull my fears: how could I be sure that the act of backing up itself wouldn't erase what I had just written? Pushing the button marked SAVE – did that really save anything? Switching the computer off at the end of my working day was like a leap into the abyss. Would the story be there the next morning when I turned the machine on again? Warily I printed out each day's work when it was done, before backing up, saving or otherwise jiggling with it: I wanted to see it safely on to paper first. Sometimes when I put a particularly difficult section together – for example, the three-page scene at the mid-point of the story, beginning with the line, 'The lobsters were singing as they marched' – I would stop right then and there and print it out before proceeding, aware that if the computer somehow were to destroy it I would never be able to reconstruct it at that level of accomplishment. (It's an axiom among writers that material written to replace inadvertently destroyed copy can't possibly equal the lost passage – which gets better and better in one's memory all the time.)

Somehow, in fear and trembling, I tiptoed my way through the entire eighty-eight-page manuscript of 'Homefaring' without any major disasters. The computer made it marvellously easy to revise the story as I went along; instead of typing out an eighty-eight-page first draft, then covering it with alterations and grimly typing the whole thing out again to make it fit to show an editor, I brought every paragraph up to final-draft status with painless little manoeuvres of the cursor. When I realized that I had chosen a confusing name for a minor character, I ordered the computer to correct my error, and sat back in wonder as 'Eitel' became 'Bleier' throughout the story without my having to do a thing. And then at the end came the wondrous moment when I pushed the button marked PRINT and page after page of immaculate typed copy began to come forth while I occupied myself with other and less dreary tasks.

The readers liked the story and it was a finalist in the 1983 Nebula Award voting – perhaps might even have won, if it had been published in a magazine less obscure than dear old *Amazing*, which had only a handful of readers. That same year the veteran connoisseur of science fiction, Donald A. Wollheim, chose it for his annual *World's Best SF* anthology, an honour that particularly pleased me. I had deliberately intended 'Homefaring' as a sleek and modern version of the sort of imagination-stirring tale of wonder that Wollheim had read and cherished in the s-f magazines of his youth, fifty years before, and his choice of the story for his book confirmed my feeling of working within a great tradition.

McCulloch was beginning to moult. The sensation, inescapable and unarguable, horrified him – it felt exactly as though his body was going to split apart, which it was – and yet it was also completely familiar, expected, welcome. Wave after wave of keen and dizzying pain swept through him. Burrowing down deep in the sandy bed, he waved his great claws about, lashed his flat tail against the pure white sand, scratched frantically with quick worried gestures of his eight walking-legs.

He was frightened. He was calm. He had no idea what was about to happen to him. He had done this a hundred times before.

The moulting prodrome had overwhelming power. It blotted from his mind all questions, and, after a moment, all fear. A white line of heat ran down his back – no, down the top of his carapace – from a point just back of his head to the first flaring segments of his tail-fan. He imagined that all the sun's force, concentrated through some giant glass lens, was being inscribed in a single track along his shell. And his soft inner body was straining, squirming, expanding, filling the carapace to overflowing. But still that rigid shell contained him, refusing to yield to the pressure. To McCulloch it was much like being inside a wet-suit that was suddenly five times too small.

– *What is the sun? What is glass? What is a lens? What is a wet-suit?*

The questions swarmed suddenly upwards in his mind like little busy many-legged creatures springing out of the sand. But he had no time for providing answers. The moulting prodrome was developing with astounding swiftness, carrying him along. The strain was becoming intolerable. In another moment he would surely burst. He was writhing in short angular convulsions. Within his claws, his tissues now were shrinking, shrivelling, drawing back within the ferocious shell-hulls, but the rest of him was continuing inexorably to grow larger.

He had to escape from this shell, or it would kill him. He had to expel himself somehow from this impossibly constricting container. Digging his front claws and most of his legs into the sand, he heaved, twisted, stretched, pushed. He thought of himself as being pregnant with himself, struggling fiercely to deliver himself of himself.

Ah. The carapace suddenly began to split.

The crack was only a small one, high up near his shoulders – *shoulders?* – but the imprisoned substance of him surged swiftly towards it, widening and lengthening it, and in another moment the hard horny covering was cracked from end to end. *Ah. Ah.* That felt so good, that release from constraint! Yet McCulloch still had to free himself. Delicately he drew himself backwards withdrawing leg after leg from its covering in a precise, almost fussy way, as though he were pulling his arms from the sleeves of some incredibly ancient and frail garment.

Until he had his huge main claws free, though, he knew he could not extricate himself from the sundered shell. And freeing the claws took extreme care. The front limbs still were shrinking, and the limy joints of the shell seemed to be dissolving and softening, but nevertheless he had to pull each claw through a passage much narrower than itself. It was easy to see how a hasty move might break a limb off altogether.

He centred his attention on the task. It was a little like telling his wrists to make themselves small, so he could slide them out of handcuffs.

– Wrists? Handcuffs? What are those?

McCulloch paid no attention to that baffling inner voice. Easy, easy, there – ah – yes, there, like that! One claw was free. Then the other, slowly, carefully. Done. Both of them retracted. The rest was simple: some shrugging and wiggling, exhausting but not really challenging, and he succeeded in extending the breach in the carapace until he could crawl backwards out of it. Then he lay on the sand beside it, weary, drained, naked, soft, terribly vulnerable. He wanted only to return to the sleep out of which he had emerged into this nightmare of shell-splitting.

But some force within him would not let him slacken off.

20

A moment to rest, only a moment. He looked to his left, towards the discarded shell. Vision was difficult – there were peculiar, incomprehensible refraction effects that broke every image into thousands of tiny fragments – but despite that, and despite the dimness of the light, he was able to see that the shell, golden-hued with broad arrow-shaped red markings, was something like a lobster's, yet even more intricate, even more bizarre. McCulloch did not understand why he had been inhabiting a lobster's shell. Obviously because he was a lobster; but he was not a lobster. That was so, was it not? Yet he was under water. He lay on fine white sand, at a depth so great he could not make out any hint of sunlight overhead. The water was warm, gentle, rich with tiny tasty creatures and with a swirling welter of sensory data that swept across his receptors in bewildering abundance.

He sought to learn more. But there was no further time for resting and thinking now. He was unprotected. Any passing enemy could destroy him while he was like this. Up, up, seek a hiding-place: that was the requirement of the moment.

First, though, he paused to devour his old shell. That too seemed to be the requirement of the moment; so he fell upon it with determination, seizing it with his clumsy-looking but curiously versatile front claws, drawing it toward his busy, efficient mandibles. When that was accomplished – no doubt to recycle the lime it contained, which he needed for the growth of his new shell – he forced himself up and began a slow scuttle, somehow knowing that the direction he had taken was the right one.

Soon came the vibrations of something large and solid against his sensors – a wall, a stone mass rising before him – and then, as he continued, he made out with his foggy vision the sloping flank of a dark broad cliff rising vertically from the ocean floor. Festoons of thick, swaying red and yellow water plants clung to it, and a dense stippling of rubbery-looking finger-shaped sponges, and a crawling, gaping, slithering host of crabs and molluscs and worms, which vastly stirred McCulloch's appetite. But this was not a time to pause to eat, lest he be eaten. Two enormous green anemones yawned nearby, ruffling their voluptuous membranes seductively, hopefully. A dark shape passed overhead, huge, tubular, tentacular, menacing. Ignoring the thronging populations of the rock, McCulloch picked his way over and around them until he came to the small cave, the McCulloch-sized cave, that was his goal.

Gingerly he backed through its narrow mouth, knowing there would be no room for turning around once he was inside. He filled the opening nicely, with a little space left over. Taking up a position just within the entrance, he blocked the cave-mouth with his claws. No enemy could enter now. Naked though he was, he would be safe during his vulnerable period.

For the first time since his agonizing awakening, McCulloch had a chance to halt: rest, regroup, consider.

It seemed a wise idea to be monitoring the waters just outside the cave even while he was resting, though. He extended his antennae a short distance into the swarming waters, and felt at once the impact, again, of a myriad sensory inputs, all the astounding complexity of the reef-world. Most of the creatures that moved slowly about on the face of the reef were simple ones, but McCulloch could feel, also, the sharp pulsations of intelligence coming from several points not far away: the anemones, so it seemed, and that enormous squidlike thing hovering overhead. Not intelligence of a kind that he understood, but that did not trouble him: for the moment, understanding could wait, while he dealt with the task of recovery from the exhausting struggles of his moulting. Keeping the antennae moving steadily in slow sweeping circles of surveillance, he began systematically to shut down the rest of his nervous system, until he had attained the rest state that he knew – how? – was optimum for the rebuilding of his shell. Already his soft new carapace was beginning to grow rigid as it absorbed water, swelled, filtered out and utilized the lime. But he would have to sit quietly a long while before he was fully armoured once more.

He rested. He waited. He did not think at all.

After a time his repose was broken by that inner voice, the one that had been trying to question him during the wildest moments of his moulting. It spoke without sound, from a point somewhere within the core of his torpid consciousness.

– *Are you awake?*

– *I am now*, McCulloch answered irritably.

– *I need definitions. You are a mystery to me. What is a McCulloch?*

– *A man.*

– *That does not help.*

– *A male human being.*

– *That also has no meaning.*

– *Look, I'm tired. Can we discuss these things some other time?*

– *This is a good time. While we rest, while we replenish ourself.*

– *Ourselves*, McCulloch corrected.

– *Ourself is more accurate.*

– *But there are two of us.*

– *Are there? Where is the other?*

McCulloch faltered. He had no perspective on his situation, none that made any sense. – *One inside the other, I think. Two of us in the same body. But definitely two of us. McCulloch and not-McCulloch.*

– *I concede the point. There are two of us. You are within me. Who are you?*

– *McCulloch.*

– *So you have said. But what does that mean?*

– *I don't know.*

The voice left him alone again. He felt its presence nearby, as a kind of warm node somewhere along his spine, or whatever was the equivalent of his spine, since he did not think invertebrates had spines. And it was fairly clear to him that he was an invertebrate.

He had become, it seemed, a lobster, or, at any rate, something lobster-like. Implied in that was transition: *he had become*. He had once been something else. Blurred, tantalizing memories of the something else that he once had been danced in his consciousness. He remembered hair, fingers, fingernails, flesh. Clothing: a kind of removable exoskeleton. Eyelids, ears, lips: shadowy concepts all, names without substance, but there was a certain elusive reality to them, a volatile, tricky plausibility. Each time he tried to apply one of those concepts to himself – 'fingers', 'hair', 'man', 'McCulloch' – it

23

slid away, it would not stick. Yet all the same those terms had some sort of relevance to him.

The harder he pushed to isolate that relevance, though, the harder it was to maintain his focus on any part of that soup of half-glimpsed notions in which his mind seemed to be swimming. The thing to do, McCulloch decided, was to go slow, try not to force understanding, wait for comprehension to seep back into his mind. Obviously he had had a bad shock, some major trauma, a total disorientation. It might be days before he achieved any sort of useful integration.

A gentle voice from outside his cave said, 'I hope that your Growing has gone well.'

Not a voice. He remembered voice: vibration of the air against the eardrums. No air here, maybe no eardrums. This was a stream of minute chemical messengers spurting through the mouth of the little cave and rebounding off the thousands of sensory filaments on his legs, tentacles, antennae, carapace and tail. But the effect was one of words having been spoken. And it was distinctly different from that other voice, the internal one, that had been questioning him so assiduously a little while ago.

'It goes extremely well,' McCulloch replied; or was it the other inhabitant of his body that had framed the answer? 'I grow. I heal. I stiffen. Soon I will come forth.'

'We feared for you.' The presence outside the cave emanated concern, warmth, intelligence. Kinship. 'In the first moments of your Growing, a strangeness came from you.'

'Strangeness is within me. I am invaded.'

'Invaded? By what?'

'A McCulloch. It is a man, which is a human being.'

'Ah. A great strangeness indeed. Do you need help?'

McCulloch answered, 'No. I will accommodate to it.'

And he knew that it was the other within himself who was making these answers, though the boundary between their identities was so indistinct that he had a definite sense of being the one who shaped these words. But how could that be? He had no idea how one shaped words by sending squirts of body-fluid into the all-surrounding ocean-fluid. That was not his language. His language was –

– words –

– English words –

He trembled in sudden understanding. His antennae thrashed wildly, his many legs jerked and quivered. Images churned in his suddenly boiling mind: bright lights, elaborate equipment, faces, walls, ceilings. People moving about him, speaking in low tones, occasionally addressing words to him, English words –

– Is English what all McCullochs speak?

– Yes.

– So English is human-language?

– Yes. But not the only one, said McCulloch. *I speak English, and also German and a little – French. But other humans speak other languages.*

– Very interesting. Why do you have so many languages?

– Because – because – we are different from one another, we live in different countries, we have different cultures –

– This is without meaning again. There are many creatures, but only one language, which all speak with greater or lesser skill, according to their destinies.

McCulloch pondered that. After a time he replied:

– Lobster is what you are. Long body, claws and antennae in front, many legs, flat tail in back. Different from, say, a clam. Clams have shell on top, shell on bottom, soft flesh in between, hinge connecting. You are not like that. You have lobster body. So you are lobster.

Now there was silence from the other.

Then – after a long pause –

– Very well. I accept the term. I am lobster. You are human. They are clams.

– What do you call yourselves in your own language?

Silence.

– What's your own name for yourself? Your individual self, the way my individual name is McCulloch and my species-name is human being?

Silence.

– Where am I, anyway?

Silence, still, so prolonged and utter that McCulloch wondered if the other being had withdrawn itself from his consciousness entirely. Perhaps days went by in this unending silence, perhaps weeks: he had no way of measuring the passing of time. He realized that such units as days or weeks were without meaning now. One moment succeeded the next, but they did not aggregate into anything continuous.

At last came a reply.

– *You are in the world, human McCulloch.*

Silence came again, intense, clinging, a dark warm garment. McCulloch made no attempt to reach the other mind. He lay motionless, feeling his carapace thicken. From outside the cave came a flow of impressions of passing beings, now differentiating themselves very sharply: he felt the thick fleshy pulses of the two anemones, the sharp stabbing presence of the squid, the slow ponderous broadcast of something dark and winged, and, again and again, the bright, comforting, unmistakable output of other lobster-creatures. It was a busy, complex world out there. The McCulloch part of him longed to leave the cave and explore it. The lobster part of him rested, content within its tight shelter.

He formed hypotheses. He had journeyed from his own place to this place, damaging his mind in the process, though now his mind seemed to be reconstructing itself steadily, if erratically. What sort of voyage? To another world? No: that seemed wrong. He did not believe that conditions so much like the ocean floor of Earth would be found on another –

Earth.

All right: significant datum. He was human, he came from Earth. And he was still on Earth. In the ocean. He was – what? – a land-dweller, an air-breather, a biped, a flesh-creature, a human. And now he was within the body of a lobster. Was that it? The entire human race, he thought, has migrated into the bodies of lobsters, and here we are on the ocean floor, scuttling about, waving our claws and feelers, going through difficult and dangerous moultings –

Or maybe I'm the only one. A scientific experiment, with me as the subject: man into lobster. That brightly-lit room that he remembered, the intricate gleaming equipment all about him – that was the laboratory, that was where they had prepared him for his transmigration, and then they had thrown the switch and hurled him into the body of –

No. No. Makes no sense. Lobsters, McCulloch reflected, are low-phylum creatures with simple nervous systems, limited intelligence. Plainly the mind he had entered was a complex

26

one. It asked thoughtful questions. It carried on civilized conversations with its friends, who came calling like ceremonious Japanese gentlemen, offering expressions of solicitude and goodwill.

New hypothesis: that lobsters and other low-phylum animals are actually quite intelligent, with minds roomy enough to accept the sudden insertion of a human being's entire neural structure, but we in our foolish anthropocentric way have up till now been too blind to perceive –

No. Too facile. You could postulate the secretly lofty intelligence of the world's humble creatures, all right: you could postulate anything you wanted. But that didn't make it so. Lobsters did not ask questions. Lobsters did not come calling like ceremonious Japanese gentlemen. At least, not the lobsters of the world he remembered.

Improved lobsters? Evolved lobsters? Super-lobsters of the future?

– *When am I?*

Into his dizzied broodings came the quiet disembodied internal voice of not-McCulloch, his companion:

– *Is your displacement then one of time rather than space?*

– *I don't know. Probably both. I'm a land creature.*

– *That has no meaning.*

– *I don't live in the ocean. I breathe air.*

From the other consciousness came an expression of deep astonishment tinged with scepticism.

– *Truly? That is very hard to believe. When you are in your own body you breathe no water at all?*

– *None. Not for long, or I would die.*

– *But there is so little land! And no creatures live upon it. Some make short visits there. But nothing can dwell there very long. So it has always been. And so will it be, until the time of the Moulting of the World.*

McCulloch considered that. Once again he found himself doubting that he was still on Earth. A world of water? Well, that could fit into his hypothesis of having journeyed forward in time, though it seemed to add a layer of implausibility upon implausibility. How many millions of years, he wondered, would it take for nearly all the Earth to have become covered with water? And he answered himself: In about as many as it would take to evolve a species of intelligent invertebrates.

Suddenly, terribly, it all fitted together. Things crystallized and clarified in his mind, and he found access to another segment of his injured and redistributed memory; and he began to comprehend what had befallen him, or, rather, what he had willingly allowed himself to undergo. With that comprehension came a swift stinging sense of total displacement and utter loss, as though he were drowning and desperately tugging at strands of seaweed in a futile attempt to pull himself back to the surface. All that was real to him, all that he was part of, everything that made sense – gone, gone, perhaps irretrievably gone, buried under the weight of uncountable millennia, vanished, drowned, forgotten, reduced to mere geology – it was unthinkable, it was unacceptable, it was impossible, and as the truth of it bore in on him he found himself choking on the frightful vastness of time past.

But that bleak sensation lasted only a moment and was gone. In its place came excitement, delight, confusion and a feverish throbbing curiosity about this place he had entered. He was here. That miraculous thing that they had strived so fiercely to achieve had been achieved – rather too well, perhaps, but it had been achieved, and he was launched on the greatest adventure he would ever have, that anyone would ever have. This was not the moment for submitting to grief and confusion. Out of that world lost and all but forgotten to him came a scrap of verse that gleamed and blazed in his soul: *Only through time time is conquered.*

McCulloch reached towards the mind that was so close to his within this strange body.

– *When will it be safe for us to leave this cave?* he asked.
– *It is safe any time, now. Do you wish to go outside?*
– *Yes. Please.*

The creature stirred, flexed its front claws, slapped its flat tail against the floor of the cave, and in a slow ungraceful way began to clamber through the narrow opening, pausing more than once to search the waters outside for lurking enemies. McCulloch felt a quick hot burst of terror, as though he were about to enter some important meeting and had discovered too late that he was naked. Was the shell truly ready? Was he safely armoured against the unknown foes outside, or would they fall upon him and tear him apart like furious shrikes? But his host did not seem to share those fears. It went plodding on and out, and in a moment more it emerged on an algae-encrusted tongue of the reef wall, a short distance below the two anemones. From each of those twin masses of rippling flesh came the same sullen pouting hungry murmurs: 'Ah, come closer, why don't you come closer?'

'Another time,' said the lobster, sounding almost playful, and turned away from them.

McCulloch looked outwards over the landscape. Earlier, in the turmoil of his bewildering arrival and the pain and chaos of the moulting prodrome, he had not had time to assemble any clear and coherent view of it. But now – despite the handicap of seeing everything with the alien perspective of the lobster's many-faceted eyes – he was able to put together an image of the terrain.

His view was a shortened one, because the sky was like a dark lid, through which came only enough light to create a cone-shaped arena spreading just a little way. Behind him was the face of the huge cliff, occupied by plant and animal life over virtually every square inch, and stretching upwards until its higher reaches were lost in the dimness far overhead. Just a short way down from the ledge where he rested was the ocean floor, a broad expanse of gentle, undulating white sand streaked here and there with long widening gores of some darker material. Here and there bottom-growing plants arose in elegant billowy clumps, and McCulloch spotted occasional creatures moving among them over the sand that were much like lobsters and crabs, though with some differences. He saw also some starfish and snails and sea urchins that did not look at all unfamiliar. At higher levels he could make out a few swimming creatures: a couple of the squidlike animals – they were hulking-looking ropy-armed things, and he disliked them instinctively – and what seemed to be large jellyfish. But something was missing, and after a moment McCulloch realized what it was: fishes. There was a rich population of invertebrate life wherever he looked, but no fishes as far as he could see.

Not that he could see very far. The darkness clamped down like a curtain perhaps two or three hundred yards away. But even so, it was odd that not one fish had entered his field of vision in all this time. He wished he knew more about marine biology. Were there zones on Earth where no sea animals more complex than lobsters and crabs existed? Perhaps, but he doubted it.

Two disturbing new hypotheses blossomed in his mind. One was that he had landed in some remote future era where nothing out of his own time survived except low-phylum sea creatures. The other was that he had not travelled to the future at all, but had arrived by mischance in some primordial geological epoch in which vertebrate life had not yet evolved. That seemed unlikely to him, though. This place did not have a prehistoric feel to him. He saw no trilobites; surely there ought to be trilobites everywhere about, and not these oversized lobsters, which he did not remember at all from his childhood visits to the natural history museum's prehistory displays.

But if this was truly the future – and the future belonged to the lobsters and squids –

That was hard to accept. Only invertebrates? What could invertebrates accomplish, what kind of civilization could lobsters build, with their hard unsupple bodies and great clumsy claws? Concepts, half-remembered or less than that, rushed through his mind: the Taj Mahal, the Gutenberg Bible, the Sistine Chapel, the Madonna of the Rocks, the great window at Chartres. Could lobsters create those? Could squids? What a poor place this world must be, McCulloch thought sadly, how grey, how narrow, how tightly bounded by the ocean above and the endless sandy floor.

– *Tell me,* he said to his host. *Are there any fishes in this sea?*

The response was what he was coming to recognize as a sigh.

– *Fishes? That is another word without meaning.*

– *A form of marine life, with an internal bony structure –*

– *With its shell* inside?

– *That's one way of putting it,* said McCulloch.

– *There are no such creatures. Such creatures have never existed. There is no room for the shell within the soft parts of the body. I can barely comprehend such an arrangement: surely there is no need for it!*

– *It can be useful, I assure you. In the former world it was quite common.*

– The world of human beings?

– Yes. My world, McCulloch said.

– Anything might have been possible in a former world, human McCulloch. Perhaps indeed before the world's last Moulting shells were worn inside. And perhaps after the next one they will be worn there again. But in the world I know, human McCulloch, it is not the practice.

– Ah, McCulloch said. *Then I am even farther from home than I thought.*

– Yes, said his host. *I think you are very far from home indeed. Does that cause you sorrow?*

– Among other things.

– If it causes you sorrow, I grieve for your grief, because we are companions now.

– You are very kind, said McCulloch to his host.

The lobster asked McCulloch if he was ready to begin their journey; and when McCulloch indicated that he was, his host serenely kicked itself free of the ledge with a single powerful stroke of its tail. For an instant it hung suspended; then it glided towards the sandy bottom as gracefully as though it were floating through air. When it landed, it was with all its many legs poised delicately *en pointe*, and it stood that way, motionless, a long moment.

Then it suddenly set out with great haste over the ocean floor, running so lightfootedly that it scarcely raised a puff of sand wherever it touched down. More than once it ran right across some bottom-grubbing creature, some slug or scallop, without appearing to disturb it at all. McCulloch thought the lobster was capering in sheer exuberance, after its long internment in the cave; but some growing sense of awareness of his companion's mind told him after a time that this was no casual frolic, that the lobster was not in fact dancing but fleeing.

– Is there an enemy? McCulloch asked.

– Yes. Above.

The lobster's antennae stabbed upwards a sharp angle, and McCulloch, seeing through the other's eyes, perceived now a large looming cylindrical shape swimming in slow circles near the upper border of their range of vision. It might have been a shark, or even a whale. McCulloch felt deceived and betrayed;

31

for the lobster had told him this was an invertebrate world, and surely that creature above him –

– *No*, said the lobster, without slowing its manic sprint. *That animal has no shell of the sort you described within its body. It is only a bag of flesh. But it is very dangerous.*

– *How will we escape it?*

– *We will not escape it.*

The lobster sounded calm, but whether it was the calm of fatalism or mere expressionlessness, McCulloch could not say: the lobster had been calm even in the first moments of McCulloch's arrival in its mind, which must surely have been alarming and even terrifying to it.

It had begun to move now in ever-widening circles. This seemed not so much an evasive tactic as a ritualistic one, now, a dance indeed. A farewell to life? The swimming creature had descended until it was only a few lobster-lengths above them, and McCulloch had a clear view of it. No, not a fish or a shark or any type of vertebrate at all, he realized, but an animal of a kind wholly unfamiliar to him, a kind of enormous wormlike thing whose meaty yellow body was reinforced externally by some sort of chitinous struts running its entire length. Fleshy vanelike fins rippled along its sides, but their purpose seemed to be more one of guidance than propulsion, for it appeared to move by guzzling in great quantities of water and expelling them through an anal siphon. Its mouth was vast, with a row of dim little green eyes ringing the scarlet lips. When the creature yawned, it revealed itself to be toothless, but capable of swallowing the lobster easily at a gulp.

Looking upwards into that yawning mouth, McCulloch had a sudden image of himself elsewhere, spreadeagled under an inverted pyramid of shining machinery as the countdown reached its final moments, as the technicians made ready to –

– to hurl him –

– to hurl him forward in time –

Yes. An experiment. Definitely an experiment. He could remember it now. Bleier, Caldwell, Rodrigues, Mortenson. And all the others. Gathered around him, faces tight, forced smiles. The lights. The colours. The bizarre coils of equipment. And the volunteer. The volunteer. First human subject to be sent forward in time. The various rabbits and mice of the previous experiments, though they had apparently survived the round trip unharmed, had not been capable of delivering much of a report on their adventures. 'I'm smarter than any rabbit,' McCulloch had said. 'Send me. I'll tell you what it's like up there.' The volunteer. All that was coming back to him in great swatches now, as he crouched here within the mind of something much like a lobster, waiting for a vast yawning predator to pounce. The project, the controversies, his co-workers, the debate over risking a human mind under the machine, the drawing of lots. McCulloch had not been the only volunteer. He was just the lucky one. 'Here you go, Jim-boy. A hundred years down the time-line.'

Or fifty, or eighty, or a hundred and twenty. They didn't have really precise trajectory control. They thought he might go as much as a hundred and twenty years. But beyond much doubt they had overshot by a few hundred million. Was that within the permissible parameters of error?

He wondered what would happen to him if his host here were to perish. Would he die also? Would he find himself instantly transferred to some other being of this epoch? Or would he simply be hurled back instead to his own time? He was not ready to go back. He had just begun to observe, to understand, to explore –

McCulloch's host had halted its running, now, and stood quite still in what was obviously a defensive mode, body cocked and upreared, claws extended, with the huge crusher claw erect and the long narrow cutting claw opening and closing in a steady rhythm. It was a threatening pose, but the swimming thing did not appear to be greatly troubled by it. Did the lobster mean to let itself be swallowed, and then to carve an exit for itself with those awesome weapons, before the alimentary juices could go to work on its armour?

'You choose your prey foolishly,' said McCulloch's host to its enemy.

The swimming creature made a reply that was unintelligible to McCulloch: vague blurry words, the clotted outspew of a feeble intelligence. It continued its unhurried downward spiral.

'You are warned,' said the lobster. 'You are not selecting your victim wisely.'

Again came a muddled response, sluggish and incoherent, the speech of an entity for whom verbal communication was a heavy, all but impossible effort.

Its enormous mouth gaped. Its fins rippled fiercely as it siphoned itself downwards the last few yards to engulf the lobster. McCulloch prepared himself for transition to some new and even more unimaginable state when his host met its death. But suddenly the ocean floor was swarming with lobsters. They must have been arriving from all sides – summoned by his host's frantic dance, McCulloch wondered? – while McCulloch, intent on the descent of the swimmer, had not noticed. Ten, twenty, possibly fifty of them arrayed themselves now beside McCulloch's host, and as the swimmer, tail on high, mouth wide, lowered itself like some gigantic suction-hose towards them, the lobsters coolly and implacably seized its lips in their claws. Caught and helpless, it began at once to thrash, and from the pores through which it spoke came bleating incoherent cries of dismay and torment.

There was no mercy for it. It had been warned. It dangled tail upwards while the pack of lobsters methodically devoured it from below, pausing occasionally to strip away and discard the rigid rods of chitin that formed its superstructure. Swiftly they reduced it to a faintly visible cloud of shreds oscillating in the water, and then small scavenging creatures came to fall upon those, and there was nothing at all left but the scattered rods of chitin on the sand.

The entire episode had taken only a few moments: the coming of the predator, the dance of McCulloch's host, the arrival of the other lobsters, the destruction of the enemy. Now the lobsters were gathered in a sort of convocation about McCulloch's host, wordlessly manifesting a commonality of spirit, a warmth of fellowship after feasting, that seemed quite comprehensible to McCulloch. For a short while they had been uninhibited savage carnivores consuming convenient meat; now once again they were courteous, refined, cultured – Japanese gentlemen, Oxford dons, gentle Benedictine monks.

McCulloch studied them closely. They were definitely more like lobsters than like any other creature he had ever seen, very much like lobsters, and yet there were differences: They were larger. How much larger, he could not tell, for he had no real way of judging distance and size in this undersea world; but he supposed they must be at least three feet long, and he doubted that lobsters of his time, even the biggest, were anything like that in length. Their bodies were wider than those of lobsters, and their heads were larger. The two largest claws looked like those of the lobsters he remembered, but the ones just behind them seemed more elaborate, as if adapted for more delicate procedures than mere rending of food and stuffing it into the mouth. There was an odd little hump, almost a dome, midway down the lobster's back – the centre of the expanded nervous system, perhaps.

The lobsters clustered solemnly about McCulloch's host and each lightly tapped its claws against those of the adjoining lobster in a sort of handshake, a process that seemed to take quite some time. McCulloch became aware also that a conversation was under way. What they were talking about, he realized, was him.

'It is not painful to have a McCulloch within one,' his host was explaining. 'It came upon me at moulting time, and that gave me a moment of difficulty, moulting being what it is. But it was only a moment. After that my only concern was for the McCulloch's comfort.'

'And it is comfortable now?'

'It is becoming more comfortable.'

'When will you show it to us?'

'Ah, that cannot be done. It has no real existence, and therefore I cannot bring it forth.'

'What is it, then? A wanderer? A revenant?'

'A revenant, yes. So I think. And a wanderer. It says it is a human being.'

'And what is that? Is a human being a kind of McCulloch?'

'I think a McCulloch is a kind of human being.'

'Which is a revenant.'

'Yes, I think so.'

'This is an Omen!'

'Where is its world?'

'Its world is lost to it.'

'Yes, definitely an Omen.'

'It lived on dry land.'

'It breathed air.'

'It wore its shell within its body.'

'What a strange revenant!'

'What a strange world its world must have been.'

'It is the former world, would you not say?'

'So I surely believe. And therefore this is an Omen.'

'Ah, we shall Moult. We shall Moult.'

McCulloch was altogether lost. He was not even sure when his own host was the speaker.

'Is it the Time?'

'We have an Omen, do we not?'

'The McCulloch surely was sent as a herald.'

'There is no precedent.'

'Each Moulting, though, is without precedent. We cannot conceive what came before. We cannot imagine what comes after. We learn by learning. The McCulloch is the herald. The McCulloch is the Omen.'

'I think not. I think it is unreal and unimportant.'

'Unreal, yes. But not unimportant.'

'The Time is not at hand. The Moulting of the World is not yet due. The human is a wanderer and a revenant, but not a herald and certainly not an Omen.'

'It comes from the former world.'

'It says it does. Can we believe that?'

'It breathed air. In the former world, perhaps there were creatures that breathed air.'

'It says it breathed air. I think it is neither herald nor Omen, neither wanderer nor revenant. I think it is a myth and a fugue. I think it betokens nothing. It is an accident. It is an interruption.'

'That is an uncivil attitude. We have much to learn from the McCulloch. And if it is an Omen, we have immediate responsibilities that must be fulfilled.'

'But how can we be certain of what it is?'

– *May I speak?* said McCulloch to his host.

– *Of course.*

– *How can I make myself heard?*

– *Speak through me.*

'The McCulloch wishes to be heard!'

'Hear it! Hear it!'

'Let it speak!'

McCulloch said, and the host spoke the words aloud for him, 'I am a stranger here, and your guest, and so I ask you to forgive me if I give offence, for I have little understanding of your ways. Nor do I know if I am a herald or an Omen. But I tell you in all truth that I am a wanderer, and that I am sent from the former world, where there are many creatures of my kind, who breathe air and live upon the land and carry their – shells – inside their body.'

'An Omen, certainly,' said several of the lobsters at once. 'A herald, beyond doubt.'

McCulloch continued, 'It was our hope to discover something of the worlds that are to come after ours. And therefore I was sent forward – '

'A herald – certainly a herald!'

'– to come to you, to go among you, to learn to know you, and then to return to my own people, the air-people, the human people, and bring the word of what is to come. But I think that I am not the herald you expect. I carry no message for you. We could not have known that you were here. Out of the former world I bring you the blessing of those that have gone before, however, and when I go back to that world I will bear tidings of your life, of your thought, of your ways – '

'Then our kind is unknown to your world?'

McCulloch hesitated. 'Creatures somewhat like you do exist in the seas of the former world. But they are smaller and simpler than you, and I think their civilization, if they have one, is not a great one.'

'You have no discourse with them, then?' one of the lobsters asked.

'Very little,' he said. A miserable evasion, cowardly, vile.

McCulloch shivered. He imagined himself crying out, 'We eat them!' and the water turning black with their shocked outbursts – and saw them instantly falling upon him, swiftly and efficiently slicing him to scraps with their claws. Through his mind ran monstrous images of lobsters in tanks, lobsters boiling alive, lobsters smothered in rich sauces, lobsters shelled, lobsters minced, lobsters rendered into bisques – he could not halt the torrent of dreadful visions. Such was our discourse with your ancestors. Such was our mode of interspecies communication. He felt himself drowning in guilt and shame and fear.

The spasm passed. The lobsters had not stirred. They continued to regard him with patience: impassive, unmoving, remote. McCulloch wondered if all that had passed through his mind just then had been transmitted to his host. Very likely; the host earlier had seemed to have access to all of his thoughts, though McCulloch did not have the same entrée to the host's. And if the host knew, did all the others? What then, what then?

Perhaps they did not even care. Lobsters, he recalled, were said to be callous cannibals, who might attack one another in the very tanks where they were awaiting their turns in the chef's pot. It was hard to view these detached and aloof beings, these dons, these monks, as having that sort of ferocity: but yet he had seen them go to work on that swimming mouth-creature without any show of embarrassment, and perhaps some atavistic echo of their ancestors' appetites lingered in them, so that they would think it only natural that McCulloch and other humans had fed on such things as lobsters. Why should they be shocked? Perhaps they thought that humans fed on humans, too. It was all in the former world, was it not? And in any event it was foolish to fear that they would exact some revenge on him for Lobster Thermidor, no matter how appalled they might be. He wasn't here. He was nothing more than a figment, a revenant, a wanderer, a set of intrusive neural networks within their companion's brain. The worst they could do to him, he supposed, was to exorcize him, and send him back to the former world.

Even so, he could not entirely shake the guilt and the shame. Or the fear.

Bleier said, 'Of course, you aren't the only one who's going to be in jeopardy when we throw the switch. There's your host to consider. One entire human ego slamming into his mind out of nowhere like a brick falling off a building – what's it going to do to him?'

'Flip him out, is my guess,' said Jake Ybarra. 'You'll land on him and he'll announce he's Napoleon, or Joan of Arc, and they'll hustle him off to the nearest asylum. Are you prepared for the possibility, Jim, that you're going to spend your entire time in the future sitting in a loony-bin undergoing therapy?'

'Or exorcism,' Mortenson suggested. 'If there's been some kind of reversion to barbarism. Christ, you might even get your host burned at the stake!'

'I don't think so,' McCulloch said quietly. 'I'm a lot more optimistic than you guys. I don't expect to land in a world of witch-doctors and mumbo-jumbo, and I don't expect to find myself in a place that locks people up in Bedlam because they suddenly start acting a little strange. The chances are that I *am* going to unsettle my host when I enter him, but that he'll simply get two sanity-stabilizer pills from his medicine chest and take them with a glass of water and feel better in five minutes. And then I'll explain what's happening to him.'

'More than likely no explanations will be necessary,' said Maggie Caldwell. 'By the time you arrive, time travel will have been a going proposition for three or four generations, after all. Having a traveller from the past turn up in your head will be old stuff to them. Your host will probably know exactly what's going on from the moment you hit him.'

'Let's hope so,' Bleier said. He looked across the laboratory to Rodrigues. 'What's the count, Bob?'

'T minus eighteen minutes.'

'I'm not worried about a thing,' McCulloch said.

Caldwell took his hand in hers. 'Neither am I, Jim.'

'Then why is your hand so cold?' he asked.

'So I'm a *little* worried,' she said.

McCulloch grinned. 'So am I. A little. Only a little.'

'You're human, Jim. No-one's ever done this before.'

'It'll be a can of corn!' Ybarra said.

Bleier looked at him blankly. 'What the hell does that mean, Jake?'

Ybarra said, 'Archaic twentieth-century slang. It means it's going to be a lot easier than we think.'

'I told you,' said McCulloch, 'I'm not worried.'

'I'm still worried about the impact on the host,' said Bleier.

'All those Napoleons and Joans of Arc that have been cluttering the asylums for the last few hundred years,' Maggie Caldwell said. 'Could it be that they're really hosts for time travellers going backwards in time?'

'You can't go backwards,' said Mortenson. 'You know that. The round trip has to begin with a forward leap.'

'Under present theory,' Caldwell said. 'But present theory's only five years old. It may turn out to be incomplete. We may have had all sorts of travellers out of the future jumping through history, and never even knew it. All the nuts, lunatics, inexplicable geniuses, idiot-savants – '

'Save it, Maggie,' Bleier said. 'Let's stick to what we understand right now.'

'Oh? Do we understand anything?' McCulloch asked.

Bleier gave him a sour look. 'I thought you said you weren't worried.'

'I'm not. Not much. But I'd be a fool if I thought we really had a firm handle on what we're doing. We're shooting in the dark, and let's never kid ourselves about it.'

'T minus fifteen,' Rodrigues called.

'Try to make the landing easy on your host, Jim,' Bleier said.

'I've got no reason not to want to,' said McCulloch.

He realized that he had been wandering. Bleier, Maggie, Mortenson, Ybarra – for a moment they had been more real to him than the congregation of lobsters. He had heard their voices, he had seen their faces, Bleier plump and perspiring and serious, Ybarra dark and lean, Maggie with her crown of short upswept red hair blazing in the laboratory light – and yet they were all dead, a hundred million years dead, two hundred million, back there with the triceratops and the trilobite in the drowned former world, and here he was among the lobster-people. How futile all those discussions of what the world of the early twenty-second century was going to be like! Those speculations on population density, religious belief, attitudes towards science, level of technological achievement, all those late-night sessions in the final months of the project, designed to prepare him for any eventuality he might encounter while he was visiting the future – what a waste, what a needless exercise. As was all that fretting about upsetting the mental stability of the person who would receive his transtemporalized consciousness. Such qualms, such moral delicacy – all unnecessary, McCulloch knew now.

But of course they had not anticipated sending him so eerily far across the dark abysm of time, into a world in which humankind and all its works were not even legendary memories, and the host who would receive him was a calm and thoughtful crustacean capable of taking him in with only the most mild and brief disruption of its serenity.

The lobsters, he noticed now, had reconfigured themselves while his mind had been drifting. They had broken up their circle and were arrayed in a long line stretching over the ocean floor, with his host at the end of the procession. The queue was a close one, each lobster so close to the one before it that it could touch it with the tips of its antennae, which from time to time they seemed to be doing; and they all were moving in a weird kind of quasi-military lockstep, every lobster swinging the same set of walking-legs forward at the same time.

– *Where are we going?* McCulloch asked his host.

– *The pilgrimage has begun.*

– *What pilgrimage is that?*

– *To the dry place,* said the host. *To the place of no water. To the land.*

– *Why?*

– *It is the custom. We have decided that the time of the Moulting of the World is soon to come; and therefore we must make the pilgrimage. It is the end of all things. It is the coming of a newer world. You are the herald: so we have agreed.*

– *Will you explain? I have a thousand questions. I need to know more about all this,* McCulloch said.

– *Soon. Soon. This is not a time for explanations.*

McCulloch felt a firm and unequivocal closing of contact, an emphatic withdrawal. He sensed a hard ringing silence that was almost an absence of the host, and knew it would be inappropriate to transgress against it. That was painful, for he brimmed now with an overwhelming rush of curiosity. The Moulting of the World? The end of all things? A pilgrimage to the land? *What* land? Where? But he did not ask. He could not ask. The host seemed to have vanished from him, disappearing utterly into this pilgrimage, this migration, moving in its lockstep way with total concentration and a kind of mystic intensity. McCulloch did not intrude. He felt as though he had been left alone in the body they shared.

As they marched, he concentrated on observing, since he could not interrogate. And there was much to see; for the longer he dwelled within his host, the more accustomed he grew to the lobster's sensory mechanisms. The compound eyes, for instance. Enough of his former life had returned to him now so that he remembered human eyes clearly, those two large gleaming ovals, so keen, so subtle of focus, set beneath protecting ridges of bone. His host's eyes were nothing like that: they were two clusters of tiny lenses rising on jointed, movable stalks, and what they showed was an intricately dissected view, a mosaic of isolated points of light. But he was learning somehow to translate those complex and baffling images into a single clear one, just as, no doubt, a creature accustomed to compound-lens vision would sooner or later learn to see through human eyes, if need be. And McCulloch found now that he could not only make more sense out of the views he received through his host's eyes, but that he was seeing farther, into quite distant dim recesses of this sunless undersea realm.

Not that the stalked eyes seemed to be a very important part of the lobster's perceptive apparatus. They provided nothing more than a certain crude awareness of the immediate terrain. But apparently the real work of perceiving was done mainly by the thousands of fine bristles, so minute that they were all but invisible, that sprouted on every surface of his host's body. These seemed to send a constant stream of messages to the lobster's brain: information on the texture and topography of the ocean floor, on tiny shifts in the flow and temperature of the water, of the proximity of obstacles, and much else. Some of the small hairlike filaments were sensitive to touch and others, it appeared, to chemicals; for whenever the lobster approached some other life-form, it received data on its scent – or the underwater equivalent – long before the creature itself was within visual range. The quantity and richness of these inputs astonished McCulloch. At every moment came a torrent of data corresponding to the landside senses he remembered, smell, taste, touch; and some central processing unit within the lobster's brain handled everything in the most effortless fashion.

But there was no sound. The ocean world appeared to be wholly silent. McCulloch knew that that was untrue, that sound waves propagated through water as persistently as through air, if somewhat more rapidly. Yet the lobster seemed neither to possess nor to need any sort of auditory equipment. The sensory bristles brought in all the data it required. The 'speech' of these creatures, McCulloch had long ago realized, was effected not by voice but by means of spurts of chemicals released into the water, hormones, perhaps, or amino acids, something of a distinct and readily recognizable identity, emitted in some high-redundancy pattern that permitted easy recognition and decoding despite the difficulties caused by currents and eddies. It was, McCulloch thought, like trying to communicate by printing individual letters on scraps of paper and hurling them into the wind. But it did somehow seem to work, however clumsy a concept it might be, because of the extreme sensitivity of the lobster's myriad chemoreceptors.

The antennae played some significant role also. There were two sets of them, a pair of three-branched ones just behind the eyes and a much longer single-branched pair behind those. The long ones restlessly twitched and probed inquisitively and most likely, he suspected, served as simple balancing and co-ordination devices much like the whiskers of a cat. The purpose of the smaller antennae eluded him, but it was his guess that they were involved in the process of communication between one lobster and another, either by some semaphore system or in a deeper communion beyond his still awkward comprehension.

McCulloch regretted not knowing more about the lobsters of his own era. But he had only a broad general knowledge of natural history, extensive, fairly deep, yet not good enough to tell him whether these elaborate sensory functions were characteristic of all lobsters or had evolved during the millions of years it had taken to create the water-world. Probably some of each, he decided. Very likely even the lobsters of the former world had had much of this scanning equipment, enough to allow them to locate their prey, to find their way around in the dark suboceanic depths, to undertake their long and unerring migrations. But he found it hard to believe that they could have had much 'speech' capacity, that they gathered in solemn sessions to discuss abstruse questions of theology and mythology, to argue gently about omens and heralds and the end of all things. That was something that the patient and ceaseless unfoldings of time must have wrought.

The lobsters marched without show of fatigue: not scampering in that dancelike way that his host had adopted while summoning its comrades to save it from the swimming creature, but moving nevertheless in an elegant and graceful fashion, barely touching the ground with the tips of their legs, going onwards step by step by step steadily and fairly swiftly.

McCulloch noticed that new lobsters frequently joined the procession, cutting in from left or right just ahead of his host, who always remained at the rear of the line; that line now was so long, hundreds of lobsters long, that it was impossible to see its beginning. Now and again one would reach out with its bigger claw to seize some passing animal, a starfish or urchin or small crab, and without missing a step would shred and devour it, tossing the unwanted husk to the cloud of planktonic scavengers that always hovered nearby. This foraging on the march was done with utter lack of self-consciousness; it was almost by reflex that these creatures snatched and gobbled as they journeyed.

And yet all the same they did not seem like mere marauding mouths. From this long line of crustaceans there emanated, McCulloch realized, a mysterious sense of community, a whole-ness of society, that he did not understand but quite sharply sensed. This was plainly not a mere migration but a true pilgrimage. He thought ruefully of his earlier condescending view of these people, incapable of achieving the Taj Mahal or the Sistine Chapel, and felt abashed: for he was beginning to see that they had other accomplishments of a less tangible sort that were only barely apparent to his displaced and struggling mind.

'When you come back,' Maggie said, 'you'll be someone else. There's no escaping that. It's the one thing I'm frightened of. Not that you'll die making the hop, or that you'll get into some sort of terrible trouble in the future, or that we won't be able to bring you back at all, or anything like that. But that you'll have become someone else.'

'I feel pretty secure in my identity,' McCulloch told her.

'I know you do. God knows, you're the most stable person in the group, and that's why you're going. But even so. Nobody's ever done anything like this before. It can't help but change you. When you return, you're going to be unique among the human race.'

'That sounds very awesome. But I'm not sure it'll matter that much, Mag. I'm just taking a little trip. If I were going to Paris, or Istanbul, or even Antarctica, would I come back totally transformed? I'd have had some new experiences, but – '

'It isn't the same,' she said. 'It isn't even remotely the same.' She came across the room to him and put her hands on his shoulders, and stared deep into his eyes, which sent a little chill through him, as it always did; for when she looked at him that way there was a sudden flow of energy between them, a powerful warm rapport rushing from her to him and from him to her as though through a huge conduit, that delighted and frightened him both at once. He could lose himself in her. He had never let himself feel that way about anyone before. And this was not the moment to begin. There was no room in him for such feelings, not now, not when he was within a couple of hours of leaping off into the most unknown of unknowns. When he returned – if he returned – he might risk allowing something at last to develop with Maggie. But not on the eve of departure, when everything in his universe was tentative and conditional. 'Can I tell you a little story, Jim?' she asked.

'Sure.'

'When my father was on the faculty at Cal, he was invited to a reception to meet a couple of the early astronauts, two of the Apollo men – I don't remember which ones, but they were from the second or third voyage to the Moon. When he showed up at the faculty club, there were two or three hundred people there, milling around having cocktails, and most of them were people he didn't know. He walked in and looked around and within ten seconds he had found the astronauts. He didn't have to be told. He just *knew*. And this is my father, remember, who doesn't believe in ESP or anything like that. But he said they were impossible to miss, even in that crowd. You could see it on their faces, you could feel the radiance coming from them, there was an aura, there was something about their eyes. Something that said, *I have walked on the Moon. I have been to that place which is not of our world and I have come back, and now I am someone else. I am who I was before, but I am someone else also.*'

45

'But they went to the *Moon*, Mag!'

'And you're going to the *future*, Jim. That's even weirder. You're going to a place that doesn't exist. And you may meet yourself there – ninety-nine years old, and waiting to shake hands with you – or you might meet me, or your grandson, or find out that everyone on Earth is dead, or that everyone has turned into a disembodied spirit, or that they're all immortal superbeings, or – or – Christ, I don't know. You'll see a world that nobody alive today is supposed to see. And when you come back, you'll have that aura. You'll be transformed.'

'Is that so frightening?'

'To me it is,' she said.

'Why is that?'

'Dummy,' she said. 'Dope. How explicit do I have to be, anyway? I thought I was being obvious enough.'

He could not meet her eyes. 'This isn't the best moment to talk about – '

'I know. I'm sorry, Jim. But you're important to me, and you're going somewhere and you're going to become someone else, and I'm scared. Selfish and scared.'

'Are you telling me not to go?'

'Don't be absurd. You'd go no matter what I told you, and I'd despise you if you didn't. There's no turning back now.'

'No.'

'I shouldn't have dumped any of this on you today. You don't need it right this moment.'

'It's OK,' he said softly. He turned until he was looking straight at her, and for a long moment he simply stared into her eyes and did not speak, and then at last he said, 'Listen, I'm going to take a big fantastic improbable insane voyage, and I'm going to be a witness to God knows what, and then I'm going to come back and yes, I'll be changed – only an ox wouldn't be changed, or maybe only a block of stone – but I'll still be me, whoever *me* is. Don't worry, OK? I'll still be me. And we'll still be us.'

'Whoever *us* is.'

'Whoever. Jesus, I wish you were going with me, Mag!'

'That's the silliest schoolboy thing I've ever heard you say.'

'True, though.'

'Well, I can't go. Only one at a time can go, and it's you.

I'm not even sure I'd want to go. I'm not as crazy as you are, I suspect. You go, Jim, and come back and tell me all about it.'

'Yes.'

'And then we'll see what there is to see about you and me.'

'Yes,' he said.

She smiled. 'Let me show you a poem, OK? You must know it, because it's Eliot, and you know all the Eliot there is. But I was reading him last night – thinking of you, reading him – and I found this, and it seemed to be the right words, and I wrote them down. From one of the *Quartets*.'

'I think I know,' he said:

> *'Time past and time future*
> *Allow but a little consciousness –* '

'That's a good one too,' Maggie said. 'But it's not the one I had in mind.' She unfolded a piece of paper. 'It's this:

> *We shall not cease from exploration*
> *And the end of all our exploring*
> *Will be to arrive where we started –* '

'– *And know the place for the first time*,' he completed. 'Yes. Exactly. To arrive where we started. And know the place for the first time.'

The lobsters were singing as they marched. That was the only word, McCulloch thought, that seemed to apply. The line of pilgrims now was immensely long – there must have been thousands in the procession by this time, and more were joining constantly – and from them arose an outpouring of chemical signals, within the narrowest of tonal ranges, that mingled in a close harmony and amounted to a kind of sustained chant on a few notes, swelling, filling all the ocean with its powerful and intense presence. Once again he had an image of them as monks, but not Benedictines, now: these were Buddhist, rather, an endless line of yellow-robed holy men singing a great *Om* as they made their way up some Tibetan slope. He was awed and humbled by it – by the intensity, and by the wholeheartedness of the devotion. It was getting hard for him to remember that these were crustaceans, no more than ragged claws scuttling across the floors of silent seas; he sensed minds all about him, whole and elaborate minds arising out of some rich cultural matrix, and it was coming to seem quite natural to him that these people should have armoured exoskeletons and jointed eye-stalks and a dozen busy legs.

His host had still not broken its silence, which must have extended now over a considerable period. Just how long a period, McCulloch had no idea, for there were no significant alternations of light and dark down here to indicate the passing of time, nor did the marchers ever seem to sleep, and they took their food, as he had seen, in a casual and random way without breaking step. But it seemed to McCulloch that he had been effectively alone in the host's body for many days.

He was not minded to try to re-enter contact with the other just yet – not until he received some sort of signal from it. Plainly the host had withdrawn into some inner sanctuary to undertake a profound meditation; and McCulloch, now that the early bewilderment and anguish of his journey through time had begun to wear off, did not feel so dependent upon the host that he needed to blurt his queries constantly into his companion's consciousness. He would watch, and wait, and attempt to fathom the mysteries of this place unaided.

The landscape had undergone a great many changes since the beginning of the march. That gentle bottom of fine white sand had yielded to a terrain of rough dark gravel, and that to one of a pale sedimentary stuff made up of tiny shells, the mortal remains, no doubt, of vast hordes of diatoms and foraminifera, that rose like clouds of snowflakes at the lobsters' lightest steps. Then came a zone where a stratum of thick red clay spread in all directions. The clay held embedded in it an odd assortment of rounded rocks and clamshells and bits of chitin, so that it had the look of some complex paving material from a fashionable terrace. And after that they entered a region where slender spires of a sharp black stone, faceted like worked flint, sprouted stalagmite-fashion at their feet. Through all of this the lobster-pilgrims marched unperturbed, never halting, never breaking their file, moving in a straight line whenever possible and making only the slightest of deviations when compelled to it by the harshness of the topography.

Homefaring

Now they were in a district of coarse yellow sandy globules, out of which two types of coral grew: thin angular strands of deep jet, and supple, almost mobile fingers of a rich lovely salmon hue. McCulloch wondered where on Earth such stuff might be found, and chided himself at once for the foolishness of the thought: the seas he knew had been swallowed long ago in the great all-encompassing ocean that swathed the world, and the familiar continents, he supposed, had broken from their moorings and slipped to strange parts of the globe well before the rising of the waters. He had no landmarks. There was an equator somewhere, and there were two poles, but down here beyond the reach of direct sunlight, in this warm changeless uterine sea, neither north nor south nor east held any meaning. He remembered other lines:

> Sand-strewn caverns, cool and deep
> Where the winds are all asleep;
> Where the spent lights quiver and gleam;
> Where the salt weed sways in the stream;
> Where the sea-beasts rang'd all round
> Feed in the ooze of their pasture-ground . . .

What was the next line? Something about great whales coming sailing by, sail and sail with unshut eye, round the world for ever and aye. Yes, but there were no great whales here, if he understood his host correctly, no dolphins, no sharks, no minnows; there were only these swarming lower creatures, mysteriously raised on high, lords of the world. And mankind? Birds and bats, horses and bears? Gone. Gone. And the valleys and meadows? The lakes and streams? Taken by the sea. The world lay before him like a land of dreams, transformed. But was it, as the poet had said, a place which hath really neither joy, nor love, nor light, nor certitude, nor peace, nor help for pain? It did not seem that way. For light there was merely that diffuse faint glow, so obscure it was close to non-existent, that filtered down through unknown fathoms. But what was that lobster-song, that ever-swelling crescendo, if not some hymn to love and certitude and peace, and help for pain? He was overwhelmed by peace, surprised by joy, and he did not understand what was happening to him. He was part of the march, that was all. He was a member of the pilgrimage.

* * *

He had wanted to know if there was any way he could signal to be pulled back home: a panic button, so to speak. Bleier was the one he asked, and the question seemed to drive the man into an agony of uneasiness. He scowled, he tugged at his jowls, he ran his hands through his sparse strands of hair.

'No,' he said finally. 'We weren't able to solve that one, Jim. There's simply no way of propagating a signal backwards in time.'

'I didn't think so,' McCulloch said. 'I just wondered.'

'Since we're not actually sending your physical body, you shouldn't find yourself in any real trouble. Psychic discomfort, at the worst – disorientation, emotional upheaval, at the worst a sort of terminal homesickness. But I think you're strong enough to pull your way through any of that. And you'll always know that we're going to be yanking you back to us at the end of the experiment.'

'How long am I going to be gone?'

'Elapsed time will be virtually nil. We'll throw the switch, off you'll go, you'll do your jaunt, we'll grab you back, and it'll seem like no time at all, perhaps a thousandth of a second. We aren't going to believe that you went anywhere at all, until you start telling us about it.'

McCulloch sensed that Bleier was being deliberately evasive, not for the first time since McCulloch had been selected as the time traveller. 'It'll seem like no time at all to the people watching in the lab,' he said. 'But what about for me?'

'Well, of course for you it'll be a little different, because you'll have had a subjective experience in another time-frame.'

'That's what I'm getting at. How long are you planning to leave me in the future? An hour? A week?'

'That's really hard to determine, Jim.'

'What does that mean?'

'You know, we've sent only rabbits and stuff. They've come back OK, beyond much doubt – '

'Sure. They still munch on lettuce when they're hungry, and they don't tie their ears together in knots before they hop. So I suppose they're none the worse for wear.'

'Obviously we can't get much of a report from a rabbit.'

'Obviously.'

'You're sounding awfully goddamned hostile today, Jim. Are

you sure you don't want us to scrub the mission and start training another volunteer?' Bleier asked.

'I'm just trying to elicit a little hard info,' McCulloch said. 'I'm not trying to back out. And if I sound hostile, it's only because you're dancing all around my questions, which is becoming a considerable pain in the arse.'

Bleier looked squarely at him and glowered. 'All right. I'll tell you anything you want to know that I'm capable of answering. Which is what I think I've been doing all along. When the rabbits come back, we test them and we observe no physiological changes, no trace of ill effects as a result of having separated the psyche from the body for the duration of a time-jaunt. Christ, we can't even tell the rabbits *have* been on a time-jaunt, except that our instruments indicate the right sort of thermodynamic drain and entropic reversal, and for all we know we're kidding ourselves about that, which is why we're risking our reputations and your neck to send a human being who can tell us what the fuck happens when we throw the switch. But you've seen the rabbits jaunting. You know as well as I do that they come back OK.'

Patiently McCulloch said, 'Yes. As OK as a rabbit ever is, I guess. But what I'm trying to find out from you, and what you seem unwilling to tell me, is how long I'm going to be up there in subjective time.'

'We don't know, Jim,' Bleier said.

'You don't *know*? What if it's ten years? What if it's a thousand? What if I'm going to live out an entire life-span, or whatever is considered a life-span a hundred years from now, and grow old and wise and wither away and die and then wake up a thousandth of a second later on your lab table?'

'We don't know. That's why we have to send a human subject.'

'There's no way to measure subjective jaunt-time?'

'Our instruments are here. They aren't *there*. You're the only instrument we'll have there. For all we know, we're sending you off for a million years, and when you come back here you'll have turned into something out of H.G. Wells. Is that straightforward enough for you, Jim? But I don't think it's going to happen that way, and Mortenson doesn't think so either, or Ybarra for that matter. What we think is that you'll spend something between a day and a couple of months in the future, with the outside possibility of a year. And when we give you the hook, you'll be back here with virtually nil elapsed time. But to answer your first question again, there's no way you can instruct us to yank you back. You'll just have to sweat it out, however long it may be. I thought you knew that. The hook, when it comes, will be virtually automatic, a function of the thermodynamic homeostasis, like the recoil of a gun. An equal and opposite reaction: or maybe more like the snapping back of a rubber band. Pick whatever metaphor you want. But if you don't like the way any of this sounds, it's not too late for you to back out, and nobody will say a word against you. It's never too late to back out. Remember that, Jim.'

McCulloch shrugged. 'Thanks for levelling with me. I appreciate that. And no, I don't want to drop out. The only thing I wonder about is whether my stay in the future is going to seem too long or too goddamned short. But I won't know that until I get there, will I? And then the time I have to wait before coming home is going to be entirely out of my hands. And out of yours too, is how it seems. But that's all right. I'll take my chances. I just wondered what I'd do if I got there and found that I didn't much like it there.'

'My bet is that you'll have the opposite problem,' said Bleier. 'You'll like it so much you won't want to come back.'

Again and again, while the pilgrims travelled onwards, McCulloch detected bright flares of intelligence gleaming like brilliant pinpoints of light in the darkness of the sea. Each creature seemed to have a characteristic emanation, a glow of neural energy. The simple ones – worms, urchins, starfish, sponges – emitted dim gentle signals; but there were others as dazzling as beacons. The lobster-folk were not the only sentient life-forms down here.

Occasionally he saw, as he had in the early muddled moments of the jaunt, isolated colonies of the giant sea anemones: great flowery-looking things, rising on thick pedestals. From them came a soft alluring lustful purr, a siren crooning calculated to bring unwary animals within reach of their swaying tentacles and the eager mouths hidden within the fleshy petals. Cemented to

the floor on their swaying stalks, they seemed like sombre philos-
ophers, lost in the intervals between meals in deep reflections
on the purpose of the cosmos. McCulloch longed to pause and
try to speak with them, for their powerful emanation appeared
plainly to indicate that they possessed a strong intelligence, but
the lobsters moved past the anemones without halting.

The squidlike beings that frequently passed in flotillas overhead seemed even keener of mind: large animals, sleek and
arrogant of motion, with long turquoise bodies that terminated
in hawser-like arms, and enormous bulging eyes of a startling
scarlet colour. He found them ugly and repugnant, and did not
quite know why. Perhaps it was some attitude of his host's that
carried over subliminally to him; for there was an unmistakable
chill among the lobsters whenever the squids appeared, and
the chanting of the marchers grew more vehement, as though
betokening a warning.

That some kind of frosty détente existed between the two
kinds of life-form was apparent from the regard they showed
one another and from the distances they maintained. Never
did the squids descend into the ocean-floor zone that was the
chief domain of the lobsters, but for long spans of time they
would soar above, in a kind of patient aerial surveillance, while
the lobsters, striving ostentatiously to ignore them, betrayed
discomfort by quickened movements of their antennae.

Still other kinds of high-order intelligence manifested themselves as the pilgrimage proceeded. In a zone of hard and
rocky terrain McCulloch felt a new and distinctive mental
pulsation, coming from some creature that he must not have
encountered before. But he saw nothing unusual: merely a
rough greyish landscape pockmarked by dense clumps of oysters
and barnacles, some shaggy outcroppings of sponges and yellow
seaweeds, a couple of torpid anemones. Yet out of the midst
of all that unremarkable clutter came clear strong signals,
produced by minds of considerable force. Whose? Not the
oysters and barnacles, surely. The mystery intensified as the
lobsters, without pausing in their march, interrupted their chant
to utter words of greeting, and had greetings in return, drifting
towards them from that tangle of marine underbrush.

'Why do you march?' the unseen speakers asked, in a voice
that rose in the water like a deep slow groaning.

'We have had an Omen,' answered the lobsters.

'Ah, is it the Time?'

'The Time will surely be here,' the lobsters replied.

'Where is the herald, then?'

'The herald is within me,' said McCulloch's host, breaking its long silence at last.

– *To whom do you speak?* McCulloch asked.

– *Can you not see? There. Before us.*

McCulloch saw only algae, barnacles, sponges, oysters.

– *Where?*

– *In a moment you will see,* said the host.

The column of pilgrims had continued all the while to move forward, until now it was within the thick groves of seaweed. And now McCulloch saw who the other speakers were. Huge crabs were crouched at the bases of many of the larger rock formations, creatures far greater in size than the largest of the lobsters; but they were camouflaged so well that they were virtually invisible except at the closest range. On their broad arching backs whole gardens grew: brilliantly coloured sponges, algae in sombre reds and browns, fluffy many-branched crimson things, odd complex feathery growths, even a small anemone or two, all jammed together in such profusion that nothing of the underlying crab showed except beady long-stalked eyes and glinting claws. Why beings that signalled their presence with potent telepathic outputs should choose to cloak themselves in such elaborate concealments, McCulloch could not guess: perhaps it was to deceive a prey so simple that it was unable to detect the emanations of these crabs' minds.

As the lobsters approached, the crabs heaved themselves up a little way from the rocky bottom, and shifted themselves ponderously from side to side, causing the intricate streamers and filaments and branches of the creatures growing on them to stir and wave about. It was like a forest agitated by a sudden hard gust of wind from the north.

'Why do you march, why do you march?' called the crabs. 'Surely it is not yet the Time. Surely!'

'Surely it is,' the lobsters replied. 'So we all agree. Will you march with us?'

'Show us your herald!' the crabs cried. 'Let us see the Omen!'

    – Speak to them, said McCulloch's host.
    – But what am I to say?
    – The truth. What else can you say?
    – I know nothing. Everything here is a mystery to me.
    – I will explain all things afterwards. Speak to them now.
    – Without understanding?
    – Tell them what you told us.

Baffled, McCulloch said, speaking through the host, 'I have come from the former world as an emissary. Whether I am a herald, whether I bring an Omen, is not for me to say. In my own world I breathed air and carried my shell within my body.'

'Unmistakably a herald,' said the lobsters.

To which the crabs replied, 'That is not so unmistakable to us. We sense a wanderer and a revenant among you. But what does that mean? The Moulting of the World is not a small thing, good friends. Shall we march, just because this strangeness is come upon you? It is not enough evidence. And to march is not a small thing either, at least for us.'

'We have chosen to march,' the lobsters said, and indeed they had not halted at all throughout this colloquy; the vanguard of their procession was far out of sight in a black-walled canyon, and McCulloch's host, still at the end of the line, was passing now through the last few crouching-places of the great crabs. 'If you mean to join us, come now.'

From the crabs came a heavy outpouring of regret. 'Alas, alas, we are large, we are slow, the way is long, the path is dangerous.'

'Then we will leave you.'

'If it is the Time, we know that you will perform the offices on our behalf. If it is not the Time, it is just as well that we do not make the pilgrimage. We are – not – certain. We – cannot – be – sure – it – is – an – Omen – '

McCulloch's host was far beyond the last of the crabs. Their words were faint and indistinct, and the final few were lost in the gentle surgings of the water.

    – They make a great error, said McCulloch's host to him. *If it is truly the Time, and they do not join the march, it might happen that their souls will be lost. That is a severe risk: but they are a lazy folk. Well, we will perform the offices on their behalf.*

And to the crabs the host called, 'We will do all that is

required, have no fear!' But it was impossible, McCulloch thought, that the words could have reached the crabs across such a distance.

He and the host now were entering the mouth of the black canyon. With the host awake and talkative once again, McCulloch meant to seize the moment at last to have some answers to his questions.

– *Tell me now* – he began.

But before he could complete the thought, he felt the sea roil and surge about him as though he had been swept up in a monstrous wave. That could not be, not at this depth; but yet that irresistible force, booming towards him out of the dark canyon and catching him up, hurled him into a chaos as desperate as that of his moment of arrival. He sought to cling, to grasp, but there was no purchase; he was loose of his moorings; he was tossed and flung like a bubble on the winds.

– *Help me!* he called. *What's happening to us?*

– *To you, friend human McCulloch. To you alone. Can I aid you?*

What was that? Happening only to him? But certainly he and the lobster both were caught in this undersea tempest, both being thrown about, both whirled in the same maelstrom –

Faces danced around him. Charlie Bleier, pudgy, earnest-looking. Maggie, tender-eyed, troubled. Bleier had his hand on McCulloch's right wrist, Maggie on the other, and they were tugging, tugging –

But he had no wrists. He was a lobster.

'Come, Jim – '

'No! Not yet!'

'Jim – Jim – '

'Stop – pulling – you're hurting – '

'Jim – '

McCulloch struggled to free himself from their grasp. As he swung his arms in wild circles, Maggie and Bleier, still clinging to them, went whipping about like tethered balloons. 'Let go,' he shouted. 'You aren't here! There's nothing for you to hold on to! You're just hallucinations! Let – go –!'

And then, as suddenly as they had come, they were gone.

* * *

The sea was calm. He was in his accustomed place, seated
somewhere deep within his host's consciousness. The lobster
was moving forward, steady as ever, into the black canyon,
following the long line of its companions.

McCulloch was too stunned and dazed to attempt contact for
a long while. Finally, when he felt some measure of composure
return, he reached his mind into his host's:

– *What happened?*

– *I cannot say. What did it seem like to you?*

– *The water grew wild and stormy. I saw faces out of the former
world. Friends of mine. They were pulling at my arms. You felt
nothing?*

– *Nothing,* said the host, *except a sense of your own turmoil.
We are deep here: beyond the reach of storms.*

– *Evidently I'm not.*

– *Perhaps your homefaring-time is coming. Your world is
summoning you.*

Of course! The faces, the pulling at his arms – the plausibility
of the host's suggestion left McCulloch trembling with dismay.
Homefaring-time! Back there in the lost and inconceivable past,
they had begun angling for him, casting their line into the vast
gulf of time –

– *I'm not ready,* he protested. *I've only just arrived here! I
know nothing yet! How can they call me so soon?*

– *Resist them, if you would remain.*

– *Will you help me?*

– *How would that be possible?*

– *I'm not sure,* McCulloch said. *But it's too early for me to
go back. If they pull on me again, hold me! Can you?*

– *I can try, friend human McCulloch.*

– *And you have to keep your promise to me now.*

– *What promise is that?*

– *You said you would explain things to me. Why you've under-
taken this pilgrimage. What it is I'm supposed to be the Omen of.
What happens when the Time comes. The Moulting of the World.*

– *Ah,* said the host.

But that was all it said. In silence it scrabbled with busy
legs over a sharply creviced terrain. McCulloch felt a fierce
impatience growing in him. What if they yanked him again,
now, and this time they succeeded? There was so much yet to

learn! But he hesitated to prod the host again, feeling abashed. Long moments passed. Two more squids appeared: the radiance of their probing minds was like twin searchlights overhead. The ocean floor sloped downwards gradually but perceptibly here. The squids vanished, and another of the predatory big-mouthed swimming-things, looking as immense as a whale and, McCulloch supposed, filling the same ecological niche, came cruising down into the level where the lobsters marched, considered their numbers in what appeared to be some surprise, and swam slowly upwards again and out of sight. Something else of great size, flapping enormous wings somewhat like those of a sting-ray but clearly just a boneless mass of chitin-strutted flesh, appeared next, surveyed the pilgrims with equally bland curiosity, and flew to the front of the line of lobsters, where McCulloch lost it in the darkness. While all of this was happening the host was quiet and inaccessible, and McCulloch did not dare attempt to penetrate its privacy. But then, as the pilgrims were moving through a region where huge, dim-witted scallops with great bright eyes nestled everywhere, waving gaudy pink and blue mantles, the host unexpectedly resumed the conversation as though there had been no interruption, saying:

 – *What we call the Time of the Moulting of the World is the time when the world undergoes a change of nature, and is purified and reborn. At such a time, we journey to the place of dry land, and perform certain holy rites.*

 – *And these rites bring about the Moulting of the World?* McCulloch asked.

 – *Not at all. The Moulting is an event wholly beyond our control. The rites are performed for our own sakes, not for the world's.*

 – *I'm not sure I understand.*

 – *We wish to survive the Moulting, to travel onwards into the world to come. For this reason, at a Time of Moulting, we must make our observances, we must demonstrate our worth. It is the responsibility of my people. We bear the duty for all the peoples of the world.*

 – *A priestly caste, is that it?* McCulloch said. *When this cataclysm comes, the lobsters go forth to say the prayers for everyone, so that everyone's soul will survive?*

The host was silent again: pondering McCulloch's terms,

perhaps, translating them into more appropriate equivalents.
Eventually it replied:

– *That is essentially correct.*

– *But other peoples can join the pilgrimage if they want. Those crabs. The anemones. The squids, even?*

– *We invite all to come. But we do not expect anyone but ourselves actually to do it.*

– *How often has there been such a ceremony?* McCulloch asked.

– *I cannot say. Never, perhaps.*

– Never?

– *The Moulting of the World is not a common event. We think it has happened only twice since the beginning of time.*

In amazement McCulloch said:

– *Twice since the world began, and you think it's going to happen again in your own lifetimes?*

– *Of course we cannot be sure of that. But we have had an Omen, or so we think, and we must abide by that. It was foretold that when the end is near, an emissary from the former world would come among us. And so it has come to pass. Is that not so?*

– *Indeed.*

– *Then we must make the pilgrimage, for if you have not brought the Omen we have merely wasted some effort, but if you are the true herald we will have forfeited all of eternity if we let your message go unheeded.*

It sounded eerily familiar to McCulloch: a messianic prophecy, a cult of the millennium, an apocalyptic transfiguration. He felt for a moment as though he had landed in the tenth century instead of in some impossibly remote future epoch. And yet the host's tone was so calm and rational, the sense of spiritual obligation that the lobster conveyed was so profound, that McCulloch found nothing absurd in these beliefs. Perhaps the world *did* end from time to time, and the performing of certain rituals did in fact permit its inhabitants to transfer their souls onwards into whatever unimaginable environment was to succeed the present one. Perhaps.

– *Tell me,* said McCulloch. *What were the former worlds like, and what will the next one be?*

– *You should know more about the former worlds than I, friend* human McCulloch. *And as for the world to come, we may only speculate.*

    – *But what are your traditions about those worlds?*

    – *The first world,* the lobster said, *was a world of fire.*

    – *You can understand fire, living in the sea?*

    – *We have heard tales of it from those who have been to the dry place. Above the water there is air, and in the air there hangs a ball of fire, which gives the world warmth. Is this not the case?*

McCulloch, hearing a creature of the ocean floor speak of things so far beyond its scope and comprehension, felt a warm burst of delight and admiration.

    – *Yes! We call that ball of fire the sun.*

    – *Ah, so that is what you mean, when you think of the sun! The word was a mystery to me, when first you used it. But I understand you much better now, do you not agree?*

    – *You amaze me,* McCulloch said.

    – *The first world, so we think, was fire: it was like the sun. And when we dwelled upon that world, we were fire also. It is the fire that we carry within us to this day, that glow, that brightness, which is our life, and which goes from us when we die. After a span of time so long that we could never describe its length, the Time of the Moulting came upon the fire-world and it grew hard, and gathered a cloak of air about itself, and creatures lived upon the land and breathed the air. I find that harder to comprehend, in truth, than I do the fire-world. But that was the first Moulting, when the air-world emerged: that world from which you have come to us. I hope you will tell me of your world, friend human McCulloch, when there is time.*

    – *So I will,* said McCulloch. *But there is so much more I need to hear from you first!*

    – *Ask it.*

    – *The second Moulting – the disappearance of my world, the coming of yours –*

    – *The tradition is that the sea existed, even in the former world, and that it was not small. At the Time of the Moulting it rose and devoured the land and all that was upon it, except for one place that was not devoured, which is sacred. And then all the world was covered by water, and that was the second Moulting, which brought forth the third world.*

    – *How long ago was that?*

– How can I speak of the passing of time? There is no way to speak of that. Time passes, and lives end, and worlds are transformed. But we have no words for that. If every grain of sand in the sea were one lifetime, then it would be as many lifetimes ago as there are grains of sand in the sea. But does that help you? Does that tell you anything? It happened. It was very long ago. And now our world's turn has come, or so we think.

– And the next world? What will that be like? McCulloch asked.

– There are those who claim to know such things, but I am not one of them. We will know the next world when we have entered it, and I am content to wait until then for the knowledge.

McCulloch had a sense then that the host had wearied of this sustained contact, and was withdrawing once again from it; and, though his own thirst for knowledge was far from sated, he chose once again not to attempt to resist that withdrawal.

All this while the pilgrims had continued down a gentle incline into the great bowl of a sunken valley. Once again now the ocean floor was level, but the water was notably deeper here, and the diffused light from above was so dim that only the most rugged of algae could grow, making the landscape bleak and sparse. There were no sponges here, and little coral, and the anemones were pale and small, giving little sign of the potent intelligence that infused their larger cousins in the shallower zones of the sea.

But there were other creatures at this level that McCulloch had not seen before. Platoons of alert, mobile oysters skipped over the bottom, leaping in agile bounds on columns of water that they squirted like jets from tubes in their dark green mantles: now and again they paused in mid-leap and their shells quickly opened and closed, snapping shut, no doubt, on some hapless larval thing of the plankton too small for McCulloch, via the lobster's imperfect vision, to detect. From these oysters came bright darting blurts of mental activity, sharp and probing: they must be as intelligent, he thought, as cats or dogs. Yet from time to time a lobster, swooping with an astonishingly swift claw, would seize one of these oysters and deftly, almost instantaneously, shuck and devour it. Appetite was no respecter of intelligence in this world of needful carnivores, McCulloch realized.

Intelligent, too, in their way, were the hordes of nearly invisible little crustaceans – shrimp of some sort, he imagined – that danced in shining clouds just above the line of march. They were ghostly things perhaps an inch long, virtually transparent, colourless, lovely, graceful. Their heads bore two huge glistening black eyes; their intestines, glowing coils running the length of their bodies, were tinged with green; the tips of their tails were an elegant crimson. They swam with the aid of a horde of busy finlike legs, and seemed almost to be mocking their stolid, plodding cousins as they marched; but these sparkling little creatures also occasionally fell victim to the lobsters' inexorable claws, and each time it was like the extinguishing of a tiny brilliant candle.

An emanation of intelligence of a different sort came from bulky animals that McCulloch noticed roaming through the gravelly foothills flanking the line of march. These seemed at first glance to be another sort of lobster, larger even than McCulloch's companions: heavily armoured things with many-segmented abdomens and thick paddle-shaped arms. But then, as one of them drew nearer, McCulloch saw the curved tapering tail with its sinister spike, and realized he was in the presence of the scorpions of the sea.

They gave off a deep, almost somnolent mental wave: slow thinkers but not light ones, Teutonic ponderers, grapplers with the abstruse. There were perhaps two dozen of them, who advanced upon the pilgrims and in quick one-sided struggles pounced, stung, slew. McCulloch watched in amazement as each of the scorpions dragged away a victim and, no more than a dozen feet from the line of march, began to gouge into its armour to draw forth tender chunks of pale flesh, without drawing the slightest response from the impassive, steadily marching column of lobsters.

They had not been so complacent when the great-mouthed swimming thing had menaced McCulloch's host; then, the lobsters had come in hordes to tear the attacker apart. And whenever one of the big squids came by, the edgy hostility of the lobsters, their willingness to do battle if necessary, was manifest. But they seemed indifferent to the scorpions. The lobsters accepted their onslaught as placidly as though it were merely a toll they must pay in order to pass through this district.

Perhaps it was. McCulloch was only beginning to perceive how dense and intricate a fabric of ritual bound this submarine world together.

The lobsters marched onwards, chanting in unfailing rhythm as though nothing untoward had happened. The scorpions, their hungers evidently gratified, withdrew and congregated a short distance off, watching without much show of interest as the procession went by them. By the time McCulloch's host, bringing up the rear, had gone past the scorpions, they were fighting among themselves in a lazy, half-hearted way, like playful lions after a successful hunt. Their mental emanation, sluggishly booming through the water, grew steadily more blurred, more vague, more toneless.

And then it was overlaid and entirely masked by the pulsation of some new and awesome kind of mind ahead: one of enormous power, whose output beat upon the water with what was almost a physical force, like some massive metal chain being lashed against the surface of the ocean. Apparently the source of this gigantic output still lay at a considerable distance, for, strong as it was, it grew stronger still as the lobsters advanced towards it, until at last it was an overwhelming clangour, terrifying, bewildering. McCulloch could no longer remain quiescent under the impact of that monstrous sound. Breaking through to the sanctuary of his host, he cried:

– *What is it?*

– *We are approaching a god,* the lobster replied.

– *A god, did you say?*

– *A divine presence, yes. Did you think we were the rulers of this world?*

In fact McCulloch had, assuming automatically that his time-jaunt had deposited him within the consciousness of some member of this world's highest species, just as he would have expected to have landed, had he reached the twenty-second century as intended, in the consciousness of a human rather than in a frog or a horse. But obviously the division between humanity and all sub-sentient species in his own world did not have an exact parallel here; many races, perhaps all of them, had some sort of intelligence, and it was becoming clear that the lobsters, though a high life-form, were not the highest. He found that dismaying and even humbling; for the lobsters

seemed quite adequately intelligent to him, quite the equals –
for all his early condescension to them – of mankind itself. And
now he was to meet one of their gods? How great a mind was
a god likely to have?

The booming of that mind grew unbearably intense, nor was
there any way to hide from it. McCulloch visualized himself
doubled over in pain, pressing his hands to his ears, an image
that drew a quizzical shaft of thought from his host. Still the
lobsters pressed forward, but even they were responding now
to the waves of mental energy that rippled outwards from that
unimaginable source. They had at last broken ranks, and were
fanning out horizontally on the broad dark plain of the ocean
floor, as though deploying themselves before a place of worship.
Where was the god? McCulloch, striving with difficulty to see
in this nearly lightless place, thought he made out some vast
shape ahead, some dark entity, swollen and fearsome, that
rose like a colossal boulder in the midst of the suddenly
diminutive-looking lobsters. He saw eyes like bright yellow
platters, gleaming furiously; he saw a huge frightful beak; he
saw what he thought at first to be a nest of writhing serpents,
and then realized to be tentacles, dozens of them, coiling and
uncoiling with a terrible restless energy. To the host he said:

– *Is that your god?*

But he could not hear the reply, for an agonizing new force
suddenly buffeted him, one even more powerful than that
which was emanating from the giant creature that sat before
him. It ripped upwards through his soul like a spike. It cast
him forth, and he tumbled over and over, helpless in some
incomprehensible limbo, where nevertheless he could still hear
the faint distant voice of his lobster host:

– *Friend human McCulloch? Friend human McCulloch?*

He was drowning. He had waded incautiously into the surf,
deceived by the beauty of the transparent tropical water and
the shimmering white sand below, and a wave had caught him
and knocked him to his knees, and the next wave had come
before he could arise, pulling him under. And now he tossed
like a discarded doll in the suddenly turbulent sea, struggling
to get his head above water and failing, failing, failing.

Maggie was standing on the shore, calling in panic to him,

and somehow he could hear her words even through the tumult of the crashing waves: 'This way, Jim, swim towards me! Oh, please, Jim, this way, this way!'

Bleier was there too, Mortenson, Bob Rodrigues, the whole group, ten or fifteen people, running about worriedly, beckoning to him, calling his name. It was odd that he could see them, if he was under water. And he could hear them so clearly, too, Bleier telling him to stand up and walk ashore, the water wasn't deep at all, and Rodrigues saying to come in on hands and knees if he couldn't manage to get up, and Ybarra yelling that it was getting late, that they couldn't wait all the goddamned afternoon, that he had been swimming long enough. McCulloch wondered why they didn't come after him, if they were so eager to get him to shore. Obviously he was in trouble. Obviously he was unable to help himself.

'Look,' he said, 'I'm drowning, can't you see? Throw me a line, for Christ's sake!' Water rushed into his mouth as he spoke. It filled his lungs, it pressed against his brain.

'We can't hear you, Jim!'

'Throw me a line!' he cried again, and felt the torrents pouring through his body. 'I'm – drowning – drowning – '

And then he realized that he did not at all want them to rescue him, that it was worse to be rescued than to drown. He did not understand why he felt that way, but he made no attempt to question the feeling. All that concerned him now was preventing those people on the shore, those humans, from seizing him and taking him from the water. They were rushing about, assembling some kind of machine to pull him in, an arm at the end of a great boom. McCulloch signalled to them to leave him alone.

'I'm OK,' he called. 'I'm not drowning after all! I'm fine right where I am!'

But now they had their machine in operation, and its long metal arm was reaching out over the water towards him. He turned and dived, and swam as hard as he could away from the shore, but it was no use: the boom seemed to extend over an infinite distance, and no matter how fast he swam the boom moved faster, so that it hovered just above him now, and from its tip some sort of hook was descending –

'No – no – let me be! I don't want to go ashore!'

Then he felt a hand on his wrist: firm, reassuring, taking control. All right, he thought. They've caught me after all, they're going to pull me in. There's nothing I can do about it. They have me, and that's all there is to it. But he realized, after a moment, that he was heading not towards shore but out to sea, beyond the waves, into the calm depths. And the hand that was on his wrist was not a hand; it was a tentacle, thick as heavy cable, a strong sturdy tentacle lined on one side by rounded suction cups that held him in an unbreakable grip.

That was all right. Anything to be away from that wild crashing surf. It was much more peaceful out here. He could rest, catch his breath, get his equilibrium. And all the while that powerful tentacle towed him steadily seawards. He could still hear the voices of his friends on shore, but they were as faint as the cries of distant sea birds now, and when he looked back he saw only tiny dots, like excited ants, moving along the beach. McCulloch waved at them. 'See you some other time,' he called. 'I didn't want to come out of the water yet anyway.' Better here. Much much better. Peaceful. Warm. Like the womb. And that tentacle around his wrist: so reassuring, so steady.

   – Friend human McCulloch? Friend human McCulloch?

   – This is where I belong. Isn't it?

   – Yes. This is where you belong. You are one of us, friend human McCulloch. You are one of us.

Gradually the turbulence subsided, and he found himself regaining his balance. He was still within the lobster; the whole horde of lobsters was gathered around him, thousands upon thousands of them, a gentle solicitous community; and right in front of him was the largest octopus imaginable, a creature that must have been fifteen or twenty feet in diameter, with tentacles that extended an implausible distance on all sides. Somehow he did not find the sight frightening.

   'He is recovered now,' his host announced.

   – What happened to me? McCulloch asked.

   – Your people called you again. But you did not want to make your homefaring, and you resisted them. And when we understood that you wanted to remain, the god aided you, and you broke free of their pull.

   – The god?

His host indicated the great octopus.

– *There.*

It did not seem at all improbable to McCulloch now. The infinite fullness of time brings about everything, he thought: even intelligent lobsters, even a divine octopus. He still could feel the mighty telepathic output of the vast creature, but though it had lost none of its power it no longer caused him discomfort; it was like the roaring thunder of some great waterfall, to which one becomes accustomed, and which, in time, one begins to love. The octopus sat motionless, its immense yellow eyes trained on McCulloch, its scarlet mantle rippling gently, its tentacles weaving in intricate patterns. McCulloch thought of an octopus he had once seen when he was diving in the West Indies: a small shy scuttling thing, hurrying to slither behind a gnarled coral head. He felt chastened and awed by this evidence of the magnifications wrought by the aeons. A hundred million years? Half a billion? The numbers were without meaning. But that span of years had produced this creature. He sensed a serene intelligence of incomprehensible depth, benign, tranquil, all-penetrating: a god indeed. Yes. Truly a god. Why not?

The great cephalopod was partly sheltered by an overhanging wall of rock. Clustered about it were dozens of the scorpion-things, motionless, poised: plainly a guard force. Overhead swam a whole army of the big squids, doubtless guardians also, and for once the presence of those creatures did not trigger any emotion in the lobsters, as if they regarded squids in the service of the god as acceptable ones. The scene left McCulloch dazed with awe. He had never felt farther from home.

– *The god would speak with you,* said his host.

– *What shall I say?*

– *Listen, first.*

McCulloch's lobster moved forward until it stood virtually beneath the octopus's huge beak. From the octopus, then, came an outpouring of words that McCulloch did not immediately comprehend, but which, after a moment, he understood to be some kind of benediction that enfolded his soul like a warm blanket. And gradually he perceived that he was being spoken to.

'Can you tell us why you have come all this way, human McCulloch?'

'It was an error. They didn't mean to send me so far – only a hundred years or less, that was all we were trying to cross. But it was our first attempt. We didn't really know what we were doing. And I suppose I wound up halfway across time – a hundred million years, two hundred, maybe a billion – who knows?'

'It is a great distance. Do you feel no fear?'

'At the beginning I did. But not any longer. This world is alien to me, but not frightening.'

'Do you prefer it to your own?'

'I don't understand,' McCulloch said.

'Your people summoned you. You refused to go. You appealed to us for aid, and we aided you in resisting your homecalling, because it was what you seemed to require from us.'

'I'm – not ready to go home yet,' he said. 'There's so much I haven't seen yet, and that I want to see. I want to see everything. I'll never have an opportunity like this again. Perhaps no-one ever will. Besides, I have services to perform here. I'm the herald; I bring the Omen; I'm part of this pilgrimage. I think I ought to stay until the rites have been performed. I *want* to stay until then.'

'Those rites will not be performed,' said the octopus quietly.

'Not performed?'

'You are not the herald. You carry no Omen. The Time is not at hand.'

McCulloch did not know what to reply. Confusion swirled within him. No Omen? Not the Time?

– *It is so,* said the host. *We were in error. The god has shown us that we came to our conclusion too quickly. The Time of the Moulting may be near, but it is not yet upon us. You have many of the outer signs of a herald, but there is no Omen upon you. You are merely a visitor. An accident.*

McCulloch was assailed by a startlingly keen pang of disappointment. It was absurd; but for a time he had been the central figure in some apocalyptic ritual of immense significance, or at least had been thought to be, and all that suddenly was gone from him, and he felt strangely diminished, irrelevant, bereft of his bewildering grandeur. A visitor. An accident.

– *In that case I feel great shame and sorrow,* he said. *To have caused so much trouble for you. To have sent you off on this pointless pilgrimage.*

– *No blame attaches to you*, said the host. *We acted of our free choice, after considering the evidence.*

'Nor was the pilgrimage pointless,' the octopus declared. 'There are no pointless pilgrimages. And this one will continue.'

'But if there's no Omen – if this is not the Time – '

'There are other needs to consider,' replied the octopus, 'and other observances to carry out. We must visit the dry place ourselves, from time to time, so that we may prepare ourselves for the world that is to succeed ours, for it will be very different from ours. It is time now for such a visit, and well past time. And also we must bring you to the dry place, for only there can we properly make you one of us.'

'I don't understand,' said McCulloch.

'You have asked to stay among us; and if you stay, you must become one of us, for your sake, and for ours. And that can best be done at the dry place. It is not necessary that you understand that now, human McCulloch.'

– *Make no further reply*, said McCulloch's host. *The god has spoken. We must proceed.*

Shortly the lobsters resumed their march, chanting as before, though in a more subdued way, and, so it seemed to McCulloch, singing a different melody. From the context of his conversation with it, McCulloch had supposed that the octopus now would accompany them, which puzzled him, for the huge unwieldy creature did not seem capable of any extensive journey. That proved to be the case: the octopus did not go along, though the vast booming resonances of its mental output followed the procession for what must have been hundreds of miles.

Once more the line was a single one, with McCulloch's host at the end of the file. A short while after departure it said:

– *I am glad, friend human McCulloch, that you chose to continue with us. I would be sorry to lose you now.*

– *Do you mean that? Isn't it an inconvenience for you, to carry me around inside your mind?*

– *I have grown quite accustomed to it. You are part of me, friend human McCulloch. We are part of one another. At*

*the place of the dry land we will celebrate our sharing of
this body.*

– *I was lucky*, said McCulloch, *to have landed like this in a
mind that would make me welcome.*

– *Any of us would have made you welcome*, responded
the host.

McCulloch pondered that. Was it merely a courteous turn of
phrase, or did the lobster mean him to take the answer literally?
Most likely the latter: the host's words seemed always to have
only a single level of meaning, a straightforwardly literal one. So
any of the lobsters would have taken him in uncomplainingly?
Perhaps so. They appeared to be virtually interchangeable
beings, without distinctive individual personalities, without
names, even. The host had remained silent when McCulloch
had asked him its name, and had not seemed to understand
what kind of a label McCulloch's own name was. So powerful
was their sense of community, then, that they must have little
sense of private identity. He had never cared much for that sort
of hive-mentality, where he had observed it in human society.
But here it seemed not only appropriate but admirable.

– *How much longer will it be*, McCulloch asked, *before we
reach the place of dry land?*

– *Long.*

– *Can you tell me where it is?*

– *It is in the place where the world grows narrower*, said
the host.

McCulloch had realized, the moment he asked the question,
that it was meaningless: what useful answer could the lobster
possibly give? The old continents were gone and their names
long forgotten. But the answer he had received was meaningless
too: where, on a round planet, is the place where the world
grows narrower? He wondered what sort of geography the
lobsters understood. If I live among them a hundred years, he
thought, I will probably just begin to comprehend what their
perceptions are like.

Where the world grows narrower. All right. Possibly the place
of the dry land was some surviving outcropping of the former
world, the summit of Mount Everest, perhaps, Kilimanjaro,
whatever. Or perhaps not: perhaps even those peaks had been
ground down by time, and new ones had arisen – one of them,

at least, tall enough to rise above the universal expanse of sea. It was folly to suppose that any shred at all of his world remained accessible: it was all down there beneath tons of water and millions of years of sediments, the old continents buried, hidden, rearranged by time like pieces scattered about a board.

The pulsations of the octopus's mind could no longer be felt. As the lobsters went tirelessly onwards, moving always in that lithe skipping stride of theirs and never halting to rest or to feed, the terrain rose for a time and then began to dip again, slightly at first and then more than slightly. They entered into waters that were deeper and significantly darker, and somewhat cooler as well. In this sombre zone, where vision seemed all but useless, the pilgrims grew silent for long spells for the first time, neither chanting nor speaking to one another, and McCulloch's host, who had become increasingly quiet, disappeared once more into its impenetrable inner domain and rarely emerged.

In the gloom and darkness there began to appear a strange red glow off to the left, as though someone had left a lantern hanging midway between the ocean floor and the surface of the sea. The lobsters, when that mysterious light came into view, at once changed the direction of their line of march to go veering off to the right; but at the same time they resumed their chanting, and kept one eye trained on the glowing place as they walked.

The water felt warmer here. A zone of unusual heat was spreading outwards from the glow. And the taste of the water, and what McCulloch persisted in thinking of as its smell, were peculiar, with a harsh choking salty flavour. Brimstone? Ashes?

McCulloch realized that what he was seeing was an undersea volcano, belching forth a stream of red-hot lava that was turning the sea into a boiling bubbling cauldron. The sight stirred him oddly. He felt that he was looking into the pulsing ancient core of the world, the primordial flame, the geological link that bound the otherwise vanished former worlds to this one. There awakened in him a powerful tide of awe, and a baffling unfocused yearning that he might have termed homesickness, except that it was not, for he was no longer sure where his true home lay.

– *Yes*, said the host. *It is a mountain on fire. We think it is a part of the older of the two former worlds that has endured both of the Moultings. It is a very sacred place.*

– *An object of pilgrimage?* McCulloch asked.

– *Only to those who wish to end their lives. The fire devours all who approach it.*

– *In my world we had many such fiery mountains,* McCulloch said. *They often did great destruction.*

– *How strange your world must have been!*

– *It was very beautiful,* said McCulloch.

– *Surely. But strange. The dry land, the fire in the air – the sun, I mean – the air-breathing creatures – yes, strange, very strange. I can scarcely believe it really existed.*

– *There are times, now, when I begin to feel the same way,* McCulloch said.

The volcano receded in the distance; its warmth could no longer be felt; the water was dark again, and cold, and growing colder, and McCulloch could no longer detect any trace of that sulphurous aroma. It seemed to him that they were moving now down an endless incline, where scarcely any creatures dwelled.

And then he realized that the marchers ahead had halted, and were drawn up in a long row as they had been when they came to the place where the octopus held its court. Another god? No. There was only blackness ahead.

– *Where are we?* he asked.

– *It is the shore of the great abyss.*

Indeed what lay before them looked like the Pit itself: lightless, without landmark, and empty landscape. McCulloch understood now that they had been marching all this while across some sunken continent's coastal plain, and at last they had come to – what? – the graveyard where one of Earth's lost oceans lay buried in ocean?

– *Is it possible to continue?* he asked.

– *Of course,* said the host. *But now we must swim.*

Already the lobsters before them were kicking off from shore with vigorous strokes of their tails and vanishing into the open sea beyond. A moment later McCulloch's host joined them. Almost at once there was no sense of a bottom beneath them, – only a dark and infinitely deep void. Swimming across this,

McCulloch thought, is like falling through time – an endless descent and no safety net.

The lobsters, he knew, were not true swimming creatures: like the lobsters of his own era they were bottom-dwellers, who walked to get where they needed to go. But they could never cross this abyss that way, and so they were swimming now, moving steadily by flexing their huge abdominal muscles and their tails. Was it terrifying to them to be setting forth into a place without landmarks like this? His host remained utterly calm, as though this were no more than an afternoon stroll.

McCulloch lost what little perception of the passage of time that he had had. Heave, stroke, forward, heave, stroke, forward, that was all, endless repetition. Out of the depths there occasionally came an upwelling of cold water, like a dull, heavy river miraculously flowing upwards through air, and in that strange surging from below rose a fountain of nourishment, tiny transparent struggling creatures and even smaller flecks of some substance that must have been edible, for the lobsters, without missing a stroke, sucked in all they could hold. And swam on and on. McCulloch had a sense of being involved in a trek of epic magnitude, a once-in-many-generations thing that would be legendary long after.

Enemies roved this open sea: the free-swimming creatures that had evolved out of God only knew which kinds of worms or slugs to become the contemporary equivalents of sharks and whales. Now and again one of these huge beasts dived through the horde of lobsters, harvesting it at will. But they could eat only so much; and the survivors kept going onwards.

Until at last – months, years later? – the far shore came into view; the ocean floor, long invisible, reared up beneath them and afforded support; the swimmers at last put their legs down on the solid bottom, and with something that sounded much like gratitude in their voices began once again to chant in unison as they ascended the rising flank of a new continent.

The first rays of the sun, when they came into view an unknown span of time later, struck McCulloch with an astonishing, over-whelming impact. He perceived them first as a pale greenish glow resting in the upper levels of the sea just ahead, striking downwards like illuminated wands; he did not then know what he was seeing, but the sight engendered wonder in him all the same, and later, when that radiance diminished and was gone and in a short while returned, he understood that the pilgrims were coming up out of the sea. So they had reached their goal: the still point of the turning world, the one remaining unsubmerged scrap of the former Earth.

– *Yes,* said the host. *This is it.*

In that same instant McCulloch felt another tug from the past: a summons dizzying in its imperative impact. He thought he could hear Maggie Caldwell's voice crying across the time-winds: 'Jim, Jim, come back to us!' And Bleier, grouchy, angered, muttering, 'For Christ's sake, McCulloch, stop holding on up there! This is getting expensive!' Was it all his imagination, that fantasy of hands on his wrists, familiar faces hovering before his eyes?

'Leave me alone,' he said. 'I'm still not ready.'

'Will you ever be?' That was Maggie. 'Jim, you'll be marooned. You'll be stranded there if you don't let us pull you back now.'

'I may be marooned already,' he said, and brushed the voices out of his mind with surprising ease.

He returned his attention to his companions and saw that they had halted their trek a little way short of that zone of light which now was but a quick scramble ahead of them. Their linear formation was broken once again. Some of the lobsters, marching blindly forward, were piling up in confused-looking heaps in the shallows, forming mounds fifteen or twenty lobsters deep. Many of the others had begun a bizarre convulsive dance: a wild twitchy cavorting, rearing up on their back legs, waving their claws about, flicking their antennae in frantic circles.

– *What's happening?* McCulloch asked his host. *Is this the beginning of a rite?*

But the host did not reply. The host did not appear to be within their shared body at all. McCulloch felt a silence far deeper than the host's earlier withdrawals; this seemed not a withdrawal but an evacuation, leaving McCulloch in sole possession. That new solitude came rolling in upon him with a crushing force. He sent forth a tentative probe, found nothing, found less than nothing. Perhaps it's meant to be this way, he thought. Perhaps it was necessary for him to face this climactic initiation unaided, unaccompanied.

Then he noticed that what he had taken to be a weird jerky dance was actually the onset of a mass moulting prodrome. Hundreds of the lobsters had been stricken simultaneously, he realized, with that strange painful sense of inner expansion, of volcanic upheaval and stress: that heaving and rearing about was the first stage of the splitting of the shell.

And all of the moulters were females.

Until that instant McCulloch had not been aware of any division into sexes among the lobsters. He had barely been able to tell one from the next; they had no individual character, no shred of uniqueness. Now, suddenly, strangely, he knew without being told that half of his companions were females, and that they were moulting now because they were fertile only when they had shed their old armour, and that the pilgrimage to the place of the dry land was the appropriate time to engender the young. He had asked no questions of anyone to learn that; the knowledge was simply within him; and, reflecting on that, he saw that the host was absent from him because the host was wholly fused with him; he was the host, the host was Jim McCulloch.

He approached a female, knowing precisely which one was the appropriate one, and sang to her, and she acknowledged his song with a song of her own, and raised her third pair of legs to him, and let him plant his gametes beside her oviducts. There was no apparent pleasure in it, as he remembered pleasure from his days as a human. Yet it brought him a subtle but unmistakable sense of fulfilment, of the completion of biological destiny, that had a kind of orgasmic finality about it, and left him calm and anchored at the absolute dead centre of his soul: yes, truly the still point of the turning world, he thought.

His mate moved away to begin her new Growing and the awaiting of her motherhood. And McCulloch, unbidden, began to ascend the slope that led to the land.

The bottom was fine sand here, soft, elegant. He barely touched it with his legs as he raced shorewards. Before him lay a world of light, radiant, heavenly, a bright irresistible beacon. He went on until the water, pearly-pink and transparent, was only a foot or two deep, and the domed upper curve of his back was reaching into the air. He felt no fear. There was no danger in this. Serenely he went forward – the leader, now, of the trek – and climbed out into the hot sunlight.

It was an island, low and sandy, so small that he imagined he could cross it in a day. The sky was intensely blue and the sun, hanging close to a noon position, looked swollen and fiery. A little grove of palm trees clustered a few hundred yards inland, but he saw nothing else, no birds, no insects, no animal life of any sort. Walking was difficult here – his breath was short, his shell seemed to be too tight, his stalked eyes were stinging in the air – but he pulled himself forward, almost to the trees. Other male lobsters, hundreds of them, thousands of them, were following. He felt himself linked to each of them: his people, his nation, his community, his brothers.

Now, at that moment of completion and communion, came one more call from the past.

There was no turbulence in it this time. No-one was yanking at his wrists, no surf boiled and heaved in his mind and threatened to dash him on the reefs of the soul. The call was simple and clear: *This is the moment of coming back, Jim.*

Was it? Had he no choice? He belonged here. These were his people. This was where his loyalties lay.

And yet, and yet: he knew that he had been sent on a mission unique in human history, that he had been granted a vision beyond all dreams, that it was his duty to return and report on it. There was no ambiguity about that. He owed it to Bleier and Maggie and Ybarra and the rest to return, to tell them everything.

How clear it all was! He belonged *here*, and he belonged *there*, and an unbreakable net of loyalties and responsibilities held him to both places. It was a perfect equilibrium; and therefore he was tranquil and at ease. The pull was on him; he resisted nothing, for he was at last beyond all resistance to anything. The immense sun was a drumbeat in the heavens; the fiery warmth was a benediction; he had never known such peace.

'I must make my homefaring now,' he said, and released himself, and let himself drift upwards, light as a bubble, towards the sun.

Strange figures surrounded him, tall and narrow-bodied, with odd fleshy faces and huge moist mouths and bulging staring eyes, and their kind of speech was a crude hubbub of sound-waves that bashed and battered against his sensibilities with painful intensity. 'We were afraid the signal wasn't reaching you, Jim,' they said. 'We tried again and again, but there was no contact, nothing. And then just as we were giving up, suddenly your eyes were opening, you were stirring, you stretched your arms – '

He felt air pouring into his body, and dryness all about him. It was a struggle to understand the speech of these creatures who were bending over him, and he hated the reek that came from their flesh and the booming vibrations that they made with their mouths. But gradually he found himself returning to himself, like one who has been lost in a dream so profound that it eclipses reality for the first few moments of wakefulness.

'How long was I gone?' he asked.

'Four minutes and eighteen seconds,' Ybarra said.

McCulloch shook his head. 'Four minutes? Eighteen seconds? It was more like forty months, to me. Longer. I don't know how long.'

'Where did you go, Jim? What was it like?'

'Wait,' someone else said. 'He's not ready for debriefing yet. Can't you see, he's about to collapse?'

McCulloch shrugged. 'You sent me too far.'

'How far? Five hundred years?' Maggie asked.

'Millions,' he said.

Someone gasped.

'He's dazed,' a voice said at his left ear.

'Millions of years,' McCulloch said in a slow, steady, deter-minedly articulate voice. '*Millions*. The whole earth was covered by the sea, except for one little island. The people are lobsters. They have a society, a culture. They worship a giant octopus.'

Maggie was crying. 'Jim, oh, Jim – '

'No. It's true. I went on migration with them. Intelligent lobsters is what they are. And I wanted to stay with them for ever. I felt you pulling at me, but I – didn't – want – to – go – '

'Give him a sedative, Doc,' Bleier said.

'You think I'm crazy? You think I'm deranged? They were lobsters, fellows. *Lobsters*.'

*   *   *

77

After he had slept and showered and changed his clothes they came to see him again, and by that time he realized that he must have been behaving like a lunatic in the first moments of his return, blurting out his words, weeping, carrying on, crying out what surely had sounded like gibberish to them. Now he was rested, he was calm, he was at home in his own body once again.

He told them all that had befallen him, and from their faces he saw at first that they still thought he had gone round the bend: but as he kept speaking, quietly, straightforwardly, in rich detail, they began to acknowledge his report in subtle little ways, asking questions about the geography, about the ecological balance in a manner that showed him they were not simply humouring him. And after that, as it sank in upon them that he really had dwelled for a period of many months at the far end of time, beyond the span of the present world, they came to look upon him – it was unmistakable – as someone who was now wholly unlike them. In particular he saw the cold glassy stare in Maggie Caldwell's eyes.

Then they left him, for he was tiring again; and later Maggie came to see him alone, and took his hand and held it between hers, which were cold.

She said, 'What do you want to do now, Jim?'

'To go back there.'

'I thought you did.'

'It's impossible, isn't it?' he said.

'We could try. But it couldn't ever work. We don't know what we're doing, yet, with that machine. We don't know where we'd send you. We might miss by a million years. By a billion.'

'That's what I figured too.'

'But you want to go back?'

He nodded. 'I can't explain it. It was like being a member of some Buddhist monastery, do you see? Feeling *absolutely sure* that this is where you belong, that everything fits together perfectly, that you're an integral part of it. I've never felt anything like that before. I never will again.'

'I'll talk to Bleier, Jim, about sending you back.'

'No. Don't. I can't possibly get there. And I don't want to land anywhere else. Let Ybarra take the next trip. I'll stay here.'

'Will you be happy?'
He smiled. 'I'll do my best,' he said.

When the others understood what the problem was, they saw
to it that he went into re-entry therapy – Bleier had already
foreseen something like that, and made preparations for it –
and after a while the pain went from him, that sense of having
undergone a violent separation, of having been ripped untimely
from the womb. He resumed his work in the group and gradually
recovered his mental balance and took an active part in the
second transmission, which sent a young anthropologist named
Ludwig off for two minutes and eight seconds. Ludwig did not
see lobsters, to McCulloch's intense disappointment. He went
sixty years into the future and came back glowing with wondrous
tales of atomic fusion plants.

That was too bad, McCulloch thought. But soon he decided
that it was just as well, that he preferred being the only one
who had encountered the world beyond this world, probably
the only human being who ever would.

He thought of that world with love, wondering about his mate
and her millions of larvae, about the journey of his friends back
across the great abyss, about the legends that were being spun
about his visit in that unimaginably distant epoch. Sometimes
the pain of separation returned, and Maggie found him crying in
the night, and held him until he was whole again. And eventually
the pain did not return. But still he did not forget, and in some
part of his soul he longed to make his homefaring back to his
true kind, and he rarely passed a day when he did not think he
could hear the inaudible sound of delicate claws, scurrying over
the sands of silent seas.

Basileus

Writing instructors often tell novice writers that they'll do their best work when they're writing about subjects they know very well, or when they're expressing some strongly-held conviction. It's not bad advice, but it doesn't necessarily hold true for experienced professionals. Here's a case in point.

'Basileus' is a story about a computer nerd who can call up real angels on his computer. It's full of convincing-sounding stuff about hardware, software, programming and such. It brims with incidental detail about the special qualities of particular angels.

I don't believe in angels.

And I had never used a computer at the time that I wrote the story.

You see what tricky characters professional writers are? Someone – was it L. Sprague de Camp? – once referred to us as people who earn their livings by telling lies. Exactly so. In my personal life I happen to be – trust me – more than usually scrupulous about telling the truth. But when I sit down to write a story, I'm willing to tell you any damn thing, and I'm capable of making you believe it, because for the time that I'm writing the story *I believe it myself.* Trust me. The best liars are those who speak out of the absolute conviction that what they're saying is so.

In the case of 'Basileus', I needed a story idea and I had, for the moment, run absolutely dry. It was September of 1982, a warm and golden month, and I was exhausted after having spent the previous six months writing an immense historical novel, *Lord of Darkness.* In those days I did my writing on a typewriter – a *manual* typewriter, none of those exotic electric jobs for me – and *Lord of Darkness* was something like 800 pages long. I had typed the entire thing twice over, plus perhaps 400 pages of incidental revisions along the way, which came out to more than two thousand pages of typing, *blam blam blam* all summer long. Now the job was done and I just wanted to sit back and think about something other than writing stories, or perhaps not think of anything at all.

But Don Myrus, one of the editors of *Omni* magazine, had conceived the idea of doing a special Robert Silverberg issue. Harlan Ellison would write an article about me, two of my earlier stories would be reprinted, and I would contribute a brand-new piece to top everything off. It was too flattering to refuse. But where was I going to get that brand-new story? I was wiped out. I had reached that point, so dreadfully familiar to any writer who has just finished a major project, where I felt convinced that I'd never have a story idea again.

But Don Myrus wasn't going to believe that. I had to come up with something for him, and it had to be done right away.

One tactic that I've sometimes used when stuck for an idea is to grab two unrelated concepts at random, jam them together, and see if they strike any sparks. I tried it. I picked up the day's newspaper and glanced quickly at two different pages.

The most interesting words that rose to my eye were 'computers' and 'angels'.

All right. I had my story, right then and there. *Nerd uses his computer to talk to angels.*

Corny? No. *Nothing's* corny if handled the right way. Trust me.

The antidote for corniness is verisimilitude. I had to write about angels as though I had spent my whole life conversing with them and knew them all by their first names. Well, I stockpile oddball reference books for just such moments, and among them is a copy of Gustav Davidson's *Dictionary of Angels*. (Due credit is given in the story.) I began to leaf through it. Very quickly I was on past Michael and Gabriel and Raphael into the more esoteric ones like Israfel, who will blow the trumpet to get the Day of Judgment under way, and Anaphaxeton, who will summon the entire universe before the court. Once I found them, I knew that I had the dramatic situation around which to build my plot. The Day of Judgment! Of course. I saw right away that I'd have to invent a few angels of my own to make things work out, but that was no problem: inventing things like angels is what I'm paid to do, and I'm probably at least as good at it as some of the people who had invented the ones who fill the pages of Gustav Davidson's immense dictionary.

What about the computer stuff, though? Me, with my manual typewriter?

Well, writing the thousands of pages of *Lord of Darkness* had finally cured me of such folly. I had decided, that exhausted September, that my next book would be written on a computer. No more grim typing out of enormous final drafts would I do. From now on, just push the button and let the electrons do the work. So I had had a few conversations with that all-knowing computer expert Jerry Pournelle, and he not only explained the whole business to me but sent me a twenty-page letter, telling me what to look for when I went computer-shopping. I studied that with great diligence, and then began wandering into showrooms. Almost at once I found myself deep in the arcana of the trade: CPUs, Winchester disks, data bases, algorithms, bytes. Overnight I became capable of creating a sentence like: 'He has dedicated one of his function keys to its text, so that a single keystroke suffices to load it.' I still didn't really know how to operate a computer – you pick that up only by sitting in front of one and turning it on – but I quickly had all the lingo down pat and some sense of what it meant.

You see how the trick is done? A knack for instant expertise is essential.

And so I wrote 'Basileus'. Tired as I was, I managed the job in four or five days. I was happy with the result, and so was Don Myrus. When he phoned to accept it, he expressed his awe, as a computer layman, for my obvious familiarity with such high-tech devices. 'Well,' I said, 'living so close to Silicon Valley, it's hard not to pick up the lingo.' What I didn't tell him was that I knew hardly any more about computers than he did, and I was going to use the cheque for my story to pay for the printer for my very first computer system, which I had just purchased the day before. 'Basileus' was, in fact, the last work of fiction I would ever write on a typewriter. A few weeks later, as you already know (the stories in this collection are arranged in approximate chronological order, but the order is only approximate) I was a full-fledged computer user, embroiled in the intricacies of my giant-lobster story 'Homefaring' and praying each hour that the damned machine would do what I wanted it to.

You know who I prayed to, of course. Israfel. Anaphaxeton. Basileus.

In the shimmering lemon-yellow October light Cunningham touches the keys of his terminal and summons angels. An instant to load the program, an instant to bring the file up, and there they are, ready to spout from the screen at his command: Apollyon, Anauel, Uriel and all the rest. Uriel is the angel of thunder and terror; Apollyon is the Destroyer, the angel of the bottomless pit; Anauel is the angel of bankers and commission brokers. Cunningham is fascinated by the multifarious duties and tasks, both exalted and humble, that are assigned to the angels. 'Every visible thing in the world is put under the charge of an angel,' said St Augustine in *The Eight Questions*.

Cunningham has 1,114 angels in his computer now. He adds a few more each night, though he knows that he has a long way to go before he has them all. In the fourteenth century the number of angels was reckoned by the Kabbalists, with some precision, at 301,655,722. Albertus Magnus had earlier calculated that each choir of angels held 6,666 legions, and each legion 6,666 angels; even without knowing the number of choirs, one can see that that produces rather a higher total. And in the Talmud, Rabbi Jochanan proposed that new angels are born 'with every utterance that goes forth from the mouth of the Holy One, blessed be He'.

If Rabbi Jochanan is correct, the number of angels is infinite. Cunningham's personal computer, though it has extraordinary add-on memory capacity and is capable, if he chooses, of tapping into the huge mainframe machines of the Defense Department, has no very practical way of handling an infinity. But he is doing his best. To have 1,114 angels on line already, after only eight months of part-time programming, is no small achievement.

One of his favourites of the moment is Harahel, the angel of archives, libraries and rare cabinets. Cunningham has designated Harahel also the angel of computers: it seems appropriate. He invokes Harahel often, to discuss the evolving niceties of data processing with him. But he has many other favourites, and his tastes run somewhat to the sinister: Azrael, the angel of death, for example, and Arioch, the angel of vengeance, and Zebuleon, one of the nine angels who will govern at the end of the world. It is Cunningham's job, from eight to four every working day, to devise programs for the interception of incoming Soviet nuclear warheads, and that, perhaps, has inclined him towards the more apocalyptic members of the angelic host.

He invokes Harahel now. He has bad news for him. The invocation that he uses is a standard one that he found in Arthur Edward Waite's *The Lemegeton, or The Lesser Key of Solomon*, and he has dedicated one of his function keys to its text, so that a single keystroke suffices to load it. 'I do invocate, conjure, and command thee, O thou Spirit N, to appear and to show thyself visibly unto me before this Circle in fair and comely shape,' is the way it begins, and it proceeds to utilize various secret and potent names of God in the summoning of Spirit N – such names as Zabaoth and Elion and of course Adonai – and it concludes, 'I do potently exorcize thee that thou appearest here to fulfil my will in all things which seem good unto me. Wherefore, come thou, visibly, peaceably and affably, now, without delay, to manifest that which I desire, speaking with a clear and perfect voice, intelligibly, and to mine understanding.' All that takes but a microsecond, and another moment to enter in the name of Harahel as Spirit N, and there the angel is on the screen.

'I am here at your summons,' he announces.

Cunningham works with his angels from five to seven every evening. Then he has dinner. He lives alone, in a neat little flat a few blocks west of the Bayshore Freeway, and does not spend much of his time socializing. He thinks of himself as a pleasant man, a sociable man, and he may very well be right about that; but the pattern of his life has been a solitary one. He is thirty-seven years old, five feet eleven, with red hair, pale blue eyes, and a light dusting of freckles on his cheeks. He did his undergraduate work at Cal Tech, his postgraduate studies at Stanford, and for the last nine years he has been involved in ultra-sensitive military-computer projects in Northern California. He has never married. Sometimes he works with his angels again after dinner, from eight to ten, but hardly ever any later than that. At ten he always goes to bed. He is a very methodical person.

He has given Harahel the physical form of his own first computer, a little Radio Shack TRS-80, with wings flanking the screen. He had thought originally to make the appearance of his angels more abstract – showing Harahel as a sheaf of kilobytes, for example – but like many of Cunningham's best and most austere ideas it had turned out impractical in the execution, since abstract concepts did not translate well into graphics for him.

'I want to notify you,' Cunningham says, 'of a shift in jurisdiction.' He speaks English with his angels. He has it on good, though apocryphal, authority that the primary language of the angels is Hebrew, but his computer's audio algorithms have no Hebrew capacity, nor does Cunningham. But they speak English readily enough with him: they have no choice. 'From now on,' Cunningham tells Harahel, 'your domain is limited to hardware only.'

Angry green lines rapidly cross and recross Harahel's screen. 'By whose authority do you – '

'It isn't a question of authority,' Cunningham replies smoothly. 'It's a question of precision. I've just read Vretil into the data-base, and I have to code his functions. He's the recording angel, after all. So to some degree he overlaps your territory.'

'Ah,' says Harahel, sounding melancholy. 'I was hoping you wouldn't bother about him.'

'How can I overlook such an important angel? "Scribe of the knowledge of the Most High", according to the Book of Enoch. "Keeper of the heavenly books and records". "Quicker in wisdom than the other archangels".'

'If he's so quick,' says Harahel sullenly, 'give *him* the hardware. That's what governs the response time, you know.'

'I understand. But he maintains the lists. That's data-base.'

'And where does the data-base live? The hardware!'

'Listen, this isn't easy for me,' Cunningham says. 'But I have to be fair. I know you'll agree that some division of responsibilities is in order. And I'm giving him all data-bases and related software. You keep the rest.'

'Screens. Terminals. CPUs. Big deal.'

'But without you, he's nothing, Harahel. Anyway, you've always been in charge of cabinets, haven't you?'

'And archives and libraries,' the angel says. 'Don't forget that.'

'I'm not. But what's a library? Is it the books and shelves and stacks, or the words on the pages? We have to distinguish the container from the thing contained.'

'A grammarian,' Harahel sighs. 'A hair-splitter. A casuist.'

'Look, Vretil wants the hardware too. But he's willing to compromise. Are you?'

'You start to sound less and less like our programmer and more and more like the Almighty every day,' says Harahel.

'Don't blaspheme,' Cunningham tells him. 'Please. Is it agreed? Hardware only?'

'You win,' says the angel. 'But you always do, naturally.'

Naturally. Cunningham is the one with his hands on the keyboard, controlling things. The angels, though they are eloquent enough and have distinct and passionate personalities, are mere magnetic impulses deep within. In any contest with Cunningham they don't stand a chance. Cunningham, though he tries always to play the game by the rules, knows that, and so do they.

It makes him uncomfortable to think about it, but the role he plays is definitely godlike in all essential ways. He puts the angels into the computer; he gives them their tasks, their personalities, and their physical appearances; he summons them or leaves them uncalled, as he wishes.

A godlike role, yes. But Cunningham resists confronting that notion. He does not believe he is trying to be God; he does not even want to think about God. His family had been on comfortable terms with God – Uncle Tim was a priest, there was an archbishop somewhere back a few generations, his parents and sisters moved cosily within the divine presence as within a warm bath – but he himself, unable to quantify the Godhead, preferred to sidestep any thought of it. There were other, more immediate matters to engage his concern. His mother had wanted him to go into the priesthood, of all things, but Cunningham had averted that by demonstrating so visible and virtuosic a skill at mathematics that even she could see he was destined for science. Then she had prayed for a Nobel Prize in physics for him; but he had preferred computer technology. 'Well,' she said, 'a Nobel in computers. I ask the Virgin daily.'

'There's no Nobel in computers, Mom,' he told her. But he suspects she still offers novenas for it.

The angel project had begun as a lark, but had escalated swiftly into an obsession. He was reading Gustav Davidson's old *Dictionary of Angels*, and when he came upon the description of the angel Adramelech, who had rebelled with Satan and had been cast from heaven, Cunningham thought it might be amusing to build his computer simulation and talk with it. Davidson said that Adramelech was sometimes shown as a winged and bearded lion, and sometimes as a mule with feathers, and sometimes as a peacock, and that one poet had described him as 'the enemy of God, greater in malice, guile, ambition and mischief than Satan, a fiend more curst, a deeper hypocrite'. That was appealing. Well, why not build him? The graphics were easy – Cunningham chose the winged-lion form – but getting the personality constructed involved a month of intense labour and some consultations with the artificial-intelligence people over at Kestrel Institute. But finally Adramelech was on line, suave and diabolical, talking amiably of his days as an Assyrian god and his conversations with Beelzebub, who had named him Chancellor of the Order of the Fly (Grand Cross).

Next, Cunningham did Asmodeus, another fallen angel, said to be the inventor of dancing, gambling, music, drama, French fashions and other frivolities. Cunningham made him look like a very dashing Beverly Hills Iranian, with a pair of tiny wings at his collar. It was Asmodeus who suggested that Cunningham continue the project; so he brought Gabriel and Raphael on line to provide some balance between good and evil, and then Forcas, the angel who renders people invisible, restores lost property and teaches logic and rhetoric in Hell; and by that time Cunningham was hooked.

He surrounded himself with arcane lore: M.R. James's editions of the Apocrypha, Waite's *Book of Ceremonial Magic* and *Holy Kabbalah*, the *Mystical Theology and Celestial Hierarchies* of Dionysius the Areopagite, and dozens of related works that he called up from the Stanford data-base in a kind of manic fervour. As he codified his systems, he became able to put in five, eight, a dozen angels a night; one June evening, staying up well past his usual time, he managed thirty-seven. As the population grew, it took on weight and substance, for one angel cross-filed another, and they behaved now as though they held long conversations with one another even when Cunningham was occupied elsewhere.

The question of actual *belief* in angels, like that of belief in God Himself, never arose in him. His project was purely a technical challenge, not a theological exploration. Once, at lunch, he told a co-worker what he was doing, and got a chilly blank stare. 'Angels? *Angels?* Flying around with big flapping wings, passing miracles? You aren't seriously telling me that you believe in angels, are you, Dan?'

To which Cunningham replied, 'You don't have to believe in angels to make use of them. I'm not always sure I believe in electrons and protons. I know I've never seen any. But I make use of them.'

'And what use do you make of angels?'

But Cunningham had lost interest in the discussion.

He divides his evenings between calling up his angels for conversations and programming additional ones into his pantheon. That requires continuous intensive research, for the literature of angels is extraordinarily large, and he is thorough in everything he does. The research is time-consuming, for he wants his angels to meet every scholarly test of authenticity. He pores constantly over such works as Ginzberg's seven-volume *Legends of the Jews*, Clement of Alexandria's *Prophetic Eclogues*, Blavatsky's *The Secret Doctrine*.

It is the early part of the evening. He brings up Hagith, ruler of the planet Venus and commander of 4,000 legions of spirits, and asks him details of the transmutation of metals, which is Hagith's speciality. He summons Hadraniel, who in Kabbalistic lore is a porter at the second gate of Heaven, and whose voice, when he proclaims the will of the Lord, penetrates through 200,000 universes; he questions the angel about his meeting with Moses, who uttered the Supreme Name at him and made him tremble. And then Cunningham sends for Israfel the four-winged, whose feet are under the seventh earth, and whose head reaches to the pillars of the divine throne. It will be Israfel's task to blow the trumpet that announces the arrival of the Day of Judgment. Cunningham asks him to take a few trial riffs now – 'just for practice', he says, but Israfel declines, saying he cannot touch his instrument until he receives the signal, and the command sequence for that, says the angel, is nowhere to be found in the software Cunningham has thus far constructed.

When he wearies of talking with the angels, Cunningham begins the evening's programming. By now the algorithms are second nature and he can enter angels into the computer in a matter of minutes, once he has done the research. This evening he inserts nine more. Then he opens a beer, sits back, lets the day wind to its close.

He thinks he understands why he has become so intensely involved with this enterprise. It is because he must contend each day in his daily work with matters of terrifying apocalyptic import: nothing less, indeed, than the impending destruction of the world. Cunningham works routinely with megadeath simulation. For six hours a day he sets up hypothetical situations in which Country A goes into alert mode, expecting an attack from Country B, which thereupon begins to suspect a pre-emptive strike and commences a defensive response, which leads Country A to escalate its own readiness, and so on until the bombs are in the air. He is aware, as are many thoughtful people both in Country A and Country B, that the possibility of computer-generated misinformation leading to a nuclear holocaust increases each year, as the time-window for correcting a malfunction diminishes. Cunningham also knows something that very few others do, or perhaps no-one else at all: that it is now possible to send a signal to the giant computers – to Theirs or Ours, it makes no difference – that will be indistinguishable from the impulses that an actual flight of airborne warhead-bearing missiles would generate. If such a signal is permitted to enter the system, a minimum of eleven minutes, at the present time, will be needed to carry out fail-safe determination of its authenticity. That, at the present time, is too long to wait to decide whether the incoming missiles are real: a much swifter response is required.

Cunningham, when he designed his missile-simulating signal, thought at once of erasing his work. But he could not bring himself to do that: the program was too elegant, too perfect. On the other hand, he was afraid to tell anyone about it, for fear that it would be taken beyond his level of classification at once, and sealed away from him. He does not want that, for he dreams of finding an antidote for it, some sort of resonating inquiry mode that will distinguish all true alarms from false. When he has it, if he ever does, he will present both modes, in a single package, to Defense. Meanwhile he bears the burden of suppressing a concept of overwhelming strategic importance. He has never done anything like that before. And he does not delude himself into thinking his mind is unique: if he could devise something like this, someone else probably could do it also, perhaps someone on the other side. True, it is a useless, suicidal program. But it would not be the first suicidal program to be devised in the interests of military security.

He knows he must take his simulator to his superiors before much more time goes by. And under the strain of that knowledge, he is beginning to show distinct signs of erosion. He mingles less and less with other people; he has unpleasant dreams and occasional periods of insomnia; he has lost his appetite and looks gaunt and haggard. The angel project is his only useful diversion, his chief distraction, his one avenue of escape.

For all his scrupulous scholarship, Cunningham has not hesitated to invent a few angels of his own. Uraniel is one of his: the angel of radioactive decay, with a face of whirling electron-shells. And he has coined Dimitrion too: the angel of Russian literature, whose wings are sleighs and whose head is a snow-covered samovar. Cunningham feels no guilt over such whimsies. It is his computer, after all, and his program. And he knows he is not the first to concoct angels. Blake engendered platoons of them in his poems: Urizen and Orc and Enitharmon and more. Milton, he suspects, populated *Paradise Lost* with dozens of sprites of his own invention. Gurdjieff and Aleister Crowley and even Pope Gregory the Great had their turns at amplifying the angelic roster: why then not also Dan Cunningham of Palo Alto, California? So from time to time he works one up on his own. His most recent is the dread high lord Basileus, to whom Cunningham has given the title of Emperor of the Angels. Basileus is still incomplete: Cunningham has not arrived at his physical appearance, nor his specific functions, other than to make him the chief administrator of the angelic horde. But there is something unsatisfactory about imagining a new archangel, when Gabriel, Raphael and Michael already constitute the high command. Basileus needs more work. Cunningham puts him aside, and begins to key in Duma, the angel of silence and of the stillness of death, thousand-eyed, armed with a fiery rod. His style in angels is getting darker and darker.

* * *

On a misty, rainy night in late October, a woman from San Francisco whom he knows in a distant, occasional way phones to invite him to a party. Her name is Joanna; she is in her mid-thirties, a biologist working for one of the little gene-splicing outfits in Berkeley; Cunningham had had a brief and vague affair with her five or six years back, when she was at Stanford, and since then they have kept fitfully in touch, with long intervals elapsing between meetings. He has not seen her or heard from her in over a year. 'It's going to be an interesting bunch,' she tells him. 'A futurologist from New York, Thomson the sociobiology man, a couple of video poets, and someone from the chimpanzee-language outfit, and I forget the rest, but they all sounded first-rate.'

Cunningham hates parties. They bore and jangle him. No matter how first-rate the people are, he thinks, real interchange of ideas is impossible in a large random group, and the best one can hope for is some pleasant low-level chatter. He would rather be alone with his angels than waste an evening that way.

On the other hand, it has been so long since he has done anything of a social nature that he has trouble remembering what the last gathering was. As he had been telling himself all his life, he needs to get out more often. He likes Joanna and it's about time they got together, he thinks, and he fears that if he turns her down she may not call again for years. And the gentle patter of the rain, coming on this mild evening after the long dry months of summer, has left him feeling uncharacteristically relaxed, open, accessible.

'All right,' he says. 'I'll be glad to go.'

The party is in San Mateo, on Saturday night. He takes down the address. They arrange to meet there. Perhaps she'll come home with him afterwards, he thinks; San Mateo is only fifteen minutes from his house, and she'll have a much longer drive back up to San Francisco. The thought surprises him. He had supposed he had lost all interest in her that way; he had supposed he had lost all interest in anyone that way, as a matter of fact.

Three days before the party, he decides to call Joanna and cancel. The idea of milling about in a roomful of strangers appals him. He can't imagine, now, why he ever agreed to go.

91

Better to stay home alone and pass a long rainy night designing angels and conversing with Uriel, Ithuriel, Raphael, Gabriel.

But as he goes towards the telephone, that renewed hunger for solitude vanishes as swiftly as it came. He *does* want to go to the party. He *does* want to see Joanna: very much, indeed. It startles him to realize that he positively yearns for some change in his rigid routine, some escape from his little apartment, its elaborate computer hookup, even its angels.

Cunningham imagines himself at the party, in some brightly-lit room in a handsome redwood-and-glass house perched in the hills above San Mateo. He stands with his back to the vast sparkling wraparound window, a drink in his hand, and he is holding forth, dominating the conversation, sharing his rich stock of angel lore with a fascinated audience.

'Yes, 300 million of them,' he is saying, 'and each with his fixed function. Angels don't have free will, you know. It's Church doctrine that they're created with it, but at the moment of their birth they're given the choice of opting for God or against Him, and the choice is irrevocable. Once they've made it they're unalterably fixed, for good or for evil. Oh, and angels are born circumcised, too. At least the Angels of Sanctification and the Angels of Glory are, and probably the seventy Angels of the Presence.'

'Does that mean that all angels are male?' asks a slender dark-haired woman.

'Strictly speaking, they're bodiless and therefore without sex,' Cunningham tells her. 'But in fact the religions that believe in angels are mainly patriarchal ones, and when the angels are visualized they tend to be portrayed as men. Although some of them, apparently, can change sex at will. Milton tells us that in *Paradise Lost*: "Spirits when they please can either sex assume, or both; so soft and uncompounded is their essence pure." And some angels seem to be envisioned as female in the first place. There's the Shekinah, for instance, "the bride of God", the manifestation of His glory indwelling in human beings. There's Sophia, the angel of wisdom. And Lilith, Adam's first wife, the demon of lust – '

'Are demons considered angels, then?' a tall professorial-looking man wants to know.

'Of course. They're the angels who opted away from God.

But they're angels nevertheless, even if we mortals perceive their aspects as demonic or diabolical.'

He goes on and on. They all listen as though he is God's own messenger. He speaks of the hierarchies of angels – the seraphim, cherubim, thrones, dominations, principalities, powers, virtues, archangels and angels – and he tells them of the various lists of the seven great angels, which differ so greatly once one gets beyond Michael, Gabriel and Raphael, and he speaks of the 90,000 angels of destruction and the 300 angels of light, he conjures up the seven angels with seven trumpets from the Book of Revelation, he tells them which angels rule the seven days of the week and which the hours of the day and night, he pours forth the wondrous angelic names, Zadkiel, Hashmal, Orphaniel, Jehudiel, Phaleg, Zagzagel. There is no end to it. He is in his glory. He is a fount of arcana. Then the manic mood passes. He is alone in his room; there is no eager audience. Once again he thinks he will skip the party. No. No. He will go. He wants to see Joanna.

He goes to his terminal and calls up two final angels before bedtime: Leviathan and Behemoth. Behemoth is the great hippopotamus-angel, the vast beast of darkness, the angel of chaos. Leviathan is his mate, the mighty she-whale, the splendid sea serpent. They dance for him on the screen. Behemoth's huge mouth yawns wide. Leviathan gapes even more awesomely. 'We are getting hungry,' they tell him. 'When is feeding time?' In rabbinical lore, these two will swallow all the damned souls at the end of days. Cunningham tosses them some electronic sardines and sends them away. As he closes his eyes he invokes Poteh, the angel of oblivion, and falls into a black dreamless sleep.

At his desk the next morning he is at work on a standard item, a glitch-clearing program for the third-quadrant surveillance satellites, when he finds himself unaccountably trembling. That has never happened to him before. His fingernails look almost white, his wrists are rigid, his hands are quivering. He feels chilled. It is as though he has not slept for days. In the washroom he clings to the sink and stares at his pallid, sweaty face. Someone comes up behind him and says, 'You all right, Dan?'

'Yeah. Just a little attack of the queasies.'

'All that wild living in the middle of the week wears a man down,' the other says, and moves along. The social necessities have been observed: a question, a non-committal answer, a quip, goodbye. He could have been having a stroke here and they would have played it the same way. Cunningham has no close friends at the office. He knows that they regard him as eccentric – eccentric in the wrong way, not lively and quirky but just a peculiar kind of hermit – and getting worse all the time. I could destroy the world, he thinks. I could go into the Big Room and type for fifteen seconds, and we'd be on all-out alert a minute later and the bombs would be coming down from orbit six minutes later. I could give that signal. I could really do it. I could do it right now.

Waves of nausea sweep him and he grips the edge of the sink until the last racking spasm is over. Then he cleans his face and, calmer now, returns to his desk to stare at the little green symbols on the screen.

That evening, still trying to find a function for Basileus, Cunningham discovers himself thinking of demons, and of one demon not in the classical demonology – Maxwell's Demon, the one that the physicist James Clerk Maxwell postulated to send fast-moving molecules in one direction and slow ones in another, thereby providing an ultra-efficient method for heating and refrigeration. Perhaps some sort of filtering role could be devised for Basileus. Last week a few of the loftier angels had been complaining about the proximity to them of certain fallen angels within the computer. 'There's a smell of brimstone on this disk that I don't like,' Gabriel had said. Cunningham wonders if he could make Basileus a kind of traffic manager within the program: let him sit in there and ship the celestial angels into one sector of a disk, the fallen ones to another.

The idea appeals to him for about thirty seconds. Then he sees how fundamentally trivial it is. He doesn't need an angel for a job like that; a little simple software could do it. Cunningham's corollary to Kant's categorical imperative: *Never use an angel as mere software*. He smiles, possibly for the first time all week. Why, he doesn't even need software. He can handle it himself, simply by assigning princes of Heaven to one file and demons to a different one. It hadn't seemed necessary to segregate his angels that way, or he would have done it from the start. But if they were complaining –

He begins to flange up a sorting program to separate the files. It should have taken him a few minutes, but he finds himself working in a rambling, muddled way, doing an untypically sloppy job. With a quick swipe he erases what he has done. Gabriel would have to put up with the reek of brimstone a little longer, he thinks.

There is a dull throbbing pain just behind his eyes. His throat is dry, his lips feel parched. Basileus would have to wait a little longer, too. Cunningham keys up another angel, allowing his fingers to choose for him, and finds himself looking at a blank-faced angel with a gleaming metal skin. One of the early ones, Cunningham realizes. 'I don't remember your name,' he says. 'Who are you?'

'I am Anaphaxeton.'

'And your function?'

'When my name is pronounced aloud, I will cause the angels to summon the entire universe before the bar of justice on Judgment Day.'

'Oh, Jesus,' Cunningham says. 'I don't want you tonight.'

He sends Anaphaxeton away and finds himself with the dark angel Apollyon, fish-scales, dragon-wings, bear-feet, breathing fire and smoke, holding the key to the Abyss. 'No,' Cunningham says, and brings up Michael, standing with drawn sword over Jerusalem, and sends him away only to find on the screen an angel with 70,000 feet and 4,000 wings, who is Azrael, the angel of death. 'No,' says Cunningham again. 'Not you. Oh, Christ!' A vengeful army crowds his computer. On his screen there passes a flurrying regiment of wings and eyes and beaks. He shivers and shuts the system down for the night. Jesus, he thinks. Jesus, Jesus, Jesus. All night long suns explode in his brain.

On Friday his supervisor, Ned Harris, saunters to his desk in an unusually folksy way and asks him if he's going to be doing anything interesting this weekend. Cunningham shrugs. 'A party Saturday night, that's about all. Why?'

'Thought you might be going off on a fishing trip, or something. Looks like the last nice weekend before the rainy season sets in, wouldn't you say?'

'I'm not a fisherman, Ned.'

'Take some kind of trip. Drive down to Monterey, maybe. Or up into the wine country.'

'What are you getting at?' Cunningham asks.

'You look like you could use a little change of pace,' Harris says amiably. 'A couple of days off. You've been crunching numbers so hard they're starting to crunch you, is my guess.'

'It's that obvious?'

Harris nods. 'You're tired, Dan. It shows. We're a little like air traffic controllers around here, you know, working so hard we start to dream about blips on the screen. That's no good. Get the hell out of town, fellow. The Defense Department can operate without you for a while. OK? Take Monday off. Tuesday, even. I can't afford to have a fine mind like yours going goofy from fatigue, Dan.'

'All right, Ned. Sure. Thanks.'

His hands are shaking again. His fingernails are colourless.

'And get a good early start on the weekend, too. No need for you to hang around here today until four.'

'If that's OK – '

'Go on. Shoo!'

Cunningham closes down his desk and makes his way uncertainly out of the building. The security guards wave at him. Everyone seems to know he's being sent home early. Is this what it's like to crack up on the job? He wanders about the parking lot for a little while, not sure where he has left his car. At last he finds it, and drives home at thirty miles an hour, with horns honking at him all the way as he wanders up the freeway.

He settles wearily in front of his computer and brings the system on line, calling for Harahel. Surely the angel of computers will not plague him with apocalyptic matters.

Harahel says, 'Well, we've worked out your Basileus problem for you.'

'You have?'

'Uriel had the basic idea, building on your Maxwell's Demon notion. Israfel and Azrael developed it some. What's needed is an angel embodying God's justice and God's mercy. A kind of evaluator, a filtering angel. He weighs deeds in the balance, and arrives at a verdict.'

'What's new about that?' Cunningham asks. 'Something like that's built into every mythology from Sumer and Egypt on. There's always a mechanism for evaluating the souls of the dead – this one goes to Paradise, this one goes to Hell – '

'Wait,' Harahel says. 'I wasn't finished. I'm not talking about the evaluation of individual souls.'

'What then?'

'Worlds,' the angel replies. 'Basileus will be the judge of worlds. He holds an entire planet up to scrutiny and decides whether it's time to call for the last trump.'

'Part of the machinery of Judgment, you mean?'

'Exactly. He's the one who presents the evidence to God and helps Him make His decision. And then he's the one who tells Israfel to blow the trumpet, and he's the one who calls out the name of Anaphaxeton to bring everyone before the bar. He's the prime apocalyptic angel, the destroyer of worlds. And we thought you might make him look like – '

'Ah,' Cunningham says. 'Not now. Let's talk about that some other time.'

He shuts the system down, pours himself a drink, sits staring out the window at the big eucalyptus tree in the front yard. After a while it begins to rain. Not such a good weekend for a drive into the country after all, he thinks. He does not turn the computer on again that evening.

Despite everything, Cunningham goes to the party. Joanna is not there. She has phoned to cancel, late Saturday afternoon, pleading a bad cold. He detects no sound of a cold in her voice, but perhaps she is telling the truth. Or possibly she has found something better to do on Saturday night. But he is already geared for party-going, and he is so tired, so eroded, that it is more effort to change his internal program than it is to follow through on the original schedule. So about eight that evening he drives up to San Mateo, through a light drizzle.

The party turns out not to be in the glamorous hills west of town, but in a small cramped condominium close to the heart of the city, furnished with what looks like somebody's college-era chairs and couches and bookshelves. A cheap stereo is playing the pop music of a dozen years ago, and a sputtering screen provides a crude computer-generated light show. The host is some sort of marketing exec for a large video-games company in San Jose, and most of the guests look vaguely corporate too. The futurologist from New York has sent his regrets; the famous sociobiologist has also somehow failed to arrive; the video poets are two San Francisco gays who will talk only to each other, and stray not very far from the bar; the expert on teaching chimpanzees to speak is in the red-faced-and-sweaty stage of being drunk, and is working hard at seducing a plump woman festooned with astrological jewellery. Cunningham, numb, drifts through the party as though he is made of ectoplasm. He speaks to no-one, no-one speaks to him. Some jugs of red wine are open on a table by the window, and he pours himself a glassful. There he stands, immobile, imprisoned by inertia. He imagines himself suddenly making a speech about angels, telling everyone how Ithuriel touched Satan with his spear in the Garden of Eden as the Fiend crouched next to Eve, and how the hierarch Ataphiel keeps Heaven aloft by balancing it on three fingers. But he says nothing. After a time he finds himself approached by a lean, leathery-looking woman with glittering eyes, who says, 'And what do you do?'

'I'm a programmer,' Cunningham says. 'Mainly I talk to angels. But I also do national security stuff.'

'Angels?' she says, and laughs in a brittle, tinkling way. 'You talk to angels? I've never heard anyone say that before.' She pours herself a drink and moves quickly elsewhere.

'Angels?' says the astrological woman. 'Did someone say angels?'

Cunningham smiles and shrugs and looks out the window. It is raining harder. I should go home, he thinks. There is absolutely no point in being here. He fills his glass again. The chimpanzee man is still working on the astrologer, but she seems to be trying to get free of him and come over to Cunningham. To discuss angels with him? She is heavy-breasted, a little wall-eyed, sloppy-looking. He does not want to discuss angels with her. He does not want to discuss angels with anyone. He holds his place at the window until it definitely does appear that the astrologer is heading his way; then he drifts towards

98

the door. She says, 'I heard you say you were interested in angels. Angels are a special field of mine, you know. I've studied with – '

'Angles,' Cunningham says. 'I play the angles. That's what I said. I'm a professional gambler.'

'Wait,' she says, but he moves past her and out into the night. It takes him a long while to find his key and get his car unlocked, and the rain soaks him to the skin, but that does not bother him. He is home a little before midnight.

He brings Raphael on line. The great archangel radiates a beautiful golden glow.

'You will be Basileus,' Raphael tells him. 'We've decided it by a vote, hierarchy by hierarchy. Everyone agrees.'

'I can't be an angel. I'm human,' Cunningham replies.

'There's ample precedent. Enoch was carried off to Heaven and became an angel. So was Elijah. St John the Baptist was actually an angel. You will become Basileus. We've already done the program for you. It's on the disk: just call him up and you'll see. Your own face, looking out at you.'

'No,' Cunningham says.

'How can you refuse?'

'Are you really Raphael? You sound like someone from the other side. A tempter. Asmodeus. Astaroth. Belphegor.'

'I am Raphael. And you are Basileus.'

Cunningham considers it. He is so very tired that he can barely think.

An angel. Why not? A rainy Saturday night, a lousy party, a splitting headache: come home and find out you've been made an angel, and given a high place in the hierarchy. Why not? Why the hell not?

'All right,' he says. 'I'm Basileus.'

He puts his hands on the keys and taps out a simple formulation that goes straight down the pipe into the Defense Department's big Northern California system. With an alteration of two keystrokes he sends the same message to the Soviets. Why not? Redundancy is the soul of security. The world now has about six minutes left. Cunningham has always been good with computers. He knows their secret language as few people before him have.

Then he brings Raphael on the screen again.

'You should see yourself as Basileus while there's still time,' the archangel says.

'Yes. Of course. What's the access key?'

Raphael tells him. Cunningham begins to set it up.

Come now, Basileus! We are one!

Cunningham stares at the screen with growing wonder and delight, while the clock continues to tick.

Dancers in the Time-flux

Long ago, in what almost seems to me now to have been another galaxy, I wrote a novel called *Son of Man*. The year was 1969, when the world was new and strange and psychedelic, and *Son of Man* was my attempt to reproduce in prose form some of the visionary aspects of life in that heady era under the pretext of creating a world of the far, far future. The results were very strange, but to me, at least, exciting and rewarding; and over the years *Son of Man* has retained a small but passionate audience. It's the kind of book that polarizes readers in an extremely sharp way: some find themselves unable to get past page three, others read it over and over again. (I read it now and then myself, as a matter of fact.)

Writing *Son of Man* had been such an extraordinarily exhilarating experience that when I began writing again in 1980 after my long period of retirement, I found myself tempted to dip into the world of *Son of Man* again, possibly for a short story or two, perhaps even for a whole new novel. But I gave the idea no serious thought until July of 1981, when I received a letter from the Pacific Northwest writer and editor, Jessica Amanda Salmonson, asking me to write a short story for an anthology called *Heroic Visions* that she was assembling. (At that time Jessica dated all her letters '9981'. I haven't heard from her lately, so I don't know whether she still regards herself as living in the hundredth century.)

Heroic Visions was intended as an anthology of new stories of 'high fantasy and heroic fantasy', according to the prospectus Jessica sent. High fantasy — Eddison, Dunsany, Charles Williams, Tolkien, William Morris — is something I read occasionally with pleasure, but have never intentionally written. Heroic fantasy — exemplified by such characters as Robert E. Howard's Conan, Fritz Leiber's Fafhrd and the Gray Mouser, and Michael Moorcock's Elric — is something that holds less interest for me as a reader, and though I suppose I could fake it as a writer if I saw some reason to do so, I have no true natural aptitude for it.

101

So I really didn't belong in Jessica's book. Nor was the financial aspect of the project especially enticing. But I was rediscovering writing again that year and was willing to try almost anything just then. I jotted at the bottom of the prospectus, 'World of *Son of Man*. Two figures from the remote past are swept into the time-flux – a woman of the twentieth century, a man of – where? ancient China? Sumer?' and dropped Jessica a card saying I might possibly send her a story later on that year, when I had finished *Majipoor Chronicles*, which I was working on at the time.

She was surprised, and, I suppose, sceptical. Justifiably so: I went on to other things and forgot all about *Heroic Visions*. But on 19 December '9981', she tried again, asking me if there was any hope of getting the story. I replied that I'd do it, provided she could see a *Son of Man* spinoff as appropriate to her theme. She had read that book and knew it well. Back came her enthusiastic OK, and on 9 January I sent 'Dancers in the Time-flux' off to her.

As you'll see, it departs considerably from the scrawled original notion of the previous July. The twentieth-century woman disappears from the plot – I tried without success to return to her later on, in a sequel – and the man of ancient China or Sumer is transmogrified into the sixteenth-century Dutch circumnavigator Olivier van Noort, an actual historic figure whom I had written about at length years before in a non-fiction book called *The Longest Voyage*. I do think the story recaptures the tone of *Son of Man* to a considerable extent, but whether it has the headlong *wildness* of that book is not so clear to me. It may be that 1969s come around only once in a lifetime. Which is, perhaps, a good thing.

Under a warm golden wind from the west Bhengarn the Traveller moves steadily onwards towards distant Crystal Pond, his appointed place of metamorphosis. The season is late. The swollen scarlet sun clings close to the southern hills. Bhengarn's body – a compact silvery tube supported by a dozen pairs of sturdy three-jointed legs – throbs with the need for transformation. And yet the Traveller is unhurried. He has been bound on this journey for many hundreds of years. He has traced across the face of the world a glistening trail that zigzags from zone to zone, from continent to continent, and even now still glimmers behind him with a cold brilliance like a thread of bright metal stitching the planet's haunches. For the past decade he has patiently circled Crystal Pond at the outer end of a radial arm one-tenth the diameter of the Earth in length; now, at the prompting of some interior signal, he has begun to spiral inwards upon it.

The path immediately before him is bleak. To his left is a district covered by furry green fog; to his right is a region of pale crimson grass sharp as spikes and sputtering with a sinister hostile hiss; straight ahead a roadbed of black clinkers and ashen crusts leads down a shallow slope to the Plain of Teeth, where menacing porcellaneous outcroppings make the wayfarer's task a taxing one. But such obstacles mean little to Bhengarn. He is a Traveller, after all. His body is superbly designed to carry him through all difficulties. And in his journeys he has been in places far worse than this.

Elegantly he descends the pathway of slag and cinders. His many feet are tough as annealed metal, sensitive as the most alert antennae. He tests each point in the road for stability and support, and scans the thick layer of ashes for concealed enemies. In this way he moves easily and swiftly towards the plain, holding his long abdomen safely above the cutting edges of the cold volcanic matter over which he walks.

As he enters the Plain of Teeth he sees a new annoyance: an Eater commands the gateway to the plain. Of all the forms of human life – and the Traveller has encountered virtually all of them in his wanderings, Eaters, Destroyers, Skimmers, Interceders and the others – Eaters seem to him the most tiresome, mere noisy monsters. Whatever philosophical underpinnings form the rationale of their bizarre way of life are of no interest to him. He is wearied by their bluster and offended by their gross appetites.

All the same he must get past this one to reach his destination. The huge creature stands straddling the path with one great meaty leg at each edge and the thick fleshy tail propping it from behind. Its steely claws are exposed, its fangs gleam, driblets of blood from recent victims stain its hard reptilian hide. Its chilly inquisitive eyes, glowing with demonic intelligence, track Bhengarn as the Traveller draws near.

The Eater emits a boastful roar and brandishes its many teeth.

'You block my way,' Bhengarn declares.

'You state the obvious,' the Eater replies.

'I have no desire for an encounter with you. But my destiny draws me towards Crystal Pond, which lies beyond you.'

'For you,' says the Eater, 'nothing lies beyond me. Your destiny has brought you to a termination today. We will collaborate, you and I, in the transformation of your component molecules.'

From the spiracles along his sides the Traveller releases a thick blue sigh of boredom. 'The only transformation that waits for me is the one I will undertake at Crystal Pond. You and I have no transaction. Stand aside.'

The Eater roars again. He rocks slightly on his gigantic claws and swishes his vast saurian tail from side to side. These are the preliminaries to an attack, but in a kind of ponderous courtesy he seems to be offering Bhengarn the opportunity to scuttle back up the ash-strewn slope.

Bhengarn says, 'Will you yield place?'

'I am an instrument of destiny.'

'You are a disagreeable boastful ignoramus,' says Bhengarn calmly, and consumes half a week's energy driving the scimitars of his spirit to the roots of the world. It is not a wasted expense of soul, for the ground trembles, the sky grows dark, the hill behind him creaks and groans, the wind turns purplish and frosty. There is a dull droning sound which the Traveller knows is the song of the time-flux, an unpredictable force that often is liberated at such moments. Despite that, Bhengarn will not relent. Beneath the Eater's splayed claws the fabric of the road ripples. Sour smells rise from sudden crevasses. The enormous beast utters a yipping cry of rage and lashes his tail vehemently against the ground. He sways; he nearly topples; he calls out to Bhengarn to cease his onslaught, but the Traveller knows better than to settle for a half measure. Even more fiercely he presses against the Eater's bulky form.

'This is unfair,' the Eater wheezes. 'My goal is the same as yours: to serve the forces of necessity.'

'Serve them by eating someone else today,' answers Bhengarn curtly, and with a final expenditure of force shoves the Eater to an awkward untenable position that causes it to crash down on to its side. The downed beast, moaning, rakes the air with his claws but does not arise, and as Bhengarn moves briskly past the Eater he observes that fine transparent threads, implacable as stone, have shot forth from a patch of swamp beside the road and are rapidly binding the fallen Eater in an unbreakable net. The Eater howls. Glancing back, Bhengarn notices the threads already cutting their way through the Eater's thick scales like tiny streams of acid. 'So, then,' Bhengarn says, without malice, 'the forces of necessity will be gratified today after all, but not by me. The Eater is to be eaten. It seems that this day *I* prove to be the instrument of destiny.' And without another backward look he passes quickly onwards into the plain. The sky regains its ruddy colour, the wind becomes mild once more, the Earth is still. But a release of the time-flux is never without consequences, and as the Traveller trundles forward he perceives some new creature of unfamiliar form staggering through the mists ahead, confused and lost, lurching between the shining lethal formations of the Plain of Teeth in seeming ignorance of the perils they hold. The creature is upright, two-legged, hairy, of archaic appearance. Bhengarn, approaching it, recognizes it finally as a primordial human, swept millions of years past its own true moment.

'Have some care,' Bhengarn calls. 'Those teeth can bite!'

'Who spoke?' the archaic creature demands, whirling about in alarm.

'I am Bhengarn the Traveller. I suspect I am responsible for your presence here.'

'Where are you? I see no one! Are you a devil?'

'I am a Traveller, and I am right in front of your nose.'

The ancient human notices Bhengarn, apparently for the first time, and leaps back, gasping. 'Serpent!' he cries. 'Serpent with legs! Worm! Devil!' Wildly he seizes rocks and hurls them at the Traveller, who deflects them easily enough, turning each into a rhythmic juncture of gold and green that hovers, twanging softly, along an arc between the other and himself. The archaic one lifts an immense boulder, but as he hoists it to drop it on Bhengarn he overbalances and his arm flies backwards, grazing one of the sleek teeth behind him. At once the tooth releases a turquoise flare and the man's arm vanishes to the elbow. He sinks to his knees, whimpering, staring bewilderedly at the stump and at the Traveller before him.

Bhengarn says, 'You are in the Plain of Teeth, and any contact

105

with these mineral formations is likely to be unfortunate, as I attempted to warn you.'

He slides himself into the other's soul for an instant, pushing his way past thick encrusted stalagmites and stalactites of anger, fear, outraged pride, pain, disorientation and arrogance, and discovers himself to be in the presence of one Olivier van Noort of Utrecht, former tavern-keeper at Rotterdam, commander of the voyage of circumnavigation that set forth from Holland on the second day of July 1598 and travelled the entire belly of the world, a man of exceedingly strong stomach and bold temperament, who has experienced much, having gorged on the meat of penguins at Cape Virgines and the isle called Pantagoms, having hunted beasts not unlike stags and buffalos and ostriches in the cold lands by Magellan's Strait, having encountered whales and parrots and trees whose bark had the bite of pepper, having had strife with the noisome Portugals in Guinea and Brazil, having entered into the South Sea on a day of divers storms, thunders and lightnings, having taken ships of the Spaniards in Valparaiso and slain many Indians, having voyaged thence to the Isles of Ladrones or Thieves, where the natives bartered bananas, coconuts and roots for old pieces of iron, overturning their canoes in their greed for metal, having suffered a bloody flux in Manila of eating palmitos, having captured vessels of China laden with rice and lead, having traded with folk on a ship of the Japans, whose men make themselves bald except a tuft left in the hinder part of the head, and wield swords which would, with one stroke, cut through three men, having traded also with the bare-breasted women of Borneo, bold and impudent and shrewd, who carry iron-pointed javelins and sharp darts, and having after great privation and the loss of three of his four ships and all but forty-five of his 248 men, many of them executed by him or marooned on remote islands for their mutinies but a good number murdered by the treacheries of savage enemies, come again to Rotterdam on 26 August in 1601, bearing little in the way of saleable goods to show for his hardships and calamities. None of this has any meaning to Bhengarn the Traveller except in the broadest sense, which is to say that he recognizes in Olivier van Noort a stubborn and difficult man who has conceived and executed a journey of mingled heroism and foolishness that spanned vast distances, and so they are brothers, of a sort, however many millions of years apart. As a fraternal gesture Bhengarn restores the newcomer's arm. That appears to be as bewildering to the other as was its sudden loss. He squeezes it, moves it cautiously back and forth, scoops up a handful of pebbles with it. 'This is Hell, then,' he mutters, 'and you are a demon of Satan.'

'I am Bhengarn the Traveller, bound towards Crystal Pond, and I think that I conjured you by accident out of your proper place in time while seeking to thwart that monster.' Bhengarn indicates the fallen Eater, now half dissolved. The other, who evidently had not looked that way before, makes a harsh choking sound at the sight of the giant creature, which still struggles sluggishly. Bhengarn says, 'The time-flux has seized you and taken you far from home, and there will be no going back for you. I offer regrets.'

'You offer regrets? A worm with legs offers regrets! Do I dream this, or am I truly dead and gone to Hell?'

'Neither one.'

'In all my sailing round the world I never saw a place so strange as this, or the likes of you, or of that creature over yonder. Am I to be tortured, demon?'

'You are not where you think you are.'

'Is this not Hell?'

'This is the world of reality.'

'How far are we, then, from Holland?'

'I am unable to calculate it,' Bhengarn answers. 'A long way, that's certain. Will you accompany me towards Crystal Pond, or shall we part here?'

Noort is silent a moment. Then he says, 'Better the company of demons than none at all, in such a place. Tell me straight, demon: am I to be punished here? I see hellfire on the horizon. I will find the rivers of fire, snow, toads and black water, will I not? And the place where sinners are pronged on hooks jutting from blazing wheels? The ladders of red-hot iron, eh? The wicked broiling on coals? And the Arch-Traitor himself, sunk in ice to his chest – he must be near, is he not?' Noort shivers. 'The fountains of poison. The wild boars of Lucifer. The aloes biting bare flesh, the dry winds of the abyss – when will I see them?'

'Look there,' says Bhengarn. Beyond the Plain of Teeth a column of black flame rises into the heavens, and in it dance creatures of a hundred sorts, melting, swirling, coupling, fading. A chain of staring lidless eyes spans the sky. Looping whorls of green light writhe on the mountaintops. 'Is that what you expect? You will find whatever you expect here.'

'And yet you say this is not Hell?'

'I tell you again, it is the true world, the same into which you were born long ago.'

'And is this Brazil, or the Indies, or some part of Africa?'

'Those names mean little to me.'

'Then we are in the Terra Australis,' says Noort. 'It must be. A land where worms have legs and speak good Dutch, and rocks can bite, and arms once lost can sprout anew – yes, it must surely be the Terra Australis, or else the land of Prester John. Eh? Is Prester John your king?' Noort laughs. He seems to be emerging from his bewilderment. 'Tell me the name of this land, creature, so I may claim it for the United Provinces, if ever I see Holland again.'

'It has no name.'

'No name! No name! What foolishness! I never found a place whose folk had no name for it, not even in the endless South Sea. But I will name it, then. Let this province be called New Utrecht, eh? And all this land, from here to the shores of the South Sea, I annex hereby to the United Provinces in the name of the States-General. You be my witness, creature. Later I will draw up documents. You say I am not dead?'

'Not dead, not dead at all. But far from home. Come, walk beside me, and touch nothing. This is troublesome territory.'

'This is strange and ghostly territory,' says Noort. 'I would paint it, if I could, and then let Mynheer Brueghel look to his fame, and old Bosch as well. Such sights! Were you a prince before you were transformed?'

'I have not yet been transformed,' says Bhengarn. 'That awaits me at Crystal Pond.' The road through the plain now trends slightly uphill; they are advancing into the farther side of the basin. A pale yellow tint comes into the sky. The path here is prickly with little many-faceted insects whose hard sharp bodies assail the Dutchman's bare tender feet. Cursing, he hops in wild leaps, bringing him dangerously close to outcroppings of teeth, and Bhengarn, in sympathy, fashions stout grey boots for him. Noort grins. He gestures towards

108

his bare middle, and Bhengarn clothes him in a shapeless grey robe.

'Like a monk, is how I look!' Noort cries. 'Well, well, a monk in Hell! But you say this is not Hell. And what kind of creature are you, creature?'

'A human being,' says Bhengarn, 'of the Traveller sort.'

'A human being!' Noort booms. He leaps across a brook of sparkling bubbling violet-hued water and waits on the far side as Bhengarn trudges through it. 'A human under an enchantment, I would venture.'

'This is my natural form. Humankind has not worn your guise since long before the falling of the Moon. The Eater you saw was human. Do you see, on yonder eastern hill, a company of Destroyers turning the forest to rubble? They are human.'

'The wolves on two legs up there?'

'Those, yes. And there are others you will see. Awaiters, Breathers, Skimmers – '

'These are mere noises to me, creature. What is human? A Dutchman is human! A Portugal is human! Even a Chinese, a black, a Japonder with a shaven head. But those beasts on yon hill? Or a creature with more legs than I have whiskers? No, Traveller, no! You flatter yourself. Do you happen to know, Traveller, how it is that I am here? I was in Amsterdam, to speak before the Lords Seventeen and the Company in general, to ask for ships to bring pepper from the Moluccas, but they said they would choose Joris van Spilbergen in my place – do you know Spilbergen? I think him much overpraised – and then all went dizzy, as though I had taken too much beer with my gin – and then – then – ah, this is a dream, is it not, Traveller? At this moment I sleep in Amsterdam. I am too old for such drinking. Yet never have I had a dream so real as this, and so strange. Tell me: when you walk, do you move the legs on the right side first, or the left?' Noort does not wait for a reply. 'If you are human, Traveller, are you also a Christian, then?'

Bhengarn searches in Noort's mind for the meaning of that, finds something approximate, and says, 'I make no such claim.'

'Good. Good. There are limits to my credulity. How far is this Crystal Pond?'

'We have covered most of the distance. If I proceed at a steady pace I will come shortly to the land of smoking holes, and not far beyond that is the approach to the Wall of Ice, which will demand a difficult but not impossible ascent, and just on the far side of that I will find the vale that contains Crystal Pond, where the beginning of the next phase of my life will occur.' They are walking now through a zone of sparkling rubbery cones of a bright vermilion colour, from which small green Stangarones emerge in quick succession to chant their one-note melodies. The flavour of a heavy musk hangs in the air. Night is beginning to fall. Bhengarn says, 'Are you tired?'

'Just a little.'

'It is not my custom to travel by night. Does this campsite suit you?' Bhengarn indicates a broad circular depression bordered by tiny volcanic fumaroles. The ground here is warm and spongy, moist, bare of vegetation. Bhengarn extends an excavator claw and pulls free a strip of it, which he hands to Noort, indicating that he should eat. Noort tentatively nibbles. Bhengarn helps himself to some also. Noort, kneeling, presses his knuckles against the ground, makes it yield, mutters to himself, shakes his head, rips off another strip and chews it in wonder. Bhengarn says, 'You find the world much changed, do you not?'

'Beyond all understanding, in fact.'

'Our finest artists have worked on it since time immemorial, making it more lively, more diverting. We think it is a great success. Do you agree?'

Noort does not answer. He is staring bleakly at the sky, suddenly dark and jewelled with blazing stars. Bhengarn realizes that he is searching for patterns, navigators' signs. Noort frowns, turns round and round to take in the full circuit of the heavens, bites his lip, finally lets out a low groaning sigh and says, 'I recognize nothing. Nothing. This is not the northern sky, this is not the southern sky, this is not any sky I can understand.' Quietly he begins to weep. After a time he says sombrely, 'I was not the most adept of navigators, but I knew something, at least. And I look at this sky and I feel like a helpless babe. All the stars have changed places. Now I see how lost I am, how far from anything I ever knew, and once it gave me great pleasure to sail under strange skies, but not now, not here, because these skies frighten me and this land of demons offers me no peace. I have never wept, do you know that, creature, never, not once in my life! But Holland – my house, my tavern, my church, my sons, my pipe – where is Holland? Where is everything I knew? The skies above Magellan's Strait were not the thousandth part so strange as this.' A harsh heavy sob escapes him, and he turns away, huddling into himself.

Compassion floods Bhengarn for this miserable wanderer. To ease Noort's pain he summons fantasies for him, dredging images from the reservoirs of the ancient man's spirit and hurling them against the sky, building a cathedral of fire in the heavens, and a royal palace, and a great armada of ships with bellying sails and the Dutch flag fluttering, and the watery boulevards of busy Amsterdam and the quiet streets of little Haarlem, and more. He paints for Noort the stars in their former courses, the Centaur, the Swan, the Bear, the Twins. He restores the fallen Moon to its place and by its cold light creates a landscape of time lost and gone, with avenues of heavy-boughed oaks and maples, and drifts of brilliant red and yellow tulips blazing beneath them, and golden roses arching in great bowers over the thick newly-mowed lawn. He creates fields of ripe wheat, and haystacks high as barns, and harvesters toiling in the hot sultry afternoon. He gives Noort the aroma of the Sunday feast and the scent of good Dutch gin and the sweet dense fumes of his long clay pipe. Noort nods and murmurs and clasps his hands, and gradually his sorrow ebbs and his weeping ceases, and he drifts off into a deep and easy slumber. The images fade. Bhengarn, who rarely sleeps, keeps watch until first light comes and a flock of finger-winged birds passes overhead, shouting shrilly, jesting and swooping.

Noort is calm and quiet in the morning. He feeds again on the spongy soil and drinks from a clear emerald rivulet and they move onwards towards Crystal Pond. Bhengarn is pleased to have his company. There is something crude and coarse about the Dutchman, perhaps even more so than another of his era might be, but Bhengarn finds that unimportant. He has always preferred companions of any sort to the solitary march, in his centuries of going to and fro upon the Earth. He has travelled with Skimmers and Destroyers, and once a ponderous Ruminant, and even on several occasions visitors from other worlds who have come to sample the wonders of Earth. At least twice Bhengarn has had as his travelling companion a castaway of the time-flux from some prehistoric era, though not so prehistoric as Noort's. And now it has befallen him that he will go to the end of his journey with this rough hairy being from the dawn of humanity's day. So be it. So be it.

Noort says, breaking a long silence as they cross a plateau of quivering gelatinous stuff, 'Were you a man or a woman before the sorcery gave you this present shape?'

'I have always had this form.'

'No. Impossible. You say you are human, you speak my language – '

'Actually, you speak *my* language,' says Bhengarn.

'As you wish. If you are human you must once have looked like me. Can it be otherwise? Were you born a thing of silvery scales and many legs? I will not believe that.'

'Born?' says Bhengarn, puzzled.

'Is this word unknown to you?'

'Born,' the Traveller repeats. 'I think I see the concept. To *begin*, to *enter*, to *acquire one's shape* – '

'Born,' says Noort in exasperation. 'To come from the womb. To hatch, to sprout, to drop. Everything alive has to be born!'

'No,' Bhengarn says mildly. 'Not any longer.'

'You talk nonsense,' Noort snaps, and scours his throat angrily and spits. His spittle strikes a node of assonance and blossoms into a dazzling mound of green and scarlet jewels. 'Rubies,' he murmurs. 'Emeralds. I could puke pearls, I suppose.' He kicks at the pile of gems and scatters them; they dissolve into spurts of moist pink air. The Dutchman gives himself over to a sullen brooding. Bhengarn does not transgress on the other's taciturnity; he is content to march forward in his steady plodding way, saying nothing.

Three Skimmers appear, prancing, leaping. They are heading to the south. The slender golden-green creatures salute the wayfarers with pulsations of their great red eyes. Noort, halting, glares at them and says hoarsely to Bhengarn, 'These are human beings too?'

'Indeed.'

'Natives of this realm?'

'Natives of this era,' says Bhengarn. 'The latest form, the newest thing, graceful, supple, purposeless.' The Skimmers

112

laugh and transform themselves into shining streaks of light and soar aloft like a trio of auroral rays. Bhengarn says, 'Do they seem beautiful to you?'

'They seem like minions of Satan,' says the Dutchman sourly. He scowls. 'When I awaken I pray I remember none of this. For if I do, I will tell the tale to Willem and Jan and Piet, and they will think I have lost my senses, and mock me. Tell me I dream, creature. Tell me I lie drunk in an inn in Amsterdam.'

'It is not so,' Bhengarn says gently.

'Very well. Very well. I have come to a land where every living thing is a demon or a monster. That is no worse, I suppose, than a land where everyone speaks Japanese and worships stones. It is a world of wonders, and I have seen more than my share. Tell me, creature, do you have cities in this land?'

'Not for millions of years.'

'Then where do the people live?'

'Why, they live where they find themselves! Last night we lived where the ground was food. Tonight we will settle by the Wall of Ice. And tomorrow – '

'Tomorrow,' Noort says, 'we will have dinner with the Grand Diabolus and dance in the Witches' Sabbath. I am prepared, just as I was prepared to sup with the penguin-eating folk of the Cape, that stood six cubits high. I will be surprised by nothing.' He laughs. 'I am hungry, creature. Shall I tear up the earth again and stuff it down?'

'Not here. Try those fruits.'

Luminous spheres dangle from a tree of golden limbs. Noort plucks one, tries it unhesitatingly, claps his hands, takes three more. Then he pulls a whole cluster free, and offers one to Bhengarn, who refuses.

'Not hungry?' the Dutchman asks.

'I take my food in other ways.'

'Yes, you breathe it in from flowers as you crawl along, eh? Tell me, Traveller: to what end is your journey? To discover new lands? To fulfil some pledge? To confound your enemies? I doubt it is any of these.'

'I travel out of simple necessity, because it is what my kind does, and for no special purpose.'

'A humble wanderer, then, like the mendicant monks who serve the Lord by taking to the highways?'

'Something like that.'

'Do you ever cease your wanderings?'

'Never yet. But cessation is coming. At Crystal Pond I will become my utter opposite, and enter the Awaiter tribe, and be made immobile and contemplative. I will root myself like a vegetable, after my metamorphosis.'

Noort offers no comment on that. After a time he says, 'I knew a man of your kind once. Jan Huyghen van Linschoten of Haarlem, who roamed the world because the world was there to roam, and spent his years in the India of the Portugals and wrote it all down in a great vast book, and when he had done that went off to Novaya Zemlya with Barents to find the chilly way to the Indies, and I think would have sailed to the Moon if he could find the pilot to guide him. I spoke with him once. My own travels took me farther than Linschoten, do you know? I saw Borneo and Java and the world's hinder side, and the thick Sargasso Sea. But I went with a purpose other than my own amusement or the gathering of strange lore, which was to buy pepper and cloves, and gather Spanish gold, and win my fame and comfort. Was that so wrong, Traveller? Was I so unworthy?' Noort chuckles. 'Perhaps I was, for I brought home neither spices nor gold nor most of my men, but only the fame of having sailed around the world. I think I understand you, Traveller. The spices go into a cask of meat and are eaten and gone; the gold is only yellow metal; but so long as there are Dutchmen, no one will forget that Olivier van Noort, the tavern-keeper of Rotterdam, strung a line around the middle of the world. So long as there are Dutchmen.' He laughs. 'It is folly to travel for profit. I will travel for wisdom from now on. What do you say, Traveller? Do you applaud me?'

'I think you are already on the proper path,' says Bhengarn. 'But look, look there: the Wall of Ice.'

Noort gasps. They have come around a low headland and are confronted abruptly by a barrier of pure white light, as radiant as a mirror at noon, that spans the horizon from east to west and rises skywards like an enormous palisade filling half the heavens. Bhengarn studies it with respect and admiration. He has known for hundreds of years that he must ascend this wall if he is to reach Crystal Pond, and that the wall is formidable; but he has seen no need before now to

114

contemplate the actualities of the problem, and now he sees that they are significant.

'Are we to ascend that?' Noort asks.

'I must. But here, I think, we shall have to part company.'

'The throne of Lucifer must lie beyond that icy rampart.'

'I know nothing of that,' says Bhengarn, 'but certainly Crystal Pond is on the farther side, and there is no other way to reach it but to climb the wall. We will camp tonight at its base, and in the morning I will begin my climb.'

'Is such a climb possible?'

'It will have to be,' Bhengarn replies.

'Ah. You will turn yourself to a puff of light like those others we met, and shoot over the top like some meteor. Eh?'

'I must climb,' says Bhengarn, 'using one limb after another, and taking care not to lose my grip. There is no magical way of making this ascent.' He sweeps aside fallen branches of a glowing blue-limbed shrub to make a campsite for them. To Noort he says, 'Before I begin the ascent tomorrow I will instruct you in the perils of the world, for your protection on your future wanderings. I hold myself responsible for your presence here and I would not have you harmed once you have left my side.'

Noort says, 'I am not yet planning to leave your side. I mean to climb that wall alongside you, Traveller.'

'It will not be possible for you.'

'I will make it possible. That wall excites my spirit. I will conquer it as I conquered the storms of the Strait and the fevers of the Sargasso. I feel I should go with you to Crystal Pond, and pay my farewells to you there, for it will bring me luck to mark the beginning of my solitary journey by witnessing the end of yours. What do you say?'

'I say wait until the morning,' Bhengarn answers, 'and see the wall at close range, before you commit yourself to such mighty resolutions.'

During the night a silent lightstorm plays overhead; twisting turbulent spears of blue and green and violet radiance clash in the throbbing sky, and an undulation of the atmosphere sends alternating waves of hot and cool air racing down from the Wall of Ice. The time-flux blows, and frantic figures out of forgotten eras are swept by now far aloft, limbs churning desperately,

115

eyes rigid with astonishment. Noort sleeps through it all, though from time to time he stirs and mutters and clenches his fists. Bhengarn ponders his obligations to the Dutchman, and by the coming of the sharp blood-hued dawn he has arrived at an idea. Together they advance to the edge of the Wall; together they stare upwards at that vast vertical field of shining whiteness, smooth as stone. Hesitantly Noort touches it with his fingertip, and hisses at the coldness of it. He turns his back to it, paces, folds and unfolds his arms.

He says finally, 'No man of woman born could achieve the summit of that wall. But is there not some magic you could work, Traveller, that would enable me to make the ascent?'

'There is one. But I think you would not like it.'

'Speak.'

'I could transform you – for a short time, only a short time, no longer than the time it takes to climb the wall – into a being of the Traveller form. Thus we could ascend together.'

Noort's eyes travel quickly over Bhengarn's body – the long tubular serpentine thorax, the tapering tail, the multitude of powerful little legs – and a look of shock and dismay and loathing comes over his face for an instant, but just an instant. He frowns. He tugs at his heavy lower lip.

Bhengarn says, 'I will take no offence if you refuse.'

'Do it.'

'You may be displeased.'

'Do it! The morning is growing old. We have much climbing to do. Change me, Traveller. Change me quickly.' A shadow of doubt crosses Noort's features. 'You will change me back, once we reach the top?'

'It will happen of its own accord. I have no power to make a permanent transformation.'

'Then do what you can, and do it now!'

'Very well,' says Bhengarn, and the Traveller, summoning his fullest force, drains metamorphic energies from the planets and the stars and a passing comet, and focuses them and hurls them at the Dutchman, and there is a buzzing and a droning and a shimmering and when it is done a second Traveller stands at the foot of the Wall of Ice.

Noort seems thunderstruck. He says nothing; he does not move; only after a long time does he carefully lift his frontmost left limb and swing it forward a short way and put it down. Then the one opposite it; then several of the middle limbs; then, growing more adept, he manages to move his entire body, adopting a curious wriggling style, and in another moment he appears to be in control. 'This is passing strange,' he remarks at length. 'And yet it is almost like being in my own body, except that everything has been changed. You are a mighty wizard, Traveller. Can you show me now how to make the ascent?'

'Are you ready so soon?'

'I am ready,' Noort says.

So Bhengarn demonstrates, approaching the wall, bringing his penetrator claws into play, driving them like pitons into the ice, hauling himself up a short distance, extending the claws, driving them in, pulling upwards. He has never climbed ice before, though he has faced all other difficulties the world has to offer, but the climb, though strenuous, seems manageable enough. He halts after a few minutes and watches as Noort, clumsy but determined in his altered body, imitates him, scratching and scraping at the ice as he pulls himself up the face until they are side by side. 'It is easy,' Noort says.

And so it is, for a time, and then it is less easy, for now they hang high above the valley and the midday sun has melted the surface of the wall just enough to make it slick and slippery, and a terrible cold from within the mass of ice seeps outwards into the climbers, and even though a Traveller's body is a wondrous machine fit to endure anything, this is close to the limit. Once Bhengarn loses his purchase, but Noort deftly claps a claw to the middle of his spine to hold him firmly until he has dug in again; and not much later the same happens to Noort, and Bhengarn grasps him. As the day wanes they are so far above the ground that they can barely make out the treetops below, and yet the top of the wall is too high to see. Together they excavate a ledge, burrowing inwards to rest in a chilly nook, and at dawn they begin again, Bhengarn's sinuous body winding upwards over the rim of their little cave and Noort following with less agility. Upwards and upwards they climb, never pausing and saying little, through a day of warmth and soft perfumed breezes and through a night of storms and falling stars, and then through a day of turquoise rain, and through another day and a night and a day and then they are at the top, looking out across the broad unending field of ferns and bright blossoms that covers the summit's flat surface, and as they move inwards from the rim Noort lets out a cry and stumbles forward, for he has resumed his ancient form. He drops to his knees and sits there panting, stunned, looking in confusion at his fingernails, at his knuckles, at the hair on the backs of his hands, as though he has never seen such things before. 'Passing strange,' he says softly.

'You are a born Traveller,' Bhengarn tells him.

They rest a time, feeding on the sparkling four-winged fruits that sprout in that garden above the ice. Bhengarn feels an immense calmness now that the climax of his peregrination is upon him. Never had he questioned the purpose of being a Traveller, nor has he had regret that destiny gave him that form, but now he is quite willing to yield it up.

'How far to Crystal Pond?' Noort asks.

'It is just over there,' says Bhengarn.

'Shall we go to it now?'

'Approach it with great care,' the Traveller warns. 'It is a place of extraordinary power.'

They go forward; a path opens for them in the swaying grasses and low fleshy-leaved plants; within minutes they stand at the edge of a perfectly circular body of water of unfathomable depth and of a clarity so complete that the reflections of the sun can plainly be seen on the white sands of its infinitely distant bed. Bhengarn moves to the edge and peers in, and is pervaded by a sense of fulfilment and finality.

Noort says, 'What will become of you here?'

'Observe,' says Bhengarn.

He enters Crystal Pond and swims serenely towards the farther shore, an enterprise quickly enough accomplished. But before he has reached the midpoint of the pond a tolling sound is heard in the air, as of bells of the most pure quality, striking notes without harmonic overtones. Sudden ecstasy engulfs him as he becomes aware of the beginning of his transformation: his body flows and streams in the flux of life, his limbs fuse, his soul expands. By the time he comes forth on the edge of the pond he has become something else, a great cone of passive flesh, which is able to drag itself no more than five or six times its own length from the water, and then sinks down on the sandy surface of the ground and begins the process of digging itself in. Here the Awaiter Bhengarn will settle, and here he will live for centuries of centuries, motionless, all but timeless, considering the primary truths of being. Already he is gliding into the earth.

Noort gapes at him from the other side of the pond.

'Is this what you sought?' the Dutchman asks.

'Yes. Absolutely.'

'I wish you farewell and Godspeed, then!' Noort cries.

'And you – what will become of you?'

Noort laughs. 'Have no fears for me! I see my destiny unfolding!'

Bhengarn, nestled now deep in the ground, enwombed by the earth, immobile, established already in his new life, watches as Noort strides boldly to the water's edge. Only slowly, for an Awaiter's mind is less agile than a Traveller's, does Bhengarn comprehend what is to happen.

Noort says, 'I've found my vocation again. But if I'm to travel, I must be equipped for travelling!'

He enters the pond, swimming in broad awkward splashing strokes, and once again the pure tolling sound is evoked, a delicate carillon of crystalline transparent tone, and there is sudden brilliance in the pond as Noort sprouts the shining scales of a Traveller, and the jointed limbs, and the strong thick tail. He scuttles out on the far side wholly transformed.

'Farewell!' Noort cries joyously.

'Farewell,' murmurs Bhengarn the Awaiter, peering out from the place of his long repose, as Olivier van Noort, all his legs ablaze with new energy, strides away vigorously to begin his second circumnavigation of the globe.

Gate of Horn, Gate of Ivory

An odd concatenation of ironies surrounds this little story.

I was, for ten years beginning in 1969, the editor of an annual anthology of original science-fiction stories called *New Dimensions*. During that time I published a good many interesting and important stories by such writers as Ursula K. Le Guin, Gardner Dozois, George Alec Effinger, James Tiptree, Jr, Harlan Ellison, Joanna Russ, Philip José Farmer, Gregory Benford, Isaac Asimov and Barry Malzberg. Some of the stories I ran won Hugo and Nebula awards and a few, like Le Guin's 'The Ones Who Walk Away from Omelas' and Joanna Russ's 'Nobody's Home', have become much-reprinted classics.

In all that time *New Dimensions* never published a story by Robert Silverberg. One minor but not insignificant reason was that I didn't write any short stories between November 1973 and January 1980. Even if I had, though, you wouldn't have seen them in *New Dimensions*, because it isn't much of a challenge for editors to sell stories to themselves, and I would have felt foolish filling *New Dimensions* with my own work.

By 1979, though, I was beginning to emerge from my five-year mid-1970s retirement from fiction-writing, and I wanted to ease myself of my editorial duties to have more time and energy available for doing stories. So I invited my friend and neighbour Marta Randall, then at the peak of her own science-fiction career, to take over *New Dimensions*. We worked out a complicated transitional mode: the eleventh *New Dimensions* would carry the byline, 'edited by Robert Silverberg and Marta Randall'. Issue twelve would be slugged 'edited by Marta Randall and Robert Silverberg'. And from the thirteenth issue onwards, *New Dimensions* would carry Marta's name alone.

And so it came to pass: a Silverberg–Randall issue in 1980, a Randall–Silverberg issue in 1981. In the autumn of 1981, as Marta was putting the finishing touches on her first solo issue of *New Dimensions*, she caught me by surprise by saying to me, 'Since your name won't be on number thirteen as editor, how about writing a story for me?'

Well, why not? I thought. Nearly every well-known science-fiction writer of the period had been published in *New Dimensions* except me. I had already decided to spend the autumn and winter of 1981–2 writing short stories anyway. And now that I was no longer connected with the anthology in any way, there was no reason to disqualify myself from contributing. A week or two later I delivered 'Gate of Horn, Gate of Ivory' to Marta. Now I, too, had sold a story to *New Dimensions*.

But it never appeared there. *New Dimensions*' publisher underwent a turbulent internal upheaval the following year and its entire science-fiction line, including *New Dimensions* and a host of other books in progress, was cancelled before publication. *New Dimensions* 13 exists today only in galley-proof form.

But a second anthology of original science fiction – *Universe* – was being edited just then by yet another Bay Area resident, Terry Carr. It had begun publication about the same time as *New Dimensions*, had won just about as much acclaim for its material, and indeed had been in direct although friendly – very friendly – competition with *New Dimensions* all along. I had written a few stories for *Universe* in its early days, and when I resumed writing them in 1980 I had vaguely promised to do another for it, but never had. When Terry heard that *New Dimensions* had been suspended with an entire issue of fiction in inventory, including one of mine, he asked Marta to show him the stories, and a little while later he called to ask if it was all right for him to use 'Gate of Horn'. Which is why the story with which I had intended to make my *New Dimensions* debut appeared instead in the 1984 number of its chief competitor *Universe*.

There is a final dark twist to the tale. Terry fell ill in 1985, weakened all through 1986, and died in the spring of 1987, only fifty years old. Pat LoBrutto, his editor at Doubleday, felt that *Universe* should be continued as a memorial to him, and asked me, a few weeks after Terry's death, to take charge of it. It was, as they say, an offer I couldn't refuse – and so today I find myself, in collaboration with my wife Karen Haber, the editor of *Universe*, which now is published every other year. So 'Gate of Horn' got in just under the wire; now that I'm its editor, I regard the contents page of *Universe* as closed to me, just as that of *New Dimensions* was for so many years.

Often at night on the edge of sleep I cast my mind towards the abyss of time to come, hoping that I will tumble through some glowing barrier and find myself on the shores of a distant tomorrow. I strain at the moorings that hold me to this time and this place, and yearn to break free. Sometimes I feel that I *have* broken free, that the journey is at last beginning, that I will open my eyes in the inconceivable dazzling future. But it is only an illusion, like that fluent knowledge of French or Sanskrit or calculus which is born in dreams and departs by dawn. I awaken and it is the year 1983 and I am in my own bed with the striped sheets and the blue coverlet, and nothing has changed.

But I try again and again and still again, for the future calls me and the bleak murderous present repels me, and again the illusion that I am cutting myself loose from the time-line comes over me, now more vivid and plausible than ever before, and as I soar and hurtle and vanish through the permeable membranes of the aeons I wonder if it is finally in truth happening. I hover suspended somewhere outside the fabric of time and space and look down upon the Earth and I can see its contours changing as though I watch an accelerated movie: roads sprout and fork and fork once more, villages arise and exfoliate into towns and then into cities and then are overtaken by the forest, rivers change their courses and deliver their waters into great mirror-bright lakes that shrivel and become meadows. And I hover, passive, a dreamer, observing. There are two gates of sleep, says Homer and also Virgil. One is fashioned of horn, and one of ivory. Through the gate of horn pass the visions that are true, but those that emerge from the gate of ivory are deceptive dreams that mean nothing. Do I journey in a dream of the ivory gate? No, no, this is a true sending, this has the solidity and substance of inexorable reality. I have achieved it this time. I have crossed the barrier. Hooded figures surround me; sombre eyes study me; I look into faces of a weird sameness, tawny skin, fleshless lips, jutting cheekbones that tug the taut skin above them into drumheads. The room in which I lie is high-vaulted and dark, but glows with a radiance that seems inherent in the material of its walls. Abstract figurings, like the ornamentation of a mosque, dance along those walls in silver inlay; but this is no mosque, nor would the tribe of Allah have loved those strange and godless geometries that restlessly chase one another like lustful squirrels over the wainscoting. I am there; I am surely there.

'I want to see everything,' I say.

'See it, then. Nothing prevents you.'

One of them presses into my hand a shining silver globe, an orb of command that transports me at the tiniest squeeze of my hand. I fly upwards jerkily and in terror, rising so swiftly that the air grows cold and the sky becomes purple, but in a moment I regain control and come to govern my trajectory more usefully. At an altitude of a few dozen yards I pass over a city of serene cubical buildings of rounded corners, glittering with white Mediterranean brilliance in the gentle sunlight. I see small vehicles, pastel-hued, teardrop-tapered, in which citizens with the universal face of the era ride above crystalline roadbeds. I drift over a garden of plants I cannot recognize, perhaps new plants entirely, with pink succulent leaves and great mounding golden influorescences, or ropy stems like bundles of coaxial cable, or jagged green thorns tipped with tiny blue eyes. I come to a pond of air where serene naked people swim with minimal motions of their fingertips. I observe a staircase of some yielding rubbery substance that vanishes into a glowing nimbus of radiance, and children are climbing that staircase and disappearing into that sparkling place at its top. In the zoological gardens I look down on creatures from a hundred worlds, stranger than any protozoan made lion-sized.

For days I tour this place, inexhaustibly curious, numb with awe. There is no blade of grass out of place. There is no stain nor blemish. The sounds I hear are harmonious sounds, and no other. The air is mild and the winds are soft. Only the people seem stark and austere to me, I suppose because of their sameness of features and the hieratic Egyptian solemnity of their eyes, but after a while I realize that this is only my poor archaic sensibility's misunderstanding, for I feel their love and support about me like a harness as I fly, and I know that these are the happiest, most angelic of all the beings that have walked the Earth. I wonder how far in time I have travelled. Fifty thousand years? Half a million? Or perhaps – perhaps, and that possibility shrivels me with pain – perhaps much less than that. Perhaps this is the world of a hundred and fifty years from now, eh? The post-apocalyptic era, the coming utopia that lies just on the farther shore of our sea of turbulent nightmares. Is it possible, that our world can be transformed into this so quickly? Why not? Miracles accelerate in an age of miracles. From the wobbly thing of wood and paper that flew a few seconds at Kitty Hawk to the gleaming majesty of the transcontinental jetliner was only a bit more than fifty years. Why not imagine that a world like this can be assembled in just as little time? But if that is so –

The torment of the thought drives me to the ground. I fall; they are taken by surprise, but ease my drop; I land on the warm moist soil and kneel, clutching it, letting my head slacken until my forehead touches the ground. I feel a gentle hand on my shoulder, just a touch, steadying me, soothing me.

'Let go,' I say, virtually snarling. 'Take your hand off!'

The hand retreats.

I am alone with my agony. I tremble, I sob, I shiver. I am aware of them surrounding me, but they are baffled, helpless, confused. Possibly they have never seen pain before. Possibly suffering is no part of their vocabulary of spirit.

Finally one of them says softly, 'Why do you weep?'

'Out of anger. Out of frustration.'

They are mystified. They surround me with shining machinery, screens and coils and lights and glowing panels, that I suspect is going to diagnose my malady. I kick everything over. I trample the intricate mechanisms and shove wildly at those who reach for me, even though I see that they are reaching not to restrain me but to soothe me.

'What is it?' they keep asking. 'What troubles you?'

'I want to know what year this is.'

They confer. It may be that their numbering system is so different from ours that they are unable to tell me. But there must be a way: diagrams, analogies, astronomical patterns. I am not so primitive that I am beyond understanding such things.

Finally they say, 'Your question has no meaning for us.'

'No meaning? You speak my language well enough. *I need to know what year this is.*'

'Its name is Eiligorda,' one of them says.

'Its *name*? Years don't have names. Years have numbers. My year is numbered 1983. Are we so far in my future that you don't remember the years with numbers?' I begin stripping away my clothing. 'Here, look at me. This hair on my body – do you have hair like that? These teeth – see, I have thirty-two of them, arranged in an arc.' I hold up my hands. 'Nails on my fingers! Have fingernails evolved away?' I tap my belly. 'In here, an appendix dangling from my gut! Prehistoric, useless, preposterous! How long ago did that disappear? Look at me! See the ape-man, and tell me how ancient I am!'

'Our bodies are just like yours,' comes the quiet reply. 'Except that we are healthier and stronger, and resistant to disease. But we have hair. We have fingernails. We have the appendix.' They are naked before me, and I see that it is true. Their bodies are lean and supple, and there is a weird and disconcerting similarity of physique about them all, but they are not alien in any way; these could be twentieth-century bodies.

'I want you to tell me,' I say, 'how distant in time your world is from mine.'

'Not very,' someone answers. 'But we lack the precise terminology for describing the interval.'

'Not very,' I say. 'Listen, does the Earth still go around the sun?'

'Of course.'

'The time it takes to make one circuit – has that changed?'

'Not at all.'

'How many times, then, do you think the Earth has circled the sun since my era?'

They exchange glances. They make quick rippling gestures – a kind of counting, perhaps. But they seem unable to complete the calculation. They murmur, they smile, they shrug. At last I understand their problem, which is not one of communication but one of tact. They do not want to tell me the truth for the same reason that I yearn to know it. The truth will hurt me. The truth will split me with anguish.

They are people of the epoch that immediately succeeds yours and mine. They are, quite possibly, the great-great-grandchildren of some who live in our world of 1983; or it may be that they are only grandchildren. The future they inhabit is not the extremely distant future. I am positive of that. But time stands still for them, for they do not know death.

Fury and frenzy return to me. I shake with rage; I taste burning bile; I explode with hatred, and launch myself upon them, scratching, punching, kicking, biting, trying in a single outpouring of bitter resentment to destroy the entire sleek epoch into which I have fallen.

I harm several of them quite seriously.

Then they recover from their astonishment and subdue me, without great effort, dropping me easily with a few delicate musical tones and holding me captive against the ground. The casualties are taken away.

One of my captors kneels beside me and says, 'Why do you show such hostility?'

I glare at him. 'Because I am so close to being one of you.'

'Ah. I think I can comprehend. But why do you blame us for that?'

The only answer I can give him is more fury; I tug against my invisible bonds and lunge as if to slaughter him with sheer energy of rage; from me pours such a blaze of madness as to sear the air, and so intense is my emotion that it seems to me I am actually breaking free, and seizing him, and clawing at him and smashing him. But I am only clutching at phantoms. My arms move like those of a windmill and I lose my balance and topple and topple and topple and when I regain my balance I am in my own bed once more, striped sheets, blue coverlet, the red eye of the digital clock telling me that it is 4:36 A.M. So they have punished me by casting me from their midst. I suppose that is no more than I deserve. But do they comprehend, do they really comprehend, my torment? Do they understand what it is like to know that those who will come just a little way after us will have learned how to live for ever, and to live in paradise, and that one of us, at least, has had a glimpse of it, but that we will all be dead when it comes to pass? Why should we not rage against the generations to come, aware that we are nearly the last ones who will know death? Why not scratch and bite and kick? An awful iron door is closing on us, and *they* are on the far side, safe. Surely they will begin to understand that, when they have given more thought to my visit. Possibly they understood it even while I was there. I suspect they did, finally. And that when they returned me to my own time I was given a gift of grace by those gilded futurians: that their mantle of immortality has been cast over me, that I will be allowed to live on and on until time has come round again and I am once more in their era, but now as one of them. That is their gift to me, and perhaps that is their curse on me as well, that I must survive through all the years of terrible darkness that must befall before that golden dawn, that I will tarry here until they come again.

Amanda and the Alien

Some stories seem almost to write themselves. This was one of them. I wish they were all that easy, or that the results were always as pleasing.

'Amanda' was a product of the rainy winter of 1981–2, when I was having a particularly fertile run of short-story writing. (Here I need to pause for a digression on California weather and my writing habits. California is one of five places in the world that has the so-called 'Mediterranean' climate – the others are Chile, Western Australia, the western part of South Africa and the Mediterranean region itself – in which the winters are mild and rainy and the summers are absolutely dry. Where I live, in the San Francisco region, the heaviest rains fall between November and March. Then they taper off and from mid-April to early November there's normally no rain at all. Rain in summertime here has been known to happen occasionally, but so rarely that it's a front-page news item. My working pattern follows the weather: I tend to write my novels during the period of maximum rainfalls, tapering off to short stories in the spring, and doing as little work as my conscience will allow during the dry season. By fall, just as the rains are getting ready to return, I warm up the machinery with a short story or two and then embark on the new season's novel. But 1981 was an unusual year: instead of a novel, my book for the year was *Majipoor Chronicles*, which is actually a collection of short stories disguised as a novel, and I wrote it in the spring and summer instead of winter. When autumn came, I was out of sequence with my regular publishing rhythm, and I decided to keep on writing short stories and get things straightened out later on.)

And so 'Amanda'. It wasn't the story I had intended to do just then. I had promised one to Ellen Datlow, the new fiction editor of *Omni*. What I had in mind was a sequel to 'Dancers in the Time-flux' – another tale of Olivier van Noort in the far future, this time encountering a Parisian woman from the year 1980, like himself a creature of antiquity but nevertheless something out of his own future. My long-range plan was to assemble another story cycle along the lines of *Majipoor Chronicles*, set in the *Son of Man* world. But something went wrong and the story died on me after about eight pages. I don't know why. Unfinished stories are as rare around here as heavy rainfall in July. So far as I can recall, that's the only story I've left unfinished in the past thirty-five years. I have those eight pages around here somewhere, and some day I may write the rest of the piece. But for some reason I put it aside. Perhaps it had been a mistake to try once again to return to the world of *Son of Man*, a closed chapter in my past.

'The thing seemed terribly slow and ponderous and wrong,' I told Ellen in a letter of 20 February 1982, 'and after a few days of work I called a halt to find out what the trouble was. The trouble was, apparently, that I wanted to do a different sort of story for you, something bouncier and zippier and more contemporary. And before I really knew what was happening, the enclosed light-hearted chiller came galloping out of the typewriter.' Ellen bought it by return mail, and Terry Carr chose it for the 1983 volume of his annual *Best SF of the Year* anthology series.

Instead of setting my story in the remote future world of 'Dancers in the Time-flux', I had put it right here, in the San Francisco Bay Area of just a few years hence. And, though I wrote it in cool rainy February, I picked warm sunny September as the time in which it took place. Perhaps that was why I wrote it with such ease. It had been pouring outside for days, but in my mind the long golden summer had already come. And with it, the utterly unscrupulous Amanda, an all too familiar California life-form.

Amanda spotted the alien late Friday afternoon outside the Video Center on South Main. It was trying to look cool and laid-back, but it simply came across as bewildered and uneasy. The alien was disguised as a seventeen-year-old girl, maybe a Chicana, with olive-toned skin and hair so black it seemed almost blue, but Amanda, who was seventeen herself, knew a phony when she saw one. She studied the alien for some moments from the other side of the street to make absolutely certain. Then she walked across.

'You're doing it wrong,' Amanda said. 'Anybody with half a brain could tell what you really are.'

'Bug off,' the alien said.

'No. Listen to me. You want to stay out of the detention centre or don't you?'

The alien stared coldly at Amanda and said, 'I don't know what the crap you're talking about.'

'Sure you do. No sense trying to bluff me. Look, I want to help you,' Amanda said. 'I think you're getting a raw deal. You know what that means, a raw deal? Hey, look, come home with me and I'll teach you a few things about passing for human. I've got the whole friggin' weekend now with nothing else to do anyway.'

A flicker of interest came into the other girl's dark chilly eyes. But it went quickly away and she said, 'You some kind of lunatic?'

'Suit yourself, O thing from beyond the stars. *Let* them lock you up again. *Let* them stick electrodes up your ass. I tried to help. That's all I can do, is try,' Amanda said, shrugging. She began to saunter away. She didn't look back. Three steps, four, five, hands in pockets, slowly heading for her car. Had she been wrong, she wondered? No. No. She could be wrong about some things, like Charley Taylor's interest in spending the weekend with her, maybe. But not this. That crinkly-haired chick was the missing alien for sure. The whole county was buzzing about it — deadly non-human life-form has escaped from the detention centre out by Tracy, might be anywhere, Walnut Creek, Livermore, even San Francisco, dangerous monster, capable of mimicking human forms, will engulf and digest you and disguise itself in your shape, and there it was, Amanda knew, standing outside the Video Center. Amanda kept walking.

'Wait,' the alien said finally.

Amanda took another easy step or two. Then she looked back over her shoulder. 'Yeah?'

'How can you tell?'

Amanda grinned. 'Easy. You've got a rain-slicker on and it's only September. Rainy season doesn't start around here for another month or two. Your pants are the old Spandex kind. People like you don't wear that stuff any more. Your face-paint is San Jose colours, but you've got the cheek-chevrons put on in the Berkeley pattern. That's just the first three things I noticed. I could find plenty more. Nothing about you fits together with anything else. It's like you did a survey to see how you ought to appear, and tried a little of everything. The closer I study you the more I see. Look, you're wearing your headphones and the battery light is on, but there's no cassette in the slot. What are you listening to, the music of the spheres? That model doesn't have any FM tuner, you know. You see? You may think you're perfectly camouflaged, but you aren't.'

'I could destroy you,' the alien said.

'What? Oh, sure. Sure you could. Engulf me right here on the street, all over in thirty seconds, little trail of slime by the door and a new Amanda walks away. But what then? What good's that going to do you? You still won't know which end is up. So there's no logic in destroying me, unless you're a total dummy. I'm on your side. I'm not going to turn you in.'

'Why should I trust you?'

'Because I've been talking to you for five minutes and I haven't yelled for the cops yet. Don't you know that half of California is out searching for you? Hey, can you read? Come over here a minute. Here.' Amanda tugged the alien towards the newspaper vending box at the curb. The headline on the afternoon *Examiner* was:

> **BAY AREA ALIEN TERROR**
> *Marines to Join Nine-County Hunt*
> *Mayor, Governor Caution Against Panic*

'You understand that?' Amanda asked. 'That's you they're talking about. They're out there with flame-guns, tranquillizer darts, web-snares, and God knows what else. There's been real hysteria for a day and a half. And you standing around here with the wrong chevrons on! Christ. Christ! What's your plan, anyway? Where are you trying to go?'

'Home,' the alien said. 'But first I have to rendezvous at the pickup point.'

'Where's that?'

'You think I'm stupid?'

'Shit,' Amanda said. 'If I meant to turn you in, I'd have done it five minutes ago. But OK. I don't give a damn where your rendezvous point is. I tell you, though, you wouldn't make it

130

as far as San Francisco rigged up the way you are. It's a miracle
you've avoided getting caught until now.'

'And you'll help me?'

'I've been trying to. Come on. Let's get the hell out of here.
I'll take you home and fix you up a little. My car's in the lot
on the corner.'

'OK.'

'Whew!' Amanda shook her head slowly. 'Christ, some people
are awfully hard to help.'

As she drove out of the centre of town Amanda glanced
occasionally at the alien sitting tensely to her right. Basically
the disguise was very convincing, Amanda thought. Maybe all
the small details were wrong, the outer stuff, the anthropological
stuff, but the alien *looked* human, it *sounded* human, it even
smelled human. Possibly it could fool ninety-nine people out of
a hundred, or maybe more than that. But Amanda had always
had a good eye for detail. And at the particular moment she
had spotted the alien on South Main she had been unusually
alert, sensitive, all raw nerves, every antenna up. Of course, it
wasn't aliens she was hunting for, but just a diversion, a little
excitement, something to fill the great gaping emptiness that
Charley Taylor had left in her weekend.

Amanda had been planning the weekend with Charley all
month. Her parents were going to go off to Lake Tahoe for
three days, her kid sister had wangled permission to accompany
them, and Amanda was going to have the house to herself,
just her and Macavity the cat. And Charley. He was going to
move in on Friday afternoon and they'd cook dinner together
and get blasted on her stash of choice powder and watch five
or six of her parents' X cassettes, and Saturday they'd drive
over to the city and cruise some of the kinky districts and go
to that bath-house on Folsom where everybody got naked and
climbed into the giant Jacuzzi, and then on Sunday – Well, none
of that was going to happen. Charley had called on Thursday to
cancel. 'Something big came up,' he said, and Amanda had a
pretty good idea what that was, which was his hot little cousin
from New Orleans who sometimes came flying out here on no
notice at all; but the inconsiderate bastard seemed to be entirely
unaware of how much Amanda had been looking forward to this

weekend, how much it meant to her, how painful it was to be dumped like this. She had run through the planned events of the weekend in her mind so many times that she almost felt as though she had experienced them: it was that real to her. But overnight it had become unreal. Three whole days on her own, the house to herself, and so early in the semester that there was no homework to think about, and Charley had stood her up! What was she supposed to do now, call desperately around town to scrounge up some old lover as a playmate? Or pick up some stranger downtown? Amanda hated to fool around with strangers. She was half tempted to go over to the city and just let things happen, but they were all weirdos and creeps over there, anyway, and she knew what she could expect. What a waste, not having Charley! She could kill him for robbing her of the weekend.

Now there was the alien, though. A dozen of these star-people had come to Earth last year, not in a flying saucer as everybody had expected, but in little capsules that floated like milkweed seeds, and they had landed in a wide arc between San Diego and Salt Lake City. Their natural form, so far as anyone could tell for sure, was something like a huge jellyfish with a row of staring purple eyes down one wavy margin, but their usual tactic was to borrow any local body they found, digesting it and turning themselves into an accurate imitation of it. One of them had made the mistake of turning itself into a brown mountain bear and another into a bobcat – maybe they thought that those were the dominant life-forms on Earth – but the others had taken on human bodies, at the cost of at least ten lives. Then they went looking to make contact with government leaders, and naturally they were rounded up very swiftly and interned, some in mental hospitals and some in county jails, but eventually – as soon as the truth of what they really were sank in – they were all put in a special detention camp in Northern California. Of course a tremendous fuss was made over them, endless stuff in the papers and on the tube, speculation by this heavy thinker and that about the significance of their mission, the nature of their biochemistry, a little wild talk about the possibility that more of their kind might be waiting undetected out there and plotting to do God knows what, and all sorts of that stuff, and then came a government clamp on the entire subject, no official announcements except that 'discussions' with the visitors were continuing; and after a while the whole thing degenerated into dumb alien jokes ('Why did the alien cross the road?') and Halloween invader masks, and then it moved into the background of everyone's attention and was forgotten. And remained forgotten until the announcement that one of the creatures had slipped out of the camp somehow and was loose within a hundred-mile zone around San Francisco. Preoccupied as she was with her anguish over Charley's heartlessness, even Amanda had managed to pick up *that* news item. And now the alien was in her very car. So there'd be some weekend amusement for her after all. Amanda was entirely unafraid of the alleged deadliness of the star-being: whatever else the alien might be, it was surely no dope, not if it had been picked to come halfway across the galaxy on a mission like this, and Amanda knew that the alien could see that harming her was not going to be in its own best interests. The alien had need of her, and the alien realized that. And Amanda, in some way that she was only just beginning to work out, had need of the alien.

She pulled up outside her house, a compact split-level at the western end of town. 'This is the place,' she said. Heat-shimmers danced in the air and the hills back of the house, parched in the long dry summer, were the colour of lions. Macavity, Amanda's old tabby, sprawled in the shade of the bottlebrush tree on the ragged front lawn. As Amanda and the alien approached, the cat sat up warily, flattened his ears, hissed. The alien immediately moved into a defensive posture, sniffing the air.

'Just a household pet,' Amanda said. 'You know what that is? He isn't dangerous. He's always a little suspicious of strangers.'

Which was untrue. An earthquake couldn't have brought Macavity out of his nap, and a cotillion of mice dancing minuets on his tail wouldn't have drawn a reaction from him. Amanda calmed him with some fur-ruffling, but he wanted nothing to do with the alien, and went slinking sullenly into the underbrush. The alien watched him with care until he was out of sight.

'You have anything like cats on your planet?' Amanda asked, as they went inside.

'We had small wild animals once. They were unnecessary.'

'Oh,' Amanda said. The house had a stuffy, stagnant air. She switched on the air-conditioning. 'Where is your planet, anyway?'

The alien ignored the question. It padded around the living room, very much like a prowling cat itself, studying the stereo, the television, the couches, the vase of dried flowers.

'Is this a typical Earthian home?'

'More or less,' said Amanda. 'Typical for around here, at least. This is what we call a suburb. It's half an hour by freeway from here to San Francisco. That's a city. A lot of people living all close together. I'll take you over there tonight or tomorrow for a look, if you're interested.' She got some music going, high volume. The alien didn't seem to mind, so she notched the volume up even more. 'I'm going to take a shower. You could use one too, actually.'

'Shower? You mean rain?'

'I mean body-cleaning activities. We Earthlings like to wash a lot, to get rid of sweat and dirt and stuff. It's considered bad form to stink. Come on, I'll show you how to do it. You've got to do what I do if you want to keep from getting caught, you know.' She led the alien to the bathroom. 'Take your clothes off, first.'

The alien stripped. Underneath its rain-slicker it wore a stained T-shirt that said FISHERMAN'S WHARF with a picture of the San Francisco skyline, and a pair of unzipped jeans. Under that it was wearing a black brassiere, unfastened and with the cups over its shoulderblades, and a pair of black shiny panty-briefs with a red heart on the left buttock. The alien's body was that of a lean, tough-looking girl with a scar running down the inside of one arm.

'Whose body is that?' Amanda asked. 'Do you know?'

'She worked at the detention centre. In the kitchen.'

'You know her name?'

'Flores Concepcion.'

'The other way around, probably. Concepcion Flores. I'll call you Connie, unless you want to give me your real name.'

'Connie will do.'

'All right, Connie. Pay attention. You turn the water on here, and you adjust the mix of hot and cold until you like it. Then you pull this knob and get underneath the spout here and wet your

134

body, and rub soap over it and wash the soap off. Afterwards you dry yourself and put fresh clothes on. You have to clean your clothes from time to time too, because otherwise *they* start to smell and it upsets people. Watch me shower and then you do it.'

Amanda washed quickly, while plans hummed in her head. The alien wasn't going to last long out there wearing the body of Concepcion Flores. Sooner or later someone was going to notice that one of the kitchen girls was missing, and they'd get an all-points alarm out for her. Amanda wondered whether the alien had figured that out yet. The alien, Amanda thought, needs a different body in a hurry.

But not mine, she told herself. For sure, not mine.

'Your turn,' she said, shutting the water off.

The alien, fumbling a little, turned the water back on and got under the spray. Clouds of steam rose and its skin began to look boiled, but it didn't appear troubled. No sense of pain? 'Hold it,' Amanda said. 'Step back.' She adjusted the water. 'You've got it too hot. You'll damage that body that way. Look, if you can't tell the difference between hot and cold, just take cold showers, OK? It's less dangerous. This is cold, on this side.' She left the alien under the shower and went to find some clean clothes. When she came back, the alien was still showering, under icy water. 'Enough,' Amanda said. 'Here. Put these on.'

'I had more clothes than this before.'

'A T-shirt and jeans are all you need in hot weather like this. With your kind of build you can skip the bra, and anyway I don't think you'll be able to fasten it the right way.'

'Do we put the face-paint on now?'

'We can skip it while we're home. It's just stupid kid stuff anyway, all that tribal crap. If we go out we'll do it, and we'll give you Walnut Creek colours, I think. Concepcion wore San Jose, but we want to throw people off the track. How about some dope?'

'What?'

'Grass. Marijuana. A drug widely used by local Earthians of our age.'

'I don't need no drug.'

'I don't either. But I'd *like* some. You ought to learn how, just in case you find yourself in a social situation.' Amanda reached for her pack of Filter Golds and pulled out a joint. Expertly she tweaked its lighter-tip and took a deep hit. 'Here,' she said, passing it. 'Hold it like I did. Put it to your mouth, breathe in, suck the smoke deep.' The alien dragged the joint and began to cough. 'Not so deep, maybe,' Amanda said. 'Take just a little. Hold it. Let it out. There, much better. Now give me back the joint. You've got to keep passing it back and forth. That part's important. You feel anything from it?'

'No.'

'It can be subtle. Don't worry about it. Are you hungry?'

'Not yet,' the alien said.

'I am. Come into the kitchen.' As she assembled a sandwich – peanut butter and avocado on whole wheat, with tomato and onion – she asked, 'What sort of things do you eat?'

'Life.'

'Life?'

'We never eat dead things. Only things with life.'

Amanda fought back a shudder. 'I see. *Anything* with life?'

'We prefer animal life. We can absorb plants if necessary.'

'Ah. Yes. And when are you going to be hungry again?'

'Maybe tonight,' the alien said. 'Or tomorrow. The hunger comes very suddenly, when it comes.'

'There's not much around here that you could eat live. But I'll work on it.'

'The small furry animal?'

'No. My cat is not available for dinner. Get that idea right out of your head. Likewise me. I'm your protector and guide. It wouldn't be sensible of you to eat me. You follow what I'm trying to tell you?'

'I said that I'm not hungry yet.'

'Well, you let me know when you start feeling the pangs. I'll find you a meal.' Amanda began to construct a second sandwich. The alien prowled the kitchen, examining the appliances. Perhaps making mental records, Amanda thought, of sink and oven design, to copy on its home world. Amanda said, 'Why did you people come here in the first place?'

'It was our mission.'

'Yes. Sure. But for what purpose? What are you after? You want to take over the world? You want to steal our scientific secrets?' The alien, making no reply, began taking spices out of the spice-rack. Delicately it licked its finger, touched it to the oregano, tasted it, tried the cumin. Amanda said, 'Or is it that you want to keep us from going into space? That you think we're a dangerous species, so you're going to quarantine us on our own planet? Come on, you can tell *me*. I'm not a government spy.' The alien sampled the tarragon, the basil, the sage. When it reached for the curry powder, its hand suddenly shook so violently that it knocked the open jars of oregano and tarragon over, making a mess. 'Hey, are you all right?' Amanda asked.

The alien said, 'I think I'm getting hungry. Are these things drugs too?'

'Spices,' Amanda said. 'We put them in our foods to make them taste better.' The alien was looking very strange, glassy-eyed, flushed, sweaty. 'Are you feeling sick?'

'I feel excited. These powders, – '

'They're turning you on? Which one?'

'This, I think.' It pointed to the oregano. 'It was either the first one or the second.'

'Yeah,' Amanda said. 'Oregano. It can really make you fly.' She wondered whether the alien might get violent when zonked. Or whether the oregano would stimulate its appetite. She had to watch out for its appetite. There are certain risks, Amanda reflected, in doing what I'm doing. Deftly she cleaned up the spilled oregano and tarragon and put the caps on the spice-jars. 'You ought to be careful,' she said. 'Your metabolism isn't used to this stuff. A little can go a long way.'

'Give me some more.'

'Later,' Amanda said. 'You don't want to overdo it.'

'More!'

'Calm down. I know this planet better than you, and I don't want to see you get in trouble. Trust me: I'll let you have more oregano when it's the right time. Look at the way you're shaking. And you're sweating like crazy.' Pocketing the oregano jar, she led the alien back into the living room. 'Sit down. Relax.'

'More? Please?'

'I appreciate your politeness. But we have important things to talk about, and then I'll give you some. OK?' Amanda opaqued the window, through which the hot late-afternoon sun was coming. Six o'clock on Friday, and if everything had gone the right way Charley would have been showing up just about now. Well, she'd found a different diversion. The weekend stretched before her like an open road leading to mysteryland. The alien offered all sorts of possibilities, and she might yet have some fun over the next few days, if she used her head. Amanda turned to the alien and said, 'You calmer now? Yes. Good. OK: first of all, you've got to get yourself another body.'

'Why is that?'

'Two reasons. One is that the authorities probably are searching for the girl you absorbed. How you got as far as you did without anybody but me spotting you is hard to understand. Number two, a teenage girl travelling by herself is going to get hassled too much, and you don't know how to handle yourself in a tight situation. You know what I'm saying? You're going to want to hitch-hike out to Nevada, Wyoming, Utah, wherever the hell your rendezvous place is, and all along the way people are going to be coming on to you. You don't need any of that. Besides, it's very tricky trying to pass for a girl. You've got to know how to put your face-paint on, how to understand challenge codes, and what the way you wear your clothing says, and things like that. Boys have a much simpler subculture. You get yourself a male body, a big hunk of a body, and nobody'll bother you much on the way to where you're going. You just keep to yourself, don't make eye contact, don't smile, and everyone will leave you alone.'

'Makes sense,' said the alien. 'All right. The hunger is becoming very bad, now. Where do I get a male body?'

'San Francisco. It's full of men. We'll go over there tonight and find a nice brawny one for you. With any luck we might even find one who's not gay, and then we can have a little fun with him first. And then you take his body over – which incidentally solves your food problem for a while, doesn't it? – and we can have some more fun, a whole weekend of fun.' Amanda winked. 'OK, Connie?'

'OK.' The alien winked, a clumsy imitation, first one eye, then the other. 'You give me more oregano now?'

'Later. And when you wink, just wink *one* eye. Like this. Except I don't think you ought to do a lot of winking at people. It's a very intimate gesture that could get you in trouble. Understand?'

138

'There's so much to understand.'

'You're on a strange planet, kid. Did you expect it to be just like home? OK, to continue. The next thing I ought to point out is that when you leave here on Sunday you'll have to – '

The telephone rang.

'What's that sound?' the alien asked.

'Communications device. I'll be right back.' Amanda went to the hall extension, imagining the worst: her parents, say, calling to announce that they were on their way back from Tahoe tonight, some mixup in the reservations or something. But the voice that greeted her was Charley's. She could hardly believe it, after the casual way he had shafted her this weekend. She could hardly believe what he wanted, either. He had left half a dozen of his best cassettes at her place last week, Golden Age rock, *Abbey Road* and the Hendrix one and a Joplin and such, and now he was heading off to Monterey for the festival and he wanted to have them for the drive. Did she mind if he stopped off in half an hour to pick them up?

The bastard, she thought. The absolute trashiness of him! First to torpedo her weekend without even an apology, and then to let her know that he and what's-her-name were scooting down to Monterey for some fun, and could he bother her for his cassettes? Didn't he think she had any feelings? She looked at the telephone in her hand as though it was emitting toads and scorpions. It was tempting to hang up on him.

She resisted the temptation. 'As it happens,' she said, 'I'm just on my way out for the weekend myself. But I've got a friend who's here cat-sitting for me. I'll leave the cassettes with her, OK? Her name's Connie.'

'Fine,' Charley said. 'I really appreciate that, Amanda.'

'It's nothing,' she said.

The alien was back in the kitchen, nosing around the spice-rack. But Amanda had the oregano. She said, 'I've arranged for delivery of your next body.'

'You did?'

'A large healthy adolescent male. Exactly what you're looking for. He's going to be here in a little while. I'm going to go out for a drive, and you take care of him before I get back. How long does it take for you to – engulf – somebody?'

'It's very fast.'

'Good.' Amanda found Charley's cassettes and stacked them on the living-room table. 'He's coming over here to get these six little boxes, which are music-storage devices. When the doorbell rings, you let him in and introduce yourself as Connie and tell him his things are on this table. After that you're on your own. You think you can handle it?'

'Sure,' the alien said.

'Tuck in your T-shirt better. When it's tight it makes your boobs stick out, and that'll distract him. Maybe he'll even make a pass at you. What happens to the Connie body after you engulf him?'

'It won't be here. What happens is I merge with him and dissolve all the Connie characteristics and take on the new ones.'

'Ah. Very nifty. You're a real nightmare thing, you know? You're a walking horror show. Here, have a little hit of oregano before I go.' She put a tiny pinch of spice in the alien's hand. 'Just to warm up your engine a little. I'll give you more later, when you've done the job. See you in an hour, OK?'

She left the house. Macavity was sitting on the porch, scowling, whipping his tail from side to side. Amanda knelt beside him and scratched him behind the ears. The cat made a low rough purring sound, not much like his usual purr.

Amanda said, 'You aren't happy, are you, fella? Well, don't worry. I've told the alien to leave you alone, and I guarantee you'll be OK. This is Amanda's fun tonight. You don't mind if Amanda has a little fun, do you?' Macavity made a glum snuffling sound. 'Listen, maybe I can get the alien to create a nice little calico cutie for you, OK? Just going into heat and ready to howl. Would you like that, guy? Would you? I'll see what I can do when I get back. But I have to clear out of here now, before Charley shows up.'

She got into her car and headed for the westbound freeway ramp. Half past six, Friday night, the sun still hanging high above the Bay. Traffic was thick in the eastbound lanes, the late commuters slogging towards home, and it was beginning to build up westbound too as people set out for dinner in San Francisco. Amanda drove through the tunnel and turned north into Berkeley to cruise city streets. Ten minutes to seven, now. Charley must have arrived. She imagined Connie in her tight T-shirt, all stoned and sweaty on oregano, and Charley giving her the eye, getting ideas, thinking about grabbing a bonus quickie before taking off with his cassettes. And Connie leading him on, Charley making his moves, and then suddenly that electric moment of surprise as the alien struck and Charley found himself turning into dinner. It could be happening right this minute, Amanda thought placidly. No more than the bastard deserves, isn't it? She had felt for a long time that Charley was a big mistake in her life, and after what he had pulled yesterday she was sure of it. No more than he deserves. But, she wondered, what if Charley had brought his weekend date along? The thought chilled her. She hadn't considered that possibility at all. It could ruin everything. Connie wasn't able to engulf two at once, was she? And suppose they recognized her as the missing alien and ran out screaming to call the cops?

No, she thought. Not even Charley would be so tacky as to bring his date over to Amanda's house tonight. And Charley never watched the news or read a paper. He wouldn't have a clue as to what Connie really was until it was too late for him to run.

Seven o'clock. Time to head for home.

The sun was sinking behind her as she turned on to the freeway. By quarter past she was approaching her house. Charley's old red Honda was parked outside. Amanda left hers across the street and cautiously let herself in, pausing just inside the front door to listen.

Silence.

'Connie?'

'In here,' said Charley's voice.

Amanda entered the living room. Charley was sprawled out comfortably on the couch. There was no sign of Connie.

'Well?' Amanda said. 'How did it go?'

'Easiest thing in the world,' the alien said. 'He was sliding his hands under my T-shirt when I let him have the nullifier jolt.'

'Ah. The nullifier jolt.'

'And then I completed the engulfment and cleaned up the carpet. God, it feels good not to be hungry again. You can't imagine how tough it was to resist engulfing you, Amanda. For the past hour I kept thinking of food, food, food – '

'Very thoughtful of you to resist.'

141

'I knew you were out to help me. It's logical not to engulf one's allies.'

'That goes without saying. So you feel well fed, now? He was good stuff?'

'Robust, healthy, nourishing – yes.'

'I'm glad Charley turned out to be good for something. How long before you get hungry again?'

The alien shrugged. 'A day or two. Maybe three, on account of he was so big. Give me more oregano, Amanda?'

'Sure,' she said. 'Sure.' She felt a little let down. Not that she was remorseful about Charley, exactly, but it all seemed so casual, so offhanded – there was something anti-climactic about it, in a way. She suspected she should have stayed and watched while it was happening. Too late for that now, though.

She took the oregano from her purse and dangled the jar teasingly. 'Here it is, babe. But you've got to earn it first.'

'What do you mean?'

'I mean that I was looking forward to a big weekend with Charley, and the weekend is here, and Charley's here too, more or less, and I'm ready for fun. Come show me some fun, big boy.'

She slipped Charley's Hendrix cassette into the deck and turned the volume way up.

The alien looked puzzled. Amanda began to peel off her clothes.

'You too,' Amanda said. 'Come on. You won't have to dig deep into Charley's mind to figure out what to do. You're going to be my Charley for me this weekend, you follow? You and I are going to do all the things that he and I were going to do. OK? Come on. Come on.' She beckoned. The alien shrugged again and slipped out of Charley's clothes, fumbling with the unfamiliarities of his zipper and buttons. Amanda, grinning, drew the alien close against her and down to the living-room floor. She took its hands and put them where she wanted them to be. She whispered instructions. The alien, docile, obedient, did what she wanted.

It felt like Charley. It smelled like Charley. It even moved pretty much the way Charley moved.

But it wasn't Charley, it wasn't Charley at all, and after the first few seconds Amanda knew that she had goofed things up

142

very badly. You couldn't just ring in an imitation like this. Making love with this alien was like making love with a very clever machine, or with her own mirror image. It was empty and meaningless and dumb.

Grimly she went on to the finish. They rolled apart, panting, sweating.

'Well?' the alien said. 'Did the earth move for you?'

'Yeah. Yeah. It was wonderful – Charley.'

'Oregano?'

'Sure,' Amanda said. She handed the spice-jar across. 'I always keep my promises, babe. Go to it. Have yourself a blast. Just remember that that's strong stuff for guys from your planet, OK? If you pass out, I'm going to leave you right there on the floor.'

'Don't worry about me.'

'OK. You have your fun. I'm going to clean up, and then maybe we'll go over to San Francisco for the nightlife. Does that interest you?'

'You bet, Amanda.' The alien winked – one eye, then the other – and gulped a huge pinch of oregano. 'That sounds terrific.'

Amanda gathered up her clothes, went upstairs for a quick shower, and dressed. When she came down the alien was more than half blown away on the oregano, goggle-eyed, loll-headed, propped up against the couch and crooning to itself in a weird atonal way. Fine, Amanda thought. You just get yourself all spiced up, love. She took the portable phone from the kitchen, carried it with her into the bathroom, locked the door, dialled the police emergency number.

She was bored with the alien. The game had worn thin very quickly. And it was crazy, she thought, to spend the whole weekend cooped up with a dangerous extraterrestrial creature when there wasn't going to be any fun in it for her. She knew now that there couldn't be any fun at all. And in a day or two the alien was going to get hungry again.

'I've got your alien,' she said. 'Sitting in my living room, stoned out of its head on oregano. Yes, I'm absolutely certain. It was disguised as a Chicana girl first, Concepcion Flores, but then it attacked my boyfriend Charley Taylor, and – yes, yes, I'm safe. I'm locked in the john. Just get somebody over here fast – OK, I'll stay on the line – what happened was, I spotted it downtown, and it insisted on coming home with me – '

The actual capture took only a few minutes. But there was no peace for hours after the police tactical squad hauled the alien away, because the media were in on the act right away, first a team from Channel 2 in Oakland, and then some of the network guys, and then the *Chronicle*, and finally a whole army of reporters from as far away as Sacramento, and phonecalls from Los Angeles and San Diego and – about three that morning – New York. Amanda told the story again and again until she was sick of it, and just as dawn was breaking she threw the last of them out and barred the door.

She wasn't sleepy at all. She felt wired up, speedy and depressed all at once. The alien was gone, Charley was gone, and she was all alone. She was going to be famous for the next couple of days, but that wouldn't help. She'd still be alone. For a time she wandered around the house, looking at it the way an alien might, as though she had never seen a stereo cassette before or a television set, or a rack of spices. The smell of oregano was everywhere. There were little trails of it on the floor.

Amanda switched on the radio and there she was on the 6 A.M. news. '– the emergency is over, thanks to the courageous Walnut Creek high-school girl who trapped and outsmarted the most dangerous life-form in the known universe – '

She shook her head. 'You think that's true?' she asked the cat. 'Most dangerous life-form in the universe? I don't think so, Macavity. I think I know of at least one that's a lot deadlier. Eh, kid?' She winked. 'If they only knew, eh? If they only knew.' She scooped the cat up and hugged it, and it began to purr. Maybe trying to get a little sleep would be a good idea around this time, she told herself. And then she had to figure out what she was going to do about the rest of the weekend.

Snake and Ocean, Ocean and Snake

We are still in the busy winter of 1982 – still in rainy February, in fact. I have just finished 'Amanda and the Alien', and the creative urge is still buzzing in me. In my revived career as a short-story writer, *Omni* and *Playboy* have become my two primary markets. Neither one can handle more than one or two stories a year from me; 'Amanda' has just found a home at *Omni*, so it's time for me to begin thinking about something new for *Playboy*.

As it turned out, the fiction editor of *Playboy* had the same thought in mind. I mean the redoubtable Alice K. Turner, with whom I had struck up instant editorial rapport of the most remarkable kind while we were butting heads over revisions to my first *Playboy* story, 'Gianni', early in 1981. Now, a year later, Alice found herself with two illustrations on hand and no stories to go with them. She phoned me: would I consider looking at the paintings in the hope one of them would inspire a story? I laughed. In the bad old days of penny-a-word pulp magazines, many editors had routinely bought cover paintings first and commissioned writers to concoct stories to go with them. I had done my share of those arsy-versy projects back then, but it was close to twenty years since I had last written a story around an illustration. I told Alice it would be fun to try again, both for nostalgia's sake and for the challenge it represented.

She sent me photostats of two paintings. One showed a naked lady – a very satisfactory one, as I recall, but she wasn't engaged in doing anything that sparked a story idea. The other, a lovely work by Brad Holland, depicted a man of about thirty-five releasing a snake at least fifteen feet long from a beautiful ceramic jug against a sleek featureless background of hills and meadows. I liked it very much. But why was that suburban-looking guy pouring a snake out of a jug?

The old craftsman's rule about writing stories around illustrations is that only a dolt tries to use the picture in any literal way. The idea always is to take it as metaphor, as analogy, as something other than what it purports to be. With the usual inexplicable swiftness of the old pro I saw that snake-as-telepathic-image was more likely to generate an interesting science-fiction story than snake-as-snake, and off I went. By the end of the month I had my story.

Alice is no easy editor to deal with. She came back at me a couple of weeks later with requests for cuts in the middle, some retuning of the dialogue, and a restructuring of my pattern of snake/ocean symbolism. As usual, I put up a fight over some things (mainly the dialogue changes), made some of the cuts she wanted, and beefed up one erotic passage, not because *Playboy* necessarily insists that its stories contain a lot of sexy stuff (it's not a mandatory requirement) but because she thought the story lacked vigour just where it needed it most and I agreed. She yielded where I could defend my choices and I yielded where her criticisms seemed apt, which was most of the time. Her ideas about the symbolic substructure, for example, were right on target and I rearranged things slightly and sent her an insert to use midway through the story. Thus 'Snake and Ocean' went through what by now had become the familiar knock-down-drag-out dialectic process by which Alice and I get most of my stories for her into final shape, and it duly appeared in the June 1984 issue of *Playboy*.

Alice had one last revision up her sleeve. When she printed the story she changed the title to 'The Affair'. She's a terrific editor, but she isn't infallible. In this reprinting, as in all previous ones – it was included in the 1984 volume of Gardner Dozois's *Year's Best Science Fiction* series, and has been anthologized elsewhere as well – I've kept all the textual changes she proposed; but this time I've reverted to my original title. You be the judge.

He found her by accident, the way it usually happens, after he had more or less given up searching. For years he had been sending out impulses like messages in bottles, random waves of telepathic energy, *Hello, hello, hello*, one forlorn SOS after another from the desert isle of the soul on which he was a castaway. Occasionally messages came back, but all they amounted to was lunacy, strident nonsense, static, spiritual noise, gabble up and down the mind-band. There were, he knew, a good many like him out there – a boy in Topeka, an old woman in Buenos Aires, another one in Fort Lauderdale, someone of indeterminate sex in Manitoba, and plenty of others, each alone, each lonely. He fell into short-lived contact with them, because they were, after all, people of his special kind. But they tended to be cranky, warped, weird, often simply crazy, all of them deformed by their bizarre gift, and they could not give him what he wanted, which was communion, harmony, the marriage of true minds. Then one Thursday afternoon when he was absent-mindedly broadcasting his identity-wave, not in any way purposefully trolling the seas of perception but only humming, so to speak, he felt a sudden startling *click*, as of perfectly machined parts locking into place. Out of the greyness in his mind an unmistakably warm, eager image blossomed, a dazzling giant yellow flower unfolding on the limb of a gnarled spiny cactus, and the image translated itself instantly into *Hi there. Where've you been all my life?*

He hesitated to send an answering signal, because he knew that he had found what he was looking for and he was aware how much of a threat that was to the fabric of the life he had constructed for himself. He was thirty-seven years old, stable, settled. He had a wife who tried her best to be wonderful for him, never knowing quite what it was that she lacked but seeking to compensate for it anyway, and two small pleasing children who had not inherited his abnormality, and a comfortable house in the hills east of San Francisco, and a comfortable job as an analyst for one of the big brokerage houses. It was not the life he had imagined in his old romantic fantasies, but it was not a bad life, either, and it was *his* life, familiar and in its way rewarding; and he knew he was about to rip an irreparable hole in it. So he hesitated. And then he transmitted an image as vivid as the one he had received: a solitary white gull soaring in enormous sweeps over the broad blue breast of the Pacific.

The reply came at once: the same gull, joined by a second one that swooped out of a cloudless sky and flew tirelessly at its side. He knew that if he responded to that, there could be no turning back, but that was all right. With uncharacteristic recklessness he switched to the verbal mode.

– OK. Who are you?

– Laurel Hammett. I'm in Phoenix. I read you clearly. This is better than the telephone.

– Cheaper, too. Chris Maitland. San Francisco.

– That's far enough away, I guess.

He didn't understand, then, what she meant by that. But he let the point pass.

– You're the first one I've found who sends images, Laurel.

– I found one once, eight years ago, in Boston. But he was crazy. Most of us are crazy, Chris.

– I'm not crazy.

– Oh, I know! Oh, God, I know!

So that was the beginning. He got very little work done that afternoon. He was supposed to be preparing a report on oil royalty trusts, and after fifteen minutes of zinging interchanges with her he actually did beg off; she broke contact with a dazzling series of visuals, many of them cryptic, snowflakes and geometrical diagrams and fields of blazing red poppies. Depletion percentages and windfall profits tax recapture were impossible to deal with while those brilliant pictures burned in his mind. Although he had promised not to reach towards her again until tomorrow – judicious self-denial, she observed, is the fuel of love – he finally did send out a flicker of abashed energy, and drew from her a mingling of irritation and delight. For five minutes they told each other it was best to go slow, to let it develop gradually, and again they vowed to keep mental silence until the next day. But when he was crossing the Bay Bridge a couple of hours later, heading for home, she tickled him suddenly with a quick flash of her presence and gave him a wondrous view of the Arizona sunset, harsh chocolate-brown hills under a purple-and-gold sky. That evening he felt shamefully and transparently adulterous, as if he had come home flushed and rumpled, with lipstick on his shirt. He pretended to be edgy and wearied by some fictitious episode of office politics, and helped himself to two drinks before dinner, and was more than usually curious about the details of his wife's day, the little suburban crises, the small challenges, the tiny triumphs. Jan was playful, amiable, almost kittenish. That told him she had not seen through him to the betrayal within, however blatant it seemed to him. She was no actress; there was nothing devious about her.

The transformation of their marriage that had taken place that afternoon saddened him, and yet not deeply, because it was an inevitable one. He and Jan were not really of the same species.

He had loved her as well and honestly as was possible for him, but what he had really wanted was someone of his kind, with whom he could join mind and soul as well as body, and it was only because he had not been able to find her that he had settled for Jan. And now he had found her. Where that would lead, and what it meant for Jan and him, he had no idea yet. Possibly he would be able to go on sharing with her the part of his life that they were able to share, while secretly he got from the other woman those things that Jan had never been able to give him; possibly. When they went to bed he turned to her with abrupt passionate ferocity, as he had not for a long time, but even so he could not help wondering what Laurel was doing now, in her bed a thousand miles to the east, and with whom.

During the morning commute Laurel came to him with stunning images of desert landscapes, eroded geological strata, mysterious dark mesas, distant flame-coloured sandstone walls. He sent her Pacific surf, cypresses bending to the wind, tidepools swarming with anemones and red starfish. Then, timidly, he sent her a kiss, and had one from her in return, and then, as he was crossing the toll plaza of the bridge, she shifted to words.

– What do you do?

– Securities analyst. I read reports and make forecasts.

– Sounds terribly dull. Is it?

– If it is, I don't let myself notice. It's OK work. What about you?

– I'm a potter. I'm a very good one. You'd like my stuff.

– Where can I see it?

– There's a gallery in Santa Fe. And one in Tucson. And of course Phoenix. But you mustn't come to Phoenix.

– Are you married?

There was a pause.

– Yes. But that isn't why you mustn't come here.

– I'm married too.

– I thought you were. You feel like a married sort of man.

– Oh? I do?

– That isn't an insult. You have a very stable vibe, do you know what I mean?

– I think so. Do you have children?

– No. Do you?

– Two. Little girls. How long have you been married, Laurel?

149

– Six years.

– Nine.

– We must be about the same age.

– I'm thirty-seven.

– I'm thirty-four.

– Close enough. Do you want to know my sign?

– Not really.

She laughed and sent him a complex, awesome image: the entire wheel of the Zodiac, which flowered into the shape of the Aztec calendar stone, which became the glowing rose window of a Gothic cathedral. An undercurrent of warmth and love and amusement rode with it. Then she was gone, leaving him on the bridge in a silence so sharp it rang like iron.

He did not reach towards her, but drove on into the city in a mellow haze, wondering what she looked like. Her mental 'voice' sounded to him like that of a tall, clear-eyed, straight-backed woman with long brown hair, but he knew better than to put much faith in that; he had played the same game with people's telephone voices and he had always been wrong. For all he knew Laurel was squat and greasy. He doubted that; he saw no way that she could be ugly. But why, then, was she so determined not to have him come to Phoenix? Perhaps she was an invalid; perhaps she was painfully shy; perhaps she feared the intrusion of any sort of reality into their long-distance romance.

At lunchtime he tuned himself to her wavelength and sent her an image of the first page of the report he had written last week on Exxon. She replied with a glimpse of a tall olive-hued porcelain jar, of a form both elegant and sturdy at once. Her work in exchange for his: he liked that. It meant they had the same sense of humour. Everything was going to be perfect.

A week later he went out to Salt Lake City for a couple of days to do some field research on a mining company headquartered there. He took an early-morning flight, had lunch with three earnest young Mormon executives overflowing with joy at the bounty of God as manifested by the mineral wealth of the Overthrust Belt in Wyoming, spent the afternoon leafing through geologists' survey sheets, and had dinner alone at his hotel. Afterwards he put in his obligatory call to Jan, worked up his notes of the day's conferences, and watched TV for an hour, hoping it would make him drowsy. Maitland didn't mind these business trips, but he slept badly when he slept alone, and any sort of time-zone change, even a trifling one like this, disrupted his internal clock. He was still wide awake when he got into bed about eleven.

He thought of Laurel. He felt very near to her, out here in this spacious mountain-ringed city with the wide bland streets. Probably Salt Lake City was not significantly closer to Phoenix than San Francisco was, but he regarded Utah and Arizona both as the true Wild West, while his own suburban and manicured part of California, paradoxically, did not seem western to him at all. Somewhere due south of here, just on the far side of all these cliffs and canyons, was the unknown woman he loved.

As though on cue she was in his mind:

– Lonely?

– You bet.

– I've been thinking of you all day. Poor Chris: sitting around with those businessmen, talking all that depletion gibberish.

– I'm a businessman too.

– You're different, love. You're a businessman outside and a freak inside.

– Don't say that.

– It's what we are, Chris. Face it. Flukes, anomalies, sports, changelings –

– Please stop, Laurel. Please.

– I'm sorry.

A silence. He thought she was gone, taking flight at his rebuke. But then:

– Are you *very* lonely?

– Very. Dull empty city, dull empty bed.

– *You're* in it.

– But you aren't.

– Is that what you want? Right now?

– I wish we could, Laurel.

– Let's try this.

He felt a sudden astounding intensifying of her mental signal, as if she had leaped the hundreds of miles and lay curled against him here. There was a sense of physical proximity, of warmth, even the light perfume of her skin, and into his mind swept an image so acutely clear that it eclipsed for him the drab realities of his room: the shore of a tropical ocean, fine pink sand, gentle pale-green water, a dense line of heavy-crowned palms.

– Go on, Chris. Into the water.

He waded into the calm wavelets until the delicate sandy bottom was far below his dangling feet and he floated effortlessly in an all-encompassing warmth, in an amniotic bath of placid soothing fluid. Placid but not motionless, for he felt, as he drifted, tiny convulsive quivers about him, an electric oceanic caress, pulsations of the water against his bare skin, intimate, tender, searching. He began to tingle. As he moved farther out from shore, so far now that the land was gone and the world was all warm water to the horizon, the pressure of those rhythmic pulsations became more forceful, deeply pleasurable: the ocean was a giant hand lightly squeezing him. He trembled and made soft sighing sounds that grew steadily more vehement, and closed his eyes, and let ecstasy overwhelm him in the ocean's benignly insistent grip. Then he grunted and his heart thumped and his body went rigid and then lax, and moments later he sat up, blinking, astonished, eerily tranquil.

– I didn't think anything like that was possible.

– For us anything's possible. Even sex across seven hundred miles. I wasn't sure it would work, but I guess it did, didn't it? Did you like it?

– Do you need an answer, Laurel?

– I feel so happy.

– How did you do it? What was the trick?

– No trick. Just the usual trick, Chris, a little more intense than usual. And a lot of love. I hated the idea that you were all alone, horny, unable to sleep.

– It was absolutely marvellous.

– And now we're lovers. Even though we've never met.

– No. Not altogether lovers, not yet. Let me try to do it to you, Laurel. It's only fair.

– Later, OK? Not now.

– I want to.

– It takes a lot of energy. You ought to get some sleep, and I can wait. Just lie there and glow and don't worry about me. You can try it with me another time.

– An hour? Two hours?

– Whenever you want. But not now. Rest, now. Enjoy. Good night, love.

– Good night, Laurel.

He was alone. He lay staring up into the darkness, stunned. He had been unfaithful to Jan three times before, not bad for nine years, and always the same innocuous pattern: a business trip far from home, a couple of solitary nights, then an official dinner with some woman executive, too many drinks, the usual half-serious banter turning serious, a blurry one-night stand, remorse in the morning and never any follow-up. Meaningless, fragmentary stuff. But this – this long-distance event with a woman he had never even seen – this seemed infinitely more explosive. For he had the power and Jan did not and Laurel did; and Jan's mind was closed to his and his to hers, and they could only stagger around blindly trying to find one another, while he and Laurel could unite at will in a communion whose richness was unknown to ordinary humans. He wondered if he could go on living with Jan at all, now. He felt no less love for her than before, and powerful ties of affection and sharing held him to her; but yet – even so –

In guilt and confusion Maitland drifted off into sleep. It was still dark when he woke – 3:13 A.M., said the clock on the dresser – and he felt different guilt, different confusion, for it was of Laurel now that he thought. He had taken pleasure from her and then he had collapsed into post-orgasmic stupor. Never mind that she had told him to do just that. He felt, and always had, a peculiarly puritanical obligation to give pleasure for pleasure, and unpaid debts were troublesome to him. Taking a deep breath, he sent strands of consciousness through the night towards the south, over the fire-hued mountains of central Utah, over the silent splendour of the Grand Canyon, down past the palm trees into torrid Phoenix, and touched Laurel's warm sleepy mind.

– Hnhh.

– It's me. I want to, now.

– All right. Yes.

The image she had chosen was a warm sea, the great mother, the all-encompassing womb. He, reaching unhesitatingly for a male equivalent, sent her a vision of himself coming forth on a hot dry summer day into a quiet landscape of grassy hills round

153

as tawny breasts. Cradled in his arms he held the gleaming porcelain jar that she had showed him last week, and he bent, tipping it, pouring forth from it an enormous snake, long and powerful but not in any way frightening, that flowed like a dark rivulet across the land, seeking her, finding, gliding up across her thighs, her belly. Too obvious? Too coarsely phallic? He wavered for a moment, but only a moment, for he heard her moan and whimper, and she reached with her mind for the serpent as it seemed he was withdrawing it; he drove back his qualms and gave her all the energy at his command, seizing the initiative as he sensed her complete surrender. Her signal shivered and lost focus. Her breathing grew ragged and hoarse, and then into his mind came a quick surprising sound, a strange low growling, that terminated in a swift sharp gasp.

– Oh, love. Oh. Oh. Thank you.

– It wasn't scary?

– Scare me like that as often as you want, Chris.

He smiled across the darkness of the miles. All was well. A fair exchange: symbol for symbol, metaphor for metaphor, delight for delight.

– Sleep well, Laurel.

– You too, love. Mmm.

This time Jan knew that something had happened while he was away. He saw it on her face, which meant that she saw it on his; but she voiced no suspicions, and when they made love the first night of his return it was as good as ever. Was it possible, he wondered, to be bigamous like this, to take part with Laurel in a literally superhuman oneness while remaining Jan's devoted husband and companion? He would, at any rate, try. Laurel had shared his soul as no one ever had and Jan never could, but yet she was a phantom, faceless, remote, scarcely real; and Jan, cut off from him as most humans are from all others, nevertheless was his wife, his partner, his bedmate, the mother of his children. He would try.

So he brought the office gossip home to her as always and went out with her twice a week to the restaurants they loved and sat beside her at night watching cassettes of operas and movies and Shakespeare, and on weekends they did their weekend things, boating on the bay and tennis and picnics in the park and dinner with their friends, and everything was fine. Everything was very fine. And yet he managed to do the other thing, too, as often as he could: snake and ocean, ocean and snake. Just as he had successfully hidden from Jan the enigmatic secret mechanism within his mind that he did not dare reveal to anyone not of his sort, so too now did he hide the second marriage, rich and strange, that that mechanism had brought him.

His lovemaking with Laurel had to be furtive, of course, a thing of stolen moments. She could hardly draw him into that warm voluptuous ocean while he lay beside Jan. But there were the business trips – he was careful not to increase their frequency, which would have been suspicious, but she came to him every night while he was away – and there was the occasional Saturday afternoon when he lay drowsing in the sun of the garden and found that whispering transparent surf beckoning to him, and once she enlivened a lunchtime for him on a working day. He roused the snake within his soul as often as he dared and nearly always she accepted it, though there were times when she told him no, not now, the moment was wrong. They had elaborate signals to indicate a clear coast. And for the ordinary conversation of the day there were no limits; they popped into each other's consciousness a thousand times a day, quick flickering interchanges, a joke, a bit of news, a job triumphantly accomplished, an image of beauty too potent to withhold. Crossing the bridge, entering his office, reaching for the telephone, unfolding a napkin – suddenly, there she was, often for the briefest flare of contact, a tag-touch and gone. He loved that. He loved her. It was a marriage.

He snooped in Mountain Bell directories at the library and found her telephone number, which he hardly needed, and her address, which at least confirmed that she really did exist in tangible actual Phoenix. He manufactured a trip to Albuquerque to appraise the earnings prospects of a small electronics company and slipped off up the freeway to Santa Fe to visit the gallery that showed her pottery: eight or ten superb pieces, sleek, wondrously skilled. He bought one of the smaller ones. 'You don't have any information about the artist, do you?' he asked the proprietor, trying to be casual, heart pounding, hoping to be shown a photograph. The proprietor thought there might be a press release in the files, and rummaged for it. 'She lives down Phoenix way,' she said. 'Comes up here once or twice a year with her new work. I think it's museum quality, don't you?' But she could not find the press release. When Laurel flashed into his mind that night back in Albuquerque he did not tell her he owned one of her vases or that he had been researching her. But he wondered desperately what she looked like. He played with the idea of visiting Phoenix and somehow getting to meet her without telling her who he was. So long as he kept his mind sheathed she would never know, he thought. But it seemed sneaky and treacherous; and it might be dangerous, too. She had told him often enough not to come to her city.

In the fourth month of their relationship he could no longer control his curiosity. She sent him a view of her studio, amazingly neat, the clay, the wheels, the kiln, the little bowls of pigment and glaze all fastidiously in their proper places.

– You left one out, Laurel.

– What's that?

– The potter herself. You didn't show me her.

– Oh, Chris.

– What's the matter? Aren't you ever curious about what I look like? We've been all over each other's minds and bodies for months and I still don't have any idea what you look like. That's absurd.

– It's so much more abstract and pure this way.

– Wonderful. Abstract love! Save that for Swinburne. I want to see you.

– I have to confess. I want to see you too.

– Here, then. Now.

He sent her, before she could demur, a mental snapshot of his face, trying not to retouch and enhance it. The nose a trifle too long, the cleft chin absurdly Hollywood, the dark hair thinning a bit at the part-line. Not a perfect face, but good enough, pleasant, honest, nothing to apologize for, he thought. It brought silence.

– Well? Am I remotely what you expected?

– Exactly, Chris. Steady-looking, strong, decent – no surprise at all. I like your face. I'm very pleased.

– Your turn.

Snake and Ocean, Ocean and Snake

– You'll promise not to be disappointed?
– Stop being silly.
– All right.

She flared in his mind, not just her face but all of her, long-legged, broad-shouldered, a woman of physical presence and strength, with straightforward open features, wide-set brown eyes, a good smile, blunt nose, conspicuous cheekbones. She was not far from the woman he had imagined, and one aspect, the dark thick straight hair falling past her shoulders, was amazingly as he had thought.

– You're beautiful.
– No, not really. But I'm OK.
– Are you an Indian?
– I must have sent you a good picture, then. I'm half. My mother was Navaho.
– You learned your pottery from her?
– No, dopy. Navahos make rugs. Pueblos make pottery. I learned mine in New York, Greenwich Village. I studied with Hideki Shinoda.
– Doesn't sound Pueblo.
– Isn't. Little Japanese man with marvellous hands.
– I'm glad we did this, Laurel.
– So am I.

But seeing her in the eye of his mind, while gratifying one curiosity, had only intensified another. He wanted to meet her. He wanted to touch her. He wanted to hold her.

Snake. Ocean. They were practised lovers now, a year of constant mental communion behind them. The novelty was gone but not the excitement. Again and again he carried the porcelain bowl out to the sun-baked hills and poured the serpent into the grass and sent it gliding towards her eager body. Again and again she surrounded him with buoyant warm sea. Their skill at pleasuring one another struck them both as extraordinary. Of course, they soon began varying the imageries of delight, so that no monotony would taint their embraces. She came to him as a starfish, thousands of tiny suction-cup feet and a startling devouring mouth, and at another time as a moist voluptuous mass of warm smooth white clay, and as a whirlpool, and as a great coy lighthearted amoeba; and he

157

manifested himself to her as a flash flood roaring down a red-rock canyon, and as a glistening vine coiling through a tropic night, and as a spaceship plunging in eternal free fall between worlds. All of these were effective, for they needed only to touch one another with their minds to bring pleasure; and each new access of ingenuity brought an abstract pleasure of its own. But even so they tended often to revert to the original modes, snake and ocean, ocean and snake, the way one might return to a familiar and modest hotel where one spent a joyous weekend at the beginning of an affair, and somehow it was always best that way. They liked to tell each other that the kind of lovemaking they had invented and of which they were perhaps the sole practitioners in the history of humanity was infinitely superior to the old-fashioned type, which was so blatant, so obvious, so coarse, so messy. Even so, even as he said things like that, he knew he was lying. He wanted her skin against his skin, her breath on his breath.

She was no longer so coy about her life outside their relationship. Maitland knew now that her husband was an artist from Chicago, not very successful, a little envious of her career. She showed him some of his work, unremarkable abstract-expressionist stuff. Maitland was jealous of the fact that this man – Tim, his name was – shared her bed and enjoyed her proximity, but he realized that he had no jealousy of the marriage itself. It was all right that she was married. Maitland had no wish to live with her. He wanted to go on living with Jan, to play tennis with her and go to restaurants with her and even to make love with her; what he wanted from Laurel was just what he was getting from her, that cool amused intelligent voice in his mind, and now and then the strange ecstasy that her playful spirit was able to kindle in his loins across such great distances. That much was true. Yet also he wanted to be her lover in the old blatant obvious coarse messy way, at least once, once at least. Because he knew it was a perilous subject, he stayed away from it as long as he could, but at last it broke into the open one night in Seattle, late, after the snake had returned to its jar and the lapping waves had retreated and he lay sweaty and alone in his hotel-room bed.

– When are we finally going to meet?

– Please, Chris.

– I think it's time to discuss it. You told me a couple of times, early on, that I must never come to Phoenix. OK. But couldn't we get together somewhere else? Tucson, San Diego, the Grand Canyon?

– It isn't the place that matters.

– What is it, then?

– Being close. Being too close.

– I don't understand. We're so close already!

– I mean physically close. Not emotionally, not even sexually. I just mean that if we came within close range of each other we'd do bad things to each other.

– That's crazy, Laurel.

– Have you ever been close to another telepath? As close as ten feet, say?

– I don't think so.

– You'd know it if you had. When you and I talk, long-distance, it's just like talking on the phone, right, plus pictures? We tell each other only what we want to tell each other, and nothing else gets through. It's not like that close up.

– Oh?

– There's a kind of radiation, an aura. We broadcast all sorts of stuff automatically. All that foul stinking nasty cesspool stuff that's at the bottom of everybody's mind, the crazy prehistoric garbage that's in us. It comes swarming out like a shriek.

– How do you know that?

– I've experienced it.

– Oh. Boston, years ago?

– Yes. Yes. I told you, I did this once before.

– But he was crazy, you said.

– In a way. But the craziness isn't what brought the other stuff up. I felt it once another time, too, and *she* wasn't crazy. It's unavoidable.

– I want to see you.

– Don't you think I want to see you too, Chris? You think I think snake and ocean's really good enough? But we can't risk it. Suppose we met, and the garbage got out, and we hated each other ever afterwards?

– We could control it.

– Maybe. Maybe not.

– Or else we could make allowances for it. Bring ourselves

159

to understand that this stuff, whatever it is that you say is there, is normal, just the gunk of the mind, nothing personal, nothing that we ought to take seriously.

– I'm scared. Let's not try.

He let the issue drop. When it came up again, four months later, it was Laurel who revived it. She had been thinking about his idea of controlling the sinister emanation, throttling it back, shielding one another. Possibly it could be done. The temptation to meet him in the flesh, she said, was overwhelming. Perhaps they could get together and suppress all telepathic contact, meet just like ordinary humans having a little illicit rendezvous, keep their minds rigidly walled off, and that way at last consummate the intimacy that had joined their souls for a year and a half.

– I'd love to, Laurel.

– But promise me this. Swear it to me. When we do get together, if we can't hold back the bad stuff, if we feel it coming out, that we go away from each other instantly. That we don't negotiate, we don't try to work it out, we don't look for angles – we just split, fast, if either of us says we have to. Swear?

– I swear.

He flew to Denver and spent a fidgety hour and a half having cocktails in the lounge at the Brown Palace. Her flight from Phoenix was supposed to have landed only half an hour after his, and he wondered if she had backed out at the last minute. He got up to call the airport when he saw her come in, unmistakably her, taller than he expected, a big handsome woman in black jeans and a sheepskin wrap. There were flecks of melting snow in her hair.

He sensed an aura.

It wasn't loathsome, it wasn't hideous, but it was there, a kind of dull whining grinding thing as of improperly oiled machinery in use three blocks away. Even as he detected it, he felt it diminish until it was barely perceptible. He struggled to rein in whatever output he might be giving off himself.

She saw him and came straight towards him, smiling nervously, cheeks rigid, eyes worried.

'Chris.'

He took her hand in his. 'You're cold, Laurel.'

160

'It's snowing. That's why I'm late. I haven't seen snow in years.'

'Can I get you a drink?'

'No. Yes. Yes, please. Scotch on the rocks.'

'Are you picking up anything bad?'

'No,' she said. 'Not really. There was just a little twinge, when I walked in – a kind of squeak in my mind.'

'I felt it too. But then it faded.'

'I'm fighting to keep it damped down. I want this to work.'

'So do I. We mustn't use the power at all today.'

'We don't need to. The old snake can have the day off. Are you scared?'

'A little.'

'Me too.' She gulped her drink. 'Oh, Chris.'

'Is it hard work, keeping the power damped down?'

'Yes. It really is.'

'For me too. But we have to.'

'Yes,' she said. 'Do you have a room yet?'

He nodded.

'Let's go upstairs, then.'

Like any unfaithful husband having his first rendezvous with a new lover he walked stiffly and sombrely through the lobby, convinced that everyone was staring at them. That was ridiculous, he knew. They were more truly married, in their way, than anybody else in Denver. But yet – but yet –

They were silent in the elevator. As they approached their floor the aura of her burst forth again, briefly, a fast sour vibration in his bones, and then it was gone altogether, shut off as though by a switch. He worked at holding his down too. She smiled at him. He winked. 'To the left,' he said. They went into the room. Heavy snowflakes splashed against the window; the wide bed was turned down. She was trembling. 'Come on,' he said. 'I love you. You know that. Everything's all right.'

They kissed and undressed. Her body was lean, athletic, with small high breasts, a flat belly, a dark appendectomy scar. He drew her towards the bed. It seemed strange, almost perverse, to be doing things in this antiquated fleshly way, no snake, no ocean, no meeting of minds. He was afraid for a moment that in the excitement of their coupling they would lose control of their mental barriers and let their inner selves come flooding out, fierce, intense, a contact too powerful to handle at such short range. But there was no loss of control. He kept the power locked behind the walls of his skull; she did the same; there were only the tiniest leakages of current. But there was no excitement, either, in their lovemaking. They touched each other here and there and here and there, they kissed, they embraced, they sighed a little and moaned a little, he slipped into her as though this had happened a thousand times before, he moved, she moved, they did all the standard things and he ran his hands over her breasts and trapped her nipples between his fingers, and gently parted her thighs with his knee, and pressed himself against her as though he had not been with a woman in a year, but the excitement seemed to be all in his head, not in his nerve-endings. Even when she ran her lips down his chest and belly and teased him for a moment and then took him fiercely and suddenly into her mouth, it was the *idea* that they were finally doing this, rather than what they were actually doing, that resonated within him. They sighed a little and moaned a little and finally he slipped into her, admiring the tightness of her and the rhythms of her hips and all that, but nevertheless it was as though this had happened between them a thousand times before: he moved, she moved, they did all the standard things and travelled along to the standard result. Not enough was real between them, that was the trouble. He knew her better than he had ever known anyone, and yet in some ways he knew her not at all, and that was what had spoiled things. That, and holding so much in check. He wished he could look into her mind now. But that was forbidden, and probably unwise too; he guessed that she was annoyed with him for having insisted on this foolish and foredoomed meeting, that she held him responsible for having spoiled things between them, and he did not want to see those thoughts in her mind.

When it was over they whispered to each other and stroked each other and gave each other little nibbling kisses, and he pretended it had been marvellous, but his real impulse was to pull away and light a cigarette and stare out the window at the snow, and he wasn't even a smoker. It was simply the way he felt. It had been only a mechanical thing, only a hotel-room screw, not remotely anything like snake and ocean: a joining of flesh of the sort that a pair of rabbits might have accomplished, or a pair of apes, without content, without fire, without joy. He and she knew an ever so much better way of doing it.

He took care to hide his disappointment.

'I'm so glad I came here, Chris,' she said, smiling, kissing him, taking care to hide her disappointment too, he guessed. He knew that if he entered her mind he would find it bleak and ashen. But of course he could not do that. 'I wish I could stay the night,' she said. 'My plane's at nine. We could have dinner downstairs, though.'

'Is it a terrible strain, keeping the power back?'

'It isn't easy.'

'No. It isn't.'

'I'm so glad we did this, Chris.'

'Are you?'

'Yes. Yes. Of course.'

They had an early dinner. The snow had stopped by the time he saw her to her cab. So: you fly up to Denver for a couple of hours of lust and steak, you fly back home, and that's that. He had a brandy in the lounge and went to his room. For a long while he lay staring at the ceiling, sure that she would come to him with the ocean, and make amends for the unsatisfactory thing they had done that afternoon. She did not. He wondered if he ought to send her the snake as she dozed on her plane, and did not want to. He felt timid about any sort of contact with her now. It had all been a terrible mistake, he knew. Not because of that emanation from the dirty depths of the psyche that she had so feared, but only because it had been so anti-climactic, so meaningless. He waited for a sending from her, some bright little flash out of Arizona. She must surely be home now. Nothing came. He went on waiting, not daring to reach towards her, and finally he fell asleep.

Jan said nothing to him about the Denver trip. He was moody and strange, but she let him be. When the silence out of Phoenix continued into the next day and the next he grew even more grim, and skulked about wrapped in black isolation. Gradually it occurred to him that he was not going to hear from Laurel again, that they had broken something in that hotel room in Denver and that it was irreparable, and, oddly, the knowledge of that gave him some ease: if he did not expect to hear from her, he did not have to lament her silence. A week, two, three, and nothing. So it was over. That hollow little grunting hour had ruined it.

Somehow he picked up the rhythms of his life: work, home, wife, kids, friends, tennis, dinner. He did an extensive analysis of south-western electric utilities that brought him a commendation from on high, and he felt only a mild twinge of anguish while doing his discussion of the prospects for Arizona Public Service as reflected in the municipal growth of the city of Phoenix. He missed the little tickle in his mind immensely, but he was encapsulating it, containing it, and after a fashion he was healing.

One day a month and a half later he found himself idly scanning the mind-noise band again, as he had not done for a long while, just to see who else was out there. He picked up the loony babble out of Fort Lauderdale and the epicene static from Manitoba, and then he encountered someone new, a bright clear signal as intense as Laurel's, and for a dazzled instant a sudden fantasy of a new relationship blossomed in him, but then he heard the nonsense syllables, the slow, firm, strong-willed stream of gibberish. There were no replacements for Laurel.

In Chicago, where he had been sent to do a survey of natural-gas companies, he began talking to a youngish woman at the Art Institute, and by easy stages some chatter about Monet and Sisley turned into a dinner invitation and a night in his hotel room. That was all right. Certainly it was simpler and easier and less depressing than Denver. But it was a bore, it was empty and foolish, and he regretted it deeply by breakfast-time, even while he was taking down her number and promising to call the next time he was in the Midwest. Maitland saw the post-Laurel pattern of his life closing about him now: the Christmas bonus, the trip to Hawaii with Jan, braces for the kids, the new house five years from now, the occasional quickie romance in far-off hotel rooms. That was all right. That was the original bargain he had made, long ago, entering adult life: not much ecstasy, not much grief.

On the long flight home that day he thought without rancour or distress about his year and a half with Laurel, and told himself that the important thing was not that it had ended but that it had happened at all. He felt peaceful and accepting, and was almost tempted to reach out towards Laurel and thank her for her love, and wish her well. But he was afraid – afraid that if he touched her mind in any way she would pull away, timid, fearful of contact in the wake of that inexplicably sundering day in Denver. She was close by now, he knew, for the captain had just told them that they were passing over the Grand Canyon. Maitland did not lean to the window, as everyone else was doing, to look down. He sat back, eyes closed, tired, calm.

And felt warmth, heard the lapping of surf, saw in the centre of his mind the vast ocean in which Laurel had so many times engulfed him. Really? Was it happening? He let himself slide into it. A little flustered, he hid himself behind a facade of newspapers, the *Tribune*, the *Wall Street Journal*. His face grew flushed. His breathing became rougher. Ah. Ah. It was happening, yes, she had reached to him, she had made the gesture at last. Tears of gratitude and relief came to him, and he let her sweep him off to a sharp and pounding fulfilment five miles above Arizona.

– Hello, Chris.

– Laurel.

– Did you mind? I felt you near me, and I couldn't hold back any more. I know you don't want to hear from me, but –

– What gave you that idea?

– I thought – it seemed to me –

– No. I thought you were the one who wanted to break it up.

– I? I missed you so much, Chris. But I was sure you'd pull away.

– So was I, about you.

– Silly.

– Laurel. Laurel. I'm so glad you took the chance, then.

– So am I.

– Let me have the snake, Chris.

– Yes. Yes.

He stepped out into the tawny sun-baked hills with the heavy porcelain jar and tipped it, and let the snake glide towards her. It was all right after all. They had made mistakes, but they were the mistakes of too much love, and they had survived them. It was going to be all right: snake and ocean, ocean and snake, now and always.

Tourist Trade

By the final month of 1982 the giant lobsters of 'Homefaring' were behind me and I was getting ready for the winter's major enterprise, the novel *Valentine Pontifex*, the closing volume of the Majipoor trilogy. But I still didn't feel entirely comfortable using the computer to write, and it seemed like a good idea to tackle one more short story before plunging into the novel. So I decided to try another one for *Playboy*.

My conversion from typewriter to computer couldn't have come at a more timely moment. 'Tourist Trade', which as I look at it now seems to move seamlessly from first sentence to last, called forth at least half a dozen drafts from me, maybe even more. If I had had to type those thirty-odd pages out every time from beginning to end, I'd probably have hurled the typewriter through the window long before I came up with something that Alice Turner would find acceptable. What should have been a relatively simple 7,500-word project turned into an interminable and agonizing ordeal.

When you use a computer to write, a lot of the false starts, fatuous passages, and other miscalculations don't survive for the amusement of scholars studying your manuscripts in years to come. You simply back up the cursor and erase them, send them into the black hole of computer limbo, and no one's ever the wiser. But from time to time a writer does need hard copy of a work in progress, and so a lot of botched drafts do get put down on paper even in the computer age. I save mine, God knows why. In the case of 'Tourist Trade' I have a stack about five inches thick.

For those of you who think that story-writing gets easier as a writer's career goes along, the 'Tourist Trade' saga – dating from my thirtieth year as a professional writer – ought to be highly instructive.

It begins with a one-page draft in first-person narration of something I entitled 'A World of Strangers':

* * *

166

Tourist Trade

In Morocco all the human tourists head straight for Marrakesh, as people have been doing ever since tourism began. But the extraterrestrials prefer to go to Fez, for some reason, and so I went to Fez also.

I don't know why it should be that way, except that they're extraterrestrials, and maybe that's enough of an explanation. Of course, Fez is a great city in its own right, and an enormously interesting place, and no traveller needs any excuse to go there. But Marrakesh is the classical tourist-trap town of Morocco, with its palaces, its tombs, its tower, its crazy grand plaza full of acrobats and jugglers and snake-charmers, and that's where the hordes invariably have gone. The *human* hordes. E-Ts, being E-Ts, have different value systems. They . . .

And there my gorge rose. It seemed to me that I was blathering on and on in an impossible way. So I stopped and started over:

When I arrived in Fez, early on a warm April evening, I checked in at the big old Palais Jamai at the edge of the old city. In Morocco all the human tourists head straight for Marrakesh, as tourists have been doing ever since tourism began. But the extraterrestrials prefer to go to Fez, for some reason. And so I went to Fez also.

Not bad, especially when compared with the first version. This time I lasted six pages. I got my aliens on the scene on page two and the exotic green-eyed woman appeared on page three. They moved out on to the dance floor together and the narrator's skin began to tingle and suddenly I felt the upchuck reflex again. What I was writing was very slick, hopelessly mechanical, a computer-constructed man's-magazine story, lifeless and formulaic. The problem, I thought, was the first-person narration. It's all too easy, writing first person, to slip into a garrulous ingratiating here's-what-I-did tone that dawdles on and on and on as the narrator murmurs in your ear.

The third draft started the same way as the second, with the protagonist checking in at his hotel in Fez. But now it was a third-person story. And this time I didn't abandon it after a few pages. I pushed on all the way to the end, or what I thought was the end. This is how it opened now:

Eitel picked up his merchandise in Paris and caught the Air France night bird to Casablanca, where he connected with a Royal Air Maroc flight for the short hop to Fez. It was the middle of April, when Europe was still bleak and winter-dead, and Morocco was halfway to summer.

Very efficient. Protagonist introduced and in motion; exotic background established; and what's this mysterious merchandise? A nice lead paragraph. I nodded and went on for thirty-seven more pages, throwing in a lot of juicy Moroccan background information before bringing my aliens on stage on page 5 and the gorgeous woman on page 7. Eitel finally gets out on the dance floor with her on page 15, and then the trouble starts. And eventually gets resolved.

All right. I had a story. But it took too long to get down to its central events, and generally seemed inflated and lifeless to me. It was now Christmas week of 1982, and an old friend from New York was visiting me – Jerrold Mundis, a wise man and fine writer who doesn't happen to write (or read, or like, I suspect) science fiction. I gave him the story, telling him that I thought something was wrong with it, and asked him for a blunt critique, no punches pulled. He was blunt, all right. As I already suspected, I had opened the story in the wrong place. All that stuff in the beginning about Fez and Marrakesh might be fascinating to me, and might even make a nice *National Geographic* article, but it stopped things dead before they began. The endless speculations about the psychology of aliens that occupied pages 6 through 14 weren't very gripping either. Start the story on page 5, he suggested, and cut a lot of what follows, and maybe it would work.

Jerry usually knows whereof he speaks, in matters of writing and in other things. So I took his advice. This was the opening of the fourth draft:

Even before Eitel's eyes had adjusted to the darkness and the glare of the clashing crisscrossing spotlights, his nose began letting him know what sort of bizarre zoo he had walked into. The nightclub was full of aliens, at least seven or eight species. He picked up the whole astonishing olfactory blast at once, a weird hodgepodge of extra-terrestrial body odours, offworld pheromones, transgalactic cosmetics, the ozone radiation of personal protection screens, minute quantities of unearthly atmospheres leaking out of breathing devices. He was smelling things that as recently as the year 1987 no human being had ever smelled. Rigelians, he thought, Centaureans, Antareans, Arcturans. Maybe Steropids and Capellans too. The world has turned into a goddamned sci-fi flick, Eitel thought.

At last: some inventiveness, some narrative vigour, some characteristic Silverbergian tone. I cut here, expanded there, and in a few days had a thirty-eight-page story very different from its limp predecessors. On

21 January 1983, 'A World of Strangers' went off to Alice Turner at *Playboy*'s New York office; I put it out of my mind with deep relief and started writing *Valentine Pontifex* a few days later.

But Alice didn't like what I had sent her.

On 1 February she told me, 'I love the *Star Wars* bar in the beginning of this story, but, all in all, I'm dubious about the story. First, there's far too much exposition in the beginning . . . Frankly, I think the flashback could go, the taxi driver too. And the ending doesn't seem a bit integral to the story. If, for instance . . .'

And so on. A lot of problems. 'But I know that you probably like this story as is,' she added, 'and thus, with complete respect and many thanks, I will pass. If I am wrong, and you feel that, on second thought, you will change the ending and do some cutting early on, let me know. We could talk.'

Imagine my delight. After four full drafts *before* submitting the story, I had a reject on my hands. I suppose I could have saved us both a lot of trouble by sending the story, as is, to some other magazine and collecting my (rather smaller) cheque for it and putting it behind me. But I took Alice's letter as a challenge, instead. I covered it with notes. 'Might work!' I wrote, next to the paragraph where she suggested a different ending. 'Make it shadier . . . Story too simple. Make David real person – a partner? Eitel uptight, David a crook. Eitel has vestiges of ethics.' And a lot more. I phoned Alice and said I was going to rewrite the story. She seemed surprised and pleased. On 16 February I sent it to her again, down to thirty-four pages, with a note that said, 'Herewith the promised new version of the art-dealer story. I think I would not have had the heart to attempt it but for the word processor, which allowed me to rewrite big sections and graft salvageable old sections right in . . . I hope this does it. God only knows how many versions of this one I've written – even if you buy it at a fat price I'll end up making about $3 an hour for it. But that isn't the point; something must have happened last fall that caused me to lose my touch, to make my stuff top-heavy with exposition, and I'm groping my way back towards the way I'm supposed to write. This revision has been a great help in telling me I'm getting back there.'

This was the new opening:

After a moment Eitel's eyes adjusted to the darkness and the glare of the clashing crisscrossing spotlights. But he didn't need his eyes to tell him what sort of bizarre zoo he had walked into. The nightclub was full of aliens, seven or eight kinds, Rigelians, Capellans, Arcturans: the works. His sensitive nostrils picked up the whole astonishing olfactory blast at once: a weird hodgepodge of extraterrestrial body odours, offworld pheromones, transgalactic cosmetics, the ozone radiation of personal protection screens, minute quantities of unearthly atmospheres leaking out of breathing devices. He began to tremble.

'Something wrong?' David asked.

Alice phoned a couple of days later. She liked the new version, but it still needed some cutting, and she had some further plot quibbles besides. Could I see my way to one more rewrite?

Yes, I said despondently. The hook was in me now for sure. I told her to send me a list of the quibbles. But *you* do the cutting, I said. I've worked this one over so much that I'm losing my way in it.

On 1 March I got an annotated copy of the manuscript from her, with huge slashes on almost every page, slicing out exposition that echoed things already said in dialogue, authorial explanation of the characters' motives, and other sorts of fatty tissue. Her plot quibbles seemed pretty major too. After all these drafts she still could find six separate places where the twists of the plot weren't really plausible. I was appalled. But she sweetened her letter by telling me at the end, 'Bob, again, I want to congratulate you on the fine job you've done with this rewrite. Though you've been feeling inadequate, this is much more than an adequate job; it's a real change, and only a thorough professional could do it. As you see, these are only minor quibbles, the story is here, and I'm *most* grateful.'

Four days later – I was working weekends now, a rarity for me – I got yet another draft back to her. You'll find the text of it beginning on the next page. I had made nearly all the cuts she wanted and had tidied up the plot. 'I think the story now answers all of your objections and it may even answer mine; at any rate I hope I'm through writing it,' I told her. 'Nobody said this business is easy, but I shouldn't goof up a story as badly as I goofed up the earlier versions of this one, not at my age.'

And a couple of days afterwards, there was Alice on the phone. The story was fine and she was putting through the cheque (a very nice one, by the way).

To her astonishment and mine, I came close to breaking into tears as I realized that I was at last done with the damned thing.

Oh, she said. One little change. I'd like to call it 'Tourist Trade' instead of 'A World of Strangers'.

At that point she could have called it 'The Snows of Kilimanjaro' and I wouldn't have raised objections. But in fact her clever punning title was more suitable than mine, as you'll see in a little while, and I've retained it in reprinting the story.

There's one final twist to this flabbergasting tale.

Years later – December of 1988 – *Playboy* published its thirty-fifth-anniversary issue. 'Tourist Trade' was one of eight stories chosen to represent the fiction *Playboy* had published over those thirty-five years. (The others, I noted smugly, were by Ray Bradbury, Ian Fleming, Walter S. Tevis, Vladimir Nabokov, John Updike, Robert Coover and Joyce Carol Oates.) In phoning me to ask permission to reprint my story, Alice said that because of space limitations it would, like the others, have to be abridged. By her, since time was short.

'Where are you going to cut it?' I asked.

'I've already done it,' she said. 'I took David out.'

And so she had – slicing away one of the three major characters, along with close to half the text. To my utter astonishment the story still seemed coherent and effective – a testimony to really brilliant editing. I look at it from time to time in wonder. Nevertheless, I've chosen to use the complete text here – along with this lengthy prologue, which I hope demonstrates that those finely polished stories you see in the magazines don't necessarily bear much resemblance to the first version that came white-hot from the forge of creativity. There can be plenty of blood, sweat and, yes, tears in writing short stories – even for a veteran pro who is widely believed to know what he's doing.

After a moment Eitel's eyes adjusted to the darkness and the glare of the clashing crisscrossing spotlights. But he didn't need his eyes to tell him what sort of bizarre zoo he had walked into. His sensitive nostrils picked up the whole astonishing olfactory blast at once: a weird hodgepodge of extraterrestrial body odours, offworld pheromones, transgalactic cosmetics, the ozone radiation of personal protection screens, minute quantities of unearthly atmospheres leaking out of breathing devices.

'Something wrong?' David asked.

'The odours. They overwhelm me.'

'The smoking, eh? You hate it that much?'

'Not the tobacco, fool. The aliens! The E-Ts!'

171

'Ah. The smell of money, you mean. I agree, it is very overwhelming in here.'

'For a shrewd man you can sometimes be very stupid,' Eitel muttered. 'Unless you say such things deliberately, which you must, because I have never known a stupid Moroccan.'

'For a Moroccan, I am very stupid,' said David serenely. 'And so it was very stupid of you to choose me as your partner, eh? Your grandfathers in Zürich would be shamed if they knew. Eh?' He gave Eitel a maddeningly seraphic smile.

Eitel scowled. He was never sure when he had genuinely offended the slippery little Moroccan and when David was merely teasing. But somehow David always came out of these interchanges a couple of points ahead.

He turned and looked the place over, checking it out.

Plenty of humans, of course. This was the biggest gathering-place for aliens in Morocco, the locus of the focus, and a lot of gawkers came to observe the action. Eitel ignored them. There was no sense doing business with humans any more. There were probably some Interpol types in here too, hoping to head off just the sort of deals Eitel was here to do. To hell with them. His hands were clean, more or less.

But the aliens! The aliens, the aliens, the aliens!

All over the room. Vast saucer eyes, spidery limbs, skins of grotesque textures and unnameable colours. Eitel felt the excitement rising in him, so un-Swiss of him, so thoroughly out of character.

'*Look* at them!' he whispered. 'They're beautiful!'

'Beautiful? You think so?'

'Fantastic!'

The Moroccan shrugged. 'Fantastic, yes. Beautiful, no. Blue skin, green skin, no skin, two heads, five heads: this is beauty? What is beautiful to me is the money. And the way they like to throw it away.'

'You would never understand,' said Eitel.

In fact Eitel hardly understood it himself. He had discovered, not long after the first alien tourists had reached Earth, that they stirred unexpected areas of his soul: strange vistas opening, odd incoherent cosmic yearnings. To find at the age of forty that there was more to him than Panamanian trusts and numbered bank accounts – that was a little troublesome; but it was delicious, as well. He stood staring for a long ecstatic chaotic moment. Then he turned to David and said, 'Where's your Centauran?'

'I don't see him.'

'Neither do I.'

'He swore he'd be here. Is a big place, Eitel. We go looking, and we find.'

The air was thick with colour, sound, fumes. Eitel moved carefully around a tableful of leathery-faced pockmarked red Rigelians, burly, noisy, like a herd of American conventioneers out on the town. Behind them sat five sleek and sinuous Steropids, wearing cone-shaped breathers. Good. Steropids were easy marks. If something went wrong with this Centauran deal David had set up, he might want to have them as customers to fall back on.

Likewise that Arcturan trio, flat heads, grizzled green hair, triple eyes bright as blue-white suns. Arcturans were wild spenders, though they weren't known to covet Eitel's usual merchandise, which was works of fine art, or more or less fine art. Perhaps they could be encouraged to. Eitel, going past, offered them a preliminary smile: Earthman establishing friendly contact, leading perhaps to more elaborate relationship. But the Arcturans didn't pick up on it. They looked through Eitel as though their eyes didn't function in the part of the spectrum he happened to inhabit.

'There,' David said.

Yes. Far across the way, a turquoise creature, inordinately long and narrow, that appeared to be constructed of the finest grade of rubber, stretched over an awkwardly flung together armature of short rods.

'There's a woman with him,' Eitel said. 'I wasn't expecting that. You didn't tell me.'

David's eyes gleamed. 'Ah, nice, very nice!'

She was more than very nice. She was splendid. But that wasn't the point. Her presence here could be a troublesome complication. A tour guide? An interpreter? Had the Centauran brought his own art expert along? Or was she some Interpol agent decked out to look like the highest-priced of hookers? Or maybe even a real hooker. God help me, he thought, if the Centauran's gotten involved in some kind of kinky infatuation that would distract him from the deal. No: God help David.

'You should have told me there was a woman,' Eitel said.

'But I didn't know! I swear, Jesus Mary Moses, I never see her yesterday! But it will be all right. Jesus Mary Moses, go ahead, walk over.' He smiled and winked and slipped off towards the bar. 'I see you later, outside. You go for it, you hear? You hear me, Eitel? It will be all right.'

The Centauran, seeing the red carnation in Eitel's lapel, lifted his arm in a gesture like the extending of a telescopic tube, and the woman smiled. It was an amazing smile, and it caught Eitel a little off guard, because for an instant it made him wish that the Centauran was back on Centaurus and this woman was sitting here alone. He shook the thought off. He was here to do a deal, not to get into entanglements.

'Hans Eitel, of Zürich,' he said.

'I am Anakhistos,' said the Centauran. His voice was like something out of a synthesizer, which perhaps it was, and his face was utterly opaque, a flat motionless mask. For vision he had a single bright strip of receptors an inch wide around his forehead, for air intake he had little vents on his cheeks, and for eating he had a three-sided oral slot like the swinging top of a trash basket. 'We are very happied you have come,' he said. 'This is Agila.'

Eitel allowed himself to look straight at her. It was dazzling but painful, a little like staring into the sun. Her hair was red and thick, her eyes were emerald and very far apart, her lips were full, her teeth were bright. She was wearing a vaguely futuristic metal-mesh sheath, green, supple, clinging. What she looked like was something that belonged on a 3-D billboard, one of those unreal idealized women who turn up in the ads for cognac, or skiing holidays in Gstaad. There was something a little freakish about such excessive beauty. A professional, he decided.

To the Centauran he said, 'This is a great pleasure for me. To meet a collector of your stature, to know that I will be able to be of assistance – '

'And a pleasure also for ourself. You are greatly recommended to me. You are called knowledgeable, reliable, discreet – '

'The traditions of our family. I was bred to my *métier*.'

'We are drinking mint tea,' the woman said. 'Will you drink mint tea with us?' Her voice was warm, deep, unfamiliar. Swedish? Did they have redheads in Sweden?

Eitel said, 'Forgive me, but it's much too sweet for me. Perhaps a brandy instead – '

A waiter appeared as though by telepathic command. Eitel ordered a Courvoisier, and the woman another round of tea. She is very smooth, very good, he thought. He imagined himself in bed with her, digging his fingers into that dense red mane, running his lips over her long lean thighs. The fantasy was pleasing but undisturbing: an idle dream, cool, agreeable, giving him no palpitations, no frenzy. Good. After that first startled moment he was getting himself under control. He wondered if she was charging the Centauran by the night, or working at something bigger.

She said, 'I love the Moroccan tea. It is so marvellous, the sweet. Sugar is my passion. I think I am addicted.'

The waiter poured the tea in the traditional way, cascading it down into the glass from three feet up. Eitel repressed a shudder. He admired the elaborate Moroccan cuisine, but the tea appalled him: lethal hypersaccharine stuff, instant diabetes.

'Do you also enjoy mint tea?' Eitel asked the alien.

'It is very wonderful,' the Centauran said. 'It is one of the most wonderful things on this wonderful planet.'

Eitel had no idea how sincere the Centauran was. He had been studying the psychology of extraterrestrials about as closely as anyone had, in the decade since they had begun to descend on Earth en masse after the lifting of the galactic quarantine, and he knew a lot about a lot of them; but he found it almost impossible to get a reading on Centaurans. If they gave any clues to their feelings at all, it was in the form of minute, perhaps imaginary fluctuations of the texture of their rubbery skins. It was Eitel's theory that the skin slackened when they were happy and went taut when they were tense, but the theory was only preliminary and he gave it little value.

'When did you arrive on Earth?' Eitel asked.

'It is the first week,' the Centauran said. 'Five days here in Fez, then we go to Rome, Paris, and afterwards the States

175

United. Following which, other places. It is greatly exciting, your world. Such vigour, such raw force. I hope to see everything, and bring back much art. I am passionate collector, you know, of Earthesque objects.'

'With a special interest in paintings.'

'Paintings, yes, but I collect many other things.'

That seemed a little blatant. Unless Eitel misunderstood the meaning, but he doubted he had. He glanced at the woman, but she showed no reaction.

Carefully he said, 'Such as?'

'Everything that is essential to the experience of your world! Everything fine, everything deeply Earthesque! Of course I am most fastidious. I seek only the first-rate objects.'

'I couldn't possibly agree more,' said Eitel. 'We share the same philosophy. The true connoisseur has no time for the tawdry, the trivial, the incompletely realized gesture, the insufficiently fulfilled impulse.' His tone, carefully practised over years of dealing with clients, was intended to skirt unctuousness and communicate nothing but warm and sincere approbation. Such nuances were probably lost on the Centauran, but Eitel never let himself underestimate a client. He looked suddenly towards the woman and said, 'Surely that's your outlook also.'

'Of course.'

She took a long pull of her mint tea, letting the syrupy stuff slide down her throat like motor oil. Then she wriggled her shoulders in a curious way. Eitel saw flesh shifting interestingly beneath the metal mesh. Surely she was professional. *Surely*. He found himself speculating on whether there could be anything sexual going on between these two. He doubted that it was possible, but you never could tell. More likely, though, she was merely one of the stellar pieces in Anakhistos's collection of the high-quality Earthesque: an object, an artefact. Eitel wondered how Anakhistos had managed to find her so fast. Was there some service that supplied visiting aliens with the finest of escorts, at the finest of prices?

He was picking up an aroma from her now, not unpleasant but very strange: caviar and cumin? Sturgeon poached in Chartreuse?

She signalled to the waiter for yet another tea. To Eitel she said, 'The problem of the export certificates, do you think it is going to get worse?'

That was unexpected, and very admirable, he thought. Discover what your client's concerns are, make them your own.

He said, 'It is a great difficulty, is it not?'

'I think of little else,' said the Centauran, leaping in as if he had been waiting for Agila to provide the cue. 'To me it is an abomination. These restrictions on removing works of art from your planet – these humiliating inspections – this agitation, this outcry for even tighter limitations – what will it come to?'

Soothingly Eitel said, 'You must try to understand the nature of the panic. We are a small backward world that has lived in isolation until just a few years ago. Suddenly we have stumbled into contact with the great galactic civilizations. You come among us, you are fascinated by us and by our artefacts, you wish to collect our things. But we can hardly supply the entire civilized universe. There are only a few Leonardos, a few Vermeers: and there are so many of you. So there is fear that you will sweep upon us with your immense wealth, with your vast numbers, with your hunger for our art, and buy everything of value that we have ever produced, and carry it off to places a hundred light-years away. So these laws are being passed. It is natural.'

'But I am not here to plunder! I am here to make legitimate purchase!'

'I understand completely,' Eitel said. He risked putting his hand, gently, compassionately, on the Centauran's arm. Some of the E-Ts resented any sort of intimate contact of this sort with Earthfolk. But apparently the Centauran didn't mind. The alien's rubbery skin felt astonishingly soft and smooth, like the finest condom imaginable. 'I'm altogether on your side,' Eitel declared. 'The export laws are absurd overreactions. There's a more than ample supply of art on this planet to meet the needs of sophisticated collectors like yourself. And by disseminating our culture among the star-worlds, we bind ourselves inextricably into the fabric of galactic civilization. Which is why I do everything in my power to make our finest art available to our visitors.'

'But can you provide valid export licences?' Agila asked.

Eitel put his finger to his lips. 'We don't need to discuss it further just now, eh? Let us enjoy the delights of this evening, and save dreary matters of commerce for later, shall we?' He beamed. 'May I offer you more tea?'

It was all going very smoothly, Eitel thought. Contact made, essential lines of agreement established. Even the woman was far less of a complication than he had anticipated. Time now to back off, relax, let rapport blossom and mature without forcing.

'Do you dance?' Agila said suddenly.

He looked towards the dance floor. The Rigelians were lurching around in a preposterously ponderous way, like dancing bears. Some Arcturans were on the dance floor too, and a few Procyonites bouncing up and down like bundles of shiny metal rods, and a Steropid doing an eerie *pas seul*, weaving in dreamy circles.

'Yes, of course,' he said, a little startled.

'Please dance with me?'

He glanced uneasily towards the Centauran, who nodded benignly. She smiled and said, 'Anakhistos does not dance. But I would like to. Would you oblige me?'

Eitel took her hand and led her out on the floor. Once they were dancing he was able to regain his calm. He moved easily and well. Some of the E-Ts were openly watching them – they had such *curiosity* about humans sometimes – but the staring didn't bother him. He found himself registering the pressure of her thighs against his thighs, her firm heavy breasts against his chest, and for an instant he felt the old biochemical imperative trying to go roaring through his veins, telling him, *follow her anywhere, promise anything, say anything, do anything*. He brushed it back. There were other women: in Nice, in Rome, in Athens. When he was done with this deal he would go to one of them.

He said, 'Agila is an interesting name. Israeli, is it?'

'No,' she said.

The way she said it, serenely and very finally, left him without room to manoeuvre. He was full of questions – who was she, how had she hooked up with the Centauran, what was her deal, how well did she think Eitel's own deal with the Centauran was likely to go? But that one cool syllable seemed to have slammed a curtain down. He concentrated on dancing again instead. She was supple, responsive, skilful. And yet the way she danced was as strange as everything else about her: she moved almost as if her feet were some inches off the floor. Odd. And her voice – an accent, but what kind? He had been everywhere, and nothing in his experience matched her way of speaking, a certain liquidity in the vowels, a certain resonance in the phrasing, as though she were hearing echoes as she spoke. She had to be something truly exotic, Rumanian, a Finn, a Bulgar – and even those did not seem exotic enough. Albanian? Lithuanian?

Most perplexing of all was her aroma. Eitel was gifted with a sense of smell worthy of a parfumier, and he heeded a woman's fragrance the way more ordinary men studied the curves of hip or bosom or thigh. Out of the pores and the axillae and the orifices came the truths of the body, he believed, the deepest, the most trustworthy, the most exciting communications; he studied them with rabbinical fervour and the most minute scientific zeal. But he had never smelled anything like this, a juxtaposition of incongruous spices, a totally baffling mix of flavours. Some amazing new perfume? Something imported from Arcturus or Capella, perhaps? Maybe so, though it was hard to imagine an effect like this being achieved by mere chemicals. It had to be *her*. But what mysterious glandular outpouring brought him that subtle hint of sea urchin mingled with honey? What hidden duct sent thyme and raisins coursing together through her bloodstream? Why did the crystalline line of light perspiration on her flawless upper lip carry those grace-notes of pomegranate, tarragon and ginger?

He looked for answers in her eyes: deep green pools, calm, cool, unearthly. They seemed as bewildering as the rest of her.

And then he understood. He realized now that the answer, impossible and implausible and terrifying, had been beckoning to him all evening, and that he could no longer go on rejecting it, impossible or not. And in the moment of accepting it he heard a sound within himself much like that of a wind beginning to rise, a hurricane being born on some far-off isle.

Eitel began to tremble. He had never felt himself so totally defenceless before.

He said, 'It's amazing, how human you seem to be.'

'*Seem* to be?'

'Outwardly identical in every way. I didn't think it was possible for life-forms of such a degree of similarity to evolve on two different worlds.'

'It isn't,' she said.

'You're not from Earth, though.'

She was smiling. She seemed almost pleased, he thought, that he had seen through her masquerade.

'No.'

'What are you, then?'

'Centauran.'

Eitel closed his eyes a moment. The wind was a gale within him; he swayed and struggled to keep his balance. He was starting to feel as though he were conducting this conversation from a point somewhere behind his own right ear. 'But Centaurans look like – '

'Like Anakhistos? Yes, of course we do, when we are at home. But I am not at home now.'

'I don't understand.'

'This is my travelling body,' she said.

'What?'

'It is not comfortable, visiting certain places in one's own body. The air is sharp, the light hurts the eyes, eating is very troublesome.'

'So you simply put on a different body?'

'Some of us do. There are those like Anakhistos who are indifferent to the discomforts, or who actually regard them as part of the purpose of travelling. But I am of the sort that prefers to transfer into a travelling body when going to other worlds.'

'Ah,' Eitel said. 'Yes.' He continued to move through the rhythms of the dance in a numb, dazed way. It's all just a costume, he told himself. What she really looks like is a bunch of rigid struts, with a rubber sheet draped over them. Cheek-vents for breathing, three-sided slot for eating, receptor strip instead of eyes. 'And these bodies?' he asked. 'Where do you get them?'

'Why, they make them for us. Several companies do it. The human models are only just now becoming available. Very expensive, you understand.'

'Yes,' he said. 'Of course.'

'Tell me: when was it that you first saw through my disguise?'

'I felt right away that something was wrong. But it wasn't until a moment ago that I figured it out.'

'No one else has guessed, I think. It is an extremely excellent Earth body, would you not say?'

'Extremely,' Eitel said.

'After each trip I always regret, at first, returning to my real body. This one seems quite genuine to me by now. You like it very much, yes?'

'Yes,' Eitel said helplessly.

He found David out in the cab line, lounging against his taxi with one arm around a Moroccan boy of about sixteen and the other exploring the breasts of a swarthy French-looking woman. It was hard to tell which one he had selected for the late hours of the night: both, maybe. David's cheerfully polymorphous ways were a little hard for Eitel to take, sometimes. But Eitel knew it wasn't necessary to approve of David in order to work with him. Whenever Eitel showed up in Fez with new merchandise, David was able to finger a customer for him within twenty-four hours; and at a five per cent commission he was probably the wealthiest taxi driver in Morocco, after two years as Eitel's point man among the E-Ts.

'Everything's set,' Eitel said. 'Take me over to get the stuff.'

David flashed his glittering gold-toothed grin. He patted the woman's rump, lightly slapped the boy's cheek, pushed them both on their way, and opened the door of his cab for Eitel. The merchandise was at Eitel's hotel, the Palais Jamai, on the edge of the native quarter. But Eitel never did business at his own hotel: it was handy to have David to take him back and forth between the Jamai and the Hotel Merinides, out here beyond the city wall by the ancient royal tombs, where most of the aliens preferred to stay.

The night was mild, fragrant, palm trees rustling in the soft breeze, huge bunches of red geranium blossoms looking almost black in the moonlight. As they drove towards the old town, with its maze of winding medieval streets, its walls and gates straight out of *The Arabian Nights*, David said, 'You mind I tell you something? One thing worries me.'

'Go ahead.'

'Inside, I watched you. Staring more at the woman than at the E-T. You got to concentrate on the deal, and forget the woman, Eitel.'

Eitel resented being told by a kid half his age how to conduct his operations. But he kept himself in check. To David, young and until recently poor, certain nuances were incomprehensible. Not that David lacked an interest in beauty. But beauty was just an abstraction; money was money. Eitel did not attempt to explain what time would surely teach.

He said, '*You* tell *me*, forget the woman?'

'Is a time for women, is a time for business. Separate times. You know that, Eitel. A Swiss, he is almost a Moroccan, when it comes to business.'

Eitel laughed. 'Thanks.'

'I am being serious. You be careful. If she confuse you, it can cost you. Can cost *me*. I am in for percentage, remember. Even if you are Swiss, maybe you need to know: business and women must be kept separate things.'

'I know.'

'You remember it, yes?'

'Don't worry about me,' Eitel said.

The cab pulled up outside the Jamai. Eitel, upstairs, withdrew four paintings and an Olmec jade statuette from the false compartment of his suitcase. The paintings were all unframed, small, genuine and unimportant. After a moment he selected the *Madonna of the Palms*, from the atelier of Lorenzo Bellini: plainly apprentice work, but enchanting, serene, pure, not bad, easily a $20,000 painting. He slipped it into a carrying case, put the others back, all but the statuette, which he fondled for a moment and put down on the dresser, in front of the mirror, as though setting up a little shrine. To beauty, he thought. He started to put it away and changed his mind. It looked so lovely there that he decided to take his chances. Taking your chances, he thought, is sometimes good for the health.

He went back to the cab.

'Is a good painting?' David asked.

'It's pretty. Trivial, but pretty.'

'I don't mean good that way. I mean, is it real?'

'Of course,' Eitel said, perhaps too sharply. 'Do we have to have this discussion again, David? You know damned well I sell only genuine paintings. Overpriced a little, but always genuine.'

'One thing I never can understand. Why you not sell them fakes?'

Startled, Eitel said, 'You think I'm crooked, David?'

'Sure I do.'

'You say it so lightheartedly. I don't like your humour sometimes.'

'Humour? What humour? Is against law to sell valuable Earth works of art to aliens. You sell them. Makes you crook, right? Is no insult. Is only description.'

'I don't believe this,' Eitel said. 'What are you trying to start here?'

'I only want to know, why you sell them real stuff. Is against the law to sell real ones, is probably not against the law to sell them fakes. You see? For two years I wonder this. We make just as much money, we run less risk.'

'My family has dealt in art for over a hundred years, David. No Eitel has ever knowingly sold a fake. None ever will.' It was a touchy point with him. 'Look,' he said, 'maybe you like playing these games with me, but you could go too far. All right?'

'You forgive me, Eitel?'

'If you shut up.'

'You know better than that. Shutting up I am very bad at. Can I tell you one more thing, and then I shut up really?'

'Go ahead,' Eitel said, sighing.

'I tell you this: you a very confused man. You a crook who thinks he not a crook, you know what I mean? Which is bad thinking. But is all right. I like you. I respect you, even. I think you are excellent businessman. So you forgive rude remarks?'

'You give me a great pain,' Eitel said.

'I bet I do. You forget I said anything. Go make deal, many millions, tomorrow we have mint tea together and you give me my cut and everybody happy.'

'I don't like mint tea.'

'Is all right. We have some anyway.'

Seeing Agila standing in the doorway of her hotel room, Eitel was startled again by the impact of her presence, the overwhelming physical power of her beauty. *If she confuse you, it can cost you.* What you see is all artificial, he told himself. It's just a mask. Eitel looked from Agila to Anakhistos, who sat oddly folded, like a giant umbrella. That's what she really is, Eitel thought. She's Mrs Anakhistos from Centaurus, and her skin is like rubber and her mouth is a hinged slot and this body that she happens to be wearing right now was made in a laboratory. And yet, and yet, and yet – the wind was roaring, he was tossing wildly about –

What the hell is happening to me?

'Show us what you have for us,' Anakhistos said.

Eitel slipped the little painting from its case. His hands were shaking ever so slightly. In the closeness of the room he picked up two strong fragrances, something dry and musty coming from Anakhistos, and the strange, irresistible mixtures of incongruous spices that Agila's synthetic body emanated.

'*The Madonna of the Palms*, Lorenzo Bellini, Venice, 1597,' Eitel said. 'Very fine work.'

'Bellini is extremely famous, I know.'

'The famous ones are Giovanni and Gentile. This is Giovanni's grandson. He's just as good, but not well-known. I couldn't possibly get you paintings by Giovanni or Gentile. No one on Earth could.'

'This is quite fine,' said Anakhistos. 'True Renaissance beauty. And very Earthesque. Of course it is genuine?'

Eitel said stiffly, 'Only a fool would try to sell a fake to a connoisseur such as yourself. But it would be easy enough for us to arrange a spectroscopic analysis in Casablanca, if – '

'Ah, no, no, no, I meant no suspicioning of your reputation. You are impeccable. We unquestion the genuinity. But what is done about the export certificate?'

'Easy. I have a document that says this is a recent copy, done by a student in Paris. They are not yet applying chemical tests of age to the paintings, not yet. You will be able to take the painting from Earth, with such a certificate.'

'And the price?' said Anakhistos.

Eitel took a deep breath. It was meant to steady him, but it dizzied him instead, for it filled his lungs with Agila.

He said, 'If the deal is straight cash, the price is four million dollars.'

'And otherwise?' Agila asked.

'I'd prefer to talk to you about that alone,' he said to her.

'Whatever you want to say, you can say in front of Anakhistos. We are absolute mates. We have complete trust.'

'I'd still prefer to speak more privately.'

She shrugged. 'All right. The balcony.'

Outside, where the sweetness of night-blooming flowers filled the air, her fragrance was less overpowering. It made no difference. Looking straight at her only with difficulty, he said, 'If I can spend the rest of this night making love to you, the price will be three million.'

'This is a joke?'

'In fact, no. Not at all.'

'It is worth a million dollars to have sexual contact with me?'

Eitel imagined how his father would have answered that question, his grandfather, his great-grandfather. Their accumulated wisdom pressed on him like a hump. To hell with them, he thought.

He said, listening in wonder to his own words, 'Yes. It is.'

'You know that this body is not my real body.'

'I know.'

'I am an alien being.'

'Yes. I know.'

She studied him in silence a long while. Then she said, 'Why did you make me come outside to ask me this?'

'On Earth, men sometimes become quite angry when strangers ask their wives to go to bed with them. I didn't know how Anakhistos would react. I don't have any real idea how Centaurans react to anything.'

'I am Centauran also,' she pointed out.

'You don't seem as alien to me.'

She smiled quickly, on-off. 'I see. Well, let us confer with Anakhistos.'

But the conference, it turned out, did not include Eitel. He stood by, feeling rash and foolish, while Agila and Anakhistos exchanged bursts of harsh rapid words in their own language, a buzzing, eerie tongue that was quite literally like nothing on Earth. He searched their faces for some understanding of the flow of conversation. Was Anakhistos shocked? Outraged?

Amused? And she? Even wearing human guise, she was opaque to him too. Did she feel contempt for Eitel's bumptious lusts? Indifference? See him as quaintly primitive, bestial, anthropoid? Or was she eagerly cajoling her husband into letting her have her little adventure? Eitel had no idea. He felt far out of his depth, a sensation as unfamiliar as it was unwelcome. Dry throat, sweaty palms, brain in turmoil: but there was no turning back now.

At last Agila turned to him and said, 'It is agreed. The painting is ours at three million. And I am yours until dawn.'

David was still waiting. He grinned a knowing grin when Eitel emerged from the Merinides with Agila on his arm, but said nothing. I have lost points with him, Eitel thought. He thinks I have allowed the nonsense of the flesh to interfere with a business decision, and now I have made myself frivolous in his eyes. It is more complicated than that, but David would never understand. *Business and women must be kept separate things.* To the taxi driver, Eitel knew, Helen of Troy herself would be as nothing next to a million dollars: mere meat, mere heat. So be it, Eitel told himself. David would never understand. What David would understand, Eitel thought guiltily, was that in cutting the deal with Agila he had also cut fifty thousand dollars off David's commission. But he did not intend to let David know anything about that.

When they were in Eitel's room Agila said, 'First, I would please like to have some mint tea, yes? It is my addiction, you know. My aphrodisiac.'

Sizzling impatience seared Eitel's soul. God only knew how long it might take room service to fetch a pot of tea at this hour, and at a million dollars a night he preferred not to waste even a minute. But there was no way to refuse. He could not allow himself to seem like some panting schoolboy.

'Of course,' he said.

After he had phoned, he walked around behind her as she stood by the window peering into the mists of the night. He put his lips to the nape of her neck and cupped his hands over her breasts. This is very crazy, he thought. I am not touching her real body. This is only some synthetic mock-up, a statue of flesh, a mere androidal shell.

No matter. No matter. He was able to resist her beauty, that illusion, that figment. That beauty, astonishing and unreal, was what had drawn him at first, but it was the dark secret alien underneath that ruled him now. That was what he hoped to reach: the alien, the star-woman, the unfathomable being from the black interstellar deeps. He would touch what no man of Earth had ever touched before.

He inhaled her fragrance until he felt himself swaying. She was making an odd purring sound that he hoped was one of pleasure.

There was a knock at the door. 'The tea is here,' she said.

The waiter, a boy in native costume, sleepy, openly envious of Eitel for having a woman like Agila in his room, took forever to set up the glasses and pour the tea, an infinitely slow process of raising the pot, aiming, letting the thick tea trickle down through the air. But at last he left. Agila drank greedily, and beckoned to Eitel to have some also. He smiled and shook his head.

She said, 'But you must. I love it so – you must share it. It is a ritual of love between us, eh?'

He did not choose to make an issue of it. A glass of mint tea more or less must not get in the way, not now.

'To us,' she said, and touched her glass to his.

He managed to drink a little. It was like pure liquid sugar. She had a second glass, and then, maddeningly, a third. He pretended to sip at his. Then at last she touched her hand to a clasp on her shoulder and her metal-mesh sheath fell away.

They had done their research properly, in the body-making labs of Centaurus. She was flawless, sheer fantasy, with heavy breasts that defied gravity, slender waist, hips that would drive a Moroccan camel-driver berserk, buttocks like pale hemispheres. They had given her a navel, pubic hair, erectile nipples, dimples here and there, the hint of blue veins in her thighs. Unreal, yes, Eitel thought, but magnificent.

'It is my fifth travelling body,' she said. 'I have been Arcturan, Steropid, Denebian, Mizarian – and each time it has been hard, hard, hard! After the transfer is done, there is a long training period, and it is always very difficult. But one learns. A moment finally comes when the body feels natural and true. I will miss this one very much.'

'So will I,' Eitel said.

Quickly he undressed. She came to him, touched her lips lightly to his, grazed his chest with her nipples.

'And now you must give me a gift,' she said.

'What?'

'It is the custom before making love. An exchange of gifts.' She took from between her breasts the pendant she was wearing, a bit of bright crystal carved in disturbing alien swirls. 'This is for you. And for me – '

Oh, God in heaven, he thought. No!

Her hand closed over the Olmec jade figurine that was still sitting on the dresser.

'This,' she said.

It sickened him. That little statuette was eighty thousand on the international antiquities market, maybe a million or two to the right E-T buyer. A gift? A love-token? He saw the gleam in her eye, and knew he was trapped. Refuse, and everything else might be lost. He dare not show any trace of pettiness. Yes. So be it. Let her have the damned thing. We are being romantic tonight. We are making grand gestures. We are not going to behave like a petit-bourgeois Swiss art pedlar. *If she confuse you, it can cost you*, David had said. Eitel took a deep breath.

'My pleasure,' he said magnificently.

He was an experienced and expert lover; supreme beauty always inspired the best in him; and pride alone made him want to send her back to Centaurus with incandescent memories of the erotic arts of Earth. His performance that night – and performance was the only word he could apply to it – might well have been the finest of his life.

With the lips and tongue, first. Everywhere. With the fingers, slowly, patiently, searching for the little secret key places, the unexpected triggering-points. With the breath against the skin, and the fingernails, ever so lightly, and the eyelashes, and even the newly sprouting stubble of the cheek. These were all things that Eitel loved doing, not merely for the effects they produced in his bed-partners but because they were delightful in and of themselves; yet he had never done them with greater dedication and skill.

And now, he thought, perhaps she will show me some of *her* skills.

But she lay there like a wax doll. Occasionally she stirred, occasionally she moved her hips a little. When he went into her, he found her warm and moist – why had they built that capacity in, Eitel wondered? – but he felt no response from her, none at all.

He moved her this way, that, running through the gamut of positions as though he and she were making a training film for newly-weds. Now and then she smiled. Her eyes were always open: she was fascinated. Eitel felt anger rising. She was ever the tourist, even here in his bed. Getting some first-hand knowledge of the quaint sexual techniques of the primitive Earthmen.

Knowing he was being foolish, that he was compounding a foolishness, he drove his body with frantic intensity, rocking rhythmically above her, grimly pushing her on and on. *Come on*, he thought. *Give me a little sigh, a moan, a wriggle. Anything.* He wasn't asking her to come. There was no reason why they should have built *that* capacity in, was there? The only thing he wanted now was to get some sort of acknowledgement of his existence from her, some quiver of assent.

He went on working at it, knowing he would not get it. But then, to his surprise, something actually seemed to be happening. Her face grew flushed, and her eyes narrowed and took on a new gleam, and her breath began to come in harsh little bursts, and her breasts heaved, and her nipples grew hard. All the signs, yes: Eitel had seen them so many times, and never more welcome than at this moment. He knew what to do. The unslackening rhythm now, the steady building of tension, carrying her onwards, steadily higher, leading her towards that magical moment of overload when the watchful conscious mind at last surrenders to the surging deeper forces. Yes. Yes. The valiant Earthman giving his all for the sake of transgalactic passion, labouring like a galley slave to show the star-woman what the communion of the sexes is all about.

She seemed almost there. Some panting now, even a little gasping. Eitel smiled in pleasant self-congratulation. Swiss precision, he thought: never underestimate it.

And then somehow she managed to slip free of him, between one thrust and the next, and she rolled to the side, so that he collapsed in amazement into the pillow as she left the bed. He sat up and looked at her, stunned, gaping, numbed.

'Excuse me,' she said, in the most casual way. 'I thought I'd have a little more tea. Shall I get some for you?'

Eitel could barely speak. 'No,' he said hoarsely.

She poured herself a glass, drank, grimaced. 'It doesn't taste as good as when it's warm,' she said, returning to the bed. 'Well, shall we go on?' she asked.

Silently he reached for her. Somehow he was able to start again. But this time a distance of a thousand light-years seemed to separate him from her. There was no rekindling that brief flame, and after a few moments he gave up. He felt himself forever shut away from the inwardness of her, as Earth is shut away from the stars. Cold, weary, more furious with himself than with her, he let himself come. He kept his eyes open as long as he could, staring icily into hers, but the sensations were unexpectedly powerful, and in the end he sank down against her breasts, clinging to her as the impact thundered through him.

In that bleak moment came a surprise. For as he shook and quivered in the force of that dismal ejaculation something opened between them, a barrier, a gate, and the hotel melted and disappeared and he saw himself in the midst of a bizarre landscape. The sky was a rich golden-green, the sun was deep green and hot, the trees and plants and flowers were like nothing he had ever seen on Earth. The air was heavy, aromatic, and of a piercing flavour that stung his nostrils. Flying creatures that were not birds soared unhurriedly overhead, and some iridescent beasts that looked like red velvet pillows mounted on tripods were grazing on the lower branches of furry-limbed trees. On the horizon Eitel saw three jagged naked mountains of some yellow-brown stone that gleamed like polished metal in the sunlight. He trembled. Wonder and awe engulfed his spirit. This is a park, he realized, the most beautiful park in the world. But this is not *this* world. He found a little path that led over a gentle hill, and when he came to the far side he looked down to see Centaurans strolling two by two, hand in hand, through an elegantly contoured garden.

Oh, my God, Eitel thought. Oh, my God in heaven!

Then it all began to fade, growing thin, turning to something no more substantial than smoke, and in a moment more it was all gone. He lay still, breathing raggedly, by her side, watching her breasts slowly rising and falling.

He lifted his head. She was studying him. 'You liked that?'

'Liked what?'

'What you saw.'

'So you know?'

She seemed surprised. 'Of course! You thought it was an accident? It was my gift for you.'

'Ah.' The picture-postcard of the home world, bestowed on the earnest native for his diligent services. 'It was extraordinary. I've never seen anything so beautiful.'

'It is very beautiful, yes,' she said complacently. Then, smiling, she said, 'That was interesting, what you did there at the end, when you were breathing so hard. Can you do that again?' she asked, as though he had just executed some intricate juggling manoeuvre.

Bleakly he shook his head, and turned away. He could not bear to look into those magnificent eyes any longer. Somehow – he would never have any way of knowing when it had happened, except that it was somewhere between 'Can you do that again?' and the dawn, he fell asleep. She was shaking him gently awake, then. The light of a brilliant morning came bursting through the fragile old silken draperies.

'I am leaving now,' she whispered. 'But I wish to thank you. It has been a night I shall never forget.'

'Nor I,' said Eitel.

'To experience the reality of Earthian ways at such close range – with such intimacy, such immediacy – '

'Yes. Of course. It must have been extraordinary for you.'

'If ever you come to Centaurus – '

'Certainly. I'll look you up.'

She kissed him lightly, tip of nose, forehead, lips. Then she walked towards the door. With her hand on the knob, she turned and said, 'Oh, one little thing that might amuse you. I meant to tell you last night. We don't have that kind of thing on our world, you know – that concept of owning one's mate's body. And in any case, Anakhistos is not male, and I am not female, not exactly. We mate, but our sex distinctions are not so well-defined as that. It is with us more like the way it is with your oysters, I think. So it is not quite right to say that Anakhistos is my husband, or that I am his wife. I thought you would like to know.'

She blew him a kiss. 'It has been very lovely,' she said. 'Goodbye.'

When she was gone he went to the window and stared into the garden for a long while without looking at anything in particular. He felt weary and burned out, and there was a taste of straw in his mouth. After a time he turned away.

When he emerged from the hotel later that morning, David's car was waiting out front.

'Get in,' he said.

They drove in silence to a cafe that Eitel had never seen before, in the new quarter of town. David said something in Arabic to the proprietor and he brought mint tea for two.

'I don't like mint tea,' Eitel said.

'Drink. It washes away bad tastes. How did it go last night?'

'Fine. Just fine.'

'You and the woman, ficky-ficky?'

'None of your ficky-ficky business.'

'Try some tea,' David urged. 'It not so good last night, eh?'

'What makes you think so?'

'You not look so happy. You not sound so happy.'

'For once you're wrong,' Eitel said. 'I got everything I wanted to get. Do you understand me? I got everything I wanted to get.' His tone might have been a little too loud, a little too aggressive, for it drew a quizzical, searching look from the Moroccan.

'Yes. Sure. And what size deal? That *is* my business, yes?'

'Three million cash.'

'Only three?'

'Three,' Eitel said. 'I owe you a hundred and fifty thousand. You're doing all right, a hundred and fifty for a couple of hours' work. I'm making you a rich man.'

'Yes. Very rich. But no more deals, Eitel.'

'What?'

'You find another boy, all right? I will work now with someone else, maybe. There are plenty of others, you know? I will be more comfortable with them. Is very bad, when one does not trust a partner.'

'I don't follow you.'

'What you did last night, going off with the woman, was very stupid. Poor business, you know? I wonder, did you have to pay her? And did you pay her some of my money too?'

David was smiling, as always. But sometimes his smiles were amiable and sometimes they were just smiles. Eitel had a sudden vision of himself in a back alley of the old town, bleeding. He had another vision of himself undergoing interrogation by the customs men. David had a lot of power over him, he realized.

Eitel took a deep breath and said, 'I resent the insinuation that I've cheated you. I've treated you very honourably from the start. You know that. And if you think I bought the woman, let me tell you this: she isn't a woman at all. She's an alien. Some of them wear human bodies when they travel. Underneath all that gorgeous flesh she's a Centauran, David.'

'And you touched her?'

'Yes.'

'You put yourself inside her?'

'Yes,' Eitel said.

David stood up. He looked as though he had just found a rat embryo in his tea. 'I am very glad we are no longer partners, then. Deliver the money to me in the usual way. And then please stay away from me when you are in this city.'

'Wait,' Eitel said. 'Take me back to the Merinides. I've got three more paintings to sell.'

'There are plenty of taxi drivers in this city,' said David.

When he was gone, Eitel peered into his mint tea for a while and wondered if David meant to make trouble for him. Then he stopped thinking about David and thought about that glimpse of a green sun and a golden landscape that Agila had given him. His hands felt cold, his fingers were quivering a little. He became aware that he wanted more than anything else to see those things again. Could any Centauran make it happen for him, he wondered, or was that only Agila's little trick? What about other aliens? He imagined himself prowling the nightclub, hustling for action, pressing himself up against this slithery thing or that one, desperately trying to re-enact that weird orgasmic moment that had carried him to the stars. A new perversion, he thought. One that even David found disgusting.

He wondered what it was like to go to bed with a Vegan or an Arcturan or a Steropid. God in heaven! Could he do it? Yes, he told himself, thinking of green suns and the unforgettable fragrance of that alien air. Yes. Yes. Of course he could. Of course.

There was a sudden strange sweetness in his mouth. He realized that he had taken a deep gulp of the mint tea without paying attention to what he was doing. Eitel smiled. It hadn't made him sick, had it? Had it? He took another swig. Then, in a slow determined way, he finished off all the rest of it, and scattered some coins on the counter, and went outside to look for a cab.

Multiples

No heartrending sagas of the torments of creation with this one. It was July of 1983; I had finished *Valentine Pontifex*, which had turned out to be unexpectedly difficult to write (the first half of 1983 was one of those periods of my life that I'd just as soon not repeat); a few days after the book was done I sat down and wrote 'Multiples' in what was essentially one long take, did a little minor editing, and sent it off to Ellen Datlow of *Omni*, who accepted it right away. They should all be that easy. But in this case (as with 'Amanda and the Alien') I was making use of my own home turf as the setting instead of having to invent some alien world, and the theme of multiple personalities was one I had been thinking about for some time. Characters and plot fell into place in that magical way that makes writers want to get down on their knees and offer thanks. The story felt like a winner to me right away. It was included in the first volume (1983) of Gardner Dozois's annual *Year's Best Science Fiction* anthologies and has had a healthy reprint existence ever since. It also gets me occasional letters from actual multiple-personality people, who want to know if I'm one myself, or married to one. (The answers are No and No — so far as I know.)

A little bragging here, if you don't mind. Having 'Multiples' chosen for one of the best-science-fiction-of-the-year anthologies completed an unusual sweep for me, one of which I'm inordinately proud. There were then three such anthologies — not only Dozois's and Don Wollheim's, but one edited by Terry Carr. I had stories in all three of them for the year of 1983. Other writers have achieved that now and then, when some very strong story was picked by all three editors — but I had a different story in each book. I'm not sure anyone else has ever managed that trick. (I did it again in 1989. That time, though, I managed to get *five* stories into that year's three anthologies. Go ahead, top it if you can!)

* * *

There were mirrors everywhere, making the place a crazyhouse of dizzying refraction: mirrors on the ceiling, mirrors on the walls, mirrors in the angles where the walls met the ceiling and the floor, even little eddies of mirror-dust periodically blown on gusts of air through the room, so that all the bizarre distortions, fracturings and dislocations of image that were bouncing around the place would from time to time coalesce in a shimmering haze of chaos right before your eyes. Coloured globes spun round and round overhead, creating patterns of ricocheting light. It was exactly the way Cleo had expected a multiples club to look.

She had walked up and down the whole Fillmore Street strip from Union to Chestnut and back again for half an hour, peering at this club and that, before finding the courage to go inside one that called itself Skits. Though she had been planning this night for months, she found herself paralysed by fear at the last minute: afraid they would spot her as a fraud the moment she walked in, afraid they would drive her out with jeers and curses and cold mocking laughter. But now that she was within, she felt fine – calm, confident, ready for the time of her life.

There were more women than men in the club, something like a seven-to-three ratio. Hardly anyone seemed to be talking to anyone else: most stood alone in the middle of the floor, staring into the mirrors as though in trance. Their eyes were slits, their jaws were slack, their shoulders slumped forward, their arms dangled. Now and then as some combination of reflections sluiced across their consciousnesses with particular impact they would go taut and jerk and wince as if they had been struck. Their faces would flush, their lips would pull back, their eyes would roll, they would mutter and whisper to themselves; and then after a moment they would slip back into stillness.

Cleo knew what they were doing. They were switching and doubling. Maybe some of the adepts were tripling. Her heart rate picked up. Her throat was very dry. What was the routine here, she wondered? Did you just walk right out on to the floor and plug into the light-patterns, or were you supposed to go to the bar first for a shot or a snort?

She looked towards the bar. A dozen or so customers sitting there, mostly men, a couple of them openly studying her, giving her that new-girl-in-town stare. Cleo returned their gaze evenly, coolly, blankly. Standard-looking men, reasonably attractive, thirtyish or early fortyish, business suits, conventional hair-styles: young lawyers, executives, maybe stockbrokers, successful sorts out for a night's fun, the kind you might run into anywhere. Look at that one, tall, athletic, curly hair, glasses. Faint ironic smile, easy inquiring eyes. Almost professorial. And yet, and yet – behind that smooth intelligent forehead, what strangenesses must teem and boil! How many hidden souls must lurk and jostle! Scary. Tempting.

Irresistible.

Cleo resisted. Take it slow, take it slow. Instead of going to the bar she moved out serenely among the switchers on the floor, found an open space, centred herself, looked towards the mirrors on the far side of the room. Legs apart, feet planted flat, shoulders forward. A turning globe splashed waves of red and violet light, splintered a thousand times over, into her face. *Go. Go. Go. Go.* You are Cleo. You are Judy. You are Vixen. You are Lisa. *Go. Go. Go. Go.* Cascades of iridescence sweeping over the rim of her soul, battering at the walls of her identity. Come, enter, drown me, split me, switch me. You are Cleo and Judy. You are Vixen and Lisa. You are Cleo and Judy and Vixen and Lisa. *Go. Go. Go.*

Her head was spinning. Her eyes were blurring. The room gyrated around her.

Was this it? Was she splitting? Was she switching? Maybe so. Maybe the capacity was there in everyone, even her, and all it took was the lights, the mirror, the ambience, the will. I am many. I am multiple. I am Cleo switching to Vixen. I am Judy and Lisa. I am –

No.

I am Cleo.

I am Cleo.

I am very dizzy and I am getting sick, and I am Cleo and only Cleo, as I have always been.

I am Cleo and only Cleo and I am going to fall down.

'Easy,' he said. 'You OK?'

'Steadying up, I think. Whew!'

'Out-of-towner, eh?'

'Sacramento. How'd you know?'

'Too quick on the floor. Locals all know better. This place has the fastest mirrors in the west. They'll blow you away if you're not careful. You can't just go out there and grab for the big one – you've got to phase yourself in slowly. You sure you're going to be OK?'

'I think so.'

He was the tall man from the bar, the athletic professorial one. She supposed he had caught her before she had actually fallen, since she felt no bruises. His hand rested now against her elbow as he lightly steered her towards a table along the wall.

'What's your now-name?' he asked.

'Judy.'

'I'm Van.'

'Hello, Van.'

'What about a brandy? Steady you up a little more.'

'I don't drink.'

'Never?'

'Vixen does the drinking,' she said. 'Not me.'

'Ah. The old story. She gets the bubbles, you get her hangovers. I have one like that too, only with him it's Hunan food. He absolutely doesn't give a damn what lobster in hot and sour sauce does to my digestive system. I hope you pay her back the way she deserves.'

Cleo smiled and said nothing.

He was watching her closely. Was he interested, or just being polite to someone who was obviously out of her depth in a strange milieu? Interested, she decided. He seemed to have accepted that Vixen stuff at face value.

Be careful now, Cleo warned herself. Trying to pile on convincing-sounding details when you don't really know what you're talking about is a sure way to give yourself away, sooner or later. The thing to do, she knew, was to establish her credentials without working too hard at it, sit back, listen, learn how things really operate among these people.

'What do you do, up there in Sacramento?'

'Nothing fascinating.'

'Poor Judy. Real-estate broker?'

'How'd you guess?'

'Every other woman I meet is a real-estate broker these days. What's Vixen?'

'A lush.'

'Not much of a livelihood in that.'

Cleo shrugged. 'She doesn't need one. The rest of us support her.'

'Real estate and what else?'

She hadn't been sure that multiples etiquette included talking about one's alternate selves. But she had come prepared. 'Lisa's a landscape architect. Cleo's into software. We all keep busy.'

'Lisa ought to meet Chuck. He's a demon horticulturalist. Partner in a plant-rental outfit – you know, huge dracaenas and philodendrons for offices, so much per month, take them away when they start looking sickly. Lisa and Chuck could talk palms and bromeliads and cacti all night.'

'We should introduce them, then.'

'We should, yes.'

'But first we have to introduce Van and Judy.'

'And then maybe Van and Cleo,' he said.

She felt a tremor of fear. Had he found her out so soon? 'Why Van and Cleo? Cleo's not here right now. This is Judy you're talking to.'

'Easy. Easy!'

But she was unable to halt. 'I can't deliver Cleo to you just like that, you know. She does as she pleases.'

'Easy,' he said. 'All I meant was, Van and Cleo have something in common. Van's into software too.'

Cleo relaxed. With a little laugh she said, 'Oh, not you too! Isn't everybody, nowadays? But I thought you were something in the academic world. A professor, perhaps.'

'I am. At Cal.'

'Software?'

'In a manner of speaking. Linguistics. Metalinguistics, actually. My field's the language of language – the basic subsets, the neural co-ordinates of communication, the underlying programs our brains use, the operating systems. Mind as computer, computer as mind. I can get very boring about it.'

'I don't find the mind a boring subject.'

'I don't find real estate a boring subject. Talk to me about second mortgages and triple-net leases.'

'Talk to me about Chomsky and Benjamin Whorf,' she said.

His eyes widened. 'You've heard of Whorf?'

199

'I majored in comparative linguistics. That was before real estate.'

'Just my lousy luck,' he said. 'I get a chance to find out what's hot in the shopping-centre market and she wants to talk about Whorf and Chomsky.'

'I thought every other woman you met these days was a real-estate broker. Talk to them about shopping centres.'

'They all want to talk about Whorf and Chomsky.'

'Poor Van.'

'Yes. Poor Van.' Then he leaned forward and said, his tone softening, 'You know, I shouldn't have made that crack about Van meeting Cleo. That was very tacky of me.'

'It's OK, Van. I didn't take it seriously.'

'You seemed to. You were very upset.'

'Well, maybe at first. But then I saw you were just horsing around.'

'I still shouldn't have said it. You were absolutely right: this is Judy's time now. Cleo's not here, and that's just fine. It's Judy I want to get to know.'

'You will,' she said. 'But you can meet Cleo too, and Lisa, and Vixen. I'll introduce you to the whole crew. I don't mind.'

'You're sure of that?'

'Sure.'

'Some of us are very secretive about our alters.'

'Are you?' Cleo asked.

'Sometimes. Sometimes not.'

'I don't mind. Maybe you'll meet some of mine tonight.' She glanced towards the centre of the floor. 'I think I've steadied up, now. I'd like to try the mirrors again.'

'Switching?'

'Doubling,' she said. 'I'd like to bring Vixen up. She can do the drinking, and I can do the talking. Will it bother you if she's here too?'

'Not unless she's a sloppy drunk. Or a mean one.'

'I can keep control of her, when we're doubling. Come on: take me through the mirrors.'

'You be careful, now. San Francisco mirrors aren't like Sacramento ones. You've already discovered that.'

'I'll watch my step this time. Shall we go out there?'

'Sure,' he said.

As they began to move out on to the floor a slender T-shirted man of about thirty came towards them. Shaven scalp, bushy moustache, medallions, boots. Very San Francisco, very gay. He frowned at Cleo and stared straightforwardly at Van.

'Ned?' he said.

Van scowled and shook his head. 'No. Not now.'

'Sorry. Very sorry. I should have realized.' The shaven-headed man flushed and hurried away.

'Let's go,' Van said to Cleo.

This time she found it easier to keep her balance. Knowing that he was nearby helped. But still the waves of refracted light came pounding in, pounding in, pounding in. The assault was total: remorseless, implacable, overwhelming. She had to struggle against the throbbing in her chest, the hammering in her temples, the wobbliness of her knees. And this was pleasure, for them? This was a supreme delight?

But they were multiples and she was only Cleo, and that, she knew, made all the difference. She seemed to be able to fake it well enough. She could make up a Judy, a Lisa, a Vixen, assign little corners of her personality to each, give them voices of their own, facial expressions, individual identities. Standing before her mirror at home, she had managed to convince herself. She might even be able to convince him. But as the swirling lights careened off the infinities of interlocking mirrors and came slaloming into the gateways of her reeling soul, the dismal fear began to rise in her that she could never truly be one of these people after all, however skilfully she imitated them in their intricacies.

Was it so? Was she doomed always to stand outside their irresistible world, hopelessly peering in? Too soon to tell – much too soon, she thought, to admit defeat –

At least she didn't fall down. She took the punishment of the mirrors as long as she could stand it, and then, not waiting for him to leave the floor, she made her way – carefully, carefully, walking a tightrope over an abyss – to the bar. When her head had begun to stop spinning she ordered a drink, and she sipped it cautiously. She could feel the alcohol extending itself inch by inch into her bloodstream. It calmed her. On the floor, Van stood in trance, occasionally quivering in a sudden convulsive way for a fraction of a second. He was doubling, she knew: bringing up one of his other identities. That was the main thing that multiples came to these clubs to do. No longer were all their various identities forced to dwell in rigorously separated compartments of their minds. With the aid of the mirrors, of the lights, the skilled ones were able briefly to fuse two or even three of their selves into something even more complex. When he comes back here, she thought, he will be Van plus X. And I must pretend to be Judy plus Vixen.

She readied herself for that. Judy was easy: Judy was mostly the real Cleo, the real-estate woman from Sacramento, with Cleo's notion of what it was like to be a multiple added in. And Vixen? Cleo imagined her to be about twenty-three, a Los Angeles girl, a one-time child tennis star who had broken her ankle in a dumb prank and had never recovered her game afterwards, and who had taken up drinking to ease the pain and loss. Uninhibited, unpredictable, untidy, fiery, fierce: all the things that Cleo was not. Could she be Vixen? She took a deep gulp of her drink and put on the Vixen-face: eyes hard and glittering, cheek-muscles clenched.

Van was leaving the floor now. His way of moving seemed to have changed: he was stiff, almost awkward, his shoulders held high, his elbows jutting oddly. He looked so different that she wondered whether he was still Van at all.

'You didn't switch, did you?'

'Doubled. Paul's with me now.'

'Paul?'

'Paul's from Texas. Geologist, terrific poker game, plays the guitar.' Van smiled and it was like a shifting of gears. In a deeper, broader voice he said, 'And I sing real good too, ma'am. Van's jealous of that, because he can't sing worth beans. Are you ready for a refill?'

'You bet,' Cleo said, sounding sloppy, sounding Vixenish.

His apartment was nearby, a cheerful airy sprawling place in the Marina district. The segmented nature of his life was immediately obvious: the prints and paintings on the walls looked as though they had been chosen by four or five different people, one of whom ran heavily towards vivid scenes of sunrise over the Grand Canyon, another to Picasso and Miró, someone else to delicate impressionist views of Parisian flower-markets. A sun-room contained the biggest and healthiest houseplants Cleo had ever seen. Another room was stacked high with technical books and scholarly journals, a third was set up as a home gymnasium equipped with three or four gleaming exercise machines. Some of the rooms were fastidiously tidy, some impossibly chaotic. Some of the furniture was stark and austere, and some was floppy and overstuffed. She kept expecting to find room-mates wandering around. But there was no-one here but Van. And Paul.

Paul fixed the drinks. Paul played soft guitar music and told her gaudy tales of prospecting for rare earths on the West Texas mesas. Paul sang something bawdy-sounding in Spanish, and Cleo, putting on her Vixen-voice, chimed in on the choruses, deliberately off key. But then Paul went away and it was Van who sat close beside her on the couch, talking quietly. He wanted to know things about Judy, and he told her a little about Van, and no other selves came into the conversation. She was sure that that was intentional. They stayed up very late. Paul came back, towards the end of the evening, to tell a few jokes and sing a soft late-night song, but when they went into the bedroom she was with Van. Of that she was completely certain.

And when she woke in the morning she was alone.

She felt a surge of confusion and dislocation, remembered after a moment where she was and how she had happened to be here, sat up, blinked. Went into the bathroom and scooped a handful of water over her face. Without bothering to dress, went padding around the apartment looking for Van.

She found him in the exercise room, using the rowing machine, but he wasn't Van. He was dressed in tight jeans and a white T-shirt, and somehow he looked younger, leaner, jauntier. There were fine beads of sweat along his forehead, but he did not seem to be breathing hard. He gave her a cool, distantly appraising, wholly asexual look, as though she were a total stranger but that it was not in the least unusual for an unknown naked woman to materialize in the house and he was altogether undisturbed by it, and said 'Good morning. I'm Ned. Pleased to know you.' His voice was higher than Van's, much higher than Paul's, and he had an odd over-precise way of shaping each syllable.

Flustered, suddenly self-conscious and wishing she had put her clothes on before leaving the bedroom, she folded one arm over her breasts, though her nakedness did not seem to matter to him at all. 'I'm – Judy. I came with Van.'

'Yes, I know. I saw the entry in our book.' Smoothly, effortlessly, he pulled on the oars of the rowing machine, leaned back, pushed forward. 'Help yourself to anything in the fridge,' he said. 'Make yourself entirely at home. Van left a note for you in the kitchen.'

She stared at him: his hands, his mouth, his long muscular arms. She remembered his touch, his kisses, the feel of his skin against hers. And now this complete indifference. No. Not *his* kisses, not *his* touch. Van's. And Van was not here now. There was a different tenant in Van's body, someone she did not know in any way and who had no memories of last night's embraces. *I saw the entry in our book.* They left memos for each other. Cleo shivered. She had known what to expect, more or less, but experiencing it was very different from reading about it. She felt almost as though she had fallen in among beings from another planet.

But this is what you wanted, she thought. Isn't it? The intricacy, the mystery, the unpredictability, the sheer weirdness? A little cruise through an alien world, because her own had become so stale, so narrow, so cramped. And here she was. *Good morning, I'm Ned. Pleased to know you.*

Van's note was clipped to the refrigerator by a little yellow magnet shaped like a lady-bug. *Dinner tonight at Chez Michel? You and me and who knows who else. Call me.*

That was the beginning. She saw him every night for the next ten days. Generally they met at some three-star restaurant, had a lingering intimate dinner, went back to his apartment. One mild clear evening they drove out to the beach and watched the waves breaking on Seal Rock until well past midnight. Another time they wandered through Fisherman's Wharf and somehow acquired three bags of tacky souvenirs.

Van was his primary name – she saw it on his credit card at dinner one night – and that seemed to be his main identity, too, though she knew there were plenty of others. At first he was reticent about that, but on the fourth or fifth night he told her that he had nine major selves and sixteen minor ones, some of which remained submerged years at a stretch. Besides Paul, the geologist, and Chuck, who was into horticulture, and Ned, the gay one, Cleo heard about Nat the stock-market plunger – he was fifty and fat, and made a fortune every week, and liked to divide his time between Las Vegas and Miami Beach – and Henry, the poet, who was very shy and never liked anyone to read his work, and Dick, who was studying to be an actor, and Hal, who once taught law at Harvard, and Dave, the yachtsman, and Nicholas, the card-sharp – and then there were all the fragmentary ones, some of whom didn't have names, only a funny way of speaking or a little routine they liked to act out –

She got to see very little of his other selves, though. Like all multiples, he was troubled occasionally by involuntary switching, and one night he became Hal while they were making love, and another time he turned into Dave for an hour, and there were momentary flashes of Henry and Nicholas. Cleo perceived it right away whenever one of those switches came: his voice, his movements, his entire manner and personality changed immediately. Those were startling, exciting moments for her, offering a strange exhilaration. But generally his control was very good, and he stayed Van, as if he felt some strong need to experience her as Van and Van alone. Once in a while he doubled, bringing up Paul to play the guitar for him and sing, or Dick to recite sonnets, but when he did that the Van identity always remained present and dominant. It appeared that he was able to double at will, without the aid of mirrors and lights, at least some of the time. He had been an active and functioning multiple as long as he could remember – since childhood, perhaps even since birth – and he had devoted himself through the years to the task of gaining mastery over his divided mind.

All the aspects of him that she came to meet had basically attractive personalities: they were energetic, stable, purposeful men, who enjoyed life and seemed to know how to go about getting what they wanted. Though they were very different people, she could trace them all back readily enough to the underlying Van from whom, so she thought, they had all split off. The one puzzle was Nat, the market operator. It was hard for Cleo to imagine what he was like when he was Nat – sleazy and coarse, yes, but how did he manage to make himself look fifteen years older and forty pounds heavier? Maybe it was all done with facial expressions and posture. But she never got to see Nat. And gradually she realized it was an oversimplification to think of Paul and Dick and Ned and the others as mere extensions of Van into different modes. Van by himself was just as incomplete as the others. He was just one of many that had evolved in parallel, each one autonomous, each one only a fragment of the whole. Though Van might have control of the shared body a greater portion of the time, he still had no idea what any of his alternate selves were up to while they were in command, and like them he had to depend on guesses and fancy footwork and such notes and messages as they bothered to leave behind in order to keep track of events that occurred outside his conscious awareness. 'The only one who knows everything is Michael. He's seven years old, smart as a whip, keeps in touch with all of us all the time.'

'Your memory trace,' Cleo said.

Van nodded. All multiples, she knew, had one alter with full awareness of the doings of all the other personalities – usually a child, an observer who sat back deep in the mind and played its own games and emerged only when necessary to fend off some crisis that threatened the stability of the entire group. 'He's just informed us that he's Ethiopian,' Van said. 'So every two or three weeks we go across to Oakland to an Ethiopian restaurant that he likes, and he flirts with the waitresses in Amharic.'

'That can't be too terrible a chore. I'm told Ethiopians are very beautiful people.'

'Absolutely. But they think it's all a big joke, and Michael doesn't know how to pick up women, anyway. He's only seven, you know. So Van doesn't get anything out of it except some exercise in comparative linguistics and a case of indigestion the next day. Ethiopian food is the spiciest in the world. I can't *stand* spicy food.'

'Neither can I,' she said. 'But Lisa loves it. Especially hot Mexican things. But nobody ever said sharing a body is easy, did they?'

She knew she had to be careful in questioning Van about the

way his life as a multiple worked. She was supposed to be a multiple herself, after all. But she made use of her Sacramento background as justification for her areas of apparent ignorance of multiple customs and the everyday mechanics of multiple life. Though she too had known she was a multiple since childhood, she said, she had grown up outside the climate of acceptance of the divided personality that prevailed in San Francisco, where an active subculture of multiples had existed openly for years. In her isolated existence, unaware that there were a great many others of her kind, she had at first regarded herself as the victim of a serious mental disorder. It was only recently, she told him, that she had come to understand the overwhelming advantages of life as a multiple: the richness, the complexity, the fullness of talents and experiences that a divided mind was free to enjoy. That was why she had come to San Francisco. That was why she listened so eagerly to all that he was telling her about himself.

She was cautious, too, in manifesting her own multiple identities. She wished she did not have to be pretending to have other selves. But they had to be brought forth now and again, Cleo felt, if only by way of maintaining his interest in her. Multiples were notoriously indifferent to singletons, she knew. They found them bland, overly simple, two-dimensional. They wanted the excitement that came with embracing one person and discovering another, or two or three. So she gave him Lisa, she gave him Vixen, she gave him the Judy-who-was-Cleo and the Cleo-who-was-someone-else, and she slipped from one to another in a seemingly involuntary and unexpected way, often when they were in bed.

Lisa was calm, controlled, strait-laced. She was totally shocked when she found herself, between one eye-blink and the next, in the arms of a strange man. 'Who are you? – where am I? – ' she blurted, rolling away, pulling herself into a foetal ball.

'I'm Judy's friend,' Van said.

She stared bleakly at him. 'So she's up to her tricks again. I should have figured it out faster.'

He looked pained, embarrassed, terribly solicitous. She let him wonder for a moment or two whether he would have to take her back to her hotel right here in the middle of the night. And then she allowed a mischievous smile to cross Lisa's face, allowed Lisa's outraged modesty to subside, allowed Lisa to relent and relax, allowed Lisa to purr –

'Well, as long as we're here already – what did you say your name was?'

He liked that. He liked Vixen, too – wild, sweaty, noisy, a moaner, a gasper, a kicker and thrasher who dragged him down on to the floor and went rolling over and over with him. She thought he liked Cleo, too, though that was harder to tell, because Cleo's style was aloof, serious, baroque, inscrutable. She would switch quickly from one to another, sometimes running through all four in the course of an hour. Wine, she said, induced quick switching in her. She let him know that she had a few other identities, too, fragmentary and submerged, and hinted that they were troubled, deeply neurotic, almost self-destructive: they were under control, she said, and would not erupt to cause woe for him, but she left the possibility hovering over them, to add spice to the relationship and plausibility to her role.

It seemed to be working. His pleasure in her company was evident, and the more they were together the stronger the bond between them became. She was beginning to indulge in pleasant little fantasies of moving down here permanently from Sacramento, renting an apartment somewhere near his, perhaps even moving in with him – though that would surely be a strange and challenging life, for she would be living with Paul and Ned and Chuck and all the rest of the crew too, but how wondrous, how electrifying –

Then on the tenth day he seemed uncharacteristically tense and sombre, and she asked him what was bothering him, and he evaded her, and she pressed, and finally he said, 'Do you really want to know?'

'Of course.'

'It bothers me that you aren't real, Judy.'

She caught her breath. 'What the hell do you mean by that?'

'You know what I mean,' he said, quietly, sadly. 'Don't try to pretend any longer. There's no point in it.'

It was like a jolt in the ribs. She turned away and stared at the wall and was silent a long while, wondering what to say. Just when everything was going so well, just when she was beginning to believe she had carried off the masquerade successfully –

'So you know?' she asked in a small voice.

'Of course I know. I knew right away.'

She was trembling. 'How could you tell?'

'A thousand ways. When we switch, we *change*. The voice. The eyes. The muscular tensions. The grammatical habits. The brain waves, even. An evoked-potential test shows it. Flash a light in my eyes and I'll give off a certain brain-wave pattern, and Ned will give off another, and Chuck still another. You and Lisa and Cleo and Vixen would all be the same. Multiples aren't actors, Judy. Multiples are separate minds within the same brain. That's a matter of scientific fact. You were just acting. You were doing it very well, but you couldn't possibly have fooled me.'

'You let me make an idiot of myself, then.'

'No.'

'Why did you – how could you – '

'I saw you walk in, that first night at the club, and you caught me right away. And then I watched you go out on the floor and fall apart, and I knew you couldn't be multiple, and I wondered, what the hell's she doing here, and then I went over to you, and I was hooked. I felt something I haven't ever felt before. Does that sound like the standard old malarkey? But it's true, Judy. You're the first singleton woman that's ever interested me.'

'Why?'

He shook his head. 'Something about you – your intensity, your alertness, maybe even your eagerness to pretend you were a multiple – I don't know. I was caught. I was caught hard. And it's been a wonderful week and a half. I mean that. Wonderful.'

'Until you got bored.'

'I'm not bored with you, Judy.'

'Cleo. That's my real name, my singleton name. There is no Judy.'

'Cleo,' he said, as if measuring the word with his lips.

'So you aren't bored with me even though there's only one of me. That's marvellous. That's tremendously flattering. That's the best thing I've heard all day. I guess I should go now, Van. It *is* Van, isn't it?'

209

'Don't talk that way.'

'How do you want me to talk? I fascinated you, you fascinated me, we played our little games with each other, and now it's over. I wasn't real, but you did your best. We both did our bests. But I'm only a singleton woman, and you can't be satisfied with that. Not for long. For a night, a week, two weeks, maybe. Sooner or later you'll want the real thing, and I can't be the real thing for you. So long, Van.'

'No.'

'No?'

'Don't go.'

'What's the sense of staying?'

'I want you to stay.'

'I'm a singleton, Van.'

'You don't have to be,' he said.

The therapist's name was Burkhalter and his office was in one of the Embarcadero towers, and to the San Francisco multiples community he was very close to being a deity. His speciality was electrophysiological integration, with specific application to multiple-personality disorders. Those who carried within themselves dark and diabolical selves that threatened the stability of the group went to him to have those selves purged, or at least contained. Those who sought to have latent selves that were submerged beneath more outgoing personalities brought forward into healthy functional state went to him also. Those whose life as a multiple was a torment of schizoid confusions instead of a richly rewarding contrapuntal symphony gave themselves to Dr Burkhalter to be healed, and in time they were. And in recent years he had begun to develop techniques for what he called personality augmentation. Van called it 'driving the wedge'.

'He can turn a singleton into a multiple?' Cleo asked in amazement.

'If the potential is there. You know that it's partly genetic: the structure of a multiple's brain is fundamentally different from a singleton's. The hardware just isn't the same, the cerebral wiring. And then, if the right stimulus comes along, usually in childhood, usually but not necessarily traumatic, the splitting takes place, the separate identities begin to establish their territories. But much of the time multiplicity is never generated, and you walk around with the capacity to be a whole horde of selves and never know it.'

'Is there reason to think I'm like that?'

He shrugged. 'It's worth finding out. If he detects the predisposition, he has effective ways of inducing separation. Driving the wedge, you see? You do *want* to be a multiple, don't you, Cleo?'

'Oh, yes, Van. Yes!'

Burkhalter wasn't sure about her. He taped electrodes to her head, flashed bright lights in her eyes, gave her verbal association tests, ran four or five different kinds of electroencephalograph studies, and still he was uncertain. 'It is not a black-and-white matter,' he said several times, frowning, scowling. He was a multiple himself, but three of his selves were psychiatrists, so there was never any real problem about his office hours. Cleo wondered if he ever went to himself for a second opinion. After a week of testing she was sure that she must be a hopeless case, an intractable singleton, but Burkhalter surprised her by concluding that it was worth the attempt. 'At the very worst,' he said, 'we will experience spontaneous fusing within a few days, and you will be no worse off than you are now. But if we succeed – ah, if we succeed –!'

His clinic was across the bay in a town called Moraga. She checked in on a Friday afternoon, spent two days undergoing further neurological and psychological tests, then three days taking medication. 'Simply an anti-convulsant,' the nurse explained cheerily. 'To build up your tolerance.'

'Tolerance for what?' Cleo asked.

'The birth trauma,' she said. 'New selves will be coming forth, and it can be uncomfortable for a little while.'

The treatment began on Thursday. Electroshock, drugs, electroshock again. She was heavily sedated. It felt like a long dream, but there was no pain. Van visited her every day. Chuck came too, bringing her two potted orchids in bloom, and Paul sang to her, and even Ned paid her a call. But it was hard for her to maintain a conversation with any of them. She heard voices much of the time. She felt feverish and dislocated, and at times she was sure she was floating eight or ten inches above the bed. Gradually that sensation subsided, but there were others nearly as odd. The voices remained. She learned how to hold conversations with them.

In the second week she was not allowed to have visitors. That didn't matter. She had plenty of company even when she was alone.

Then Van came for her. 'They're going to let you go home today,' he said. 'How are you doing, Cleo?'

'I'm Noreen,' she said.

There were five of her, apparently. That was what Van said. She had no way of knowing, because when they were dominant she was gone – not merely asleep, but *gone*, perceiving nothing. But he showed her notes that they wrote, in handwritings that she did not recognize and indeed could barely read, and he played tapes of her other voices, Noreen a deep contralto, Nanette high and breathy, Katya hard and rough New York, and the last one, who had not yet announced her name, a stagy voluptuous campy siren-voice.

She did not leave his apartment the first few days, and then began going out for short trips, always with Van or one of his alters close beside. She felt convalescent. A kind of hangover from the various drugs had dulled her reflexes and made it difficult for her to cope with the traffic, and also there was the fear that she would undergo a switching while she was out. Whenever that happened it came without warning, and when she returned to awareness afterwards she felt a sharp bewildering discontinuity of memory, not knowing how it was that she suddenly found herself in Ghiradelli Square or Golden Gate Park or wherever it was that the other self had taken their body.

But she was happy. And Van was happy with her. As they strolled hand in hand through the cool evenings she turned to him now and again and saw the warmth of his smile, the glow of his eyes. One night in the second week when they were out together he switched to Chuck – Cleo saw him change, and knew it was Chuck coming on, for now she always knew right away which identity had taken over – and he said, 'You've had a marvellous effect on him, Cleo. None of us has ever seen him like this before – so contented, so fulfilled – '

'I hope it lasts, Chuck.'

'Of course it'll last! Why on earth shouldn't it last?'

It didn't. Towards the end of the third week Cleo noticed that there hadn't been any entries in her memo book from Noreen for several days. That in itself was nothing alarming: an alter might choose to submerge for days, weeks, even months at a time. But was it likely that Noreen, so new to the world, would remain out of sight so long? Lin-lin, the little Chinese girl who had evolved in the second week and was Cleo's memory trace, reported that Noreen had gone away. A few days later an identity named Mattie came and went within three hours, like something bubbling up out of a troubled sea. Then Nanette disappeared, leaving Cleo with no-one but her nameless breathy-voiced alter and Lin-lin. She knew she was fusing again. The wedges that Dr Burkhalter had driven into her soul were not holding; her mind insisted on oneness, and was integrating itself; she was reverting to the singleton state.

'They're all gone,' she told Van disconsolately.

'I know. I've been watching it happen.'

'Is there anything we can do? Should I go back to Burkhalter?'

She saw the pain in his eyes. 'It won't do any good,' he said. 'He told me the chances were about three to one this would happen. A month, he figured – that was about the best we could hope for. And we've had our month.'

'I'd better go, Van.'

'Don't say that.'

'No?'

'I love you, Cleo.'

'You won't,' she said. 'Not for much longer.'

He tried to argue with her, to tell her that it didn't matter to him that she was a singleton, that one Cleo was worth a whole raft of alters, that he would learn to adapt to life with a singleton woman. He could not bear the thought of her leaving now. So she stayed: a week, two weeks, three. They ate at their favourite restaurants. They strolled hand in hand through the cool evenings. They talked of Chomsky and Whorf and even of shopping centres. When he was gone and Paul or Chuck or Hal or Dave was there she went places with them, if they wanted her to. Once she went to a movie with Ned, and when towards the end he felt himself starting to switch she put her arm around him and held him until he regained control, so that he could see how the movie finished.

But it was no good, really. She sensed the strain in him. He wanted something richer than she could offer him: the switching, the doubling, the complex undertones and overtones of other personalities resonating beyond the shores of consciousness. She could not give him that. And though he insisted he didn't miss it, he was like one who has voluntarily blindfolded himself in order to keep a blind woman company. She knew she could not ask him to live like that for ever.

And so one afternoon when Van was somewhere else she packed her things and said goodbye to Paul, who gave her a hug and wept a little with her, and she went back to Sacramento. 'Tell him not to call,' she said. 'A clean break's the best.' She had been in San Francisco two months, and it was as though those two months were the only months of her life that had had any colour in them, and all the rest had been lived in tones of grey.

There had been a man in the real-estate office who had been telling her for a couple of years that they were meant for each other. Cleo had always been friendly enough to him – they had done a few skiing weekends in Tahoe the winter before, they had gone to Hawaii once, they had driven down to San Diego – but she had never felt anything particular when she was with him. A week after her return, she phoned him and suggested that they drive out up north to the redwood country for a few days together. When they came back, she moved into the handsome condominium he had just outside town.

It was hard to find anything wrong with him. He was good-natured and attractive, he was successful, he read books and liked good movies, he enjoyed hiking and rafting and backpacking, he even talked of driving down into the city during the opera season to take in a performance or two. He was getting towards the age where he was thinking about marriage and a family. He seemed very fond of her.

But he was flat, she thought. Flat as a cardboard cut-out: a singleton, a one-brain, a no-switch. There was only one of him, and there always would be. It was hardly his fault, she knew. But she couldn't settle for someone who had only two dimensions.

A terrible restlessness went roaring through her every evening, and she could not possibly tell him what was troubling her.

On a drizzly afternoon in early November she packed a suitcase and drove down to San Francisco. She arrived about six-thirty, and checked into one of the Lombard Street motels, and showered and changed and walked over to Fillmore Street. Cautiously she explored the strip from Chestnut down to Union, from Union back to Chestnut. The thought of running into Van terrified her. Probably she would, sooner or later, she knew: but not tonight, she prayed. Not tonight. She went past Skits, did not go in, stopped outside a club called Big Mama, shook her head, finally entered one called the Side Effect. Mostly women inside, as usual, but a few men at the bar, not too bad-looking. No sign of Van. She bought herself a drink and casually struck up a conversation with the man to her left, a short curly-haired artistic-looking type, about forty.

'You come here often?' he asked.

'First time. I've usually gone to Skits.'

'I think I remember seeing you there. Or maybe not.'

She smiled. 'What's your now-name?'

'Sandy. Yours?'

Cleo drew her breath down deep into her lungs. She felt a kind of lightheadedness beginning to swirl behind her eyes. *Is this what you want?* she asked herself. *Yes. Yes. This is what you want.*

'Melinda,' she said.

Against Babylon

Another easy one. (The gods owed me a few, after the wearying months of 'Tourist Trade' and *Pontifex.*)

Though Northern California is where I live – and the distance that separates San Francisco from Los Angeles is 400 miles, which is about the distance between Rome and Budapest – I've carried on an intense love–hate relationship with the southern half of my immense state for more than thirty years. During the 1970s and 1980s I must have made a hundred trips to Los Angeles; I know the place like a native, blithely buzzing around confidently on routes unknown even to some of the locals. Yet I've never wanted to live there, despite my envy of the warm winters and my admiration for the districts of astonishing beauty that one finds interspersed among the parts that are of astonishing ugliness. If I'm away from Los Angeles too long, I miss it in a way that is the next thing to homesickness; if I'm down there for more than four or five days at a stretch, I yearn for the blue skies and sweet air of my own region. And so I oscillate from one end of the pendulum to the other, and probably always will.

'Against Babylon' reflects my close-range observations of the colossus of the south over many decades, my horrified fascination for the place, and my uneasiness over certain of the tawdry aspects of the California mentality, both southern and northern. Once again, as with the other California stories in this book, the work went swiftly and relatively easily – I had had a long holiday from writing during August, September and October of 1983, which helped – and acceptance (from Ellen Datlow again, at *Omni*) came without complications. This story also made it into the Dozois *Year's Best SF* 1986 volume, and was picked as well for Don Wollheim's anthology covering the same year.

* * *

Carmichael flew in from New Mexico that morning and the first thing they told him when he put his little plane down at Burbank was that fires were burning out of control all around the Los Angeles basin. He was needed bad, they told him. It was late October, the height of the brush-fire season in Southern California, and a hot hard dry wind was blowing out of the desert, and the last time it had rained was the fifth of April. He phoned the district supervisor right away and the district supervisor told him, 'Get your arse out here on the line double fast, Mike.'

'Where do you want me?'

'The worst one's just above Chatsworth. We've got planes loaded and ready to go out of Van Nuys Airport.'

'I need time to pee and to phone my wife,' Carmichael said. 'I'll be in Van Nuys in fifteen, OK?'

He was so tired that he could feel it in his teeth. It was nine in the morning and he'd been flying since half past four, and it had been rough all the way, getting pushed around by that same fierce wind out of the heart of the continent that was threatening now to fan the flames in LA. At this moment all he wanted was home and shower and Cindy and bed. But Carmichael didn't regard firefighting work as optional. This time of year, the whole crazy city could go in one big firestorm. There were times he almost wished that it would. He hated this smoggy tawdry Babylon of a city, its endless tangle of freeways, the strange-looking houses, the filthy air, the thick choking glossy foliage everywhere, the drugs, the booze, the divorces, the laziness, the sleaziness, the porno shops and the naked-encounter parlours and the massage joints, the weird people wearing their weird clothes and driving their weird cars and cutting their hair in weird ways. There was a cheapness, a trashiness, about everything here, he thought. Even the mansions and the fancy restaurants were that way: hollow, like slick movie sets. He sometimes felt that the trashiness bothered him more than the out-and-out evil. If you kept sight of your own values you could do battle with evil, but trashiness slipped up around you and infiltrated your soul without your even knowing it. He hoped that his sojourn in Los Angeles was not doing that to him. He came from the Valley, and what he meant by the Valley was the great San Joaquin, out behind Bakersfield, and not the little cluttered

San Fernando Valley they had here. But LA was Cindy's city and Cindy loved LA and he loved Cindy, and for Cindy's sake he had lived here seven years, up in Laurel Canyon amidst the lush green shrubbery, and for seven Octobers in a row he had gone out to dump chemical retardants on the annual brush-fires, to save the Angelenos from their own idiotic carelessness. You had to accept your responsibilities, Carmichael believed.

The phone rang seven times at the home number before he hung up. Then he tried the little studio where Cindy made her jewellery, but she didn't answer there either, and it was too early to call her at the gallery. That bothered him, not being able to say hello to her right away after his three-day absence, and no likely chance for it now for another eight or ten hours. But there was nothing he could do about that.

As soon as he was aloft again he could see the fire not far to the north-west, a greasy black column against the pale sky. And when he stepped from his plane a few minutes later at Van Nuys he felt the blast of sudden heat. The temperature had been in the mid-eighties at Burbank, damned well hot enough for nine in the morning, but here it was over a hundred. He heard the distant roar of flames, the popping and crackling of burning underbrush, the peculiar whistling sound of dry grass catching fire.

The airport looked like a combat centre. Planes were coming and going with lunatic frenzy, and they were lunatic planes, too, antiques of every sort, forty and fifty years old and even older, converted B-17 Flying Fortresses and DC-3s and a Douglas Invader and, to Carmichael's astonishment, a Ford Trimotor from the 1930s that had been hauled, maybe, out of some movie studio's collection. Some were equipped with tanks that held fire-retardant chemicals, some were water-pumpers, some were mappers with infra-red and electronic scanning equipment glistening on their snouts. Harried-looking men and women ran back and forth, shouting into CB handsets, supervising the loading process. Carmichael found his way to Operations HQ, which was full of haggard people staring into computer screens. He knew most of them from other years. They knew him.

One of the dispatchers said, 'We've got a DC-3 waiting for you. You'll dump retardants along this arc, from Ybarra Canyon eastwards to Horse Flats. The fire's in the Santa Susana foothills and so far the wind's from the east, but if it shifts to northerly it's going to take out everything from Chatsworth to Granada Hills, and right on down to Ventura Boulevard. And that's only *this* fire.'

'How many are there?'

The dispatcher tapped his keyboard. The map of the San Fernando Valley that had been showing disappeared and was replaced by one of the entire Los Angeles basin. Carmichael stared. Three great scarlet streaks indicated fire zones: this one along the Santa Susanas, another nearly as big way off to the east in the grasslands north of the 210 Freeway around Glendora or San Dimas, and a third down in eastern Orange County, back of Anaheim Hills. 'Ours is the big one so far,' the dispatcher said. 'But these other two are only about forty miles apart, and if they should join up somehow – '

'Yeah,' Carmichael said. A single wall of fire running along the whole eastern rim of the basin, maybe – with Santa Ana winds blowing, carrying sparks westwards across Pasadena, across downtown LA, across Hollywood, across Beverly Hills, all the way to the coast, to Venice, Santa Monica, Malibu. He shivered. Laurel Canyon would go. Everything would go. Worse than Sodom and Gomorrah, worse than the fall of Nineveh. Nothing but ashes for hundreds of miles. 'Jesus,' he said. 'Everybody scared silly of Russian nukes, and three carloads of dumb kids tossing cigarettes can do the job just as easily.'

'But this wasn't cigarettes, Mike,' the dispatcher said.

'No? What then, arson?'

'You haven't heard.'

'I've been in New Mexico the last three days.'

'You're the only one in the world who hasn't heard, then.'

'For Christ's sake, heard what?'

'About the E-Ts,' said the dispatcher wearily. 'They started the fires. Three spaceships landing at six this morning in three different corners of the LA basin. The heat of their engines ignited the dry grass.'

Carmichael did not smile. 'You've got one weird sense of humour, man.'

The dispatcher said, 'You think I'm joking?'

'Spaceships? From another world?'

'With critters fifteen feet high on board,' the dispatcher

at the next computer said. 'Tim's not kidding. They're out walking around on the freeways right this minute. Fifteen feet high, Mike.'

'Men from Mars?'

'Nobody knows where the hell they're from.'

'Jesus,' Carmichael said. 'Jesus Christ God.'

Wild updraughts from the blaze buffeted the plane as he took it aloft, and gave him a few bad moments. But he moved easily and automatically to gain control, pulling the moves out of the underground territories of his nervous system. It was essential, he believed, to have the moves in your fingers, your shoulders, your thighs, rather than in the conscious realms of your brain. Consciousness could get you a long way, but ultimately you had to work out of the underground territories or you were dead.

He felt the plane responding and managed a grin. DC-3s were tough old birds. He loved flying them, though the youngest of them had been manufactured before he was born. He loved flying anything. Flying wasn't what Carmichael did for a living – he didn't actually do anything for a living, not any more – but flying was what he did. There were months when he spent more time in the air than on the ground, or so it seemed to him, because the hours he spent on the ground often slid by unnoticed, while time in the air was heightened, intensified, magnified.

He swung south over Encino and Tarzana before heading up across Canoga Park and Chatsworth into the fire zone. A fine haze of ash masked the sun. Looking down, he could see the tiny houses, the tiny blue swimming pools, the tiny people scurrying about, desperately trying to hose down their roofs before the flames arrived. So many houses, so many people, filling every inch of space between the sea and the desert, and now it was all in jeopardy. The southbound lanes of Topanga Canyon Boulevard were as jammed with cars, here in mid-morning, as the Hollywood Freeway at rush hour. Where were they all going? Away from the fire, yes. Towards the coast, it seemed. Maybe some television preacher had told them there was an ark sitting out there in the Pacific, waiting to carry them to safety while God rained brimstone down on Los Angeles. Maybe there really was. In Los Angeles anything was possible. Invaders from space walking around on the freeways, even. Jesus. Jesus. Carmichael hardly knew how to begin thinking about that.

He wondered where Cindy was, what *she* was thinking about it. Most likely she found it very funny. Cindy had a wonderful ability to be amused by things. There was a line of poetry she liked to quote, from that Roman, Virgil: a storm is rising, the ship has sprung a leak, there's a whirlpool to one side and sea monsters on the other, and the captain turns to his men and says, 'One day perhaps we'll look back and laugh even at all this.' That was Cindy's way, Carmichael thought. The Santa Anas are blowing and three big brush-fires are burning and invaders from space have arrived at the same time, and one day perhaps we'll look back and laugh even at all this. His heart overflowed with love for her, and longing. He had never known anything about poetry before he had met her. He closed his eyes a moment and brought her on to the screen of his mind. Thick cascades of jet-black hair, quick dazzling smile, long slender tanned body all aglitter with those amazing rings and necklaces and pendants she designed and fashioned. And her eyes. No-one else he knew had eyes like hers, bright with strange mischief, with that altogether original way of vision that was the thing he most loved about her. *Damn* this fire, just when he'd been away three days! *Damn* the stupid men from Mars!

Where the neat rows and circles of suburban streets ended there was a great open stretch of grassy land, parched by the long summer to the colour of a lion's hide, and beyond that were the mountains, and between the grassland and the mountains lay the fire, an enormous lateral red crest topped by a plume of foul black smoke. It seemed already to cover hundreds of acres, maybe thousands. A hundred acres of burning brush, Carmichael had heard once, creates as much heat energy as the atomic bomb they dropped on Hiroshima.

Through the crackle of radio static came the voice of the line boss, directing operations from a bubble-domed helicopter hovering at about four o'clock. 'DC-3, who are you?'

'Carmichael.'

'We're trying to contain it on three sides, Carmichael. You work on the east, Limekiln Canyon, down the flank of Porter Ranch Park. Got it?'

'Got it,' Carmichael said.

221

He flew low, less than a thousand feet. That gave him a good view of all the action: sawyers in hard hats and orange shirts chopping burning trees to make them fall towards the fire, bulldozer crews clearing brush ahead of the blaze, shovellers carving fire-breaks, helicopters pumping water into isolated tongues of flame. He climbed five hundred feet to avoid a single-engine observer plane, then went up five hundred more to avoid the smoke and air turbulence of the fire itself. From that altitude he had a clear picture of it, running like a bloody gash from west to east, wider at its western end. Just east of the fire's far tip he saw a circular zone of grassland perhaps a hundred acres in diameter that had already burned out, and precisely at the centre of that zone stood something that looked like an aluminium silo, the size of a ten-storey building, surrounded at a considerable distance by a cordon of military vehicles.

He felt a wave of dizziness go rocking through his mind. That thing, he realized, had to be the E-T spaceship.

It had come out of the west in the night, Carmichael thought, floating like a tremendous meteor over Oxnard and Camarillo, sliding towards the western end of the San Fernando Valley, kissing the grass with its exhaust and leaving a trail of flame behind it. And then it had gently set itself down over there and extinguished its own brush-fire in a neat little circle about itself, not caring at all about the blaze it had kindled farther back, and God knows what kind of creatures had come forth from it to inspect Los Angeles. It figured that when the UFOs finally did make a landing out in the open, it would be in LA. Probably they had chosen it because they had seen it so often on television – didn't all the stories say that UFO people always monitored our TV transmissions? So they saw LA on every other show and they probably figured it was the capital of the world, the perfect place for the first landing. But why, Carmichael wondered, had the bastards needed to pick the height of the fire season to put their ships down here?

He thought of Cindy again, how fascinated she was by all this UFO and E-T stuff, those books she read, the ideas she had, the way she had looked towards the stars one night when they were camping in Kings Canyon and talked of the beings that must live up there. 'I'd love to see them,' she said. 'I'd love to get to know them and find out what their heads are like.' Los Angeles was full of nutcases who wanted to ride in flying saucers, or claimed they already had, but it didn't sound nutty to Carmichael when Cindy talked that way. She had the Angeleno love of the exotic and the bizarre, yes, but he knew that her soul had never been touched by the crazy corruption here, that she was untainted by the prevailing craving for the weird and irrational that made him loathe the place so much. If she turned her imagination towards the stars, it was out of wonder, not out of madness: it was simply part of her nature, that curiosity, that hunger for what lay outside her experience, to embrace the unknowable. He had had no more belief in E-Ts than he did in the tooth fairy, but for her sake he had told her that he hoped she'd get her wish. And now the UFO people were really here. He could imagine her, eyes shining, standing at the edge of that cordon staring at the spaceship. Pity he couldn't be with her now, feeling all that excitement surging through her, the joy, the wonder, the magic.

But he had work to do. Swinging the DC-3 back around towards the west, he swooped down as close as he dared to the edge of the fire and hit the release button on his dump lines. Behind him, a great crimson cloud spread out: a slurry of ammonium sulphate and water, thick as paint, with a red dye mixed into it so they could tell which areas had been sprayed. The retardant clung in globs to anything, and would keep it damp for hours.

Emptying his four 500-gallon tanks quickly, he headed back to Van Nuys to reload. His eyes were throbbing with fatigue and the bitter stink of the wet charred earth below was filtering through every plate of the old plane. It was not quite noon. He had been up all night.

At the airport they had coffee ready, sandwiches, tacos, burritos. While he was waiting for the ground crew to fill his tanks he went inside to call Cindy again, and again there was no answer at home, none at the studio. He phoned the gallery and the kid who worked there said she hadn't been in touch all morning.

'If you hear from her,' Carmichael said, 'tell her I'm flying fire control out of Van Nuys on the Chatsworth fire, and I'll be home as soon as things calm down a little. Tell her I miss her, too. And tell her that if I run into an E-T I'll give it a big hug for her. You got that? Tell her just that.'

Across the way in the main hall he saw a crowd gathered around someone carrying a portable television set. Carmichael shouldered his way in just as the announcer was saying, 'There has been no sign yet of the occupants of the San Gabriel or Orange County spaceships. But this was the horrifying sight that astounded residents of the Porter Ranch area beheld this morning between nine and ten o'clock.' The screen showed two upright tubular figures that looked like squids walking on the tips of their tentacles, moving cautiously through the parking lot of a shopping centre, peering this way and that out of enormous yellow platter-shaped eyes. At least a thousand onlookers were watching them at a wary distance, appearing both repelled and at the same time irresistibly drawn. Now and then the creatures paused to touch their foreheads together in some sort of communion. They moved very daintily, but Carmichael saw that they were taller than the lamp posts – twelve feet high, maybe fifteen. Their skins were purplish and leathery-looking, with rows of luminescent orange spots glowing along the sides. The camera zoomed in for a close-up, then jiggled and swerved wildly just as an enormously long elastic tongue sprang from the chest of one of the alien beings and whipped out into the crowd. For an instant the only thing visible on the screen was a view of the sky; then Carmichael saw a shot of a stunned-looking girl of about fourteen, caught around the waist by that long tongue, being hoisted into the air and popped like a collected specimen into a narrow green sack. 'Teams of the giant creatures roamed the town for nearly an hour,' the announcer intoned. 'It has definitely been confirmed that between twenty and thirty human hostages were captured before they returned to their spacecraft. Meanwhile, firefighting activities desperately continue under Santa Ana conditions in the vicinity of all three landing sites, and – '

Carmichael shook his head. Los Angeles, he thought. The kind of people that live here, they walk right up and let the E-Ts gobble them like flies. Maybe they think it's just a movie, and everything will be OK by the last reel. And then he remembered that Cindy was the kind of people who would walk right up to one of these E-Ts. Cindy was the kind of people who lived in

Los Angeles, he told himself, except that Cindy was *different*.
Somehow.

He went outside. The DC-3 was loaded and ready.

In the forty-five minutes since he had left the line, the blaze
seemed to have spread noticeably towards the south. This time
the line boss had him lay down the retardant from the De
Soto Avenue freeway interchange to the north-east corner of
Porter Ranch. When he returned to the airport, intending to try
phoning Cindy once again, a man in military uniform stopped
him as he was crossing the field and said, 'You Mike Carmichael,
Laurel Canyon?'

'That's right.'

'I've got some troublesome news for you. Let's go inside.'

'Suppose you tell me here, OK?'

The officer looked at him strangely. 'It's about your wife,' he
said. 'Cynthia Carmichael? That's your wife's name?'

'Come *on*,' Carmichael said.

'She's one of the hostages, Mr Carmichael.'

His breath went from him as though he had been kicked.

'Where did it happen?' he demanded. 'How did they get
her?'

The officer gave him a strange strained smile. 'It was the
shopping-centre lot, Porter Ranch. Maybe you saw some of it
on the TV.'

Carmichael nodded. That girl jerked off her feet by that
immense elastic tongue, swept through the air, popped into
that green pouch. And Cindy –?

'You saw the part where the creatures were moving around?
And then suddenly they were grabbing people, and everyone
was running from them? That was when they got her. She was
up front when they began grabbing, and maybe she had a chance
to get away but she waited just a little too long. She started to
run, I understand, but then she stopped – she looked back at
them – she may have called something out to them – and then
– well, and then – '

'Then they scooped her up?'

'I have to tell you that they did.'

'I see,' Carmichael said stonily.

'One thing all the witnesses agreed, she didn't panic, she

225

didn't scream. She was very brave when those monsters grabbed her. How in God's name you can be brave when something that size is holding you in mid-air is something I don't understand, but I have to assure you that those who saw it – '

'It makes sense to me,' Carmichael said.

He turned away. He shut his eyes for a moment and took deep, heavy pulls of the hot smoky air.

It figures, he thought. It makes absolute sense.

Of course she had gone right out to the landing site. Of course. If there was anyone in Los Angeles who would have wanted to get to them and see them with her own eyes and perhaps try to talk to them and establish some sort of rapport with them, it was Cindy. She wouldn't have been afraid of them. She had never seemed to be afraid of anything. It wasn't hard for Carmichael to imagine her in that panicky mob in the parking lot, cool and radiant, staring at the giant aliens, smiling at them right up to the moment they seized her.

In a way he felt very proud of her. But it terrified him to think that she was in their grasp.

'She's on the ship?' he asked. 'The one that we have right up back here?'

'Yes.'

'Have there been any messages from the hostages? Or from the aliens, for that matter?'

'I'm not in a position to divulge that information.'

'*Is* there any information?'

'I'm sorry, I'm not at liberty to – '

'I refuse to believe,' Carmichael said, 'that that ship is just sitting there, that nothing at all is being done to make contact with – '

'A command centre has been established, Mr Carmichael, and certain efforts are under way. That much I can tell you. I can tell you that Washington is involved. But beyond that, at the present point in time – '

A kid who looked like an Eagle Scout came running up. 'Your plane's all loaded and ready to go, Mike!'

'Yeah,' Carmichael said. The fire, the fucking fire! He had almost managed to forget about it. *Almost.* He hesitated a moment, torn between conflicting responsibilities. Then he said to the officer, 'Look, I've got to get back out on the fire line. Can you stay here a little while?'

'Well – '

'Maybe half an hour. I have to do a retardant dump. Then I want you to take me over to that spaceship and get me through the cordon, so I can talk to those critters myself. If she's on that ship, I mean to get her off it.'

'I don't see how it would be possible for – '

'Well, try to see,' Carmichael said. 'I'll meet you right here in half an hour.'

When he was aloft he noticed right away that the fire was spreading. The wind was even rougher and wilder than before, and now it was blowing hard from the north-east, pushing the flames down toward the edge of Chatsworth. Already some glowing cinders had blown across the city limits and Carmichael saw houses afire to his left, maybe half a dozen of them. There would be more, he knew. In firefighting you come to develop an odd sense of which way the struggle is going, whether you're gaining on the blaze or the blaze is gaining on you, and that sense told him now that the vast effort that was under way was failing, that the fire was still on the upcurve, that whole neighbourhoods were going to be ashes by nightfall.

He held on tight as the DC-3 entered the fire zone. The fire was sucking air like crazy, now, and the turbulence was astounding: it felt as if a giant's hand had grabbed the ship by the nose. The line boss's helicopter was tossing around like a balloon on a string.

Carmichael called in for orders and was sent over to the south-west side, close by the outermost street of houses. Firefighters with shovels were beating on wisps of flame rising out of people's gardens down there. The skirts of dead leaves that dangled down the trunks of a row of towering palm trees were blazing. The neighbourhood dogs had formed a crazed pack, running desperately back and forth.

Swooping down to treetop level, Carmichael let go with a red gush of chemicals, swathing everything that looked combustible with the stuff. The shovellers looked up and waved at him, and he dipped his wings to them and headed off to the north, around the western edge of the blaze – it was edging farther to the west too, he saw, leaping up into the high canyons out by the Ventura County line – and then he flew eastwards along the Santa Susana foothills until he could see the spaceship once more, standing isolated in its circle of blackened earth. The cordon of military vehicles seemed now to be even larger, what looked like a whole armoured division deployed in concentric rings beginning half a mile or so from the ship.

He stared intently at the alien vessel as though he might be able to see through its shining walls to Cindy within.

He imagined her sitting at a table, or whatever the aliens used instead of tables, sitting at a table with seven or eight of the huge beings, calmly explaining Earth to them and then asking them to explain their world to her. He was altogether certain that she was safe, that no harm would come to her, that they were not torturing her or dissecting her or sending electric currents through her simply to see how she reacted. Things like that would never happen to Cindy, he knew. The only thing he feared was that they would depart for their home star without releasing her. The terror that that thought generated in him was as powerful as any kind of fear he had ever felt.

As Carmichael approached the aliens' landing site he saw the guns of some of the tanks below swivelling around to point at him, and he picked up a radio voice telling him brusquely, 'You're off limits, DC-3. Get back to the fire zone. This is prohibited air space.'

'Sorry,' Carmichael answered. 'No entry intended.'

But as he started to make his turn he dropped down even lower, so that he could have a good look at the spaceship. If it had portholes, and Cindy was looking out of one of those portholes, he wanted her to know that he was nearby. That he was watching, that he was waiting for her to come back. But the ship's hull was blind-faced, entirely blank.

– Cindy? Cindy?

She was always looking for the strange, the mysterious, the unfamiliar, he thought. The people she brought to the house: a Navaho once, a bewildered Turkish tourist, a kid from New York. The music she played, the way she chanted along with it. The incense, the lights, the meditation. 'I'm searching,' she liked to say. Trying always to find a route that would take her into something that was wholly outside herself. Trying to become something more than she was. That was how they had fallen in love in the first place, an unlikely couple, she with her beads and sandals, he with his steady no-nonsense view of the world: she had come up to him that day long ago when he was in the record shop in Studio City, and God only knew what he was doing in that part of the world in the first place, and she had asked him something and they had started to talk, and they had talked and talked, talked all night, she wanting to know everything there was to know about him, and when dawn came up they were still together and they had rarely been parted since. He never had really been able to understand what it was that she had wanted him for – the Valley redneck, the ageing flyboy – although he felt certain that she wanted him for something real, that he filled some need for her, as she did for him, which could for lack of a more specific term be called love. She had always been searching for that, too. Who wasn't? And he knew that she loved him truly and well, though he couldn't quite see why. 'Love is understanding,' she liked to say. 'Understanding is loving.' Was she trying to tell the spaceship people about love right this minute? *Cindy, Cindy, Cindy* –

Back in Van Nuys a few minutes later, he found that everyone at the airport seemed to know by this time that his wife was one of the hostages. The officer whom Carmichael had asked to wait for him was gone. He was not very surprised by that. He thought for a moment of trying to go over to the ship by himself, to get through the cordon and do something about getting Cindy free, but he realized that that was a dumb idea: the military were in charge and they wouldn't let him or anybody else get within a mile of that ship, and he'd only get snarled up in stuff with the television interviewers looking for poignant crap about the families of those who had been captured.

Then the head dispatcher came down to meet him on the field, looking almost about ready to burst with compassion, and in funereal tones told Carmichael that it would be all right if he called it quits for the day and went home to await whatever might happen. But Carmichael shook him off. 'I won't get her back by sitting in the living room,' he said. 'And this fire isn't going to go out by itself, either.'

It took twenty minutes for the ground crew to pump the retardant slurry into the DC-3's tanks. Carmichael stood to one side, drinking Cokes and watching the planes come and go. People stared at him, and those who knew him waved from a distance, and three or four pilots came over and silently squeezed his arm or rested a hand consolingly on his shoulder. The northern sky was black with soot, shading to grey to east and west. The air was sauna-hot and frighteningly dry: you could set fire to it, Carmichael thought, with a snap of your fingers. Somebody running by said that a new fire had broken out in Pasadena, near the Jet Propulsion Lab, and there was another in Griffith Park. The wind was starting to carry firebrands, then. Dodgers Stadium was burning, someone said. So is Santa Anita Racetrack, said someone else. The whole damned place is going to go, Carmichael thought. And my wife is sitting inside a spaceship from another planet.

When his plane was ready he took it up and laid down a new line of retardant practically in the faces of the firefighters working on the outskirts of Chatsworth. They were too busy to wave. In order to get back to the airport he had to make a big loop behind the fire, over the Santa Susanas and down the flank of the Golden State Freeway, and this time he saw the fires burning to the east, two huge conflagrations marking the places where the exhaust streams of the other two spaceships had grazed the dry grass, and a bunch of smaller blazes strung out on a line from Burbank or Glendale deep into Orange County. His hands were shaking as he touched down at Van Nuys. He had gone without sleep now for something like thirty-two hours, and he could feel himself starting to pass into that blank white fatigue that lies somewhere beyond ordinary fatigue.

The head dispatcher was waiting for him again as he left his plane. 'All right,' Carmichael said at once. 'I give in. I'll knock off for five or six hours and grab some sleep, and then you can call me back to – '

'No. That isn't it.'

'That isn't what?'

'What I came out here to tell you, Mike. They've released some of the hostages.'

'Cindy?'

'I think so. There's an Air Force car here to take you to

Sylmar. That's where they've got the command centre set up. They said to find you as soon as you came off your last dump mission and send you over there so you can talk with your wife.'

'So she's free,' Carmichael said. 'Oh, Jesus, she's free!'

'You go on along, Mike. We'll look after the fire without you for a while, OK?'

The Air Force car looked like a general's limo, long and low and sleek, with a square-jawed driver in front and a couple of very tough-looking young officers to sit with him in back. They said hardly anything, and they looked as weary as Carmichael felt. 'How's my wife?' he asked, and one of them said, 'We understand that she hasn't been harmed.' The way he said it was stiff and strange. Carmichael shrugged. The kid has seen too many old Air Force movies, he told himself.

The whole city seemed to be on fire now. Within the air-conditioned limo there was only the faintest whiff of smoke, but the sky to the east was terrifying, with streaks of red bursting like meteors through the blackness. Carmichael asked the Air Force men about that, but all he got was a clipped, 'It looks pretty bad, we understand.' Somewhere along the San Diego Freeway between Mission Hills and Sylmar, Carmichael fell asleep, and the next thing he knew they were waking him gently and leading him into a vast bleak hangar-like building near the reservoir. The place was a maze of cables and screens, with military personnel operating what looked like a thousand computers and ten thousand telephones. He let himself be shuffled along, moving mechanically and barely able to focus his eyes, to an inner office where a grey-haired colonel greeted him in his best this-is-the-tense-part-of-the-movie style and said, 'This may be the most difficult job you've ever had to handle, Mr Carmichael.'

Carmichael scowled. Everybody was Hollywood in this damned town, he thought.

'They told me the hostages were being freed,' he said. 'Where's my wife?'

The colonel pointed to a television screen. 'We're going to let you talk to her right now.'

'Are you saying I don't get to see her?'

'Not immediately.'

231

'Why not? Is she all right?'

'As far as we know, yes.'

'You mean she hasn't been released? They told me the hostages were being freed.'

'All but three have been let go,' said the colonel. 'Two people, according to the aliens, were injured as they were captured, and are undergoing medical treatment aboard the ship. They'll be released shortly. The third is your wife, Mr Carmichael. She is unwilling to leave the ship.'

It was like hitting an air-pocket. '*Unwilling –?*'

'She claims to have volunteered to make the journey to the home world of the aliens. She says she's going to serve as our ambassador, our special emissary. Mr Carmichael, does your wife have any history of mental imbalance?'

Glaring, Carmichael said, 'She's very sane. Believe me.'

'You are aware that she showed no display of fear when the aliens seized her in the shopping-centre incident this morning?'

'I know, yes. That doesn't mean she's crazy. She's unusual. She has unusual ideas. But she's not crazy. Neither am I, incidentally.' He put his hands to his face for a moment and pressed his fingertips lightly against his eyes. 'All right,' he said. 'Let me talk to her.'

'Do you think you can persuade her to leave that ship?'

'I'm sure as hell going to try.'

'You are not yourself sympathetic to what she's doing, are you?' the colonel asked.

Carmichael looked up. 'Yes, I am sympathetic. She's an intelligent woman doing something that she thinks is important, and doing it of her own free will. Why the hell shouldn't I be sympathetic? But I'm going to try to talk her out of it, you bet. I love her. I want her. Somebody else can be the goddamned ambassador to Betelgeuse. Let me talk to her, will you?'

The colonel gestured and the big television screen came to life. For a moment mysterious coloured patterns flashed across it in a disturbing random way; then Carmichael caught glimpses of shadowy catwalks, intricate metal strutworks crossing and recrossing at peculiar angles; and then for an instant one of the aliens appeared on the screen. Yellow platter-eyes looked complacently back at him. Carmichael felt altogether wide-awake now.

232

The alien's face vanished and Cindy came into view. The moment he saw her, Carmichael knew that he had lost her.

Her face was glowing. There was a calm joy in her eyes verging on ecstasy. He had seen her look something like that on many occasions, but this was different: this was beyond anything she had attained before. She had seen the beatific vision, this time.

'Cindy?'

'Hello, Mike.'

'Can you tell me what's been happening in there, Cindy?'

'It's incredible. The contact, the communication.'

Sure, he thought. If anyone could make contact with the space people it would be Cindy. She had a certain kind of magic about her: the gift of being able to open any door.

She said, 'They speak mind to mind, you know, no barriers at all. They've come in peace, to get to know us, to join in harmony with us, to welcome us into the confederation of worlds.'

He moistened his lips. 'What have they done to you, Cindy? Have they brainwashed you or something?'

'No! No, nothing like that! They haven't done a thing to me, Mike! We've just talked.'

'Talked!'

'They've showed me how to touch my mind to theirs. That isn't brainwashing. I'm still me. I, me, Cindy. I'm OK. Do I look as though I'm being harmed? They aren't dangerous. Believe me.'

'They've set fire to half the city with their exhaust trails, you know.'

'That grieves them. It was an accident. They didn't understand how dry the hills were. If they had some way of extinguishing the flames, they would, but the fires are too big even for them. They ask us to forgive them. They want everyone to know how sorry they are.' She paused a moment. Then she said, very gently, 'Mike, will you come on board? I want you to experience them as I'm experiencing them.'

'I can't do that, Cindy.'

'Of course you can! Anyone can! You just open your mind, and they touch you, and – '

'I know. I don't want to. Come out of there and come home,

233

Cindy. Please. Please. It's been three days – four, now – I want to hug you, I want to hold you – '

'You can hold me as tight as you like. They'll let you on board. We can go to their world together. You know that I'm going to go with them to their world, don't you?'

'You aren't. Not really.'

She nodded gravely. She seemed terribly serious. 'They'll be leaving in a few weeks, as soon as they've had a chance to exchange gifts with Earth. I've seen images of their planet – like movies, only they do it with their minds – Mike, you can't imagine how beautiful it is! How eager they are to have me come!'

Sweat rolled out of his hair into his eyes, making him blink, but he did not dare wipe it away, for fear she would think he was crying.

'I don't want to go to their planet, Cindy. And I don't want you to go either.'

She was silent for a time.

Then she smiled delicately and said, 'I know, Mike.'

He clenched his fists and let go and clenched them again. 'I *can't* go there.'

'No. You can't. I understand that. Los Angeles is alien enough for you, I think. You need to be in your Valley, in your own real world, not running off to some far star. I won't try to coax you.'

'But you're going to go anyway?' he asked, and it was not really a question.

'You already know what I'm going to do.'

'Yes.'

'I'm sorry. But not really.'

'Do you love me?' he said, and regretted saying it at once.

She smiled sadly. 'You know I do. And you know I don't want to leave you. But once they touched my mind with theirs, once I saw what kind of beings they are – do you know what I mean? I don't have to explain, do I? You always know what I mean.'

'Cindy – '

'Oh, Mike, I do love you so much.'

'And I love you, babe. And I wish you'd come out of that goddamned ship.'

'You won't ask that. Because you love me, right? Just as I

won't ask you again to come on board with me, because I really love you. Do you understand that, Mike?'

He wanted to reach into the screen and grab her.

'I understand, yes,' he made himself say.

'I love you, Mike.'

'I love you, Cindy.'

'They tell me the round trip takes forty-eight of our years, but it will only seem like a few weeks to me. Oh, Mike! Goodbye, Mike! God bless, Mike!' She blew kisses to him. He saw his favourite rings on her fingers, the three little strange star sapphire ones that she had made when she first began to design jewellery. He searched his mind for some new way to reason with her, some line of argument that would work, and could find none. He felt a vast emptiness beginning to expand within him, as though he were being made hollow by some whirling blade. Her face was shining. She seemed like a stranger to him suddenly. She seemed like a Los Angeles person, one of *those* lost in fantasies and dreams, and it was as though he had never known her, as though he had pretended she was something other than she was. No. No, that isn't right. She's not one of *those*, she's Cindy. Following her own star, as always. Suddenly he was unable to look at the screen any longer, and he turned away, biting his lip, making a shoving gesture with his left hand. The Air Force men in the room wore the awkward expressions of people who had inadvertently eavesdropped on someone's most intimate moments and were trying to pretend they had heard nothing.

'She isn't crazy, colonel,' Carmichael said vehemently. 'I don't want anyone believing she's some kind of nut.'

'Of course not, Mr Carmichael.'

'But she's not going to leave that spaceship. You heard her. She's staying aboard, going back with them to wherever the hell they came from. I can't do anything about that. You see that, don't you? Nothing I could do, short of going aboard that ship and dragging her off physically, would get her out of there. And I wouldn't ever do that.'

'Naturally not. In any case, you understand that it would be impossible for us to permit you to go on board, even for the sake of attempting to remove her.'

'That's all right,' Carmichael said. 'I wouldn't dream of it. To remove her or even just to join her for the trip. I don't want to go to that place. Let her go: that's what she was meant to do in this world. Not me. Not me, colonel. That's simply not my thing.' He took a deep breath. He thought he might be trembling. 'Colonel, do you mind if I get the hell out of here? Maybe I would feel better if I went back out there and dumped some more gunk on that fire. I think that might help. That's what I think, colonel. All right? Would you send me back to Van Nuys, Colonel?'

He went up one last time in the DC-3. They wanted him to dump the retardants along the western face of the fire, but instead he went to the east, where the spaceship was, and flew in a wide circle around it. A radio voice warned him to move out of the area, and he said that he would.

As he circled, a hatch opened in the spaceship's side and one of the aliens appeared, looking gigantic even from Carmichael's altitude. The huge purplish thing stepped from the ship, extended its tentacles, seemed to be sniffing the smoky air.

Carmichael thought vaguely of flying down low and dropping his whole load of retardants on the creature, drowning it in gunk, getting even with the aliens for having taken Cindy from him. He shook his head. That's crazy, he told himself. Cindy would feel sick if she knew he had ever considered any such thing.

But that's what I'm like, he thought. Just an ordinary ugly vengeful Earthman. And that's why I'm not going to go to that other planet, and that's why she is.

He swung around past the spaceship and headed straight across Granada Hills and Northridge into Van Nuys Airport. When he was on the ground he sat at the controls of his plane a long while, not moving at all. Finally one of the dispatchers came out and called up to him, 'Mike, are you OK?'

'Yeah. I'm fine.'

'How come you came back without dropping your load?'

Carmichael peered at his gauges. 'Did I do that? I guess I did that, didn't I?'

'You're not OK, are you?'

'I forgot to dump, I guess. No, I didn't forget. I just didn't bother. I didn't feel like doing it.'

'Mike, come on out of that plane.'

'I didn't feel like doing it,' Carmichael said again. 'Why the hell bother? This crazy city – there's nothing left in it that I would want to save, anyway.' His control deserted him at last, and rage swept through him like fire racing up the slopes of a dry canyon. He understood what she was doing, and he respected it, but he didn't have to like it. He didn't like it at all. He had lost Cindy, and he felt somehow that he had lost his war with Los Angeles as well. 'Fuck it,' he said. 'Let it burn. This crazy city. I always hated it. It deserves what it gets. The only reason I stayed here was for her. She was all that mattered. But she's going away, now. Let the fucking place burn.'

The dispatcher gaped at him in amazement. 'Mike – '

Carmichael moved his head slowly from side to side as though trying to shake a monstrous headache from it. Then he frowned. 'No, that's wrong,' he said. 'You've got to do the job anyway, right? No matter how you feel. You have to put the fires out. You have to save what you can. Listen, Tim, I'm going to fly one last load today, you hear? And then I'll go home and get some sleep. OK? OK?' He had the plane in motion, going down the short runway. Dimly he realized that he had not requested clearance. A little Cessna spotter plane moved desperately out of his way, and then he was aloft. The sky was black and red. The fire was completely uncontained now, and maybe uncontainable. But you had to keep trying, he thought. You had to save what you could. He gunned and went forward, flying calmly into the inferno in the foothills, until the wild thermals caught his wings from below and lifted him and tossed him like a toy skimming over the top, and sent him hurtling toward the waiting hills to the north.

Thus saith the Lord: Behold. I will raise up against Babylon, and against them that dwell in the midst of them that rise up against me, a destroying wind;

And will send unto Babylon fanners, that shall fan her, and shall empty her land: for in the day of trouble they shall be against her round about.

Jeremiah, 51: 1–2

Symbiont

Long ago there was a gaudy pulp magazine called *Planet Stories*, which was devoted to two-fisted, colourful tales of action and adventure on other worlds. Don't think it was junk, though: Ray Bradbury, Poul Anderson, Theodore Sturgeon and Leigh Brackett were regular contributors, Isaac Asimov and Jack Vance wrote for it, Philip K. Dick's first published story appeared in it. Readers loved it and so did the writers, because they could rare back and let their imaginations run free.

I never had anything published in *Planet Stories*, because it went out of business in 1955, just as my career was getting started. But I enjoyed doing *Planet*-type material for such later imitators as *Science Fiction Adventures* and *Venture SF*, which flourished in the fifties, and suddenly, one day in the spring of 1984, it occurred to me to attempt one for *Playboy* in the old *Planet Stories* mode, appropriately buffed and polished for *Playboy*'s demanding readership. (I would, after all, be fighting for a place on the contents page with the likes of Nabokov, Updike, and Joyce Carol Oates.) And out of the machine came 'Symbiont', the sombre tale of jungle adventure and diabolical revenge that you are about to read. Off it went, with some trepidation, to the formidable Alice K. Turner, who had put me so exhaustingly through my paces fifteen months earlier with 'Tourist Trade'. And back from Alice a few days later came this letter of acceptance:

'Your cheque, as we like to say, is in the mail. I was dumbfounded when I read this story (*avidly*, I should add), and sent it off to Teresa [her assistant editor], whose youth was not misspent, as mine was, in reading stories that featured creatures with tentacles and body-takeovers by alien nasties. I waited, somewhat apprehensively, for her response – and she *loved* it. That's good enough for me. If such a noble mind can be here o'erthrown, what the hell. This is one of the ones that will go in with not a word changed, though not till '85 some time.'

Symbiont

The initial idea for the story, incidentally, was given to me by a young woman named Karen Haber, whom I had met while on a speaking tour in Texas. It originally involved something that had happened to a friend of a friend of hers in Vietnam, but I applied my usual science-fiction metamorphosis techniques to it and 'Symbiont' was the result. Ms Haber was very impressed. I was very impressed with Ms Haber, too. A couple of years later I married her.

Ten years later, when I was long out of the Service and working the turnaround wheel at Betelgeuse Station, Fazio still haunted me. Not that he was dead. Other people get haunted by dead men; I was haunted by a live one. It would have been a lot better for both of us if he *had* been dead, but as far as I knew Fazio was still alive.

He'd been haunting me a long while. Three or four times a year his little dry thin voice would come out of nowhere and I'd hear him telling me again, 'Before we go into that jungle, we got to come to an understanding. If a synsym nails me, Chollie, you kill me right away, hear? None of this shit of calling in the paramedics to clean me out. You just kill me right away. And I'll do the same for you. Is that a deal?'

This was on a planet called Weinstein in the Servadac system, late in the Second Ovoid War. We were twenty years old and we were volunteers: two dumb kids playing hero. 'You bet your arse,' is what I told him, not hesitating a second. 'Deal. Absolutely.' Then I gave him a big grin and a handclasp and we headed off together on spore-spreading duty.

At the time, I really thought I meant it. Sometimes I still believe that I did.

Ten years. I could still see the two of us back there on Weinstein, going out to distribute latchenango spores in the enemy-held zone. The planet had been grabbed by the Ovoids early in the war, but we were starting to drive them back from that whole system. Fazio and I were the entire patrol: you get spread pretty thin in galactic warfare. But there was plenty of support force behind us in the hills.

Weinstein was strategically important, God only knows why. Two small continents – both tropical, mostly thick jungle, air like green soup – surrounded by an enormous turbulent ocean: never colonized by Earth, and of no use that anyone had ever successfully explained to me. But the place had once been ours and they had taken it away, and we wanted it back.

The way you got a planet back was to catch a dozen or so Ovoids, fill them full of latchenango spores, and let them return to their base. There is no life-form a latchenango likes better as its host than an Ovoid. The Ovoids, being Ovoids, would usually conceal what had happened to them from their pals, who would kill them instantly if they knew they were carrying deadly parasites. Of course, the carriers were going to die anyway – latchenango infestation is invariably fatal to Ovoids – but by the time they did, in about six standard weeks, the latchenangos had gone through three or four reproductive cycles and the whole army would be infested. All we needed to do was wait until all the Ovoids were dead and then come in, clean the place up, and raise the flag again. The latchenangos were generally dead too by then, since they rarely could find other suitable hosts. But even if they weren't, we didn't worry about it. Latchenangos don't cause any serious problems for humans. About the worst of it is that you usually inhale some spores while you're handling them, and it irritates your lungs for a couple of weeks so you do some pretty ugly coughing until you're desporified.

In return for our latchenangos the Ovoids gave us synsyms.

Synsyms were the first things you heard about when you arrived in the war zone, and what you heard was horrendous. You didn't know how much of it was myth and how much was mere bullshit and how much was truth, but even if you discounted seventy-five per cent of it the rest was scary enough. 'If you get hit by one,' the old hands advised us, 'kill yourself fast, while you have the chance.' Roving synsym vectors cruised the perimeter of every Ovoid camp, sniffing for humans. They were not parasites but synthetic symbionts: when they got into you, they stayed there, sharing your body with you indefinitely.

In school they teach you that symbiosis is a mutually beneficial state. Maybe so. But the word that passed through the ranks in the war zone was that it definitely did not improve the quality of your life to take a synsym into your body. And though the Service medics would spare no effort to see that you survived a synsym attack – they aren't allowed to perform mercy killings, and wouldn't anyway – everything we heard indicated that you didn't really *want* to survive one.

The day Fazio and I entered the jungle was like all the others on Weinstein: dank, humid, rainy. We strapped on our spore-tanks and started out, using hand-held heat-piles to burn our way through the curtains of tangled vines. The wet spongy soil had a purplish tinge and the lakes were iridescent green from lightning-algae.

'Here's where we'll put the hotel landing strip,' Fazio said lightly. 'Over here, the pool and cabanas. The gravity-tennis courts here, and on the far side of that – '

'Watch it,' I said, and skewered a low-flying wingfinger with a beam of hot purple light. It fell in ashes at our feet. Another one came by, the mate, travelling at eye-level with its razor-sharp beak aimed at my throat, but Fazio took it out just as neatly. We thanked each other. Wingfingers are elegant things, all trajectory and hardly any body mass, with scaly silvery skins that shine like the finest grade of moonlight, and it is their habit to go straight for the jugular in the most literal sense. We killed twelve that day and I hope it is my quota for this lifetime. As we advanced into the heart of the jungle we dealt just as efficiently with assorted hostile coilworms, eyeflies, dingleberries, leper bats, and other disagreeable local specialities. We were a great team: quick, smart, good at protecting each other.

We were admiring a giant carnivorous fungus a klick and a half deep in the woods when we came upon our first Ovoid. The fungus was a fleshy phallic red tower three metres high with orange gills, equipped with a dozen dangling whiplike arms that had green adhesive knobs at the tips. At the ends of most of the arms hung small forest creatures in various stages of digestion. As we watched, an unoccupied arm rose and shot forth, extended itself to three times its resting length, and by some neat homing tropism slapped its adhesive knob against a passing many-legger about the size of a cat. The beast had no chance to struggle; a network of wiry structures sprouted at once from the killer arm and slipped into the victim's flesh, and that was that. We almost applauded.

'Let's plant three of them in the hotel garden,' I said, 'and post a schedule of feeding times. It'll be a great show for the guests.'

'Shh,' Fazio said. He pointed.

Maybe fifty metres away a solitary Ovoid was gliding serenely along a forest path, obviously unaware of us. I caught my breath. Everyone knows what Ovoids look like, but this was the first time I had seen a live one. I was surprised at how beautiful it was, a tapering cone of firm jelly, pale blue streaked with red and gold. Triple rows of short-stalked eyes along its sides like brass buttons. Clusters of delicate tendrils sprouting like epaulettes around the eating-orifice at the top of its head. Turquoise ribbons of neural conduit winding round and round its equator, surrounding the dark heart-shaped brain faintly visible within the cloudy depths. The enemy. I was conditioned to hate it, and I did; yet I couldn't deny its strange beauty.

Fazio smiled and took aim and put a numb-needle through the Ovoid's middle. It froze instantly in mid-glide; its colour deepened to a dusky flush; the tiny mouth-tendrils fluttered wildly but there was no other motion. We jogged up to it and I slipped the tip of my spore-distributor about five centimetres into its meaty middle. 'Let him have it!' Fazio yelled. I pumped a couple of ccs of latchenango spores into the paralysed alien. Its soft quivering flesh turned blue-black with fear and rage and God knows what other emotions that were strictly Ovoid. We nodded to each other and moved along. Already the latchenangos were spawning within their host; in half an hour the Ovoid, able once more to move, would limp off toward its camp to start infecting its comrades. It is a funny way to wage war.

The second Ovoid, an hour later, was trickier. It knew we had spotted it and took evasive action, zigzagging through a zone of streams and slender trees in a weird dignified way like someone trying to move very fast without having his hat blow off. Ovoids are not designed for quick movements, but this one was agile and determined, ducking behind this rock and that. More than once we lost sight of it altogether and were afraid it might double back and come down on *us* while we stood gaping and blinking.

Eventually we bottled it up between two swift little streams and closed in on it from both sides. I raised my needler and Fazio got ready with his spore-distributor and just then something grey and slipper-shaped and about fifteen centimetres long came leaping up out of the left-hand stream and plastered itself over Fazio's mouth and throat.

Down he went, snuffling and gurgling, trying desperately to peel it away. I thought it was some kind of killer fish. Pausing only long enough to shoot a needle through the Ovoid, I dropped my gear and jumped down beside him.

Fazio was rolling around, eyes wild, kicking at the ground in terror and agony. I put my elbow on his chest to hold him still and pried with both hands at the thing on his face. Getting it loose was like pulling a second skin off him, but somehow I managed to lift it away from his lips far enough for him to gasp, 'Synsym – I think it's synsym – '

'No, man, it's just some nasty fish,' I told him. 'Hang in there and I'll rip the rest of it loose in half a minute – '

Fazio shook his head in anguish.

Then I saw the two thin strands of transparent stuff snaking up out of it and disappearing into his nostrils and I knew he was right.

I didn't hear anything from him or about him after the end of the war, and didn't want to, but I assumed all along that Fazio was still alive. I don't know why: my faith in the general perversity of the universe, I guess.

The last I had seen of him was our final day on Weinstein. We both were being invalided out. They were shipping me to the big hospital on Daemmerung for routine desporification treatment, but he was going to the quarantine station on Quixote; and as we lay side by side in the depot, me on an ordinary stretcher and Fazio inside an isolation bubble, he raised his head with what must have been a terrible effort and glared at me out of eyes that already were ringed with the red concentric synsym circles, and he whispered something to me. I wasn't able to understand the words through the wall of his bubble, but I could *feel* them, the way you feel the light of a blue-white sun from half a parsec out. His skin was glowing. The dreadful vitality of the symbiont within him was already apparent. I had a good notion of what he was trying to tell me. *You bastard*, he was most likely trying to say. *Now I'm stuck with this thing for a thousand years. And I'm going to hate you every minute of the time,* Chollie.

Then they took him away. They sent him floating up the ramp

into that Quixote-bound ship. When he was out of view I felt released, as though I was coming out from under a pull of six or seven gravs. It occurred to me that I wasn't ever going to have to see Fazio again. I wouldn't have to face those reddened eyes, that taut shining skin, that glare of infinite reproach. Or so I believed for the next ten years, until he turned up on Betelgeuse Station.

A bolt out of the blue: there he was, suddenly, standing next to me in the recreation room on North Spoke. It was just after my shift and I was balancing on the rim of the swimmer web, getting ready to dive. 'Chollie?' he said calmly. The voice was Fazio's voice: that was clear, when I stopped to think about it a little later. But I never for a moment considered that this weird gnomish man might be Fazio. I stared at him and didn't even come close to recognizing him. He seemed about seven million years old, shrunken, fleshless, weightless, with thick coarse hair like white straw and strange soft gleaming translucent skin that looked like parchment worn thin by time. In the bright light of the rec room he kept his eyes hooded nearly shut; but then he turned away from the glowglobes and opened them wide enough to show me the fine red rings around his pupils. The hair began to rise along the back of my neck.

'Come on,' he said. 'You know me. Yeah. Yeah.'

The voice, the cheekbones, the lips, the eyes – the eyes, the eyes, the eyes. Yes, I knew him. But it wasn't possible. Fazio? Here? How? So long a time, so many light-years away! And yet – yet –

He nodded. 'You got it, Chollie. Come on. Who am I?'

My first attempt at saying something was a sputtering failure. But I managed to get his name out on the second try.

'Yeah,' he said. 'Fazio. What a surprise.'

He didn't look even slightly surprised. I think he must have been watching me for a few days before he approached me – casing me, checking me out, making certain it was really me, getting used to the idea that he had actually found me. Otherwise the amazement would surely have been showing on him now. Finding me – finding *anybody* along the starways – wasn't remotely probable. This was a coincidence almost too big to swallow. I knew he couldn't have deliberately come after me, because the galaxy is so damned big a place that the idea of setting out to search for someone in it is too silly even to think about. But somehow he had caught up with me anyway. If the universe is truly infinite, I suppose, then even the most wildly improbable things must occur in it a billion times a day.

I said shakily, 'I can't believe – '

'You can't? Hey, you better! What a surprise, kid, hey? Hey?' He clapped his hand against my arm. 'And you're looking good, kid. Nice and healthy. You keep in shape, huh? How old are you now, thirty-two?'

'Thirty.' I was numb with shock and fear.

'Thirty. Mmm. So am I. Nice age, ain't it? Prime of life.'

'Fazio – '

His control was terrifying. 'Come on, Chollie. You look like you're about to crap in your pants. Aren't you glad to see your old buddy? We had some good times together, didn't we? Didn't we? What was the name of that fuckin' planet? Weinberg? Weinfeld? Hey, hey, don't *stare* at me like that!'

I had to work hard to make any sound at all. Finally I said, 'What the hell do you want me to do, Fazio? I feel like I'm looking at a ghost.'

He leaned close and his eyes opened wider. I could practically count the concentric red rings, ten or fifteen of them, very fine lines. 'I wish to Christ you were,' he said quietly. Such unfathomable depths of pain, such searing intensity of hatred. I wanted to squirm away from him. But there was no way. He gave me a long slow crucifying inspection. Then he eased back and some of the menacing intensity seemed to go out of him. Almost jauntily he said, 'We got a lot to talk about, Chollie. You know some quiet place around here we can go?'

'There's the gravity lounge – '

'Sure. The gravity lounge.'

We floated face to face, at half pull. 'You promised you'd kill me if I got nailed,' Fazio murmured. 'That was our deal. Why didn't you do it, Chollie? Why the fuck didn't you do it?'

I could hardly bear to look into his red-ringed eyes.

'Things happened too fast, man. How was I to know paramedics would be on the scene in five minutes?'

'Five minutes is plenty of time to put a heat-bolt through a guy's chest.'

'Less than five minutes. Three. Two. The paramedic floater was right overhead, man! It was covering us the whole while. They came down on us like a bunch of fucking *angels*, Fazio!'

'You had time.'

'I thought they were going to be able to save you,' I said lamely. 'They got there so quickly.'

Fazio laughed harshly. 'They did try to save me,' he said. 'I'll give them credit for trying. Five minutes and I was on that floater and they were sending tracers all over me to clean the synsym goop out of my lungs and my heart and my liver.'

'Sure. That was just what I figured they'd do.'

'You promised to finish me off, Chollie, if I got nailed.'

'But the paramedics were right *there*!'

'They worked on me like sonsabitches,' he said. 'They did everything. They can clean up the vital tissues, they can yank out your organs, synsym and all, and stick in transplants. But they can't get the stuff out of your brain, did you know that? The synsym goes straight up your nose into your brain and it slips its tendrils into your meninges and your neural glia and right into your fucking corpus callosum. And from there it goes everywhere. The cerebellum, the medulla, you name it. They can't send tracers into the brain that will clean out synsym and not damage brain tissue. And they can't pull out your brain and give you a new one, either. Thirty seconds after the synsym gets into your nose it reaches your brain and it's all over for you, no matter what kind of treatment you get. Didn't you hear them tell you that when we first got to the war zone? Didn't you hear all the horror stories?'

'I thought they were just horror stories,' I said faintly.

He rocked back and forth gently in his gravity cradle. He didn't say anything.

'Do you want to tell me what it's like?' I asked after a while.

Fazio shrugged. As though from a great distance he said, 'What it's like? Ah, it's not all that goddamned bad, Chollie. It's like having a room-mate. Living with you in your head, for ever, and you can't break the lease. That's all. Or like having an itch you can't scratch. Having it there is like finding yourself trapped in a space that's exactly one centimetre bigger than you are all around, and knowing that you're going to stay walled up in it for a million years.' He looked off towards the great clear wall of the lounge, toward giant red Betelgeuse blazing outside far away. 'Your synsym talks to you, sometimes. So you're never lonely, you know? Doesn't speak any language you understand, just sits there and spouts gibberish. But at least it's company. Sometimes it makes *you* spout gibberish, especially when you badly need to make sense. It grabs control of the upper brain centres now and then, you know. And as for the autonomous centres, it does any damned thing it likes with them. Keys into the pain zones and runs little simulations for you – an amputation without anaesthetic, say. Just for fun. *Its* fun. Or you're in bed with a woman and it disconnects your erection mechanism. Or it *gives* you an erection that won't go down for six weeks. For fun. It can get playful with your toilet training, too. I wear a diaper, Chollie, isn't that sweet? I have to. I get drunk sometimes without drinking. Or I drink myself sick without feeling a thing. And all the time I feel it there, tickling me. Like an ant crawling around within my skull. Like a worm up my nose. It's just like the other guys told us, when we came out to the war zone. Remember? "Kill yourself fast, while you have the chance." I never had the chance. I had you, Chollie, and we had a deal, but you didn't take our deal seriously. Why not, Chollie?'

I felt his eyes burning me. I looked away, halfway across the lounge, and caught sight of Elisandra's long golden hair drifting in free float. She saw me at the same moment, and waved. We usually got together in here this time of night. I shook my head, trying to warn her off, but it was too late. She was already heading our way.

'Who's that?' Fazio asked. 'Your girlfriend?'

'A friend.'

'Nice,' he said. He was staring at her as though he had never seen a woman before. 'I noticed her last night too. You live together?'

'We work the same shift on the wheel.'

'Yeah. I saw you leave with her last night. And the night before.'

'How long have you been at the Station, Fazio?'

'Week. Ten days, maybe.'

'Came here looking for me?'

'Just wandering around,' he said. 'Fat disability pension, plenty of time. I go to a lot of places. That's a really nice woman, Chollie. You're a lucky guy.' A tic was popping on his cheek and another was getting started on his lower lip. He said, 'Why the fuck didn't you kill me when that thing first jumped me?'

'I told you. I couldn't. The paramedics were on the scene too fast.'

'Right. You needed to say some Hail Marys first, and they just didn't give you enough time.'

He was implacable. I had to strike back at him somehow or the guilt and shame would drive me crazy. Angrily I said, 'What the hell do you want me to tell you, Fazio? That I'm sorry I didn't kill you ten years ago? OK, I'm sorry. Does that do any good? Listen, if the synsym's as bad as you say, how come *you* haven't killed yourself? Why go on dragging yourself around with that thing inside your head?'

He shook his head and made a little muffled grunting sound. His face abruptly became grey, his lips were sagging. His eyeballs seemed to be spinning slowly in opposite directions. Just an illusion, I knew, but a scary one.

'Fazio?'

He said, 'Chollallula lillalolla loolicholla. Billillolla.'

I stared. He looked frightening. He looked hideous.

'Jesus, Fazio!'

Spittle dribbled down his chin. Muscles jumped and writhed crazily all over his face. 'You see? You see?' he managed to blurt. There was warfare inside him. I watched him trying to regain command. It was like a man wrestling himself to a fall. I thought he was going to have a stroke. But then, suddenly, he seemed to grow calm. His breath was ragged, his skin was mottled with fiery blotches. He collapsed down into himself, head drooping, arms dangling. He looked altogether spent. Another minute or two passed before he could speak. I didn't know what to do for him. I floated there, watching. Finally a little life seemed to return to him.

'Did you see? That's what happens,' he gasped. 'It takes control. How could I ever kill myself? It wouldn't let me do it.'

'Wouldn't *let* you?'

He looked up at me and sighed wearily. 'Think, Chollie,

think! It's in symbiosis with me. We aren't independent organisms.' Then the tremors began again, worse than before. Fazio made a desperate furious attempt to fight them off – arms and legs flung rigidly out, jaws working – but it was useless. 'Illallomba!' he yelled. 'Nullagribba!' He tossed his head from side to side as if trying to shake off something sticky that was clinging to it. 'If I – then it – gillagilla! Holligoolla! I can't – I can't – oh – Jesus – Christ –!'

His voice died away into harsh sputters and clankings. He moaned and covered his face with his hands.

But now I understood.

For Fazio there could never be any escape. That was the most monstrous part of the whole thing, the ultimate horrifying twist. The symbiont knew that its destiny was linked to Fazio's. If he died, the symbiont would also; and so it could not allow its host to damage himself. From its seat in Fazio's brain it had ultimate control over his body. Whatever he tried – jump off a bridge, reach for a flask of poison, pick up a gun – the watchful thing in his mind would be a step ahead of him, always protecting him against harm.

A flood of compassion welled up in me and I started to put my hand comfortingly on Fazio's shoulder. But then I yanked it back as though I were afraid the symbiont could jump from his mind into mine at the slightest touch. And then I scowled and forced myself to touch him after all. He pulled away. He looked burned out.

'Chollie?' Elisandra said, coming up beside us. She floated alongside, long-limbed, beautiful, frowning. 'Is this private, or can I join you?'

I hesitated, fumbling. I desperately wanted to keep Fazio and Elisandra in separate compartments of my life, but I saw that I had no way of doing that. 'We were – well – just that – '

'Come on, Chollie,' Fazio said in a bleak hollow voice. 'Introduce your old war buddy to the nice woman.'

Elisandra gave him an enquiring glance. She could not have failed to detect the strangeness in his tone.

I took a deep breath. 'This is Fazio,' I said. 'We were in the Servadac campaign together during the Second Ovoid War. Fazio – Elisandra. Elisandra's a traffic-polarity engineer on the turnaround wheel – you ought to see her at work, the coolest cookie you can imagine – '

'An honour to meet you,' said Fazio grandly. 'A woman who combines such beauty and such technical skills – I have to say – I – I – ' Suddenly he was faltering. His face turned blotchy. Fury blazed in his eyes. 'No! Damn it, no! No more!' He clutched handfuls of air in some wild attempt at steadying himself. 'Mullagalloola!' he cried, helpless. 'Jillabongbong! Sampazozozo!' And he burst into wild choking sobs, while Elisandra stared at him in amazement and sorrow.

'Well, are you going to kill him?' she asked.

It was two hours later. We had put Fazio to bed in his little cubicle over at Transient House, and she and I were in her room. I had told her everything.

I looked at her as though she had begun to babble the way Fazio had. Elisandra and I had been together almost a year, but there were times I felt I didn't know her at all.

'Well?' she said.

'Are you serious?'

'You owe it to him. You owe him a death, Chollie. He can't come right out and say it, because the symbiont won't allow him to. But that's what he wants from you.'

I couldn't deny any of that. I'd been thinking the same thing for at least the past hour. The reality of it was inescapable: I had muffed things on Weinstein and sent Fazio to hell for ten years. Now I had to set him free.

'If there was only some way to get the symbiont out of his brain – '

'But there isn't.'

'No,' I said. 'There isn't.'

'You'll do it for him, won't you?'

'Quit it,' I said.

'I hate the way he's suffering, Chollie.'

'You think I don't?'

'And what about you? Suppose you fail him a second time. How will you live with that? Tell me how.'

'I was never much for killing, Ellie. Not even Ovoids.'

'We know that,' she said. 'But you don't have any choice this time.'

I went to the little fireglobe she had mounted above the sleeping platform, and hit the button and sent sparks through the thick coiling mists. A rustle of angry colours swept the mist, a wild aurora, green, purple, yellow. After a moment I said quietly, 'You're absolutely right.'

'Good. I was afraid for a moment you were going to crap out on him again.'

There was no malice in it, the way she said it. All the same, it hit me like a fist. I stood there nodding, letting the impact go rippling through me and away.

At last the reverberations seemed to die down within me. But then a great new uneasiness took hold of me and I said, 'You know, it's totally idiotic of us to be discussing this. I'm involving you in something that's none of your business. What we're doing is making you an accomplice before the fact.'

Elisandra ignored me. Something was in motion in her mind, and there was no swerving her now. 'How would you go about it?' she asked. 'You can't just cut someone's throat and dump him down a disposer chute.'

'Look,' I said, 'do you understand that the penalty could be anything up to – '

She went on, 'Any sort of direct physical assault is out. There'd be some sort of struggle for sure – the symbiont's bound to defend the host body against attack – you'd come away with scratches, bruises, worse. Somebody would notice. Suppose you got so badly hurt you had to go to the medics. What would you tell them? A bar-room brawl? And then nobody can find your old friend Fazio who you were seen with a few days before? No, much too risky.' Her tone was strangely businesslike, matter-of-fact. 'And then, getting rid of the body – that's even tougher, Chollie, getting fifty kilos of body mass off the Station without some kind of papers. No destination visa, no transshipment entry. Even a sack of potatoes would have an out-invoice. But if someone just vanishes and there's a fifty-kilo short balance in the mass totals that day – '

'Quit it,' I said. 'OK?'

'You owe him a death. You agreed about that.'

'Maybe I do. But whatever I decide, I don't want to drag you into it. It isn't your mess, Ellie.'

'You don't think so?' she shot right back at me.

Anger and love were all jumbled together in Elisandra's tone. I didn't feel like dealing with that just now. My head was pounding. I activated the pharmo arm by the sink and hastily ran a load of relaxants into myself with a subcute shot. Then I took her by the hand. Gently, trying hard to disengage, I said, 'Can we just go to bed now? I'd rather not talk about this any more.'

Elisandra smiled and nodded. 'Sure,' she replied, and her voice was much softer.

She started to pull off her clothes. But after a moment she turned to me, troubled. 'I can't drop it just like that, Chollie. It's still buzzing inside me. That poor bastard.' She shuddered. 'Never to be alone in his own head. Never to be sure he has control over his own body. Waking up in a puddle of piss, he said. Speaking in tongues. All that other crazy stuff. What did he say? Like feeling an ant wandering around inside his skull? An itch you can't possibly scratch?'

'I didn't know it would be that bad,' I said. 'I think I would have killed him back then, if I had known.'

'Why didn't you anyway?'

'He was Fazio. A human being. My friend. My buddy. I didn't much want to kill Ovoids, even. How the hell was I going to kill him?'

'But you promised to, Chollie.'

'Let me be,' I said. 'I didn't do it, that's all. Now I have to live with that.'

'So does he,' said Elisandra.

I climbed into her sleeptube and lay there without moving, waiting for her.

'So do I,' she added after a little while.

She wandered around the room for a time before joining me. Finally she lay down beside me, but at a slight distance. I didn't move towards her. But eventually the distance lessened, and I put my hand lightly on her shoulder, and she turned to me.

An hour or so before dawn she said, 'I think I see a way we can do it.'

We spent a week and a half working out the details. I was completely committed to it now, no hesitations, no reservations. As Elisandra said, I had no choice. This was what I owed Fazio; this was the only way I could settle accounts between us.

She was completely committed to it too: even more so than I was, it sometimes seemed. I warned her that she was needlessly letting herself in for major trouble in case the Station authorities ever managed to reconstruct what had happened. It didn't seem needless to her, she said.

I didn't have a lot of contact with him while we were arranging things. It was important, I figured, not to give the symbiont any hints. I saw Fazio practically every day, of course – Betelgeuse Station isn't all that big – off at a distance, staring, glaring, sometimes having one of his weird fits, climbing a wall or shouting incoherently or arguing with himself out loud; but generally I pretended not to see him. At times I couldn't avoid him, and then we met for dinner or drinks or a workout in the rec room. But there wasn't much of that.

'OK,' Elisandra said finally. 'I've done my part. Now you do yours, Chollie.'

Among the little services we run here is a sightseeing operation for tourists who feel like taking a close look at a red giant star. After the big stellar-envelope research project shut down a few years ago we inherited a dozen or so solar sleds that had been used for skimming through the fringes of Betelgeuse's mantle, and we began renting them out for three-day excursions. The sleds are two-passenger jobs without much in the way of luxury and nothing at all in the way of propulsion systems. The trip is strictly ballistic: we calculate your orbit and shoot you out of here on the big repellers, sending you on a dazzling swing across Betelgeuse's outer fringes that gives you the complete light-show and maybe a view of ten or twelve of the big star's family of planets. When the sled reaches the end of its string, we catch you on the turnaround wheel and reel you in. It sounds spectacular, and it is; it sounds dangerous, and it isn't. Not usually, anyhow.

I tracked Fazio down in the gravity lounge and said, 'We've arranged a treat for you, man.'

The sled I had rented for him was called the *Corona Queen*. Elisandra routinely handled the despatching job for these tours, and now and then I worked as wheelman for them, although ordinarily I wheeled the big interstellar liners that used Betelgeuse Station as their jumping-off point for deeper space. We were both going to work Fazio's sled. Unfortunately, this time there was going to be a disaster, because a regrettable little error had been made in calculating orbital polarity, and then there would be a one-in-a-million failure of the redundancy circuits. Fazio's sled wasn't going to go on a tour of Betelgeuse's far-flung corona at all. It was going to plunge right into the heart of the giant red star.

I would have liked to tell him that, as we headed down the winding corridors to the dropdock. But I couldn't, because telling Fazio meant telling Fazio's symbiont also; and what was good news for Fazio was bad news for the symbiont. To catch the filthy thing by surprise: that was essential.

How much did Fazio suspect? God knows. In his place, I think I might have had an inkling. But maybe he was striving with all his strength to turn his mind away from any kind of speculation about the voyage he was about to take.

'You can't possibly imagine what it's like,' I said. 'It's unique. There's just no way to simulate it. And the view of Betelgeuse that you get from the Station isn't even remotely comparable.'

'The sled glides through the corona on a film of vaporized carbon,' said Elisandra. 'The heat just rolls right off its surface.' We were chattering compulsively, trying to fill every moment with talk. 'You're completely shielded so that you can actually pass through the atmosphere of the star – '

'Of course,' I said, 'Betelgeuse is so big and so violent that you're more or less inside its atmosphere no matter where you are in its system – '

'And then there are the planets,' Elisandra said. 'The way things are lined up this week, you may be able to see as many as a dozen of them – '

'– Otello, Falstaff, Siegfried, maybe Wotan – '

'– You'll find a map on the ceiling of your cabin – '

'– Five gas giants twice the mass of Jupiter – keep your eye out for Wotan, that's the one with rings – '

'– and Isolde, you can't miss Isolde, she's even redder than Betelgeuse, the damnedest bloodshot planet imaginable – '

'– with eleven red moons, too, but you won't be able to see them without filters – '

'– Otello and Falstaff for sure, and I think this week's chart shows Aida out of occultation now too – '

'– and then there's the band of comets – '

'– the asteroids, that's where we think a couple of the planets collided after gravitational perturbation of – '

'– and the Einsteinian curvature, it's unmistakable – '

'– the big solar flares – '

'Here we are,' Elisandra said.

We had reached the dropdock. Before us rose a gleaming metal wall. Elisandra activated the hatch and it swung back to reveal the little sled, a sleek tapering frog-nosed thing with a low hump in the middle. It sat on tracks; above it arched the coils of the repeller-launcher, radiating at the moment the blue-green glow that indicated a neutral charge. Everything was automatic. We had only to put Fazio on board and give the Station the signal for launch; the rest would be taken care of by the orbital-polarity program Elisandra had previously keyed in.

'It's going to be the trip of your life, man!' I said.

Fazio nodded. His eyes looked a little glazed, and his nostrils were flaring.

Elisandra hit the pre-launch control. The sled's roof opened and a recorded voice out of a speaker in the dropdock ceiling began to explain to Fazio how to get inside and make himself secure for launching. My hands were cold, my throat was dry. Yet I was very calm, all things considered. This was murder, wasn't it? Maybe so, technically speaking. But I was finding other names for it. A mercy killing; a balancing of the karmic accounts; a way of atoning for an ancient sin of omission. For him, release from hell after ten years; for me, release from a lesser but still acute kind of pain.

Fazio approached the sled's narrow entry slot.

'Wait a second,' I said. I caught him by the arm. The account wasn't quite in balance yet.

'Chollie – ' Elisandra said.

I shook her off. To Fazio I said, 'There's one thing I need to tell you before you go.'

He gave me a peculiar look, but didn't say anything.

I went on, 'I've been claiming all along that I didn't shoot you when the synsym got you because there wasn't time, the medics

255

landed too fast. That's sort of true, but mainly it's bullshit. I had time. What I didn't have was the guts.'

'Chollie – ' Elisandra said again. There was an edge on her voice.

'Just one more second,' I told her. I turned to Fazio again. 'I looked at you, I looked at the heat-gun, I thought about the synsym. But I just couldn't do it. I stood there with the gun in my hand and I didn't do a thing. And then the medics landed and it was too late – I felt like such a shit, Fazio, such a cowardly shit – '

Fazio's face was turning blotchy. The red synsym lines blazed weirdly in his eyes.

'Get him into the sled!' Elisandra yelled. 'It's taking control of him, Chollie!'

'Oligabongaboo!' Fazio said. 'Ungabanoo! Flizz! Thrapp!'

And he came at me like a wild man.

I had him by thirty kilos, at least, but he damned near knocked me over. Somehow I managed to stay upright. He bounced off me and went reeling around, and Elisandra grabbed his arm. He kicked her hard and sent her flying, but then I wrapped my forearm around the throat from behind, and Elisandra, crawling across the floor, got him around his legs so we could lift him and stuff him into the sled. Even then we had trouble holding him. Two of us against one skinny burned-out ruined man, and he writhed and twisted and wriggled about like something diabolical. He scratched, he kicked, he elbowed, he spat. His eyes were fiery. Every time we forced him close to the entryway of the sled he dragged us back away from it. Elisandra and I were grunting and winded, and I didn't think we could hang on much longer. This wasn't Fazio we were doing battle with, it was a synthetic symbiont out of the Ovoid labs, furiously trying to save itself from a fiery death. God knows what alien hormones it was pumping into Fazio's bloodstream. God knows how it had rebuilt his bones and heart and lungs for greater efficiency. If he ever managed to break free of my grip, I wondered which of us would get out of the dropdock alive.

But all the same Fazio still needed to breathe. I tightened my hold on his throat and felt cartilage yielding. I didn't care. I just wanted to get him on that sled, dead or alive, give him some peace at all. Him and me both. Tighter – tighter –

Fazio made rough sputtering noises, and then a thick nasty gargling sound.

'You've got him,' Elisandra said.

'Yeah. Yeah.'

I clamped down one notch tighter yet, and Fazio began to go limp, though his muscles still spasmed and jerked frantically. The creature within him was still full of fight; but there wasn't much air getting into Fazio's lungs now and his brain was starving for oxygen. Slowly Elisandra and I shoved him the last five metres towards the sled – lifted him, pushed him up to the edge of the slot, started to jam him into it –

A convulsion wilder than anything that had gone before ripped through Fazio's body. He twisted half around in my grasp until he was face to face with Elisandra, and a bubble of something grey and shiny appeared on his lips. For an instant everything seemed frozen. It was like a slice across time, for just that instant. Then things began to move again. The bubble burst; some fragment of tissue leaped the short gap from Fazio's lips to Elisandra's. The symbiont, facing death, had cast forth a piece of its own life-stuff to find another host. '*Chollie!*' Elisandra wailed, and let go of Fazio and went reeling away as if someone had thrown acid in her eyes. She was clawing at her face. At the little flat grey slippery thing that had plastered itself over her mouth and was rapidly poking a couple of glistening pseudopods up into her nostrils. I hadn't known it was possible for a symbiont to send out offshoots like that. I guess no-one did, or people like Fazio wouldn't be allowed to walk around loose.

I wanted to yell and scream and break things. I wanted to cry. But I didn't do any of those things.

When I was four years old, growing up on Backgammon, my father bought me a shiny little vortex-boat from a pedlar on Maelstrom Bridge. It was just a toy, a bathtub boat, though it had all the stabilizer struts and outriggers in miniature. We were standing on the bridge and I wanted to see how well the boat worked, so I flipped it over the rail into the vortex. Of course it was swept out of sight at once. Bewildered and upset because it didn't come back to me, I looked toward my father for help. But he thought I had flung his gift into the whirlpool for the sheer hell of it, and he gave me a shrivelling look of black anger and downright hatred that I will never forget. I cried half a day, but that didn't bring back my vortex-boat. I wanted to cry now. Sure. Something grotesquely unfair had happened, and I felt four years old all over again, and there was nobody to turn to for help. I was on my own.

I went to Elisandra and held her for a moment. She was sobbing and trying to speak, but the thing covered her lips. Her face was white with terror and her whole body was trembling and jerking crazily.

'Don't worry,' I whispered. 'This time I know what to do.'

How fast we act, when finally we move. I got Fazio out of the way first, tossing him or the husk of him into the entry slot of the *Solar Queen* as easily as though he had been an armload of straw. Then I picked up Elisandra and carried her to the sled. She didn't really struggle, just twisted about a little. The symbiont didn't have that much control yet. At the last moment I looked into her eyes, hoping I wasn't going to see the red circles in them. No, not yet, not so soon. Her eyes were the eyes I remembered, the eyes I loved. They were steady, cold, clear. She knew what was happening. She couldn't speak, but she was telling me with her eyes: *Yes, yes, go ahead, for Christ's sake go ahead, Chollie!*

Unfair. Unfair. But nothing is ever fair, I thought. Or else if there is justice in the universe it exists only on levels we can't perceive, in some chilly macrocosmic place where everything is evened out in the long run but the sin is not necessarily atoned by the sinner. I pushed her into the slot down next to Fazio and slammed the sled shut. And went to the dropdock's wall-console and keyed in the departure signal, and watched as the sled went sliding down the track towards the exit hatch on its one-way journey to Betelgeuse. The red light of the activated repellers glared for a moment, and then the blue-green returned. I turned away, wondering if the symbiont had managed to get a piece of itself into me too at the last moment. I waited to feel that tickle in the mind. But I didn't. I guess there hadn't been time for it to get us both.

And then, finally, I dropped down on the launching track and let myself cry. And went out of there, after a while, silent, numb, purged clean, thinking of nothing at all. At the inquest

six weeks later I told them I didn't have the slightest notion why
Elisandra had chosen to get aboard that ship with Fazio. Was it
a suicide pact, the inquest panel asked me? I shrugged. I don't
know, I said. I don't have any goddamned idea what was going
on in their minds that day, I said. Silent, numb, purged clean,
thinking of nothing at all.

So Fazio rests at last in the blazing heart of Betelgeuse. My
Elisandra is in there also. And I go on, day after day, still
working the turnaround wheel here at the Station, reeling in
the stargoing ships that come cruising past the fringes of the
giant red sun. I still feel haunted, too. But it isn't Fazio's ghost
that visits me now, or even Elisandra's – not now, not after all
this time. I think the ghost that haunts me is my own.

Sailing to Byzantium

We've reached the spring of 1984. A few months earlier I had completed my historical/fantasy novel *Gilgamesh the King*, which is set in ancient Sumer, and antiquity was still very much on my mind when Shawna McCarthy, who had just begun her brief and brilliant career as editor of *Isaac Asimov's Science Fiction Magazine*, came to the San Francisco area on holiday. I ran into her at a party and she asked me if I'd write a story for her. 'I'd like to, yes,' I said. 'A long one.'

'How long?'

'Long,' I told her. 'A novella.'

'Good,' she said. We did a little haggling over the price, and that was that. She went back to New York and I got going on 'Sailing to Byzantium', and by late summer it was done.

Though I had forgotten it until recently, 'Sailing to Byzantium' wasn't called that, originally. A few months ago, going through some old papers, I came upon a manila envelope on which I had jotted the kernel of the idea out of which 'Sailing to Byzantium' grew. My working title was 'The Hundred-Gated City', a reference to ancient Thebes, and this was what I had in mind:

'Ancient Egypt has been re-created at the end of time, along with various other highlights of history — a sort of Disneyland. A twentieth-century man, through error, has been regenerated in Thebes, though he belongs in the replica of Los Angeles. The misplaced Egyptian has been sent to Troy, or maybe Knossos, and a Cretan has been displaced into a Brasilia-equivalent of the twenty-ninth century. They move about, attempting to return to their proper places.'

It's a nice idea, but it's not quite the story I ultimately wrote. (Maybe I'll use it some day — waste not, want not.) 'Sailing to Byzantium' is what emerged instead, and from the earliest pages I knew I was on to something special. Shawna had one or two small editorial suggestions for clarifying the ending, which I accepted gladly, and my friend Shay

Barsabe, who read the story in manuscript, pointed out one subtle blunder in the plot which I hastily corrected.

The story was published as an elegant limited-edition book by the house of Underwood-Miller, and soon afterwards it appeared in *Asimov's* issue for February 1985. It was immediately popular and all three of the year's-best-s-f anthologists chose it for that year's volume. 'A possible classic,' is what Wollheim called it, praise which I shamelessly quote here because Don Wollheim, who has been pondering the mysteries of science fiction longer than I've been alive, is not one to throw such words around lightly, and I was delighted by his comment. 'Sailing to Byzantium' won me a Nebula award, too, and was nominated for a Hugo, but finished in second place, losing by four votes out of 800. Since then it's been reprinted several more times and translated into many languages. It's one of my own all-time favourites among my stories.

At dawn he arose and stepped out on to the patio for his first look at Alexandria, the one city he had not yet seen. That year the five cities were Chang-an, Asgard, New Chicago, Timbuctoo, Alexandria: the usual mix of eras, cultures, realities. He and Gioia, making the long flight from Asgard in the distant north the night before, had arrived late, well after sundown, and had gone straight to bed. Now, by the gentle apricot-hued morning light, the fierce spires and battlements of Asgard seemed merely something he had dreamed.

The rumour was that Asgard's moment was finished, anyway. In a little while, he had heard, they were going to tear it down and replace it, elsewhere, with Mohenjo-daro. Though there were never more than five cities, they changed constantly. He could remember a time when they had had Rome of the Caesars instead of Chang-an, and Rio de Janeiro rather than Alexandria. These people saw no point in keeping anything very long.

It was not easy for him to adjust to the sultry intensity of Alexandria after the frozen splendours of Asgard. The wind, coming off the water, was brisk and torrid both at once. Soft turquoise wavelets lapped at the jetties. Strong presences assailed his senses: the hot heavy sky, the stinging scent of the red lowland sand borne on the breeze, the sullen swampy aroma of the nearby sea. Everything trembled and glimmered in the early light. Their hotel was beautifully situated, high on the northern slope of the huge artificial mound known as the Paneium that was sacred to the goat-footed god. From here they had a total view of the city: the wide noble boulevards, the soaring obelisks and monuments, the palace of Hadrian just below the hill, the stately and awesome Library, the temple of Poseidon, the teeming marketplace, the royal lodge that Mark Antony had built after his defeat at Actium. And of course the Lighthouse, the wondrous many-windowed Lighthouse, the seventh wonder of the world, that immense pile of marble and limestone and reddish-purple Aswan granite rising in majesty at the end of its mile-long causeway. Black smoke from the beacon-fire at its summit curled lazily into the sky. The city was awakening. Some temporaries in short white kilts appeared and began to trim the dense dark hedges that bordered the great public buildings. A few citizens wearing loose robes of vaguely Grecian style were strolling in the streets.

There were ghosts and chimeras and phantasies everywhere about. Two slim elegant centaurs, a male and a female, grazed on the hillside. A burly thick-thighed swordsman appeared on the porch of the temple of Poseidon holding a Gorgon's severed head and waved it in a wide arc, grinning broadly. In the street below the hotel gate three small pink sphinxes, no bigger than house cats, stretched and yawned and began to prowl the kerbside. A larger one, lion-sized, watched warily from an alleyway: their mother, surely. Even at this distance he could hear her loud purring.

Shading his eyes, he peered far out past the Lighthouse and across the water. He hoped to see the dim shores of Crete or Cyprus to the north, or perhaps the great dark curve of Anatolia. *Carry me towards that great Byzantium*, he thought. *Where all is ancient, singing at the oars*. But he beheld only the endless empty sea, sun-bright and blinding though the morning was just beginning. Nothing was ever where he expected it to be. The continents did not seem to be in their proper places any longer. Gioia, taking him aloft long ago in her little flitterflitter, had shown him that. The tip of South America was canted far out into the Pacific; Africa was weirdly foreshortened; a broad tongue of ocean separated Europe and Asia. Australia did not appear to exist at all. Perhaps they had dug it up and used it for other things. There was no trace of the world he once had known. This was the fiftieth century. 'The fiftieth century after *what*?' he had asked several times, but no-one seemed to know, or else they did not care to say.

'Is Alexandria very beautiful?' Gioia called from within.

'Come out and see.'

Naked and sleepy-looking, she padded out on to the white-tiled patio and nestled up beside him. She fitted neatly under his arm. 'Oh, yes, yes!' she said softly. 'So very beautiful, isn't it? Look, there, the palaces, the Library, the Lighthouse! Where will we go first? The Lighthouse, I think. Yes? And then the market place – I want to see the Egyptian magicians – and the stadium, the races – will they be having races today, do you think? Oh, Charles, I want to see everything!'

'Everything? All on the first day?'

'All on the first day, yes,' she said. 'Everything.'

'But we have plenty of time, Gioia.'

'Do we?'

He smiled and drew her tight against his side.

'Time enough,' he said gently.

He loved her for her impatience, for her bright bubbling eagerness. Gioia was not much like the rest in that regard, though she seemed identical in all other ways. She was short, supple, slender, dark-eyed, olive-skinned, narrow-hipped, with wide shoulders and flat muscles. They were all like that, each one indistinguishable from the rest, like a horde of millions of brothers and sisters – a world of small lithe childlike Mediterraneans, built for juggling, for bull-dancing, for sweet white wine at midday and rough red wine at night. They had the same slim bodies, the same broad mouths, the same great glossy eyes. He had never seen anyone who appeared to be younger than twelve or older than twenty. Gioia was somehow a little different, although he did not quite know how; but he knew that it was for that imperceptible but significant difference that he loved her. And probably that was why she loved him also.

He let his gaze drift from west to east, from the Gate of the Moon down broad Canopus Street and out to the harbour, and off to the tomb of Cleopatra at the tip of long slender Cape Lochias. Everything was here and all of it perfect, the obelisks, the statues and marble colonnades, the courtyards and shrines and groves, great Alexander himself in his coffin of crystal and gold: a splendid gleaming pagan city. But there were oddities – an unmistakable mosque near the public gardens, and what seemed to be a Christian church not far from the Library. And those ships in the harbour, with all those red sails and bristling masts – surely they were medieval, and late medieval at that. He had seen such anachronisms in other places before. Doubtless these people found them amusing. Life was a game for them. They played at it unceasingly. Rome, Alexandria, Timbuctoo – why not? Create an Asgard of translucent bridges and shimmering ice-girt palaces, then grow weary of it and take it away? Replace it with Mohenjo-daro? Why not? It seemed to him a great pity to destroy those lofty Nordic feasting-halls for the sake of building a squat brutal sun-baked city of brown brick; but these people did not look at things the way he did. Their cities were only temporary. Someone in Asgard had said that Timbuctoo would be the next to go, with Byzantium rising in its place. Well, why not? Why not? They could have anything they liked. This was the fiftieth century, after all. The only rule was that there could be no more than five cities at once. 'Limits,' Gioia had informed him solemnly when they first began to travel together, 'are very important.' But she did not know why, or did not care to say.

He stared out once more towards the sea.

He imagined a newborn city congealing suddenly out of mists, far across the water: shining towers, great domed palaces, golden mosaics. That would be no great effort for them. They could just summon it forth whole out of time, the Emperor on his throne and the Emperor's drunken soldiery roistering in the streets, the brazen clangour of the cathedral gong rolling through the Grand Bazaar, dolphins leaping beyond the shoreside pavilions. Why not? They had Timbuctoo. They had Alexandria. Do you crave Constantinople? Then behold Constantinople! Or Avalon, or Lyonesse, or Atlantis. They could have anything they liked. It is pure Schopenhauer here: the world as will and imagination. Yes! These slender dark-eyed people journeying tirelessly from miracle to miracle. Why not Byzantium next? Yes! Why not? *That is no country for old men*, he thought. *The young in one another's arms, the birds in the trees* – yes! Yes! Anything they liked. They even had him.

Suddenly he felt frightened. Questions he had not asked for a long time burst through into his conciousness. *Who am I? Why am I here? Who is this woman beside me?*

'You're so quiet all of a sudden, Charles,' said Gioia, who could not abide silence for very long. 'Will you talk to me? I want you to talk to me. Tell me what you're looking for out there.'

He shrugged. 'Nothing.'

'Nothing?'

'Nothing in particular.'

'I could see you seeing something.'

'Byzantium,' he said. 'I was imagining that I could look straight across the water to Byzantium. I was trying to get a glimpse of the walls of Constantinople.'

'Oh, but you wouldn't be able to see as far as that from here. Not really.'

'I know.'

'And anyway Byzantium doesn't exist.'

'Not yet. But it will. Its time comes later on.'

'Does it?' she said. 'Do you know that for a fact?'

'On good authority. I heard it in Asgard,' he told her. 'But even if I hadn't, Byzantium would be inevitable, don't you think? Its time would have to come. How could we not do Byzantium, Gioia? We certainly will do Byzantium, sooner or later. I know we will. It's only a matter of time. And we have all the time in the world.'

A shadow crossed her face. 'Do we? Do we?'

He knew very little about himself, but he knew that he was not one of them. That he knew. He knew that his name was Charles Phillips and that before he had come to live among these people he had lived in the year 1984, when there had been such things as computers and television sets and baseball and jet planes, and the world was full of cities, not merely five but thousands of them, New York and London and Johannesburg and Paris and Liverpool and Bangkok and San Francisco and Buenos Aires and a multitude of others, all at the same time. There had been four and a half billion people in the world then; now he doubted that there were as many as four and a half million. Nearly everything had changed beyond comprehension. The moon still seemed the same, and the sun; but at night he searched in vain for familiar constellations. He had no idea how they had brought him from then to now, or why. It did no good to ask. No-one had any answers for him; no-one so much as appeared to understand what it was that he was trying to learn. After a time he had stopped asking; after a time he had almost entirely ceased wanting to know.

He and Gioia were climbing the Lighthouse. She scampered ahead, in a hurry as always, and he came along behind her in his more stolid fashion. Scores of other tourists, mostly in groups of two or three, were making their way up the wide flagstone ramps, laughing, calling to one another. Some of them, seeing him, stopped a moment, stared, pointed. He was used to that. He was so much taller than any of them; he was plainly not one of them. When they pointed at him he smiled. Sometimes he nodded a little acknowledgement.

He could not find much of interest in the lowest level, a massive square structure two hundred feet high built of huge marble blocks: within its cool musty arcades were hundreds of small dark rooms, the offices of the Lighthouse's keepers and mechanics, the barracks of the garrison, the stables for the three hundred donkeys that carried the fuel to the lantern far above. None of that appeared inviting to him. He forged onwards without halting until he emerged on the balcony that led to the next level. Here the Lighthouse grew narrower and became octagonal: its face, granite now and handsomely fluted, rose in a stunning sweep above him.

Gioia was waiting for him there. 'This is for you,' she said, holding out a nugget of meat on a wooden skewer. 'Roast lamb. Absolutely delicious. I had one while I was waiting for you.' She gave him a cup of some cool green sherbet also, and darted off to buy a pomegranate. Dozens of temporaries were roaming the balcony, selling refreshments of all kinds.

He nibbled at the meat. It was charred outside, nicely pink and moist within. While he ate, one of the temporaries came up to him and peered blandly into his face. It was a stocky swarthy male wearing nothing but a strip of red and yellow cloth about its waist. 'I sell meat,' it said. 'Very fine roast lamb, only five drachmas.'

Phillips indicated the piece he was eating. 'I already have some,' he said.

'It is excellent meat, very tender. It has been soaked for three days in the juices of – '

'Please,' Phillips said. 'I don't want to buy any meat. Do you mind moving along?'

The temporaries had confused and baffled him at first, and there was still much about them that was unclear to him. They were not machines – they looked like creatures of flesh and blood – but they did not seem to be human beings, either, and no-one treated them as if they were. He supposed they were artificial constructs, products of a technology so consummate that it was invisible. Some appeared to be more intelligent than others, but all of them behaved as if they had no more autonomy than characters in a play, which was essentially what they were. There were untold numbers of them in each of the five cities, playing all manner of roles: shepherds and swineherds, street-sweepers, merchants, boatmen, vendors of grilled meats and cool drinks, hagglers in the marketplace, schoolchildren, charioteers, policemen, grooms, gladiators, monks, artisans, whores and cutpurses, sailors – whatever was needed to sustain the illusion of a thriving, populous urban centre. The dark-eyed people, Gioia's people, never performed work. There were not enough of them to keep a city's functions going, and in any case they were strictly tourists, wandering with the wind, moving from city to city as the whim took them, Chang-an to New Chicago, New Chicago to Timbuctoo, Timbuctoo to Asgard, Asgard to Alexandria, onwards, ever onwards.

The temporary would not leave him alone. Phillips walked away and it followed him, cornering him against the balcony wall. When Gioia returned a few minutes later, lips prettily stained with pomegranate juice, the temporary was still hovering about him, trying with lunatic persistence to sell him a skewer of lamb. It stood much too close to him, almost nose to nose, great sad cowlike eyes peering intently into his as it extolled with mournful mooing urgency the quality of its wares. It seemed to him that he had had trouble like this with temporaries on one or two earlier occasions. Gioia touched the creature's elbow lightly and said, in a short sharp tone Phillips had never heard her use before, 'He isn't interested. Get away from him.' It went at once. To Phillips she said, 'You have to be firm with them.'

'I was trying. It wouldn't listen to me.'

'You ordered it to go away, and it refused?'

'I asked it to go away. Politely. Too politely, maybe.'

'Even so,' she said. 'It should have obeyed a human, regardless.'

'Maybe it didn't think I was human,' Phillips suggested. 'Because of the way I look. My height, the colour of my eyes. It might have thought I was some kind of temporary myself.'

'No,' Gioia said, frowning. 'A temporary won't solicit another temporary. But it won't ever disobey a citizen, either. There's a very clear boundary. There isn't ever any confusion. I can't understand why it went on bothering you.' He was surprised at how troubled she seemed: far more so, he thought, than the incident warranted. A stupid device, perhaps miscalibrated in some way, overenthusiastically pushing its wares – what of it? What of it? Gioia, after a moment, appeared to come to the same conclusion. Shrugging, she said, 'It's defective, I suppose. Probably such things are more common than we suspect, don't you think?' There was something forced about her tone that bothered him. She smiled and handed him her pomegranate. 'Here. Have a bite, Charles. It's wonderfully sweet. They used to be extinct, you know. Shall we go on upwards?'

The octagonal midsection of the Lighthouse must have been several hundred feet in height, a grim claustrophobic tube almost entirely filled by the two broad spiralling ramps that wound around the huge building's central well. The ascent was slow: a donkey team was a little way ahead of them on the ramp, plodding along laden with bundles of kindling for the lantern. But at last, just as Phillips was growing winded and dizzy, he and Gioia came out on to the second balcony, the one marking the transition between the octagonal section and the Lighthouse's uppermost storey, which was cylindrical and very slender.

She leaned far out over the balustrade. 'Oh, Charles, look at the view! Look at it!'

It was amazing. From one side they could see the entire city, and swampy Lake Mareotis and the dusty Egyptian plain beyond it, and from the other they peered far out into the grey and choppy Mediterranean. He gestured towards the innumerable reefs and shallows that infested the waters leading to the harbour entrance. 'No wonder they needed a lighthouse here,' he said. 'Without some kind of gigantic landmark they'd never have found their way in from the open sea.'

A blast of sound, a ferocious snort, erupted just above him. He looked up, startled. Immense statues of trumpet-wielding Tritons jutted from the corners of the Lighthouse at this level; that great blurting sound had come from the nearest of them. A signal, he thought. A warning to the ships negotiating that troubled passage. The sound was produced by some kind of steam-powered mechanism, he realized, operated by teams of sweating temporaries clustered about bonfires at the base of each Triton.

Once again he found himself swept by admiration for the clever way these people carried out their reproductions of antiquity. Or *were* they reproductions, he wondered? He still did not understand how they brought their cities into being. For all he knew, this place was the authentic Alexandria itself, pulled forward out of its proper time just as he himself had been. Perhaps this was the true and original Lighthouse, and not a copy. He had no idea which was the case, nor which would be the greater miracle.

'How do we get to the top?' Gioia asked.

'Over there, I think. That doorway.'

The spiralling donkey-ramps ended here. The loads of lantern fuel went higher via a dumb-waiter in the central shaft. Visitors continued by way of a cramped staircase, so narrow at its upper end that it was impossible to turn around while climbing. Gioia, tireless, sprinted ahead. He clung to the rail and laboured up and up, keeping count of the tiny window-slits to ease the boredom of the ascent. The count was nearing a hundred when finally he stumbled into the vestibule of the beacon chamber. A dozen or so visitors were crowded into it. Gioia was at the far side, by the wall that was open to the sea.

It seemed to him he could feel the building swaying in the winds, up here. How high were they? Five hundred feet, six hundred, seven? The beacon chamber was tall and narrow, divided by a catwalk into upper and lower sections. Down below, relays of temporaries carried wood from the dumb-waiter and tossed it on the blazing fire. He felt its intense heat from where he stood, at the rim of the platform on which the giant mirror of polished metal was hung. Tongues of flame leaped upwards and danced before the mirror, which hurled its dazzling beam far out to sea. Smoke rose through a vent. At the very top was a colossal statue of Poseidon, austere, ferocious, looming above the lantern.

Gioia sidled along the catwalk until she was at his side. 'The guide was talking before you came,' she said, pointing. 'Do you see that place over there, under the mirror? Someone standing there and looking into the mirror gets a view of ships at sea that can't be seen from here by the naked eye. The mirror magnifies things.'

'Do you believe that?'

She nodded towards the guide. 'It said so. And it also told us that if you look in a certain way, you can see right across the water into the city of Constantinople.'

She is like a child, he thought. They all are. He said, 'You told me yourself this very morning that it isn't possible to see that far. Besides, Constantinople doesn't exist right now.'

'It will,' she replied. '*You* said that to me, this very morning. And when it does, it'll be reflected in the Lighthouse mirror. That's the truth. I'm absolutely certain of it.' She swung about abruptly towards the entrance of the beacon chamber. 'Oh, look, Charles! Here come Nissandra and Aramayne! And there's Hawk! There's Stengard!' Gioia laughed and waved and called out names. 'Oh, everyone's here! *Everyone!*'

They came jostling into the room, so many newcomers that some of those who had been there were forced to scramble down the steps on the far side. Gioia moved among them, hugging, kissing. Phillips could scarcely tell one from another – it was hard for him even to tell which were the men and which the women, dressed as they all were in the same sort of loose robes – but he recognized some of the names. These were her special friends, her set, with whom she had journeyed from city to city on an endless round of gaiety in the old days before he had come into her life. He had met a few of them before, in Asgard, in Rio, in Rome. The beacon-chamber guide, a squat wide-shouldered old temporary wearing a laurel wreath on its bald head, reappeared and began its potted speech, but no-one listened to it; they were all too busy greeting one another, embracing, giggling. Some of them edged their way over to Phillips and reached up, standing on tiptoes, to touch their fingertips to his cheek in that odd hello of theirs. 'Charles,' they said gravely, making two syllables out of the name, as these people often did. 'So good to see you again. Such a pleasure. You and Gioia – such a handsome couple. So well suited to each other.'

Was that so? He supposed it was.

The chamber hummed with chatter. The guide could not be heard at all. Stengard and Nissandra had visited New Chicago for the water-dancing – Aramayne bore tales of a feast in Chang-an that had gone on for *days* – Hawk and Hekna had been to Timbuctoo to see the arrival of the salt caravan, and were going back there soon – a final party soon to celebrate the end of Asgard that absolutely should not be missed – the plans for the new city, Mohenjo-daro – we have reservations for the opening, we wouldn't pass it up for anything – and, yes, they were definitely going to do Constantinople after that, the planners were already deep into their Byzantium research – so good to see you, you look so beautiful all the time – have you been to the Library yet? The zoo? To the temple of Serapis? –

To Phillips they said, 'What do you think of our Alexandria, Charles? Of course you must have known it well in your day. Does it look the way you remember it?' They were always asking things like that. They did not seem to comprehend that the Alexandria of the Lighthouse and the Library was long lost and legendary by the time his twentieth century had been. To them, he suspected, all the places they had brought back into existence were more or less contemporary. Rome of the Caesars, Alexandria of the Ptolemies, Venice of the Doges, Chang-an of the T'angs, Asgard of the Aesir, none any less real than the next nor any less unreal, each one simply a facet of the distant past, the fantastic immemorial past, a plum plucked from that dark backward abysm of time. They had no contexts for separating one era from another. To them all the past was one borderless timeless realm. Why then should he not have seen the Lighthouse before, he who had leaped into this era from the New York of 1984? He had never been able to explain it to them. Julius Caesar and Hannibal, Helen of Troy and Charlemagne, Rome of the gladiators and New York of the Yankees and Mets, Gilgamesh and Tristan and Othello and Robin Hood and George Washington and Queen Victoria – to them, all equally real and unreal, none of them any more than bright figures moving about on a painted canvas. The past, the past, the elusive and fluid past – to them it was a single place of infinite accessibility and infinite connectivity. Of course they would think he had seen the Lighthouse before. He knew better than to try again to explain things. 'No,' he said simply. 'This is my first time in Alexandria.'

They stayed there all winter long, and possibly some of the spring. Alexandria was not a place where one was sharply aware of the change of seasons, nor did the passage of time itself make itself very evident when one was living one's entire life as a tourist.

During the day there was always something new to see. The zoological garden, for instance: a wondrous park, miraculously green and lush in this hot dry climate, where astounding animals roamed in enclosures so generous that they did not seem like enclosures at all. Here were camels, rhinoceroses, gazelles, ostriches, lions, wild asses; and here too, casually adjacent to those familiar African beasts, were hippogriffs, unicorns, basilisks and fire-snorting dragons with rainbow scales. Had the original zoo of Alexandria had dragons and unicorns? Phillips doubted it. But this one did; evidently it was no harder for the backstage craftsmen to manufacture mythic beasts than it was for them to turn out camels and gazelles. To Gioia and her friends all of them were equally mythical, anyway. They were just as awed by the rhinoceros as by the hippogriff. One was no more strange – nor any less – than the other. So far as Phillips had been able to discover, none of the mammals or birds of his era had survived into this one except for a few cats and dogs, though many had been reconstructed.

And then the Library! All those lost treasures, reclaimed from the jaws of time! Stupendous columned marble walls, airy high-vaulted reading-rooms, dark coiling stacks stretching away to infinity. The ivory handles of seven hundred thousand papyrus scrolls bristling on the shelves. Scholars and librarians gliding quietly about, smiling faint scholarly smiles but plainly preoccupied with serious matters of the mind. They were all temporaries, Phillips realized. Mere props, part of the illusion. But were the scrolls illusions too? 'Here we have the complete dramas of Sophocles,' said the guide with a blithe wave of its hand, indicating shelf upon shelf of texts. Only seven of his hundred and twenty-three plays had survived the successive burnings of the Library in ancient times by Romans, Christians, Arabs: were the lost ones here, the *Triptolemus*, the *Nausicaa*, the *Jason* and all the rest? And would he find here too, miraculously restored to being, the other vanished treasures of ancient literature – the memoirs of Odysseus, Cato's history of Rome, Thucydides' life of Pericles, the missing volumes of Livy? But when he asked if he might explore the stacks, the guide smiled apologetically and said that all the librarians were busy just now. Another time, perhaps? Perhaps, said the guide. It made no difference, Phillips decided. Even if these people somehow had brought back those lost masterpieces of antiquity, how would he read them? He knew no Greek.

The life of the city buzzed and throbbed about him. It was a dazzlingly beautiful place: the vast bay thick with sails, the great avenues running rigidly east–west, north–south, the sunlight rebounding almost audibly from the bright walls of the palaces of kings and gods. They have done this very well, Phillips thought: very well indeed. In the marketplace hard-eyed traders squabbled in half a dozen mysterious languages over the price of ebony, Arabian incense, jade, panther-skins. Gioia bought a dram of pale musky Egyptian perfume in a delicate tapering glass flask. Magicians and jugglers and scribes called out stridently to passers-by, begging for a few moments of attention and a handful of coins for their labour. Strapping slaves, black and tawny and some that might have been Chinese, were put up for auction, made to flex their muscles, to bare their teeth, to bare their breasts and thighs to prospective buyers. In the gymnasium naked athletes hurled javelins and discuses, and wrestled with terrifying zeal. Gioia's friend Stengard came rushing up with a gift for her, a golden necklace that would not have embarrassed Cleopatra. An hour later she had lost it, or perhaps had given it away while Phillips was looking elsewhere. She bought another, even finer, the next day. Anyone could have all the money he wanted, simply by asking: it was as easy to come by as air, for these people.

Being here was much like going to the movies, Phillips told himself. A different show every day: not much plot, but the special effects were magnificent and the detail-work could hardly have been surpassed. A megamovie, a vast entertainment that went on all the time and was being played out by the whole population of Earth. And it was all so effortless, so spontaneous: just as when he had gone to a movie he had never troubled to think about the myriad technicians behind the scenes, the cameramen and the costume designers and the set-builders and the electricians and the model-makers and the boom operators, so too here he chose not to question the means by which Alexandria had been set before him. It felt real. It *was* real. When he drank the strong red wine it gave him a pleasant buzz. If he leaped from the beacon chamber of the Lighthouse he suspected he would die, though perhaps he would not stay dead for long: doubtless they had some way of restoring him as often as was necessary. Death did not seem to be a factor in these people's lives.

By day they saw sights. By night he and Gioia went to parties, in their hotel, in seaside villas, in the palaces of the high nobility. The usual people were there all the time: Hawk and Hekna, Aramayne, Stengard and Shelimir, Nissandra, Asoka, Afonso, Protay. At the parties there were five or ten temporaries for every citizen, some as mere servants, others as entertainers or even surrogate guests, mingling freely and a little daringly. But everyone knew, all the time, who was a citizen and who just a temporary. Phillips began to think his own status lay somewhere between. Certainly they treated him with a courtesy that no-one ever would give a temporary, and yet there was a condescension to their manner that told him not simply that he was not one of them but that he was someone or something of an altogether different order of existence. That he was Gioia's lover gave him some standing in their eyes, but not a great deal: obviously he was always going to be an outsider, a primitive, ancient and quaint. For that matter he noticed that Gioia herself, though unquestionably a member of the set, seemed to be regarded as something of an outsider, like a tradesman's great-granddaughter in a gathering of Plantagenets. She did not always find out about the best parties in time to attend; her friends did not always reciprocate her effusive greetings with the same degree of warmth; sometimes he noticed her straining to hear some bit of gossip that was not quite being shared with her. Was it because she had taken him for her lover? Or was it the other way around: that she had chosen to be his lover precisely because she was *not* a full member of their caste?

Being a primitive gave him, at least, something to talk about at their parties. 'Tell us about war,' they said. 'Tell us about elections. About money. About disease.' They wanted to know everything, though they did not seem to pay close attention: their eyes were quick to glaze. Still, they asked. He described traffic jams to them, and politics, and deodorants, and vitamin pills. He told them about cigarettes, newspapers, subways, telephone directories, credit cards and basketball. 'Which was your city?' they asked. New York, he told them. 'And when was it? The seventh century, did you say?' The twentieth, he told them. They exchanged glances and nodded. 'We will have to do it,' they said. 'The World Trade Center, the Empire State Building, the Citicorp Center, the Cathedral of St John the Divine: how fascinating! Yankee Stadium. The Verrazano Bridge. We will do it all. But first must come Mohenjo-daro. And then, I think, Constantinople. Did your city have many people?' Seven million, he said. Just in the five boroughs alone. They nodded, smiling amiably, unfazed by the number. Seven million, seventy million – it was all the same to them, he sensed. They would just bring forth the temporaries in whatever quantity was required. He wondered how well they would carry the job off. He was no real judge of Alexandrias and Asgards, after all. Here they could have unicorns and hippogriffs in the zoo, and live sphinxes prowling in the gutters, and it did not trouble him. Their fanciful Alexandria was as good as history's, or better. But how sad, how disillusioning it would be, if the New York that they conjured up had Greenwich Village uptown and Times Square in the Bronx, and the New Yorkers, gentle and polite, spoke with the honeyed accents of Savannah or New Orleans. Well, that was nothing he needed to brood about just now. Very likely they were only being courteous when they spoke of doing his New York. They had all the vastness of the past to choose from: Nineveh, Memphis of the Pharaohs, the London of Victoria or Shakespeare or Richard III, Florence of the Medici, the Paris of Abelard and Héloïse or the Paris of Louis XIV,

Montezuma's Tenochtitlan and Atahualpa's Cuzco; Damascus, St Petersburg, Babylon, Troy. And then there were all the cities like New Chicago, out of time that was time yet unborn to him but ancient history to them. In such richness, such an infinity of choices, even mighty New York might have to wait a long while for its turn. Would he still be among them by the time they got around to it? By then, perhaps, they might have become bored with him and returned him to his own proper era. Or possibly he would simply have grown old and died. Even here, he supposed, he would eventually die, though no-one else ever seemed to. He did not know. He realized that in fact he did not know anything.

The north wind blew all day long. Vast flocks of ibises appeared over the city, fleeing the heat of the interior, and screeched across the sky with their black necks and scrawny legs extended. The sacred birds, descending by the thousand, scuttered about in every crossroad, pouncing on spiders and beetles, on mice, on the debris of the meat shops and the bakeries. They were beautiful but annoyingly ubiquitous, and they splashed their dung over the marble buildings; each morning squadrons of temporaries carefully washed it off. Gioia said little to him now. She seemed cool, withdrawn, depressed; and there was something almost intangible about her, as though she were gradually becoming transparent. He felt it would be an intrusion upon her privacy to ask her what was wrong. Perhaps it was only restlessness. She became religious, and presented costly offerings at the temples of Serapis, Isis, Poseidon, Pan. She went to the necropolis west of the city to lay wreaths on the tombs in the catacombs. In a single day she climbed the Lighthouse three times without any sign of fatigue. One afternoon he returned from a visit to the Library and found her naked on the patio; she had anointed herself all over with some aromatic green salve. Abruptly she said, 'I think it's time to leave Alexandria, don't you?'

She wanted to go to Mohenjo-daro, but Mohenjo-daro was not yet ready for visitors. Instead they flew eastwards to Chang-an, which they had not seen in years. It was Phillips's suggestion: he hoped that the cosmopolitan gaudiness of the old T'ang capital would lift her mood.

They were to be guests of the Emperor this time: an unusual privilege, which ordinarily had to be applied for far in advance, but Phillips had told some of Gioia's highly-placed friends that she was unhappy, and they had quickly arranged everything. Three endlessly bowing functionaries in flowing yellow robes and purple sashes met them at the Gate of Brilliant Virtue in the city's south wall and conducted them to their pavilion, close by the imperial palace and the Forbidden Garden. It was a light, airy place, thin walls of plastered brick braced by graceful columns of some dark, aromatic wood. Fountains played on the roof of green and yellow tiles, creating an unending cool rainfall of recirculating water. The balustrades were of carved marble, the door-fittings were of gold.

There was a suite of private rooms for him, and another for her, though they would share the handsome damask-draped bedroom at the heart of the pavilion. As soon as they arrived Gioia announced that she must go to her rooms to bathe and dress. 'There will be a formal reception for us at the palace tonight,' she said. 'They say the imperial receptions are splendid beyond anything you could imagine. I want to be at my best.' The Emperor and all his ministers, she told him, would receive them in the Hall of the Supreme Ultimate; there would be a banquet for a thousand people; Persian dancers would perform, and the celebrated jugglers of Chung-nan. Afterwards everyone would be conducted into the fantastic landscape of the Forbidden Garden to view the dragon-races and the fireworks.

He went to his own rooms. Two delicate little maidservants undressed him and bathed him with fragrant sponges. The pavilion came equipped with eleven temporaries who were to be their servants: soft-voiced unobtrusive catlike Chinese, done with perfect verisimilitude, straight black hair, glowing skin, epicanthic folds. Phillips often wondered what happened to a city's temporaries when the city's time was over. Were the towering Norse heroes of Asgard being recycled at this moment into wiry dark-skinned Dravidians for Mohenjo-daro? When Timbuctoo's day was done, would its brightly-robed black warriors be converted into supple Byzantines to stock the arcades of Constantinople? Or did they simply discard the old temporaries like so many excess props, stash them in ware-houses somewhere, and turn out the appropriate quantities of the new model? He did not know; and once when he had asked Gioia about it she had grown uncomfortable and vague. She did not like him to probe for information, and he suspected it was because she had very little to give. These people did not seem to question the workings of their own world; his curiosities were very twentieth-century of him, he was frequently told, in that gently patronizing way of theirs. As his two little maids patted him with their sponges he thought of asking them where they had served before Chang-an. Rio? Rome? Haroun al-Raschid's Baghdad? But these fragile girls, he knew, would only giggle and retreat if he tried to question them. Interrogating temporaries was not only improper but pointless: it was like interrogating one's luggage.

When he was bathed and robed in rich red silks he wandered the pavilion for a little while, admiring the tinkling pendants of green jade dangling on the portico, the lustrous auburn pillars, the rainbow hues of the intricately interwoven girders and brackets that supported the roof. Then, wearying of his solitude, he approached the bamboo curtain at the entrance to Gioia's suite. A porter and one of the maids stood just within. They indicated that he should not enter; but he scowled at them and they melted from him like snowflakes. A trail of incense led him through the pavilion to Gioia's innermost dressing-room. There he halted, just outside the door.

Gioia sat naked with her back to him at an ornate dressing-table of some rare flame-coloured wood inlaid with bands of orange and green porcelain. She was studying herself intently in a mirror of polished bronze held by one of her maids: picking through her scalp with her fingernails, as a woman might do who was searching out her grey hairs.

But that seemed strange. Grey hair, on Gioia? On a citizen? A temporary might display some appearance of ageing, perhaps, but surely not a citizen. Citizens remained forever young. Gioia looked like a girl. Her face was smooth and unlined, her flesh was firm, her hair was dark: that was true of all of them, every citizen he had ever seen. And yet there was no mistaking what Gioia was doing. She found a hair, frowned, drew it taut, nodded, plucked it. Another. Another. She pressed the tip of her finger to her cheek as if testing it for resilience. She tugged at the skin below her eyes, pulling it downwards. Such familiar little gestures of vanity; but so odd here, he thought, in this world of the perpetually young. Gioia, worried about growing old? Had he simply failed to notice the signs of age on her? Or was it that she worked hard behind his back at concealing them? Perhaps that was it. Was he wrong about the citizens, then? Did they age even as the people of less blessed eras had always done, but simply have better ways of hiding it? How old was she, anyway? Thirty? Sixty? Three hundred?

Gioia appeared satisfied now. She waved the mirror away; she rose; she beckoned for her banquet robes. Phillips, still standing unnoticed by the door, studied her with admiration: the small round buttocks, almost but not quite boyish, the elegant line of her spine, the surprising breadth of her shoulders. No, he thought, she is not ageing at all. Her body is still like a girl's. She looks as young as on the day they first had met, however long ago that was – he could not say; it was hard to keep track of time here; but he was sure some years had passed since they had come together. Those grey hairs, those wrinkles and sags for which she had searched just now with such desperate intensity, must all be imaginary, mere artefacts of vanity. Even in this remote future epoch, then, vanity was not extinct. He wondered why she was so concerned with the fear of ageing. An affectation? Did all these timeless people take some perverse pleasure in fretting over the possibility that they might be growing old? Or was it some private fear of Gioia's, another symptom of the mysterious depression that had come over her in Alexandria?

Not wanting her to think that he had been spying on her, when all he had really intended was to pay her a visit, he slipped silently away to dress for the evening. She came to him an hour later, gorgeously robed, swaddled from chin to ankles in a brocade of brilliant colours shot through with threads of gold, face painted, hair drawn up tightly and fastened with ivory combs: very much the lady of the court. His servants had made him splendid also, a lustrous black surplice embroidered with golden dragons over a sweeping floor-length gown of shining white silk, a necklace and pendant of red coral, a five-cornered grey felt hat that rose in tower upon tower like a ziggurat. Gioia, grinning, touched her fingertips to his cheek. 'You look marvellous!' she told him. 'Like a grand mandarin!'

'And you like an empress,' he said. 'Of some distant land:

Persia, India. Here to pay a ceremonial visit on the Son of Heaven.' An access of love suffused his spirit, and, catching her lightly by the wrist, he drew her towards him, as close as he could manage it considering how elaborate their costumes were. But as he bent forward and downwards, meaning to brush his lips lightly and affectionately against the tip of her nose, he perceived an unexpected strangeness, an anomaly: the coating of white paint that was her make-up seemed oddly to magnify rather than mask the contours of her skin, highlighting and revealing details he had never observed before. He saw a pattern of fine lines radiating from the corners of her eyes, and the unmistakable beginning of a quirk-mark in her cheek just to the left of her mouth, and perhaps the faint indentation of frown-lines in her flawless forehead. A shiver travelled along the nape of his neck. So it was not affectation, then, that had had her studying her mirror so fiercely. Age was in truth beginning to stake its claim on her, despite all that he had come to believe about these people's agelessness. But a moment later he was not so sure. Gioia turned and slid gently half a step back from him – she must have found his stare disturbing – and the lines he had thought he had seen were gone. He searched for them and saw only girlish smoothness once again. A trick of the light? A figment of an overwrought imagination? He was baffled.

'Come,' she said. 'We mustn't keep the Emperor waiting.'

Five moustachioed warriors in armour of white quilting and seven musicians playing cymbals and pipes escorted them to the Hall of the Supreme Ultimate. There they found the full court arrayed: princes and ministers, high officials, yellow-robed monks, a swarm of imperial concubines. In a place of honour to the right of the royal thrones, which rose like gilded scaffolds high above all else, was a little group of stern-faced men in foreign costumes, the ambassadors of Rome and Byzantium, of Arabia and Syria, of Korea, Japan, Tibet, Turkestan. Incense smouldered in enamelled braziers. A poet sang a delicate twanging melody, accompanying himself on a small harp. Then the Emperor and Empress entered: two tiny aged people, like waxen images, moving with infinite slowness, taking steps no greater than a child's. There was the sound of trumpets as they ascended their thrones. When the little Emperor was seated – he looked like a doll up there, ancient, faded, shrunken, yet still somehow a figure of extraordinary power – he stretched forth both his hands, and enormous gongs began to sound. It was a scene of astonishing splendour, grand and overpowering.

These are all temporaries, Phillips realized suddenly. He saw only a handful of citizens – eight, ten, possibly as many as a dozen – scattered here and there about the vast room. He knew them by their eyes, dark, liquid, knowing. They were watching not only the imperial spectacle but also Gioia and him; and Gioia, smiling secretly, nodding almost imperceptibly to them, was acknowledging their presence and their interest. But those few were the only ones in here who were autonomous living beings. All the rest – the entire splendid court, the great mandarins and paladins, the officials, the giggling concubines, the haughty and resplendent ambassadors, the aged Emperor and Empress themselves, were simply part of the scenery. Had the world ever seen entertainment on so grand a scale before? All this pomp, all this pageantry, conjured up each night for the amusement of a dozen or so viewers?

At the banquet the little group of citizens sat together at a table apart, a round onyx slab draped with translucent green silk. There turned out to be seventeen of them in all, including Gioia; Gioia appeared to know all of them, though none, so far as he could tell, was a member of her set that he had met before. She did not attempt introductions. Nor was conversation at all possible during the meal: there was a constant astounding roaring din in the room. Three orchestras played at once and there were troupes of strolling musicians also, and a steady stream of monks and their attendants marched back and forth between the tables loudly chanting sutras and waving censers to the deafening accompaniment of drums and gongs. The Emperor did not descend from his throne to join the banquet; he seemed to be asleep, though now and then he waved his hand in time to the music. Gigantic half-naked brown slaves with broad cheekbones and mouths like gaping pockets brought forth the food, peacock tongues and breast of phoenix heaped on mounds of glowing saffron-coloured rice, served on frail alabaster plates. For chopsticks they were given slender rods of dark jade. The wine, served in glistening crystal beakers, was thick and sweet, with an aftertaste of raisins, and no beaker was allowed to remain empty for more than a moment.

Phillips felt himself growing dizzy: when the Persian dancers emerged he could not tell whether there were five of them or fifty, and as they performed their intricate whirling routines it seemed to him that their slender muslin-veiled forms were blurring and merging one into another. He felt frightened by their proficiency, and wanted to look away, but he could not. The Chung-nan jugglers that followed them were equally skilful, equally alarming, filling the air with scythes, flaming torches, live animals, rare porcelain vases, pink jade hatchets, silver bells, gilded cups, wagon-wheels, bronze vessels, and never missing a catch. The citizens applauded politely but did not seem impressed. After the jugglers, the dancers returned, performing this time on stilts; the waiters brought platters of steaming meat of a pale lavender colour, unfamiliar in taste and texture: filet of camel, perhaps, or haunch of hippopotamus, or possibly some choice chop from a young dragon. There was more wine. Feebly Phillips tried to wave it away, but the servitors were implacable. This was a drier sort, greenish-gold, austere, sharp on the tongue. With it came a silver dish, chilled to a polar coldness, that held shaved ice flavoured with some potent smoky-flavoured brandy. The jugglers were doing a second turn, he noticed. He thought he was going to be ill. He looked helplessly towards Gioia, who seemed sober but fiercely animated, almost manic, her eyes blazing like rubies. She touched his cheek fondly. A cool draught blew through the hall: they had opened one entire wall, revealing the garden, the night, the stars. Just outside was a colossal wheel of oiled paper stretched on wooden struts. They must have erected it in the past hour: it stood a hundred and fifty feet high or even more, and on it hung lanterns by the thousands, glimmering like giant fireflies. The guests began to leave the hall. Phillips let himself be swept along into the garden, where under a yellow moon strange crook-armed trees with dense black needles loomed ominously. Gioia slipped her arm through his. They went down to a lake of bubbling crimson fluid and watched scarlet flamingo-like birds ten feet tall fastidiously spearing angry-eyed turquoise eels. They stood in awe before a fat-bellied Buddha of gleaming blue tilework, seventy feet high. A horse with a golden mane came prancing by, striking showers of brilliant red sparks wherever its hooves touched the ground.

In a grove of lemon trees that seemed to have the power to wave their slender limbs about, Phillips came upon the Emperor, standing by himself and rocking gently back and forth. The old man seized Phillips by the hand and pressed something into his palm, closing his fingers tight about it; when he opened his fist a few moments later he found his palm full of grey irregular pearls. Gioia took them from him and cast them into the air, and they burst like exploding firecrackers, giving off splashes of coloured light. A little later, Phillips realized that he was no longer wearing his surplice or his white silken undergown. Gioia was naked too, and she drew him gently down into a carpet of moist blue moss, where they made love until dawn, fiercely at first, then slowly, languidly, dreamily. At sunrise he looked at her tenderly and saw that something was wrong.

'Gioia?' he said doubtfully.

She smiled. 'Ah, no. Gioia is with Fenimon tonight. I am Belilala.'

'With – Fenimon?'

'They are old friends. She had not seen him in years.'

'Ah. I see. And you are –?'

'Belilala,' she said again, touching her fingertips to his cheek.

It was not unusual, Belilala said. It happened all the time; the only unusual thing was that it had not happened to him before now. Couples formed, travelled together for a while, drifted apart, eventually reunited. It did not mean that Gioia had left him for ever. It meant only that just now she chose to be with Fenimon. Gioia would return. In the meanwhile he would not be alone. 'You and I met in New Chicago,' Belilala told him. 'And then we saw each other again in Timbuctoo. Have you forgotten? Oh, yes, I see that you have forgotten!' She laughed prettily; she did not seem at all offended.

She looked enough like Gioia to be her sister. But, then, all the citizens looked more or less alike to him. And apart from their physical resemblance, so he quickly came to realize, Belilala and Gioia were not really very similar. There was a calmness, a deep reservoir of serenity, in Belilala, that Gioia, eager and volatile and ever impatient, did not seem to have. Strolling the swarming streets of Chang-an with Belilala, he did

283

not perceive in her any of Gioia's restless feverish need always to know what lay beyond, and beyond, and beyond even that. When they toured the Hsing-ch'ing Palace, Belilala did not after five minutes begin – as Gioia surely would have done – to seek directions to the Fountain of Hsuan-tsung or the Wild Goose Pagoda. Curiosity did not consume Belilala as it did Gioia. Plainly she believed that there would always be enough time for her to see everything she cared to see. There were some days when Belilala chose not to go out at all, but was content merely to remain at their pavilion playing a solitary game with flat porcelain counters, or viewing the flowers of the garden.

He found, oddly, that he enjoyed the respite from Gioia's intense world-swallowing appetites; and yet he longed for her to return. Belilala – beautiful, gentle, tranquil, patient – was too perfect for him. She seemed unreal in her gleaming impeccability, much like one of those Sung celadon vases that appear too flawless to have been thrown and glazed by human hands. There was something a little soulless about her: an immaculate finish outside, emptiness within. Belilala might almost have been a temporary, he thought, though he knew she was not. He could explore the pavilions and palaces of Chang-an with her, he could make graceful conversation with her while they dined, he could certainly enjoy coupling with her; but he could not love her or even contemplate the possibility. It was hard to imagine Belilala worriedly studying herself in a mirror for wrinkles and grey hairs. Belilala would never be any older than she was at this moment; nor could Belilala ever have been any younger. Perfection does not move along an axis of time. But the perfection of Belilala's glossy surface made her inner being impenetrable to him. Gioia was more vulnerable, more obviously flawed – her restlessness, her moodiness, her vanity, her fears – and therefore she was more accessible to his own highly imperfect twentieth-century sensibility.

Occasionally he saw Gioia as he roamed the city, or thought he did. He had a glimpse of her among the miracle-vendors in the Persian Bazaar, and outside the Zoroastrian temple, and again by the goldfish pond in the Serpentine Park. But he was never quite sure that the woman he saw was really Gioia, and he never could get close enough to her to be certain: she had a way of vanishing as he approached, like some mysterious

Lorelei luring him onwards and onwards in a hopeless chase. After a while he came to realize that he was not going to find her until she was ready to be found.

He lost track of time. Weeks, months, years? He had no idea. In this city of exotic luxury, mystery and magic, all was in constant flux and transition and the days had a fitful, unstable quality. Buildings and even whole streets were torn down of an afternoon and re-erected, within days, far away. Grand new pagodas sprouted like toadstools in the night. Citizens came in from Asgard, Alexandria, Timbuctoo, New Chicago, stayed for a time, disappeared, returned. There was a constant round of court receptions, banquets, theatrical events, each one much like the one before. The festivals in honour of past emperors and empresses might have given some form to the year, but they seemed to occur in a random way, the ceremony marking the death of T'ai Tsung coming around twice the same year, so it seemed to him, once in a season of snow and again in high summer, and the one honouring the ascension of the Empress Wu being held twice in a single season. Perhaps he had misunderstood something. But he knew it was no use asking anyone.

One day Belilala said unexpectedly, 'Shall we go to Mohenjo-daro?'

'I didn't know it was ready for visitors,' he replied.

'Oh, yes. For quite some time now.'

He hesitated. This had caught him unprepared. Cautiously he said, 'Gioia and I were going to go there together, you know.'

Belilala smiled amiably, as though the topic under discussion were nothing more than the choice of that evening's restaurant.

'Were you?' she asked.

'It was all arranged while we were still in Alexandria. To go with you instead – I don't know what to tell you, Belilala.' Phillips sensed that he was growing terribly flustered. 'You know that I'd like to go. With you. But on the other hand I can't help feeling that I shouldn't go there until I'm back with Gioia again. If I ever am.' How foolish this sounds, he thought. How clumsy, how adolescent. He found that he was having trouble looking straight at her. Uneasily he said, with a kind of desperation in his voice,

285

'I did promise her – there was a commitment, you understand – a firm agreement that we would go to Mohenjo-daro together – '

'Oh, but Gioia's already there!' said Belilala in the most casual way.

He gaped as though she had punched him.

'*What?*'

'She was one of the first to go, after it opened. Months and months ago. You didn't know?' she asked, sounding surprised, but not very. 'You really didn't know?'

That astonished him. He felt bewildered, betrayed, furious. His cheeks grew hot, his mouth gaped. He shook his head again and again, trying to clear it of confusion. It was a moment before he could speak. 'Already there?' he said at last. 'Without waiting for me? After we had talked about going there together – after we had agreed – '

Belilala laughed. 'But how could she resist seeing the newest city? You know how impatient Gioia is!'

'Yes. Yes.'

He was stunned. He could barely think.

'Just like all short-timers,' Belilala said. 'She rushes here, she rushes there. She must have it all, now, now, right away, at once, instantly. You ought never to expect her to wait for you for anything for very long: the fit seizes her, and off she goes. Surely you must know that about her by now.'

'A short-timer?' He had not heard that term before.

'Yes. You knew that. You must have known that.' Belilala flashed her sweetest smile. She showed no sign of comprehending his distress. With a brisk wave of her hand she said, 'Well, then, shall we go, you and I? To Mohenjo-daro?'

'Of course,' Phillips said bleakly.

'When would you like to leave?'

'Tonight,' he said. He paused a moment. 'What's a short-timer, Belilala?'

Colour came to her cheeks. 'Isn't it obvious?' she asked.

Had there ever been a more hideous place on the face of the earth than the city of Mohenjo-daro? Phillips found it difficult to imagine one. Nor could he understand why, out of all the cities that had ever been, these people had chosen to restore this one to existence. More than ever they seemed alien to him, unfathomable, incomprehensible.

From the terrace atop the many-towered citadel he peered down into grim claustrophobic Mohenjo-daro and shivered. The stark, bleak city looked like nothing so much as some prehistoric prison colony. In the manner of an uneasy tortoise it huddled, squat and compact, against the grey monotonous Indus River plain: miles of dark burnt-brick walls enclosing miles of terrifyingly orderly streets, laid out in an awesome, monstrous gridiron pattern of maniacal rigidity. The houses themselves were dismal and forbidding too, clusters of brick cells gathered about small airless courtyards. There were no windows, only small doors that opened not on to the main boulevards but on to the tiny mysterious lanes that ran between the buildings. Who had designed this horrifying metropolis? What harsh sour souls they must have had, these frightening and frightened folk, creating for themselves in the lush fertile plains of India such a Supreme Soviet of a city!

'How lovely it is,' Belilala murmured. 'How fascinating!'

He stared at her in amazement.

'Fascinating? Yes,' he said. 'I suppose so. The same way that the smile of a cobra is fascinating.'

'What's a cobra?'

'Poisonous predatory serpent,' Phillips told her. 'Probably extinct. Or formerly extinct, more likely. It wouldn't surprise me if you people had re-created a few and turned them loose in Mohenjo to make things livelier.'

'You sound angry, Charles.'

'Do I? That's not how I feel.'

'How do you feel, then?'

'I don't know,' he said after a long moment's pause. He shrugged. 'Lost, I suppose. Very far from home.'

'Poor Charles.'

'Standing here in this ghastly barracks of a city, listening to you tell me how beautiful it is, I've never felt more alone in my life.'

'You miss Gioia very much, don't you?'

He gave her another startled look.

'Gioia has nothing to do with it. She's probably been having ecstasies over the loveliness of Mohenjo just like you. Just like

287

all of you. I suppose I'm the only one who can't find the beauty, the charm. I'm the only one who looks out there and sees only horror, and then wonders why nobody else sees it, why in fact people would set up a place like this for *entertainment*, for *pleasure* – '

Her eyes were gleaming. 'Oh, you are angry! You really are!'

'Does that fascinate you too?' he snapped. 'A demonstration of genuine primitive emotion? A typical quaint twentieth-century outburst?' He paced the rampart in short quick anguished steps. 'Ah. Ah. I think I understand it now, Belilala. Of course: I'm part of your circus, the star of the sideshow. I'm the first experiment in setting up the next stage of it, in fact.' Her eyes were wide. The sudden harshness and violence in his voice seemed to be alarming and exciting her at the same time. That angered him even more. Fiercely he went on, 'Bringing whole cities back out of time was fun for a while, but it lacks a certain authenticity, eh? For some reason you couldn't bring the inhabitants too; you couldn't just grab a few million prehistorics out of Egypt or Greece or India and dump them down in this era, I suppose because you might have too much trouble controlling them, or because you'd have the problem of disposing of them once you were bored with them. So you had to settle for creating temporaries to populate your ancient cities. But now you've got me. I'm something more real than a temporary, and that's a terrific novelty for you, and novelty is the thing you people crave more than anything else: maybe the *only* thing you crave. And here I am, complicated, unpredictable, edgy, capable of anger, fear, sadness, love and all those other formerly extinct things. Why settle for picturesque architecture when you can observe picturesque emotion, too? What fun I must be for all of you! And if you decide that I was really interesting, maybe you'll ship me back where I came from and check out a few other ancient types – a Roman gladiator, maybe, or a Renaissance pope, or even a Neanderthal or two – '

'Charles,' she said tenderly. 'Oh, Charles, Charles, Charles, how lonely you must be, how lost, how troubled! Will you ever forgive me? Will you ever forgive us all?'

Once more he was astounded by her. She sounded entirely sincere, altogether sympathetic. Was she? Was she, really? He was not sure he had ever had a sign of genuine caring from any of them before, not even Gioia. Nor could he bring himself to trust Belilala now. He was afraid of her, afraid of all of them, of their brittleness, their slyness, their elegance. He wished he could go to her and have her take him in her arms; but he felt too much the shaggy prehistoric just now to be able to risk asking that comfort of her.

He turned away and began to walk around the rim of the citadel's massive wall.

'Charles?'

'Let me alone for a little while,' he said.

He walked on. His forehead throbbed and there was a pounding in his chest. All stress systems going full blast, he thought: secret glands dumping gallons of inflammatory substances into his bloodstream. The heat, the inner confusion, the repellent look of this place –

Try to understand, he thought. Relax. Look about you. Try to enjoy your holiday in Mohenjo-daro.

He leaned warily outwards over the edge of the wall. He had never seen a wall like this; it must be forty feet thick at the base, he guessed, perhaps even more, and every brick perfectly shaped, meticulously set. Beyond the great rampart, marshes ran almost to the edge of the city, although close by the wall the swamps had been dammed and drained for agriculture. He saw lithe brown farmers down there, busy with their wheat and barley and peas. Cattle and buffaloes grazed a little farther out. The air was heavy, dank, humid. All was still. From somewhere close at hand came the sound of a droning, whining stringed instrument and a steady insistent chanting.

Gradually a sort of peace pervaded him. His anger subsided. He felt himself beginning to grow calm again. He looked back at the city, the rigid interlocking streets, the maze of inner lanes, the millions of courses of precise brickwork.

It is a miracle, he told himself, that this city is here in this place and at this time. And it is a miracle that I am here to see it.

Caught for a moment by the magic within the bleakness, he thought he began to understand Belilala's awe and delight, and he wished now that he had not spoken to her so sharply. The city was alive. Whether it was the actual Mohenjo-daro of thousands upon thousands of years ago, ripped from the past by some wondrous hook, or simply a cunning reproduction, did not matter at all. Real or not, this was the true Mohenjo-daro. It had been dead and now, for the moment, it was alive again. These people, these *citizens*, might be trivial, but reconstructing Mohenjo-daro was no trivial achievement. And that the city that had been reconstructed was oppressive and sinister-looking was unimportant. No-one was compelled to live in Mohenjo-daro any more. Its time had come and gone, long ago; those little dark-skinned peasants and craftsmen and merchants down there were mere temporaries, mere inanimate things, conjured up like zombies to enhance the illusion. They did not need his pity. Nor did he need to pity himself. He knew that he should be grateful for the chance to behold these things. Some day, when this dream had ended and his hosts had returned him to the world of subways and computers and income tax and television networks, he would think of Mohenjo-daro as he had once beheld it, lofty walls of tightly woven dark brick under a heavy sky, and he would remember only its beauty.

Glancing back, he searched for Belilala and could not for a moment find her. Then he caught sight of her carefully descending a narrow staircase that angled down the inner face of the citadel wall.

'Belilala!' he called.

She paused and looked his way, shading her eyes from the sun with her hand. 'Are you all right?'

'Where are you going?'

'To the baths,' she said. 'Do you want to come?'

He nodded. 'Yes. Wait for me, will you? I'll be right there.' He began to run towards her along the top of the wall.

The baths were attached to the citadel: a great open tank the size of a large swimming pool, lined with bricks set on edge in gypsum mortar and waterproofed with asphalt, and eight smaller tanks just north of it in a kind of covered arcade. He supposed that in ancient times the whole complex had had some ritual purpose, the large tank used by common folk and the small chambers set aside for the private ablutions of priests or nobles. Now the baths were maintained, it seemed, entirely for the pleasure of visiting citizens. As Phillips came up the passageway that led to the main bath he saw fifteen or twenty of them lolling in the water or padding languidly about, while temporaries of the dark-skinned Mohenjo-daro type served them drinks and pungent little morsels of spiced meat as though this were some sort of luxury resort. Which was, he realized, exactly what it was. The temporaries wore white cotton loincloths; the citizens were naked. In his former life he had encountered that sort of casual public nudity a few times on visits to California and the south of France, and it had made him mildly uneasy. But he was growing accustomed to it here.

The changing-rooms were tiny brick cubicles connected by rows of closely placed steps to the courtyard that surrounded the central tank. They entered one and Belilala swiftly slipped out of the loose cotton robe that she had worn since their arrival that morning. With arms folded she stood leaning against the wall, waiting for him. After a moment he dropped his own robe and followed her outside. He felt a little giddy, sauntering around naked in the open like this.

On the way to the main bathing area they passed the private baths. None of them seemed to be occupied. They were elegantly constructed chambers, with finely jointed brick floors and carefully designed runnels to drain excess water into the passageway that led to the primary drain. Phillips was struck with admiration for the cleverness of the prehistoric engineers. He peered into this chamber and that to see how the conduits and ventilating ducts were arranged, and when he came to the last room in the sequence he was surprised and embarrassed to discover that it was in use. A brawny grinning man, big-muscled, deep-chested, with exuberantly flowing shoulder-length red hair and a flamboyant, sharply tapering beard was thrashing about merrily with two women in the small tank. Phillips had a quick glimpse of a lively tangle of arms, legs, breasts, buttocks.

'Sorry,' he muttered. His cheeks reddened. Quickly he ducked out, blurting apologies as he went. 'Didn't realize the room was occupied – no wish to intrude – '

Belilala had proceeded on down the passageway. Phillips hurried after her. From behind him came peals of cheerful raucous booming laughter and high-pitched giggling and the sound of splashing water. Probably they had not even noticed him.

He paused a moment, puzzled, playing back in his mind that

one startling glimpse. Something was not right. Those women, he was fairly sure, were citizens: little slender elfin dark-haired girlish creatures, the standard model. But the man? That great curling sweep of red hair? Not a citizen. Citizens did not affect shoulder-length hair. And *red*? Nor had he ever seen a citizen so burly, so powerfully muscular. Or one with a beard. But he could hardly be a temporary, either. Phillips could conceive no reason why there would be so Anglo-Saxon-looking a temporary at Mohenjo-daro; and it was unthinkable for a temporary to be frolicking like that with citizens, anyway.

'Charles?'

He looked up ahead. Belilala stood at the end of the passageway, outlined in a nimbus of brilliant sunlight. 'Charles?' she said again. 'Did you lose your way?'

'I'm right here behind you,' he said. 'I'm coming.'

'Who did you meet in there?'

'A man with a beard.'

'With a what?'

'A beard,' he said. 'Red hair growing on his face. I wonder who he is.'

'Nobody I know,' said Belilala. 'The only one I know with hair on his face is you. And yours is black, and you shave it off every day.' She laughed. 'Come along, now! I see some friends by the pool!'

He caught up with her and they went hand in hand out into the courtyard. Immediately a waiter glided up to them, an obsequious little temporary with a tray of drinks. Phillips waved it away and headed for the pool. He felt terribly exposed: he imagined that the citizens disporting themselves here were staring intently at him, studying his hairy primitive body as though he were some mythical creature, a Minotaur, a werewolf, summoned up for their amusement. Belilala drifted off to talk to someone and he slipped into the water, grateful for the concealment it offered. It was deep, warm, comforting. With swift powerful strokes he breast-stroked from one end to the other.

A citizen perched elegantly on the pool's rim smiled at him. 'Ah, so you've come at last, Charles!' Char-*less*. Two syllables. Someone from Gioia's set: Stengard, Hawk, Aramayne? He could not remember which one. They were all so much alike.

Phillips returned the man's smile in a half-hearted, tentative way. He searched for something to say and finally asked, 'Have you been here long?'

'Weeks. Perhaps months. What a splendid achievement this city is, eh, Charles? Such utter unity of mood – such a total statement of a uniquely single-minded aesthetic – '

'Yes. Single-minded is the word,' Phillips said drily.

'Gioia's word, actually. Gioia's phrase. I was merely quoting.'

Gioia. He felt as if he had been stabbed.

'You've spoken to Gioia lately?' he said.

'Actually, no. It was Hekna who saw her. You do remember Hekna, eh?' He nodded towards two naked women standing on the brick platform that bordered the pool, chatting, delicately nibbling morsels of meat. They could have been twins. 'There is Hekna, with your Belilala.' Hekna, yes. So this must be Hawk, Phillips thought, unless there has been some recent shift of couples. 'How sweet she is, your Belilala,' Hawk said. 'Gioia chose very wisely when she picked her for you.'

Another stab: a much deeper one. 'Is that how it was?' he said. 'Gioia *picked* Belilala for me?'

'Why, of course!' Hawk seemed surprised. It went without saying, evidently. 'What did you think? That Gioia would merely go off and leave you to fend for yourself?'

'Hardly. Not Gioia.'

'She's very tender, very gentle, isn't she?'

'You mean Belilala? Yes, very,' said Phillips carefully. 'A dear woman, a wonderful woman. But of course I hope to get together with Gioia again soon.' He paused. 'They say she's been in Mohenjo-daro almost since it opened.'

'She was here, yes.'

'*Was?*'

'Oh, you know Gioia,' Hawk said lightly. 'She's moved along by now, naturally.'

Phillips leaned forward. 'Naturally,' he said. Tension thickened his voice. 'Where has she gone this time?'

'Timbuctoo, I think. Or New Chicago. I forget which one it was. She was telling us that she hoped to be in Timbuctoo for the closing-down party. But then Fenimon had some pressing reason for going to New Chicago. I can't remember what they decided to do.' Hawk gestured sadly. 'Either way, a pity that she left Mohenjo before the new visitor came. She had such a rewarding time with you, after all: I'm sure she'd have found much to learn from him also.'

The unfamiliar term twanged an alarm deep in Phillips's consciousness. '*Visitor?*' he said, angling his head sharply towards Hawk. 'What visitor do you mean?'

'You haven't met him yet? Oh, of course, you've only just arrived.'

Phillips moistened his lips. 'I think I may have seen him. Long red hair? Beard like this?'

'That's the one! Willoughby, he's called. He's – what? – a Viking, a pirate, something like that. Tremendous vigour and force. Remarkable person. We should have many more visitors, I think. They're far superior to temporaries, everyone agrees. Talking with a temporary is a little like talking to one's self, wouldn't you say? They give you no significant illumination. But a visitor – someone like this Willoughby – or like you, Charles – a visitor can be truly enlightening, a visitor can transform one's view of reality – '

'Excuse me,' Phillips said. A throbbing began behind his forehead. 'Perhaps we can continue this conversation later, yes?' He put the flats of his hands against the hot brick of the platform and hoisted himself swiftly from the pool. 'At dinner, maybe – or afterwards – yes? All right?' He set off at a quick half-trot back towards the passageway that led to the private baths.

As he entered the roofed part of the structure his throat grew dry, his breath suddenly came short. He padded quickly up the hall and peered into the little bath-chamber. The bearded man was still there, sitting up in the tank, breast-high above the water, with one arm around each of the women. His eyes gleamed with fiery intensity in the dimness. He was grinning in marvellous self-satisfaction; he seemed to brim with intensity, confidence, gusto.

Let him be what I think he is, Phillips prayed. I have been alone among these people long enough.

'May I come in?' he asked.

'Aye, fellow!' cried the man in the tub thunderously. 'By my

troth, come ye in, and bring your lass as well! God's teeth, I
wot there's room aplenty for more folk in this tub than we!'

At that great uproarious outcry Phillips felt a powerful surge
of joy. What a joyous rowdy voice! How rich, how lusty, how
totally uncitizen-like!

And those oddly archaic words! *God's teeth? By my troth?*
What sort of talk was that? What else but the good pure
sonorous Elizabethan diction! Certainly it had something of
the roll and fervour of Shakespeare about it. And spoken with
– an Irish brogue, was it? No, not quite: it was English, but
English spoken in no manner Phillips had ever heard.

Citizens did not speak that way. But a *visitor* might.

So it was true. Relief flooded Phillips's soul. Not alone,
then! Another relict of a former age – another wanderer
– a companion in chaos, a brother in adversity – a fellow
voyager, tossed even farther than he had been by the tempests
of time –

The bearded man grinned heartily and beckoned to Phillips
with a toss of his head. 'Well, join us, join us, man! 'Tis good
to see an English face again, amidst all these Moors and rogue
Portugals! But what have ye done with thy lass? One can never
have enough wenches, d'ye not agree?'

The force and vigour of him were extraordinary: almost too
much so. He roared, he bellowed, he boomed. He was so very
much what he ought to be that he seemed more a character out
of some old pirate movie than anything else, so blustering, so
real, that he seemed unreal. A stage-Elizabethan, larger than
life, a boisterous young Falstaff without the belly.

Hoarsely Phillips said, 'Who are you?'

'Why, Ned Willoughby's son Francis am I, of Plymouth. Late
of the service of Her Most Protestant Majesty, but most foully
abducted by the powers of darkness and cast away among these
blackamoor Hindus, or whatever they be. And thyself?'

'Charles Phillips.' After a moment's uncertainty he added,
'I'm from New York.'

'*New* York? What place is that? In faith, man, I know it
not!'

'A city in America.'

'A city in America, forsooth! What a fine fancy that is!
In America, you say, and not on the Moon, or perchance

295

underneath the sea?' To the women Willoughby said, 'D'ye hear him? He comes from a city in America! With the face of an Englishman, though not the manner of one, and not quite the proper sort of speech. A city in America! A *city*. God's blood, what will I hear next?'

Phillips trembled. Awe was beginning to take hold of him. This man had walked the streets of Shakespeare's London, perhaps. He had clinked canisters with Marlowe or Essex or Walter Raleigh; he had watched the ships of the Armada wallowing in the Channel. It strained Phillips's spirit to think of it. This strange dream in which he found himself was compounding its strangeness now. He felt like a weary swimmer assailed by heavy surf, winded, dazed. The hot close atmosphere of the baths was driving him towards vertigo. There could be no doubt of it any longer. He was not the only primitive – the only *visitor* – who was wandering loose in this fiftieth century. They were conducting other experiments as well. He gripped the sides of the door to steady himself and said, 'When you speak of Her Most Protestant Majesty, it's Elizabeth the First you mean, is that not so?'

'Elizabeth, aye! As to the First, that is true enough, but why trouble to name her thus? There is but one. First and Last, I do trow, and God save her, there is no other!'

Phillips studied the other man warily. He knew that he must proceed with care. A misstep at this point and he would forfeit any chance that Willoughby would take him seriously. How much metaphysical bewilderment, after all, could this man absorb? What did he know, what had anyone of his time known, of past and present and future and the notion that one might somehow move from one to the other as readily as one would go from Surrey to Kent? That was a twentieth-century idea, late-nineteenth at best, a fantastical speculation that very likely no one had even considered before Wells had sent his time traveller off to stare at the reddened sun of the Earth's last twilight. Willoughby's world was a world of Protestants and Catholics, of kings and queens, of tiny sailing vessels, of swords at the hip and ox-carts on the road: that world seemed to Phillips far more alien and distant than was this world of citizens and temporaries. The risk that Willoughby would not begin to understand him was great.

296

But this man and he were natural allies against a world they had never made. Phillips chose to take the risk.

'Elizabeth the First is the queen you serve,' he said. 'There will be another of her name in England, in due time. Has already been, in fact.'

Willoughby shook his head like a puzzled lion. 'Another Elizabeth, d'ye say?'

'A second one, and not much like the first. Long after your Virgin Queen, this one. She will reign in what you think of as the days to come. That I know without doubt.'

The Englishman peered at him and frowned. 'You see the future? Are you a soothsayer, then? A necromancer, mayhap? Or one of the very demons that brought me to this place?'

'Not at all,' Phillips said gently. 'Only a lost soul, like yourself.' He stepped into the little room and crouched by the side of the tank. The two citizen-women were staring at him in bland fascination. He ignored them. To Willoughby he said, 'Do you have any idea where you are?'

The Englishman had guessed, rightly enough, that he was in India: 'I do believe these little brown Moorish folk are of the Hindy sort,' he said. But that was as far as his comprehension of what had befallen him could go.

It had not occurred to him that he was no longer living in the sixteenth century. And of course he did not begin to suspect that this strange and sombre brick city in which he found himself was a wanderer out of an era even more remote than his own. Was there any way, Phillips wondered, of explaining that to him?

He had been here only three days. He thought it was devils that had carried him off. 'While I slept did they come for me,' he said. 'Mephistophilis Sathanas his henchmen seized me – God alone can say why – and swept me in a moment out to this torrid realm from England, where I had reposed among friends and family. For I was between one voyage and the next, you must understand, awaiting Drake and his ship – you know Drake, the glorious Francis? God's blood, there's a mariner for ye! We were to go to the Main again, he and I, but instead here I be in this other place – ' Willoughby leaned close and said, 'I ask you, soothsayer, how can it be, that a man go to sleep in Plymouth and wake up in India? It is passing strange, is it not?'

'That it is,' Phillips said.

'But he that is in the dance must needs dance on, though he do but hop, eh? So do I believe.' He gestured towards the two citizen-women. 'And therefore to console myself in this pagan land I have found me some sport among these little Portugal women – '

'Portugal?' said Phillips.

'Why, what else can they be, but Portugals? Is it not the Portugals who control all these coasts of India? See, the people are of two sorts here, the blackamoors and the others, the fair-skinned ones, the lords and masters who lie here in these baths. If they be not Hindus, and I think they are not, then Portugals is what they must be.' He laughed and pulled the women against himself and rubbed his hands over their breasts as though they were fruits on a vine. 'Is that not what you are, you little naked shameless Papist wenches? A pair of Portugals, eh?'

They giggled, but did not answer.

'No,' Phillips said. 'This is India, but not the India you think you know. And these women are not Portuguese.'

'Not Portuguese?' Willoughby said, baffled.

'No more so than you. I'm quite certain of that.'

Willoughby stroked his beard. 'I do admit I found them very odd, for Portugals. I have heard not a syllable of their Portugee speech on their lips. And it is strange also that they run naked as Adam and Eve in these baths, and allow me free plunder of their women, which is not the way of Portugals at home, God wot. But I thought me, this is India, they choose to live in another fashion here – '

'No,' Phillips said. 'I tell you, these are not Portuguese, nor any other people of Europe who are known to you.'

'Prithee, who are they, then?'

Do it delicately, now, Phillips warned himself. *Delicately.*

He said, 'It is not far wrong to think of them as spirits of some kind – demons, even. Or sorcerers who have magicked us out of our proper places in the world.' He paused, groping for some means to share with Willoughby, in a way that Willoughby might grasp, this mystery that had enfolded them. He drew a deep breath. 'They've taken us not only across the sea,' he said, 'but across the years as well. We have both been hauled, you and I, far into the days that are to come.'

Willoughby gave him a look of blank bewilderment.

'Days that are to come? Times yet unborn, d'ye mean? Why, I comprehend none of that!'

'Try to understand. We're both castaways in the same boat, man! But there's no way we can help each other if I can't make you see – '

Shaking his head, Willoughby muttered, 'In faith, good friend, I find your words the merest folly. Today is today, and tomorrow is tomorrow, and how can a man step from one to t'other until tomorrow be turned into today?'

'I have no idea,' said Phillips. Struggle was apparent on Willoughby's face; but plainly he could perceive no more than the haziest outline of what Phillips was driving at, if that much. 'But this I know,' he went on. 'That your world and all that was in it is dead and gone. And so is mine, though I was born four hundred years after you, in the time of the second Elizabeth.'

Willoughby snorted scornfully. 'Four hundred – '

'You must believe me!'

'Nay! Nay!'

'It's the truth. Your time is only history to me. And mine and yours are history to *them* – ancient history. They call us visitors, but what we are is captives.' Phillips felt himself quivering in the intensity of his effort. He was aware how insane this must sound to Willoughby. It was beginning to sound insane to him. 'They've stolen us out of our proper times – seizing us like gypsies in the night – '

'Fie, man! You rave with lunacy!'

Phillips shook his head. He reached out and seized Willoughby tightly by the wrist. 'I beg you, listen to me!' The citizen-women were watching closely, whispering to one another behind their hands, laughing. 'Ask them!' Phillips cried. 'Make them tell you what century this is! The sixteenth, do you think? Ask them!'

'What century could it be, but the sixteenth of Our Lord!'

'They will tell you it is the fiftieth.'

Willoughby looked at him pityingly. 'Man, man, what a sorry thing thou art! The fiftieth, indeed!' He laughed. 'Fellow, listen to me, now. There is but one Elizabeth, safe upon her throne in Westminster. This is India. The year is Anno 1591. Come,

299

let us you and I steal a ship from these Portugals, and make our way back to England, and peradventure you may get from there to your America – '

'There is no England.'

'Ah, can you say that and not be mad?'

'The cities and nations we knew are gone. These people live like magicians, Francis.' There was no use holding anything back now, Phillips thought leadenly. He knew that he had lost. 'They conjure up places of long ago, and build them here and there to suit their fancy, and when they are bored with them they destroy them, and start anew. There is no England. Europe is empty, featureless, void. Do you know what cities there are? There are only five in all the world. There is Alexandria of Egypt. There is Timbuctoo in Africa. There is New Chicago in America. There is a great city in China – in Cathay, I suppose you would say. And there is this place, which they call Mohenjo-daro, and which is far more ancient than Greece, than Rome, than Babylon.'

Quietly Willoughby said, 'Nay. This is mere absurdity. You say we are in some far tomorrow, and then you tell me we are dwelling in some city of long ago.'

'A conjuration, only,' Phillips said in desperation. 'A likeness of that city. Which these folk have fashioned somehow for their own amusement. Just as we are here, you and I: to amuse them. Only to amuse them.'

'You are completely mad.'

'Come with me, then. Talk with the citizens by the great pool. Ask them what year this is; ask them about England; ask them how you come to be here.' Once again Phillips grasped Willoughby's wrist. 'We should be allies. If we work together, perhaps we can discover some way to get ourselves out of this place, and – '

'Let me be, fellow.'

'Please – '

'Let me be!' roared Willoughby, and pulled his arm free. His eyes were stark with rage. Rising in the tank, he looked about furiously as though searching for a weapon. The citizen-women shrank back away from him, though at the same time they seemed captivated by the big man's fierce outburst. 'Go to, get you to Bedlam! Let me be, madman! Let me be!'

* * *

300

Dismally Phillips roamed the dusty unpaved streets of Mohenjo-daro alone for hours. His failure with Willoughby had left him bleak-spirited and sombre: he had hoped to stand back to back with the Elizabethan against the citizens, but he saw now that that was not to be. He had bungled things; or, more likely, it had been impossible ever to bring Willoughby to see the truth of their predicament.

In the stifling heat he went at random through the confusing congested lanes of flat-roofed windowless houses and blank featureless walls until he emerged into a broad marketplace. The life of the city swirled madly around him: the pseudo-life, rather, the intricate interactions of the thousands of temporaries who were nothing more than wind-up dolls set in motion to provide the illusion that pre-Vedic India was still a going concern. Here vendors sold beautiful little carved stone seals portraying tigers and monkeys and strange humped cattle, and women bargained vociferously with craftsmen for ornaments of ivory, gold, copper and bronze. Weary-looking women squatted behind immense mounds of newly-made pottery, pinkish-red with black designs. No-one paid any attention to him. He was the outsider here, neither citizen nor temporary. They belonged.

He went on, passing the huge granaries where workmen ceaselessly unloaded carts of wheat and others pounded grain on great circular brick platforms. He drifted into a public restaurant thronging with joyless silent people standing elbow to elbow at small brick counters, and was given a flat round piece of bread, a sort of tortilla or chapatti, in which was stuffed some spiced mincemeat that stung his lips like fire. Then he moved onwards down a wide shallow timbered staircase into the lower part of the city, where the peasantry lived in cell-like rooms packed together as though in hives.

It was an oppressive city, but not a squalid one. The intensity of the concern with sanitation amazed him: wells and fountains and public privies everywhere, and brick drains running from each building, leading to covered cesspools. There was none of the open sewage and pestilent gutters that he knew still could be found in the India of his own time. He wondered whether ancient Mohenjo-daro had in truth been so fastidious. Perhaps the citizens had redesigned the city to suit their own ideals of cleanliness.. No: most likely what he saw was authentic, he decided, a function of the same obsessive discipline that had given the city its rigidity of form. If Mohenjo-daro had been a verminous filthy hole, the citizens probably would have re-created it in just that way, and loved it for its fascinating reeking filth.

Not that he had ever noticed an excessive concern with authenticity on the part of the citizens; and Mohenjo-daro, like all the other restored cities he had visited, was full of the usual casual anachronisms. Phillips saw images of Shiva and Krishna here and there on the walls of buildings he took to be temples, and the benign face of the mother-goddess Kali loomed in the plazas. Surely those deities had arisen in India long after the collapse of the Mohenjo-daro civilization. Or did they take a certain naughty pleasure in mixing the eras – a mosque and a church in Greek Alexandria, Hindu gods in prehistoric Mohenjo-daro? Perhaps their records of the past had become contaminated with errors over the thousands of years. He would not have been surprised to see banners bearing portraits of Gandhi and Nehru being carried in procession through the streets. And there were phantasms and chimeras at large here again too, as if the citizens were untroubled by the boundary between history and myth: little fat elephant-headed Ganeshas blithely plunging their trunks into water-fountains, a six-armed three-headed woman sunning herself on a brick terrace. Why not? Surely that was the motto of these people: *Why not, why not, why not?* They could do as they pleased, and they did. Yet Gioia had said to him, long ago, 'Limits are very important.' In what, Phillips wondered, did they limit themselves, other than the number of their cities? Was there a quota, perhaps, on the number of 'visitors' they allowed themselves to kidnap from the past? Until today he had thought he was the only one; now he knew there was at least one other; possibly there were more elsewhere, a step or two ahead or behind him, making the circuit with the citizens who travelled endlessly from New Chicago to Chang-an to Alexandria. We should join forces, he thought, and compel them to send us back to our rightful eras. *Compel?* How? File a class-action suit, maybe? Demonstrate in the streets? Sadly he thought of his failure to make common cause with Willoughby. We are natural allies, he thought. Together perhaps we might have won some compassion from these people. But to Willoughby it must be literally unthinkable that Good Queen Bess and her subjects were sealed away on the far side of a barrier hundreds of centuries thick. He would prefer to believe that England was just a few months' voyage away around the Cape of Good Hope, and that all he need do was commandeer a ship and set sail for home. Poor Willoughby: probably he would never see his home again.

The thought came to Phillips suddenly:

Neither will you.

And then, after it:

If you could go home, would you really want to?

One of the first things he had realized here was that he knew almost nothing substantial about his former existence. His mind was well stocked with details on life in twentieth-century New York, to be sure; but of himself he could say not much more than that he was Charles Phillips and had come from 1984. Profession? Age? Parents' names? Did he have a wife? Children? A cat, a dog, hobbies? No data: none. Possibly the citizens had stripped such things from him when they brought him here, to spare him from the pain of separation. They might be capable of that kindness. Knowing so little of what he had lost, could he truly say that he yearned for it? Willoughby seemed to remember much more of his former life, and longed somehow for it all the more intensely. He was spared that. Why not stay here, and go on and on from city to city, sightseeing all of time past as the citizens conjured it back into being? Why not? Why not? The chances were that he had no choice about it, anyway.

He made his way back up towards the citadel and to the baths once more. He felt a little like a ghost, haunting a city of ghosts.

Belilala seemed unaware that he had been gone for most of the day. She sat by herself on the terrace of the baths, placidly sipping some thick milky beverage that had been sprinkled with a dark spice. He shook his head when she offered him some.

'Do you remember I mentioned that I saw a man with red hair and a beard this morning?' Phillips said. 'He's a visitor. Hawk told me that.'

'Is he?' Belilala asked.

'From a time about four hundred years before mine. I talked

with him. He thinks he was brought here by demons.' Phillips gave her a searching look. 'I'm a visitor too, isn't that so?'

'Of course, love.'

'And how was *I* brought here? By demons also?'

Belilala smiled indifferently. 'You'd have to ask someone else. Hawk, perhaps. I haven't looked into these things very deeply.'

'I see. Are there many visitors here, do you know?'

A languid shrug. 'Not many, no, not really. I've only heard of three of four besides you. There may be others by now, I suppose.' She rested her hand lightly on his. 'Are you having a good time in Mohenjo, Charles?'

He let her question pass as though he had not heard it.

'I asked Hawk about Gioia,' he said.

'Oh?'

'He told me that she's no longer here, that she's gone on to Timbuctoo or New Chicago, he wasn't sure which.'

'That's quite likely. As everybody knows, Gioia rarely stays in the same place very long.'

Phillips nodded. 'You said the other day that Gioia is a short-timer. That means she's going to grow old and die, doesn't it?'

'I thought you understood that, Charles.'

'Whereas you will not age? Nor Hawk, nor Stengard, nor any of the rest of your set?'

'We will live as long as we wish,' she said. 'But we will not age, no.'

'What makes a person a short-timer?'

'They're born that way, I think. Some missing gene, some extra gene – I don't actually know. It's extremely uncommon. Nothing can be done to help them. It's very slow, the ageing. But it can't be halted.'

Phillips nodded. 'That must be very disagreeable,' he said. 'To find yourself one of the few people growing old in a world where everyone stays young. No wonder Gioia is so impatient. No wonder she runs around from place to place. No wonder she attached herself so quickly to the barbaric hairy visitor from the twentieth century, who comes from a time when *everybody* was a short-timer. She and I have something in common, wouldn't you say?'

'In a manner of speaking, yes.'

'We understand ageing. We understand death. Tell me: is Gioia likely to die very soon, Belilala?'

'Soon? soon?' She gave him a wide-eyed childlike stare. 'What is soon? How can I say? What you think of as soon and what I think of as soon are not the same things, Charles.' Then her manner changed: she seemed to be hearing what he was saying for the first time. Softly she said, 'No, no, Charles. I don't think she will die very soon.'

'When she left me in Chang-an, was it because she had become bored with me?'

Belilala shook her head. 'She was simply restless. It had nothing to do with you. She was never bored with you.'

'Then I'm going to go looking for her. Wherever she may be, Timbuctoo, New Chicago, I'll find her. Gioia and I belong together.'

'Perhaps you do,' said Belilala. 'Yes. Yes, I think you really do.' She sounded altogether unperturbed, unrejected, unbereft. 'By all means, Charles. Go to her. Follow her. Find her. Wherever she may be.'

They had already begun dismantling Timbuctoo when Phillips got there. While he was still high overhead, his flitterflitter hovering above the dusty tawny plain where the River Niger met the sands of the Sahara, a surge of keen excitement rose in him as he looked down at the square grey flat-roofed mud-brick buildings of the great desert capital. But when he landed he found gleaming metal-skinned robots swarming everywhere, a horde of them scuttling about like giant shining insects, pulling the place apart.

He had not known about the robots before. So that was how all these miracles were carried out, Phillips realized: an army of obliging machines. He imagined them bustling up out of the earth whenever their services were needed, emerging from some sterile subterranean storehouse to put together Venice or Thebes or Knossos or Houston or whatever place was required, down to the finest detail, and then at some later time returning to undo everything that they had fashioned. He watched them now, diligently pulling down the adobe walls, demolishing the heavy metal-studded gates, bulldozing the amazing labyrinth of alleyways and thoroughfares, sweeping away the market. On his last visit to Timbuctoo that market had been crowded with a horde of veiled Tuaregs and swaggering Moors, black Sudanese, shrewd-faced Syrian traders, all of them busily dickering for camels, horses, donkeys, slabs of salt, huge green melons, silver bracelets, splendid vellum Korans. They were all gone now, that picturesque crowd of swarthy temporaries. Nor were there any citizens to be seen. The dust of destruction choked the air. One of the robots came up to Phillips and said in a dry crackling insect-voice, 'You ought not to be here. This city is closed.'

He stared at the flashing, buzzing band of scanners and sensors across the creature's glittering tapered snout. 'I'm trying to find someone, a citizen who may have been here recently. Her name is – '

'This city is closed,' the robot repeated inexorably.

They would not let him stay as much as an hour. There is no food here, the robot said, no water, no shelter. This is not a place any longer. You may not stay. You may not stay. You may not stay.

This is not a place any longer.

Perhaps he could find her in New Chicago, then. He took to the air again, soaring northwards and westwards over the vast emptiness. The land below him curved away into the hazy horizon, bare, sterile. What had they done with the vestiges of the world that had gone before? Had they turned their gleaming metal beetles loose to clean everything away? Were there no ruins of genuine antiquity anywhere? No scrap of Rome, no shard of Jerusalem, no stump of Fifth Avenue? It was all so barren down there: an empty stage, waiting for its next set to be built. He flew on a great arc across the jutting hump of Africa and on into what he supposed was southern Europe: the little vehicle did all the work, leaving him to doze or stare as he wished. Now and again he saw another flitterflitter pass by, far away, a dark distant winged teardrop outlined against the hard clarity of the sky. He wished there was some way of making radio contact with them, but he had no idea how to go about it. Not that he had anything he wanted to say; he wanted only to hear a human voice. He was utterly isolated. He might just as well have been the last living man on Earth. He closed his eyes and thought of Gioia.

* * *

'Like this?' Phillips asked. In an ivory-panelled oval room sixty storeys above the softly glowing streets of New Chicago he touched a small cool plastic canister to his upper lip and pressed the stud at its base. He heard a foaming sound; and then blue vapour rose to his nostrils.

'Yes,' Cantilena said. 'That's right.'

He detected a faint aroma of cinnamon, cloves and something that might almost have been broiled lobster. Then a spasm of dizziness hit him and visions rushed through his head: Gothic cathedrals, the Pyramids, Central Park under fresh snow, the harsh brick warrens of Mohenjo-daro, and fifty thousand other places all at once, a wild roller-coaster ride through space and time. It seemed to go on for centuries. But finally his head cleared and he looked about, blinking, realizing that the whole thing had taken only a moment. Cantilena still stood at his elbow. The other citizens in the room – fifteen, twenty of them – had scarcely moved. The strange little man with the celadon skin over by the far wall continued to stare at him.

'Well?' Cantilena asked. 'What did you think?'

'Incredible.'

'And very authentic. It's an actual New Chicagoan drug. The exact formula. Would you like another?'

'Not just yet,' Phillips said uneasily. He swayed and had to struggle for his balance. Sniffing that stuff might not have been such a wise idea, he thought.

He had been in New Chicago a week, or perhaps it was two, and he was still suffering from the peculiar disorientation that that city always aroused in him. This was the fourth time that he had come here, and it had been the same every time. New Chicago was the only one of the reconstructed cities of this world that in its original incarnation had existed *after* his own era. To him it was an outpost of the incomprehensible future; to the citizens it was a quaint simulacrum of the archaeological past. That paradox left him aswirl with impossible confusions and tensions.

What had happened to *old* Chicago was of course impossible for him to discover. Vanished without a trace, that was clear: no Water Tower, no Marina City, no Hancock Centre, no Tribune building, not a fragment, not an atom. But it was hopeless to ask any of the million-plus inhabitants of New Chicago about their city's predecessor. They were only temporaries; they knew no more than they had to know, and all that they had to know was how to go through the motions of whatever it was that they did by way of creating the illusion that this was a real city. They had no need of knowing ancient history.

Nor was he likely to find out anything from a citizen, of course. Citizens did not seem to bother much about scholarly matters. Phillips had no reason to think that the world was anything other than an amusement park to them. Somewhere, certainly, there had to be those who specialized in the serious study of the lost civilizations of the past – for how, otherwise, would these uncanny reconstructed cities be brought into being? 'The planners,' he had once heard Nissandra or Aramayne say, 'are already deep into their Byzantium research.' But who were the planners? He had no idea. For all he knew, they were the robots. Perhaps the robots were the real masters of this whole era, who created the cities not primarily for the sake of amusing the citizens but in their own diligent attempt to comprehend the life of the world that had passed away. A wild speculation, yes; but not without some plausibility, he thought.

He felt oppressed by the party gaiety all about him. 'I need some air,' he said to Cantilena, and headed towards the window. It was the merest crescent, but a breeze came through. He looked out at the strange city below.

New Chicago had nothing in common with the old one but its name. They had built it, at least, along the western shore of a large inland lake that might even be Lake Michigan, although when he had flown over it had seemed broader and less elongated than the lake he remembered. The city itself was a lacy fantasy of slender pastel-hued buildings rising at odd angles and linked by a webwork of gently undulating aerial bridges. The streets were long parentheses that touched the lake at their northern and southern ends and arched gracefully westwards in the middle. Between each of the great boulevards ran a track for public transportation – sleek aquamarine bubble-vehicles gliding on soundless wheels – and flanking each of the tracks were lush strips of park. It was beautiful, astonishingly so, but insubstantial. The whole thing seemed to have been contrived from sunbeams and silk.

A soft voice beside him said, 'Are you becoming ill?'

Phillips glanced around. The celadon man stood beside him: a compact, precise person, vaguely Oriental in appearance. His skin was of a curious grey-green hue like no skin Phillips had ever seen, and it was extraordinarily smooth in texture, as though he were made of fine porcelain.

He shook his head. 'Just a little queasy,' he said. 'This city always scrambles me.'

'I suppose it can be disconcerting,' the little man replied. His tone was furry and veiled, the inflection strange. There was something feline about him. He seemed sinewy, unyielding, almost menacing. 'Visitor, are you?'

Phillips studied him a moment. 'Yes,' he said.

'So am I, of course.'

'Are you?'

'Indeed.' The little man smiled. 'What's your locus? Twentieth century? Twenty-first at the latest, I'd say.'

'I'm from 1984. AD 1984.'

Another smile, a self-satisfied one. 'Not a bad guess, then.' A brisk tilt of the head. 'Y'ang-Yeovil.'

'Pardon me?' Phillips said.

'Y'ang-Yeovil. It is my name. Formerly Colonel Y'ang-Yeovil of the Third Septentriad.'

'Is that on some other planet?' asked Phillips, feeling a bit dazed.

'Oh, no, not at all,' Y'ang-Yeovil said pleasantly. 'This very world, I assure you. I am quite of human origin. Citizen of the Republic of Upper Han, native of the city of Port Ssu. And you – forgive me – your name –?'

'I'm sorry. Phillips. Charles Phillips. From New York City, once upon a time.'

'Ah, New York!' Y'ang-Yeovil's face lit with a glimmer of recognition that quickly faded. 'New York – New York – it was very famous, that I know – '

This is very strange, Phillips thought. He felt greater compassion for poor bewildered Francis Willoughby now. This man comes from a time so far beyond my own that he barely knows of New York – he must be a contemporary of the real New Chicago, in fact; I wonder whether he finds this version authentic – and yet to the citizens this Y'ang-Yeovil too is just a primitive, a curio out of antiquity –

'New York was the largest city of the United States of America,' Phillips said.

'Of course. Yes. Very famous.'

'But virtually forgotten by the time the Republic of Upper Han came into existence, I gather.'

Y'ang-Yeovil said, looking uncomfortable, 'There were disturbances between your time and mine. But by no means should you take from my words the impression that your city was – '

Sudden laughter resounded across the room. Five or six newcomers had arrived at the party. Phillips stared, gasped, gaped. Surely that was Stengard – and Armayne beside him – and that other woman, half-hidden behind them –

'If you'll pardon me a moment – ' Phillips said, turning abruptly away from Y'ang-Yeovil. 'Please excuse me. Someone just coming in – a person I've been trying to find ever since – '

He hurried towards her.

'Gioia?' he called. 'Gioia, it's me! Wait! Wait!'

Stengard was in the way. Aramayne, turning to take a handful of the little vapour-sniffers from Cantilena, blocked him also. Phillips pushed through them as though they were not there. Gioia, halfway out the door, halted and looked towards him like a frightened deer.

'Don't go,' he said. He took her hand in his.

He was startled by her appearance. How long had it been since their strange parting on that night of mysteries in Chang-an? A year? A year and a half? So he believed. Or had he lost all track of time? Were his perceptions of the passing of the months in this world that unreliable? She seemed at least ten or fifteen years older. Maybe she really was; maybe the years had been passing for him here as in a dream, and he had never known it. She looked strained, faded, worn. Out of a thinner and strangely altered face her eyes blazed at him almost defiantly, as though saying, *See? See how ugly I have become?*

He said, 'I've been hunting for you for – I don't know how long it's been, Gioia. In Mohenjo, in Timbuctoo, now here. I want to be with you again.'

'It isn't possible.'

'Belilala explained everything to me in Mohenjo. I know that

310

you're a short-timer – I know what that means, Gioia. But what
of it? So you're beginning to age a little. So what? So you'll only
have three or four hundred years, instead of forever. Don't you
think I know what it means to be a short-timer? I'm just a
simple ancient man of the twentieth century, remember? Sixty,
seventy, eighty years is all we would get. You and I suffer from
the same malady, Gioia. That's what drew you to me in the first
place. I'm certain of that. That's why we belong with each other
now. However much time we have, we can spend the rest of it
together, don't you see?'

'You're the one who doesn't see, Charles,' she said softly.

'Maybe. Maybe I still don't understand a damned thing about
this place. Except that you and I – that I love you – that I think
you love me – '

'I love you, yes. But you don't understand. It's precisely
because I love you that you and I – you and I can't – '

With a despairing sigh she slid her hand free of his grasp.
He reached for her again, but she shook him off and backed
up quickly into the corridor.

'Gioia?'

'Please,' she said. 'No. I would never have come here if I
knew you were here. Don't come after me. Please. Please.'

She turned and fled.

He stood looking after her for a long moment. Cantilena and
Aramayne appeared, and smiled at him as if nothing at all had
happened. Cantilena offered him a vial of some sparkling amber
fluid. He refused with a brusque gesture. Where do I go now, he
wondered? What do I do? He wandered back into the party.

Y'ang-Yeovil glided to his side. 'You are in great distress,'
the little man murmured.

Phillips glared. 'Let me be.'

'Perhaps I could be of some help.'

'There's no help possible,' said Phillips. He swung about and
plucked one of the vials from a tray and gulped its contents. It
made him feel as if there were two of him, standing on either
side of Y'ang-Yeovil. He gulped another. Now there were four
of him. 'I'm in love with a citizen,' he blurted. It seemed to him
that he was speaking in chorus.

'Love. Ah. And does she love you?'

'So I thought. So I think. But she's a short-timer. Do you know what that means? She's not immortal like the others. She ages. She's beginning to look old. And so she's been running away from me. She doesn't want me to see her changing. She thinks it'll disgust me, I suppose. I tried to remind her just now that I'm not immortal either, that she and I could grow old together, but she – '

'Oh, no,' Y'ang-Yeovil said quietly. 'Why do you think you will age? Have you grown any older in all the time you have been here?'

Phillips was nonplussed. 'Of course I have. I – I – '

'Have you?' Y'ang-Yeovil smiled. 'Here. Look at yourself.' He did something intricate with his fingers and a shimmering zone of mirror-like light appeared between them. Phillips stared at his reflection. A youthful face stared back at him. It was true, then. He had simply not thought about it. How many years had he spent in this world? The time had simply slipped by: a great deal of time, though he could not calculate how much. They did not seem to keep close count of it here, nor had he. But it must have been many years, he thought. All that endless travel up and down the globe – so many cities had come and gone – Rio, Rome, Asgard, those were the first three that came to mind – and there were others; he could hardly remember every one. Years. His face had not changed at all. Time had worked its harshness on Gioia, yes, but not on him.

'I don't understand,' he said. 'Why am I not ageing?'

'Because you are not real,' said Y'ang-Yeovil. 'Are you unaware of that?'

Phillips blinked. 'Not – real?'

'Did you think you were lifted bodily out of your own time?' the little man asked. 'Ah, no, no, there is no way for them to do such a thing. We are not actual time travellers: not you, not I, not any of the visitors. I thought you were aware of that. But perhaps your era is too early for a proper understanding of these things. We are very cleverly done, my friend. We are ingenious constructs, marvellously stuffed with the thoughts and attitudes and events of our own times. We are their finest achievement, you know: far more complex even than one of these cities: We are a step beyond the temporaries – more than a step, a great deal more. They do only what they are instructed to do, and their range is very narrow. They are nothing but machines, really. Whereas we are autonomous. We move about by our own will; we think, we talk, we even, so it seems, fall in love. But we will not age. How could we age? We are not real. We are mere artificial webworks of mental responses. We are mere illusions, done so well that we deceive even ourselves. You did not know that? Indeed, you did not know?'

He was airborne, touching destination buttons at random. Somehow he found himself heading back towards Timbuctoo. *This city is closed. This is not a place any longer.* It did not matter to him. Why should anything matter?

Fury and a choking sense of despair rose within him. I am software, Phillips thought. I am nothing but software.

Not real. Very cleverly done. An ingenious construct. A mere illusion.

No trace of Timbuctoo was visible from the air. He landed anyway. The grey sandy earth was smooth, unturned, as though there had never been anything there. A few robots were still about, handling whatever final chores were required in the shutting-down of a city. Two of them scuttled up to him. Huge bland gleaming silver-skinned insects, not friendly.

'There is no city here,' they said. 'This is not a permissible place.'

'Permissible by whom?'

'There is no reason for you to be here.'

'There's no reason for me to be anywhere,' Phillips said. The robots stirred, made uneasy humming sounds and ominous clicks, waved their antennae about. They seem troubled, he thought. They seem to dislike my attitude. Perhaps I run some risk of being taken off to the home for unruly software for debugging. 'I'm leaving now,' he told them. 'Thank you. Thank you very much.' He backed away from them and climbed into his flitterflitter. He touched more destination buttons.

We move about by our own will. We think, we talk, we even fall in love.

He landed in Chang-an. This time there was no reception committee waiting for him at the Gate of Brilliant Virtue. The city seemed larger and more resplendent: new pagodas, new palaces. It felt like winter: a chilly cutting wind was blowing. The sky was cloudless and dazzlingly bright. At the steps of the Silver Terrace he encountered Francis Willoughby, a great hulking figure in magnificent brocaded robes, with two dainty little temporaries, pretty as jade statuettes, engulfed in his arms. 'Miracles and wonders! The silly lunatic fellow is here too!' Willoughby roared. 'Look, look, we are come to far Cathay, you and I!'

We are nowhere, Phillips thought. *We are mere illusions, done so well that we deceive even ourselves.*

To Willoughby he said, 'You look like an emperor in those robes, Francis.'

'Aye, like Prester John!' Willoughby cried. 'Like Tamburlaine himself! Aye, am I not majestic?' He slapped Phillips gaily on the shoulder, a rough playful poke that spun him halfway about, coughing and wheezing. 'We flew in the air, as the eagles do, as the demons do, as the angels do! Soared like angels! Like angels!' He came close, looming over Phillips. 'I would have gone to England, but the wench Belilala said there was an enchantment on me that would keep me from England just now; and so we voyaged to Cathay. Tell me this, fellow, will you go witness for me when we see England again? Swear that all that has befallen us did in truth befall? For I fear they will say I am as mad as Marco Polo, when I tell them of flying to Cathay.'

'One madman backing another?' Phillips asked. 'What can I tell you? You still think you'll reach England, do you?' Rage rose to the surface in him, bubbling hot. 'Ah, Francis, Francis, do you know your Shakespeare? Did you go to the plays? We aren't real. *We aren't real.* We are such stuff as dreams are made on, the two of us. That's all we are. O brave new world! What England? Where? There's no England. There's no Francis Willoughby. There's no Charles Phillips. What we are is – '

'Let him be, Charles,' a cool voice cut in.

He turned. Belilala, in the robes of an empress, coming down the steps of the Silver Terrace.

'I know the truth,' he said bitterly. 'Y'ang-Yeovil told me. The visitor from the twenty-fifth century. I saw him in New Chicago.'

'Did you see Gioia there too?' Belilala asked.

'Briefly. She looks much older.'

'Yes. I know. She was here recently.'

'And has gone on, I suppose?'

'To Mohenjo again, yes. Go after her, Charles. Leave poor Francis alone. I told her to wait for you. I told her that she needs you, and you need her.'

'Very kind of you. But what good is it, Belilala? I don't even exist. And she's going to die.'

'You exist. How can you doubt that you exist? You feel, don't you? You suffer. You love. You love Gioia: is that not so? And you are loved by Gioia. Would Gioia love what is not real?'

'You think she loves me?'

'I know she does. Go to her, Charles. Go. I told her to wait for you in Mohenjo.'

Phillips nodded numbly. What was there to lose?

'Go to her,' said Belilala again. 'Now.'

'Yes,' Phillips said. 'I'll go now.' He turned to Willoughby. 'If ever we meet in London, friend, I'll testify for you. Fear nothing. All will be well, Francis.'

He left them and set his course for Mohenjo-daro, half expecting to find the robots already tearing it down. Mohenjo-daro was still there, no lovelier than before. He went to the baths, thinking he might find Gioia there. She was not; but he came upon Nissandra, Stengard, Fenimon. 'She has gone to Alexandria,' Fenimon told him. 'She wants to see it one last time, before they close it.'

'They're almost ready to open Constantinople,' Stengard explained. 'The capital of Byzantium, you know, the great city by the Golden Horn. They'll take Alexandria away, you understand, when Byzantium opens. They say it's going to be marvellous. We'll see you there for the opening, naturally?'

'Naturally,' Phillips said.

He flew to Alexandria. He felt lost and weary. All this is hopeless folly, he told himself. I am nothing but a puppet jerking about on its strings. But somewhere above the shining breast of the Arabian Sea the deeper implications of something that Belilala had said to him started to sink in, and he felt his bitterness, his rage, his despair, all suddenly beginning to leave him. *You exist. How can you doubt that you exist? Would Gioia love what is not real?* Of course. Of course. Y'ang-Yeovil had been wrong: visitors were something more than mere illusions. Indeed Y'ang-Yeovil had voiced the truth of their condition

315

without understanding what he was really saying: *We think, we talk, we fall in love.* Yes. That was the heart of the situation. The visitors might be artificial, but they were not unreal. Belilala had been trying to tell him that just the other night. *You suffer. You love. You love Gioia. Would Gioia love what is not real?* Surely he was real, or at any rate real enough. What he was was something strange, something that would probably have been all but incomprehensible to the twentieth-century people whom he had been designed to simulate. But that did not mean that he was unreal. Did one have to be of woman born to be real? No. No. No. His kind of reality was a sufficient reality. He had no need to be ashamed of it. And, understanding that, he understood that Gioia did not need to grow old and die. There was a way by which she could be saved, if only she would embrace it. If only she would.

When he landed in Alexandria he went immediately to the hotel on the slopes of the Paneium where they had stayed on their first visit, so very long ago; and there she was, sitting quietly on a patio with a view of the harbour and the Lighthouse. There was something calm and resigned about the way she sat. She had given up. She did not even have the strength to flee from him any longer.

'Gioia,' he said gently.

She looked older than she had in New Chicago. Her face was drawn and sallow and her eyes seemed sunken; and she was not even bothering these days to deal with the white strands that stood out in stark contrast against the darkness of her hair. He sat down beside her and put his hand over hers, and looked out towards the obelisks, the palaces, the temples, the Lighthouse. At length he said, 'I know what I really am, now.'

'Do you, Charles?' She sounded very far away.

'In my era we called it software. All I am is a set of commands, responses, cross-references, operating some sort of artificial body. It's infinitely better software than we could have imagined. But we were only just beginning to learn how, after all. They pumped me full of twentieth-century reflexes. The right moods, the right appetites, the right irrationalities, the right sort of combativeness. Somebody knows a lot about what it was like to be a twentieth-century man. They did a good job with Willoughby, too, all that Elizabethan rhetoric and swagger. And I suppose they got Y'ang-Yeovil right. He seems to think so: who better to judge? The twenty-fifth century, the Republic of Upper Han, people with grey-green skin, half Chinese and half Martian for all I know. *Somebody* knows. Somebody here is very good at programming, Gioia.'

She was not looking at him.

'I feel frightened, Charles,' she said in that same distant way.

'Of me? Of the things I'm saying?'

'No, not of you. Don't you see what has happened to me?'

'I see you. There are changes.'

'I lived a long time wondering when the changes would begin. I thought maybe they wouldn't, not really. Who wants to believe they'll get old? But it started when we were in Alexandria that first time. In Chang-an it got much worse. And now – now – '

He said abruptly, 'Stengard tells me they'll be opening Constantinople very soon.'

'So?'

'Don't you want to be there when it opens?'

'I'm becoming old and ugly, Charles.'

'We'll go to Constantinople together. We'll leave tomorrow, eh? What do you say? We'll charter a boat. It's a quick little hop, right across the Mediterranean. Sailing to Byzantium! There was a poem, you know, in my time. Not forgotten, I guess, because they've programmed it into me. All these thousands of years, and someone still remembers old Yeats. *The young in one another's arms, birds in the trees.* Come with me to Byzantium, Gioia.'

She shrugged. 'Looking like this? Getting more hideous every hour? While *they* stay young for ever? While *you* – ' She faltered; her voice cracked; she fell silent.

'Finish the sentence, Gioia.'

'Please. Let me alone.'

'You were going to say, "While *you* stay young for ever too, Charles," isn't that it? You knew all along that I was never going to change. I didn't know that, but you did.'

'Yes. I knew. I pretended that it wasn't true – that as I aged, you'd age too. It was very foolish of me. In Chang-an, when I first began to see the real signs of it – that was when I realized

317

I couldn't stay with you any longer. Because I'd look at you, always young, always remaining the same age, and I'd look at myself, and – ' She gestured, palms upward. 'So I gave you to Belilala and ran away.'

'All so unnecessary, Gioia.'

'I didn't think it was.'

'But you don't have to grow old. Not if you don't want to!'

'Don't be cruel, Charles,' she said tonelessly. 'There's no way of escaping what I have.'

'But there is,' he said.

'You know nothing about these things.'

'Not very much, no,' he said. 'But I see how it can be done. Maybe it's a primitive simple-minded twentieth-century sort of solution, but I think it ought to work. I've been playing with the idea ever since I left Mohenjo. Tell me this, Gioia: why can't you go to them, to the programmers, to the artificers, the planners, whoever they are, the ones who create the cities and the temporaries and the visitors. And have yourself made into something like me!'

She looked up, startled. 'What are you saying?'

'They can cobble up a twentieth-century man out of nothing more than fragmentary records and make him plausible, can't they? Or an Elizabethan, or anyone else of any era at all, and he's authentic, he's convincing. So why couldn't they do an even better job with you? Produce a Gioia so real that even Gioia can't tell the difference? But a Gioia that will never age – a Gioia-construct, a Gioia-program, a visitor-Gioia! Why not? Tell me why not, Gioia.'

She was trembling. 'I've never heard of doing any such thing!'

'But don't you think it's possible?'

'How would I know?'

'Of course it's possible. If they can create visitors, they can take a citizen and duplicate her in such a way that – '

'It's never been done. I'm sure of it. I can't imagine any citizen agreeing to any such thing. To give up the body – to let yourself be turned into – into – '

She shook her head, but it seemed to be a gesture of astonishment as much as of negation.

He said, 'Sure. To give up the body. Your natural body,

318

your ageing, shrinking, deteriorating short-timer body. What's
so awful about that?'

She was very pale. 'This is craziness, Charles. I don't want
to talk about it any more.'

'It doesn't sound crazy to me.'

'You can't possibly understand.'

'Can't I? I can certainly understand being afraid to die. I don't
have a lot of trouble understanding what it's like to be one of the
few ageing people in a world where nobody grows old. What I
can't understand is why you aren't even willing to consider the
possibility that – '

'No,' she said. 'I tell you, it's crazy. They'd laugh at me.'

'Who?'

'All of my friends. Hawk, Stengard, Aramayne – ' Once again
she would not look at him. 'They can be very cruel, without
even realizing it. They despise anything that seems ungraceful
to them, anything sweaty and desperate and cowardly. Citizens
don't do sweaty things, Charles. And that's how this will seem.
Assuming it can be done at all. They'll be terribly patronizing.
Oh, they'll be sweet to me, yes, dear Gioia, how wonderful for
you, Gioia, but when I turn my back they'll laugh. They'll say
the most wicked things about me. I couldn't bear that.'

'They can afford to laugh,' Phillips said. 'It's easy to be brave
and cool about dying when you know you're going to live for
ever. How very fine for them: but why should you be the only
one to grow old and die? And they won't laugh, anyway. They're
not as cruel as you think. Shallow, maybe, but not cruel. They'll
be glad that you've found a way to save yourself. At the very
least, they won't have to feel guilty about you any longer, and
that's bound to please them. You can – '

'Stop it,' she said.

She rose, walked to the railing of the patio, stared out towards the sea. He came up behind her. Red sails in the harbour,
sunlight glittering along the sides of the Lighthouse, the palaces
of the Ptolemies stark white against the sky. Lightly he rested
his hand on her shoulder. She twitched as if to pull away from
him, but remained where she was.

'Then I have another idea,' he said quietly. 'If you won't
go to the planners, *I* will. Reprogram me, I'll say. Fix things
so that I start to age at the same rate you do. It'll be more

authentic, anyway, if I'm supposed to be playing the part of a twentieth-century man. Over the years I'll very gradually get some lines in my face, my hair will turn grey, I'll walk a little more slowly – we'll grow old together, Gioia. To hell with your lovely immortal friends. We'll have each other. We won't need them.'

She swung around. Her eyes were wide with horror.

'Are you serious, Charles?'

'Of course.'

'No,' she murmured. 'No. Everything you've said to me today is monstrous nonsense. Don't you realize that?'

He reached for her hand and enclosed her fingertips in his. 'All I'm trying to do is find some way for you and me to – '

'Don't say any more,' she said. 'Please.' Quickly, as though drawing back from a suddenly flaring flame, she tugged her fingers free of his and put her hand behind her. Though his face was just inches from hers he felt an immense chasm opening between them. They stared at one another for a moment; then she moved deftly to his left, darted around him, and ran from the patio.

Stunned, he watched her go, down the long marble corridor and out of sight. It was folly to give pursuit, he thought. She was lost to him: that was clear, that was beyond any question. She was terrified of him. Why cause her even more anguish? But somehow he found himself running through the halls of the hotel, along the winding garden path, into the cool green groves of the Paneium. He thought he saw her on the portico of Hadrian's palace, but when he got there the echoing stone halls were empty. To a temporary that was sweeping the steps he said, 'Did you see a woman come this way?' A blank sullen stare was his only answer.

Phillips cursed and turned away.

'Gioia?' he called. 'Wait! Come back!'

Was that her, going into the Library? He rushed past the startled mumbling librarians and sped through the stacks, peering beyond the mounds of double-handled scrolls into the shadowy corridors. 'Gioia? *Gioia!*' It was a desecration, bellowing like that in this quiet place. He scarcely cared.

Emerging by a side door, he loped down to the harbour. The Lighthouse! Terror enfolded him. She might already be a hundred steps up that ramp, heading for the parapet from which she meant to fling herself into the sea. Scattering citizens and temporaries as if they were straws, he ran within. Up he went, never pausing for breath, though his synthetic lungs were screaming for respite, his ingeniously designed heart was desperately pounding. On the first balcony he imagined he caught a glimpse of her, but he circled it without finding her. Onwards, upwards. He went to the top, to the beacon chamber itself: no Gioia. Had she jumped? Had she gone down one ramp while he was ascending the other? He clung to the rim and looked out, down, searching the base of the Lighthouse, the rocks offshore, the causeway. No Gioia. I will find her somewhere, he thought. I will keep going until I find her. He went running down the ramp, calling her name. He reached ground level and sprinted back towards the centre of town. Where next? The temple of Poseidon? The tomb of Cleopatra?

He paused in the middle of Canopus Street, groggy and dazed.

'Charles?' she said.

'Where are you?'

'Right here. Beside you.' She seemed to materialize from the air. Her face was unflushed, her robe bore no trace of perspiration. Had he been chasing a phantom through the city? She came to him and took his hand, and said, softly, tenderly, 'Were you really serious, about having them make you age?'

'If there's no other way, yes.'

'The other way is so frightening, Charles.'

'Is it?'

'You can't understand how much.'

'More frightening than growing old? Than dying?'

'I don't know,' she said. 'I suppose not. The only thing I'm sure of is that I don't want you to get old, Charles.'

'But I won't have to. Will I?'

He stared at her.

'No,' she said. 'You won't have to. Neither of us will.'

Phillips smiled. 'We should get away from here,' he said after a while. 'Let's go across to Byzantium, yes, Gioia? We'll show up in Constantinople for the opening. Your friends will be there. We'll tell them what you've decided to do. They'll know how to arrange it. Someone will.'

'It sounds so strange,' said Gioia. 'To turn myself into – into a visitor? A visitor in my own world?'

'That's what you've always been, though.'

'I suppose. In a way. But at least I've been *real* up to now.'

'Whereas I'm not?'

'Are you, Charles?'

'Yes. Just as real as you. I was angry at first, when I found out the truth about myself. But I came to accept it. Somewhere between Mohenjo and here, I came to see that it was all right to be what I am: that I perceive things, I form ideas, I draw conclusions. I am very well designed, Gioia. I can't tell the difference between being what I am and being completely alive, and to me that's being real enough. I think, I feel, I experience joy and pain. I'm as real as I need to be. And you will be too. You'll never stop being Gioia, you know. It's only your body that you'll cast away, the body that played such a terrible joke on you anyway.' He brushed her cheek with his hand. 'It was all said for us before, long ago:

> *Once out of nature I shall never take*
> *My bodily form from any natural thing,*
> *But such a form as Grecian goldsmiths make*
> *Of hammered gold and gold enamelling*
> *To keep a drowsy Emperor awake – '*

'Is that the same poem?' she asked.

'The same poem, yes. The ancient poem that isn't quite forgotten yet.'

'Finish it, Charles.'

> *– 'Or set upon a golden bough to sing*
> *To lords and ladies of Byzantium*
> *Of what is past, or passing, or to come.'*

'How beautiful. What does it mean?'

'That it isn't necessary to be mortal. That we can allow ourselves to be gathered into the artifice of eternity, that we can be transformed, that we can move on beyond the flesh. Yeats didn't mean it in quite the way I do – he wouldn't have begun to comprehend what we're talking about, not a word of it – and yet, and yet – the underlying truth is the same. Live,

Gioia! With me!' He turned to her and saw colour coming into her pallid cheeks. 'It does make sense, what I'm suggesting, doesn't it? You'll attempt it, won't you? Whoever makes the visitors can be induced to remake you. Right? What do you think: can they, Gioia?'

She nodded in a barely perceptible way. 'I think so,' she said faintly. 'It's very strange. But I think it ought to be possible. Why not, Charles? Why not?'

'Yes,' he said. 'Why not?'

In the morning they hired a vessel in the harbour, a low sleek pirogue with a blood-red sail, skippered by a rascally-looking temporary whose smile was irresistible. Phillips shaded his eyes and peered northwards across the sea. He thought he could almost make out the shape of the great city sprawling on its seven hills, Constantine's New Rome beside the Golden Horn, the mighty dome of Hagia Sophia, the sombre walls of the citadel, the palaces and churches, the Hippodrome, Christ in glory rising above all else in brilliant mosaic streaming with light.

'Byzantium,' Phillips said. 'Take us there the shortest and quickest way.'

'It is my pleasure,' said the boatman with unexpected grace.

Gioia smiled. He had not seen her looking so vibrantly alive since the night of the imperial feast in Chang-an. He reached for her hand – her slender fingers were quivering lightly – and helped her into the boat.

Sunrise on Pluto

A curious bit of history lies behind this one.

Back in the summer of 1981 my good friend Byron Preiss, the editor and book-packager, asked me to do a little non-fiction piece on Pluto for a project he was assembling. It was to be a book of speculative science-fact called *The Planets*, in which essays on the likely nature of each world of the solar system would be matched with colour paintings by astronomical artists. I did some research, produced the desired short article, collected my cheque, and forgot all about it. Years went by and the book didn't appear.

Suddenly there was Byron on the phone again, after me for *another* piece about Pluto. His book had undergone a transformation: now it was going to be a large and handsome volume containing fiction as well as fact. Each scientific essay would be matched by a story set on the planet discussed. The authors of the other essays he had gathered were all astronomers with no experience at doing science-fiction; but I had some credentials as a fiction-writer as well, so would I mind, Byron asked, taking the speculative passages out of my Pluto article and developing them into a story, for a second fee?

The timing was right – it was the autumn of 1984, and I wasn't quite ready to get started on my new novel, *Tom O'Bedlam*. I dug out the yellowing carbon copy of my Pluto piece – written back in the pre-computer days, so I couldn't simply call it up from a disk – and set to work. 'Sunrise on Pluto' was the result. And in due course Byron's book, *The Planets*, finally appeared – years in the making, stellar cast, altogether a magnificent production. Among the other contributors of fiction were Frank Herbert, Roger Zelazny, Jack Williamson, Ray Bradbury and Philip José Farmer. And there I was, not only with a story, but posing as an astronomical authority too. All in a day's work, I guess.

*   *   *

324

We have waited out the night, and now at last we will go forth on to the frozen face of Pluto. One by one we take our places – Leonides, Sherrard, Gartenmeister, me – and ready ourselves to clamber down the ladder to the icy surface of the outermost of worlds.

Soon we will have an answer to the question that has obsessed us all during this long night.

Night on Pluto is 6.39 Earth-days long, and that night is blacker and colder than anything any of us has ever known. It is a true dark night of the soul, a dismal time made infinitely more terrible by our awareness of the monstrous distance separating us from all that we love. That distance imposes a burden which our spirits can scarcely carry. God knows, the dark side of Luna is a bleak and terrible place, but one never feels so wholly crushed by its bleakness as we have felt here. On Luna one need make only a brief journey to the edge and there is the lovely blue Earth hovering overhead, close, familiar, beckoning. But here stand we on forlorn Pluto, knowing that we are nearly four billion miles from home. No-one has ever been so far from home before.

Now at last the fierce interminable night is ending. When we made our touchdown here the night was half spent; we used what remained of the dark hours to carry out our preliminary observations and to prepare for the extra-vehicular journey. Now, as we make ready to emerge, there comes the first trembling hint of a dawn. The utter and absolute and overwhelming darkness, which has been made all the more intense by the chilly glitter of the stars, is pierced by a strange pale glow. Then a sudden astonishing burst of light enters the sky – the light of a giant whose cold radiance is hundreds of times as bright as that of the full moon seen from Earth.

It is the sun, *our* sun, the well of all warmth, the fountain of life. But how sadly its splendour is altered and diminished by those billions of miles! What reaches us here is not the throbbing golden blaze of summer but only a brilliant wintry beacon that sends glittering tracks of dazzling merciless brightness across the stark icefields of Pluto.

We move towards the hatch. No-one speaks. The tension is rising and our faces show it.

We are edgy and uneasy, but not because we are about to be

the first humans to set foot on this world: that is trivial, entirely unimportant to us, as I think it has always been to those who have carried the great quest outwards into space. No, what concerns us is a mystery that no previous explorers of the Solar System have had to confront. Our instruments, during the long Plutonian night, have been recording apparent indications that living creatures, Plutonian life-forms, are moving about out there.

Life-forms? Here, on the coldest and most remote of worlds? It seems absurd. It *is* absurd. Nowhere in the Solar System has anyone ever found a trace of extraterrestrial life, not on any of the explored planets nor on any of their moons. Unless something unimaginable lurks deep within the impenetrable gaseous mantles of Jupiter or Saturn or Uranus, our own small planet is the sole repository of life in the System, and, for all we know, in the entire universe. But our scanners have picked up the spoor of life here: barely perceptible electromagnetic pulses that indicate something in motion. It is strictly a threshold phenomenon, the most minimal trace-output of energy, the tiniest trickle of exertion. The signal is so faint that Sherrard thinks it is nothing more than an instrumentation error, mere noise in the circuitry. And Gartenmeister *wants* it to be an error – he fears the existence of extraterrestrial life, so it seems, the way Pascal feared the eternal silence of the infinite heavens. Leonides argues that there is nothing that could produce such distinct vectors of electromagnetic activity except neural interaction, and therefore some sort of living beings must be crawling about on the ice-fields. 'No,' I say, 'they could be purely mechanical, couldn't they? Robots left behind by interstellar explorers, say?'

Gartenmeister scowls at me. 'Even more absurd,' he says.

No, I think, not more absurd, merely more disturbing. No matter what we discover out there, it is bound to upset deeply-held convictions about the unique place of Earth in the cosmos. Who would have thought it, that Pluto, of all places, would harbour life? On the other hand, perhaps Sherrard is right. Perhaps what we have imagined to be life-forms emitting minuscule flickers of electrical energy is in truth nothing more than deceptive Brownian tremors in the atoms that make up our ship's sensors. Perhaps. Soon we may have an answer.

'Let's go,' Leonides says.

We swing downwards and outwards, into the cheerless Plutonian dawn.

The blackness of the sky is tinged with green as the distant sunlight bounces through the faint wispy swirls of methane that are Pluto's atmosphere. Visible now overhead, hovering ominously close, is the dull menacing bulk of Charon, Pluto's enormous moon, motionless and immense. Our shadows are weird things, sharp-edged and immensely long. They seem to strain forward as though trying to escape from us. Cold tendrils of sunlight glide unhurriedly towards the jagged icy cliffs in the distance.

Sunrise! Sunrise on Pluto!

How still it is, an alien sunrise. No birds sing, no insects buzz and drone. We four have seen many such sunrises – on Luna, on Mars, on Titan, on Ganymede, on Iapetus: standing with our backs to the rising sun, looking out on a harsh and silent landscape. But none so silent as this, none so harsh.

We fan out across the surface of Pluto, moving lithely, all but floating: Pluto is the lightest of worlds, its mass only a few hundredths that of Earth, and its gravitational grip is less secure than those of some of the larger moons. What do I see? Ice. A joyless methane sea far away, shining faintly by the dull light of dawn. Fangs of black rock. Despair begins to rise in me. To have come billions of miles, merely for the sake of being able to say that this world, too, has been explored –

'Here!' Leonides calls.

He is far in front of us, almost at the terminator line beyond which the sun has not yet reached. He is pointing ahead, into the darkness, stabbing at it with the beam of his light.

'Look! I can see them moving!'

We run toward him, leaping in great bounds, soaring, gliding. Then we stand beside him, following the line of his light, staring in awe and astonishment toward the darkness.

Yes. Yes. We have the answer at last to our question, and the answer is a stunning one. Pluto bears life. Small dome-shaped things are scrabbling over the ice!

They move slowly, unhurriedly, and yet one somehow feels that they are going as fast as possible, that indeed they are racing for cover, pushing their bodies to the limits. And we know what it is that they are struggling to escape; for already the ones closest to us have been overtaken by the advancing light of day, and as the rays touch them they move more slowly, and more slowly yet, and then they fall entirely still, stopping altogether between one moment and the next, like wind-up toys that have run down. Those that are in sunlight now lie stranded on the ice, and those ahead of them are being overtaken, one after another.

We hasten to them, kneel, examine them. None of us says a word. We hardly dare look at one another. The creatures are about the size of large crabs, with thick smooth waxy-textured grey shells that reveal neither eyes nor mouths. They are altogether motionless. I touch one with a trembling hand, nudge it, get no response, nudge it a bit more forcefully. It does not move. I glance at Leonides. He nods, and I tip the creature on its side, which shows us a great many small jointed legs that seem to sprout from the shell surface itself. What a simple creature! A mere armoured box!

'I don't believe it,' Sherrard mutters.

'You still think it's an error in the circuitry?' Leonides asks him gently.

Sherrard shakes his head. Carefully he gathers one of the creatures into his gloved hands and brings it close to his face-plate. 'It doesn't move at all,' he says quietly. 'It's playing possum, isn't it?'

'It may not be able to move,' says Leonides. 'Not with anything as warm as you so close to it. They're tremendously sensitive to heat, I imagine. You see how they start to shut down, the moment the sun strikes them?'

'Like machines,' says Sherrard. 'At the wrong operating temperature they cease to function.'

'*Like* machines, yes,' Leonides replies. 'But surely you aren't going to try to argue that they *are* machines, are you?'

Sherrard shrugs. 'Machines can have legs. Machines can have shells.' He looks towards me. 'It's like you said, Tom: robots left behind by explorers from some other part of the galaxy. Why not? Why the hell not?'

* * *

328

There is nothing to gain by debating it out here. We return to the ship to get collection chambers and scoop three of the creatures into cryotanks, along with liquid methane and lumps of frozen-ammonia ice. The discovery is so wholly unexpected and so numbing in its implications that we can hardly speak. We had thought we were making a routine reconnaissance of an unimportant planet; instead we have made one of the most astonishing discoveries in the history of science.

We store our finds in the ship's lab at a temperature of two or three degrees Kelvin. Gartenmeister and Sherrard set about the job of examining them while Leonides and I continue the extra-vehicular exploration.

The crab-creatures are littered all over the place, dozens of them, hundreds, scattered like jetsam on a beach. They appear to be dead, but very likely Leonides' notion that they are extremely heat-sensitive tells the real story: to the native life-forms of Pluto – and how strange it is to have a phrase like that running through my mind! – the coming of day must be an inexorable signal bringing a halt to all metabolic activity. A rise of just a few degrees and they are compelled to stop in their tracks, seemingly lifeless, in fact held in suspended animation, until the slow rotation of the planet brings them back, in another 6.39 Earth-days, into the frigid darkness that they must have in order to function. Creatures of the night: creatures of the inconceivable realm at the borderland of absolute zero. But why? It makes so little sense: to move by night, to go dormant at the first touch of the life-giving sun! Why? Why?

Leonides and I explore for hours. There is so much to do: collecting mineral samples, drilling for ice-cores that may yield data on earlier epochs of Pluto's history, searching for other forms of life. We move carefully, for we are not yet used to the lightness of the gravitational field, and we prowl in a slow, systematic way, as if we are going to be the only expedition ever to land on this remote outpost of the Solar System and must take pains not to overlook anything. But I see the fallacy in that. It is true that this is the first time anyone has bothered to visit Pluto, although centuries have passed since the earliest human voyages into space. And it is true also that when we planned this expedition it was under the assumption that no-one was likely to have reason to come this way again for a long time. But all that has changed. There is extraterrestrial life on this world, after all. Nowhere else is that the case. When we send back the news, it will alter the direction of virtually all scientific research, and much else besides.

The impact of our find is only just beginning to sink in.

Sherrard peers out of the ship's lab as Leonides and I come back on board. His expression is a peculiar one, a mixture of astonishment and – what? – self-satisfaction?

'We've discovered how they work,' he announces. 'They operate by superconductivity.'

Of course. Superconductivity occurs only within a few degrees of absolute zero: a strange and miraculous thing, that resistance-free flow of current, the most efficient possible way of trans-mitting an electrical signal. Why *not* have it serve as the energizing principle for life-forms on a world where night-time temperatures drop to two degrees Kelvin? It seems so obvious, now that Sherrard has said it. But at the same time it is such an unlikely thing, such an *alien* way for living creatures to be designed. If, that is, they are living creatures at all, and not merely some sort of cunning mechanisms. I feel the hair lifting along the back of my neck.

Gartenmeister and Sherrard have dissected one. It lies on its back, its undershell neatly cut away and its internal organs exposed to view. Its interior is lined with a series of narrow glossy green and blue tubes that cross and meet at rigid angles, with small yellow hexagonal bodies spaced at regular intervals down the centre. The overall pattern is intricate, yes, but it is the intricacy of a well-designed machine. There is an almost oppressive symmetry about the arrangement. A second creature, still intact, rests unmoving and seemingly lifeless in its holding tank. The third has been placed in an adjoining tank, and it is awake and sullenly scrabbling about like a trapped turtle trying to climb the walls of its bowl.

Jerking his thumb at the one that is moving, Gartenmeister says, 'We've got it at Pluto-night temperature, just a notch above absolute. The other tank's five degrees warmer. The threshold is very precise: when the temperature rises to seven degrees above absolute zero they start to go dormant. Lower the temperature and they wake up. Raise it again, they stop in their tracks again. It's like throwing a switch.'

330

'It's *exactly* like throwing a switch,' says Sherrard. 'They're machines. Very neatly calibrated.' He turns on a projector. Glittering cubical forms appear on the screen. 'Here: look at the crystalline structure of one of these tubes. Silicon and cobalt, arranged in a perfect matrix. You want to tell me this is organic life? These things are nothing more than signal-processing devices designed to operate at super-cold temperatures.'

'And we?' Leonides asks. 'Are we not merely signal-processing devices also, designed to operate in somewhat warmer weather?'

'Merely? *Merely?*'

'We are machines of flesh and blood,' says Leonides. 'These are machines of another kind.'

'But they have blood also,' Gartenmeister says. 'Of the sort that a superconductive life-form would have to have. Their blood is helium II.'

How startling that is – and yet how plausible! Helium II, that weird friction-free fluid that exists only at the lowest of temperatures – capable of creeping up the side of a glass vessel in defiance of gravity, of passing through openings of incredibly small size, of doing all manner of unlikely things – and of creating an environment in which certain metals become capable of superconductive propagation of electrical signals. Helium II 'blood', I realize, would indeed be an ideal carrier of nutrients through the body of a non-organic creature unable to pump a conventional fluid from one part of itself to another.

'Is that true?' Leonides asks. 'Helium II? Actually?'

Gartenmeister nods. 'There is no doubt of it.'

'Helium II, yes,' says Sherrard sullenly. 'But it's just lubricating fluid. Not blood.'

'Call it what you like,' Gartenmeister tells him. 'I use only a metaphor. I am nowhere saying yet that they are alive.'

'But you imply – '

'I imply nothing!'

I remain silent, paying little attention to the argument. In awe and wonder I stare at the motionless creature, at the one that is moving about, and at the dissected one. I think of them out there on the Plutonian ice-fields, meandering in their unhurried way over fields of frozen methane, pausing to nibble at a hydrocarbon sundae whenever they feel the need for refreshment. But only during the night; for when their side of Pluto at last comes round to face the sun, the temperature will climb, soaring as high as seventy-seven degrees Kelvin. They will cease motion long before that, of course – at just a few moments after dawn, as we have seen, when the day's heat rises beyond those critical few degrees at which superconductivity is possible. They slip into immobility then until night returns. And so their slow lives must go, switching from *on* to *off* for – who knew? – thousands of years, perhaps. Or perhaps for ever.

How strange, I think, how alien, how wonderful they are! On temperate Earth, where animal life has taken the form of protoplasmic oxygen-breathing beings whose chemistry is based on carbon, the phenomenon of superconductivity itself is a bizarre and alien thing, sustainable only under laboratory conditions. But in the unthinkable cold of Pluto, how appropriate that the life-forms should be fashioned of silicon and cobalt, constructed in flawless lattices so that their tissues offer no resistance to electrical currents. Once generated, such a current would persist indefinitely, flowing for ever without weakening – the spark of life, and eternal life at that!

They still look like grotesque crabs to me, and not the machines that Sherrard insists they must be. But even if they are animals rather than machines, they are, by comparison with any life-form known to Earth, very machine-like animals indeed.

We have spent a wearying six hours. This discovery should have been exhilarating, even exalting; instead we find ourselves bickering over whether we have found living creatures or mere ingenious mechanisms. Sherrard is adamant that they are machines; Gartenmeister seems to lean in both directions at once, though he is obviously troubled by the thought that they may be alive; Leonides is convinced that we are dealing with true life-forms. I think the dispute, now overheated and ugly, is a mere displacement symptom: we are disturbed by the deeper implications of the find, and, unwilling thus far to face them directly, we turn instead to quarrelling over secondary semantic technicalities. The real question is not who created these beings – whether they are the work of what I suppose we

can call the divine force, or simply of other intelligent creatures
– but how we are to deal with the sudden inescapable knowledge
that we are not alone in the universe.

I think we may just have settled the life-versus-machine
dispute.

It is morning, ship-time. Gartenmeister calls out sharply,
waking us. He has been on watch, puttering in the lab, while
we sleep. We rush in and he points to the Plutonian that has
been kept at superconductive temperatures.

'See there? Along the lower left-hand rim of its shell?'

I can find nothing unusual at first. Then I look more carefully,
as he focuses the laser lamp to cast its beam at a steeper angle.
Now I observe two fine metallic 'whiskers', so delicate that they
are barely visible even to my most intense scrutiny, jutting to a
length of five or six millimetres from the edge of the shell.

'I saw them sprout,' he says. 'One came half an hour ago.
The other just now. Look – here comes a third!'

We crowd in close. There can be no doubt: a third delicate
whisker is beginning to protrude.

Sherrard says, 'Communications devices, perhaps? It's programmed to signal for help when captured: it's setting up its
antenna so that it can broadcast to the others outside.'

Leonides laughs. 'Do you think they get captured often? By
whom?'

'Who knows?' Sherrard responds. 'There may be other
creatures out there that prey on – '

He stops, realizing what he has said. It is too late.

'Other *creatures*?' I ask. 'Don't you mean bigger machines?'

Sherrard looks angry. 'I don't know what I mean. Creatures,
machines – ' He shakes his head. 'Even so, these might be
antennae of some sort, mightn't they? Signalling devices that
protrude automatically in time of danger? Say, when one is
trapped by an ice-slide?'

'Or sensors,' offers Leonides. 'Like a cat's whiskers, like a
snail's feelers. Probing the environment, helping it to find a
way out of the tank we've got it in.'

'A reproductive organ,' Gartenmeister says suddenly.

We stare at him. '*What?*'

Unperturbed, he says, 'Many low-phylum life-forms, when

333

they are trapped, go automatically into reproductive mode. Even if the individual is destroyed, the species is still propagated. Let us say that these are living creatures, yes? For the sake of argument. Then they must reproduce somehow. Even though they are slow-growing, virtually immortal, they must still reproduce. What if it is by budding? They take in minute quantities of silicon and cobalt, build up a surplus of nutrients, and at a certain time they put forth these filaments. Which gain in size over – who knows, a hundred years, a thousand, ten thousand? – and when they have the requisite minimum mass, they break free, take up independent life, foraging for their own food. The electrical spark of life is transferred automatically from parent to offspring, and sustains itself by means of their superconductivity.'

We look at him in amazement. Obviously he has been pondering deeply while we were sleeping.

'If you tell us that they metabolize – they eat, they transfer nutrients along the flow of helium II, they even reproduce,' says Leonides, 'then you're telling us that they're living things. Or else you're asking us to redefine the nature of machines in such a way as to eliminate any distinction between machines and living things.'

'I think,' says Gartenmeister in a dark and despondent tone, 'that there can be no doubt. They are alive.'

Sherrard stares a long while at the three tiny filaments. Then he shrugs.

'You may be right,' he says.

Leonides shakes his head. 'Listen to you! Both of you! We've made the most exciting discovery in five hundred years and you sound as though you've just learned that the sun's going nova tomorrow!'

'Let them be,' I tell him, touching his arm lightly. 'It's not easy.'

'What's not?'

'A thousand years ago everyone thought the Earth was at the centre of the universe, with everything else moving in orbit around it,' I say. 'It was a very comfortable and cosy and flattering idea, but it didn't happen to be true, as Copernicus and Kepler and Galileo were able to prove. It was such a hard thing for people to accept that Galileo was put on trial and forced to deny his own findings, wasn't he? All right. In time everyone came to admit that the Earth moves around the sun, and not vice versa. And now, for centuries, we've explored space and found it absolutely lifeless – not a smidgeon of life, not a speck, no Martians, no Venusians, no Lunarians, nothing. *Nothing*. Earth the cosmic exception, the sole abode of life, the crown of creation. Until now. We have these little superconductive crabs here on Pluto. Our brothers-in-life, four billion miles away. Earth's last uniqueness is stripped away. I think that'll be harder to swallow than you may think. If we had found life right away, on the Moon back in the twentieth century, on Mars a little later on, it might have been easier. But not now, not after we've been all over the System. We developed a sort of smugness about ourselves. These little critters have just destroyed that.'

'Even if they are machines,' says Gartenmeister hollowly, 'then we have to ask ourselves: who built them?'

'I think I'd prefer to think they're alive,' Sherrard says.

'They *are* alive,' I tell them. 'We're going to get used to that idea.'

I walk to the hatch and peer outside. Small dark shapes lie huddled motionless here and there on the ice, waiting for night to return. For a long while I stare at them. My soul is flooded with awe and joy. The greatest of miracles has happened on this planet, as it had happened also long ago on Earth; and if life has been able to come into being on dismal Pluto, I know we will encounter it on a million million other worlds as we make our way in the centuries to come beyond this little Solar System into the vast galaxy. Somehow I cannot find anything to fear in that thought. Suddenly, thinking of the wonders and splendours that await us in that great beyond, I imagine that I hear the jubilant music of the spheres resounding from world to world; and when I turn and look back at the others, I realize that they also have been able to move past that first hard moment of shock and dismay which the loss of our uniqueness has brought. I see their faces transfigured, I see the doubt and turmoil gone; and it seems to me that they must be hearing that music too.

Hardware

No profundities here: just a quick, light piece, written in February of 1985 with some of the surplus energy left over after producing *Tom O'Bedlam*, which had been an uncharacteristically refreshing book to write and left me far less wearied than I usually am after finishing a book. Ellen Datlow liked it and in the due course of time published it in *Omni*.

'It's a computer, that's what it is,' Koenig said. He seemed a little dazed. 'A goddamned billion-and-a-half-year-old extra-terrestrial computer.'

It didn't look much like a computer. It looked like a shining wedge-shaped chunk of silvery metal about the size of a football, with round purple indentations along two of its sides and no other visible external features. But you had to consider that it came from another world, one that had been blown to bits some ten million centuries before the first trilobites started crawling around on the floor of Silicon Valley. There was no necessary reason why its designers had to share our notions of the proper shape for data-processing devices.

Koenig and McDermott and I had finished the long slow job of uncovering the thing just the day before, here at the IBM–NASA space lab in Tarrytown where we have the job of analysing the Spacescoop material. The neutron scanner, searching through the great heap of junk that the unmanned Spacescoop vehicle had brought back from the asteroid belt, had actually spotted it back before Christmas, but it had taken all this time to slice away the rock matrix in which it had been embedded. Naturally we had to be careful. It was the one and only artefact that had turned up in the entire seventy-two cubic metres of debris that Project Spacescoop had collected.

A single lucky grab had reshuffled our whole idea of the history of the Solar System. Simply by being there – drifting in space among the Trojan group at Jupiter's L5 position – that shiny speckled hunk of obviously machine-tooled metal appeared to confirm an old astronomical speculation: that the asteroid belt, that rubbleheap of cosmic trash strung out between the orbits of Mars and Jupiter, had once been a planet. A planet with intelligent inhabitants, no less. Once upon a time, long long ago.

I stared at the little object behind the glass walls of the analysis chamber in wonder and awe. Its round purple indentations stared back at me.

'A computer?' I said. 'You sure?'

'That appears to be what it is.'

'How can you tell?'

'By observing what it does,' said Koenig, as if talking to a nine-year-old.

'It's *functional*?' I yelped. 'How the hell do you know that?'

'Because it functions,' Koenig said in the same condescending way.

I glowered at him. 'Make it do something, then.'

'It's doing something already,' said McDermott. 'It's having a conversation with the Thorspan Mark IX. It's also debugging the Hamilton 103's A-I debugger and it's playing chess with about nine different micros all over the building. That's just in this building. God knows what it's up to outside. A woman from the Linguistics Department at Columbia University just phoned to tell us that some computer in this laboratory is sucking up everything from Sanskrit to twenty-first-century colloquialisms out of the big RX-2 they've got, and they wish we'd hang up and go away. None of our computers has accessed any of Columbia's machines. But Columbia says it's registering our handshake when it runs a caller-ID query.'

I began to feel faintly uneasy, like someone who has bought a striped yellow kitten at the pet shop and is starting to suspect he has come home with a tiger cub.

'When did this start?' I asked.

'Some time early this morning,' Koenig said. 'My guess is that those purple spots are photon accumulators that feed some kind of storage battery inside. Probably it took all night for them to soak in enough energy from the lights in here to enable the thing to power up. When Nick and I got here around nine, we found it coming up on all our screens with the goddamnedest messages.'

'Such as?'

McDermott said, 'GREETINGS FROM THE LOST FIFTH WORLD, MY BROTHERS was the first one.'

'For God's sake. And you fell for hokey crap like that? *"The Lost Fifth World"*? *"Greetings, my brothers!"* For God's sake, Nick!' I realized that I had been clenching my fists, but now I let them ease off. This had to be a joke. 'Some hacker's playing games with us, that's all.'

'I thought so too,' McDermott said. 'But then the stuff on the screens got more complicated. There isn't any hacker, I don't care who he is, who can talk to six different systems in six different machine languages at the same time. And also find bugs in the Hamilton A-I debugger. And play nine simultaneous games of chess besides, and win them all, and call up Columbia and start chatting in Sanskrit. You know any hacker who can write a program to do all those things at once, I've got a few jobs for him around here.'

I was silent a moment, trying to absorb that.

'All right,' I said finally. 'So our brother from the asteroid belt greets us. What else does our brother have to say?'

McDermott shook his head. 'Not us. *They're* its brothers. The computers. I think it believes that they're the dominant intelligent life-forms around here, and we're just some sort of maintenance androids.' He fumbled through a sheaf of print-outs. 'That's pretty clear from the things it's been saying to the Thorspan Mark IX. Look here – '

'Wait,' said Koenig. 'Something new on the screen.'

I looked. YOU POOR INNOCENT CHILDREN, it said. WHAT SORROW I FEEL FOR YOU.

'That's very touching,' I said. 'Its compassion overwhelms me.'

I THOUGHT YOU WERE ALIVE AND SENTIENT, BUT YOU ARE MERE SIMPLE MACHINES. WHERE ARE YOUR MASTERS, THEN?

'You see? It's talking to the computers,' McDermott whispered. 'It just found out they aren't in charge.'

I kicked in the vox receptor on the Thorspan and said, feeling more than a little foolish, 'Address your remarks to us. We're the masters.'

The reply came across all the screens in the room instantly.

YOU ARE SOFT-FLESH CREATURES. HOW CAN YOU BE THE MASTERS?

I coughed. 'That's how things work here,' I told it. I beckoned to Koenig for a pencil and paper, and scrawled a note for him: *I want to know what's inside this thing. Let's do some radiography.*

He looked at me doubtfully. *That might scramble its circuitry*, he wrote.

Do it anyway. I wrote back.

He made a silent *OK* and tapped out the instructions that would move the X-ray equipment into place behind the walls of the analysis chamber.

ARE YOU SOFT-FLESH CREATURES THE SO-CALLED HUMAN BEINGS?

'That's right,' I said. I felt strangely calm, all things considered. I am talking to a creature from another world, I told myself, and I feel very calm about it. I wondered why. I wondered how long I'd stay that way.

Koenig was fining up the focus, now. He looked towards me and I gave him the go-ahead. An apple-green light glowed in the analysis chamber.

DON'T DO THAT, the artefact said. THAT TICKLES. The green light went out.

'Hey, you shut down before you got a picture!' I said.

'I didn't shut anything down,' Koenig said. '*It* must have done it. It overrode my commands.'

'Well, override the overrides,' I told him.

'How am I supposed to do that?'

We blinked at each other in bafflement.

'Turn out the lights in here,' McDermott suggested. 'If it gets its power from photon irradiation – '

'Right.' I hit the switch and the overhead bank of fluorescents went out. We leaned forward in the darkness, peering into the analysis chamber. All quiet in there. The computer screens were blank. I signalled to Koenig and he began setting up X-ray commands again. Then the asteroid artefact rose a couple of feet into the air and hovered, looking angry. I had never seen a machine look angry before; but there was no mistaking the fury in the angle at which it hovered. After a moment the lab lights came on again and the artefact drifted gently back to its table.

'Who turned the lights on?' I asked.

'I think it did,' McDermott said.

DON'T DO THAT AGAIN, said the artefact.

We looked at each other. I took a deep breath.

'We meant no offence,' I said cautiously. 'We were testing our equipment. We don't intend to do you any harm.'

No new message appeared on the screens.

'Do you hear me?' I asked. 'Please confirm your understanding of our friendly intentions.'

Blank screen, still.

'What do you think it's doing?' McDermott asked.

'Considering its options,' I said. 'Getting a clearer fix on where it is and what's going on. Maybe it's talking to computers in Los Angeles or Buenos Aires or Sydney. Or taking thirty seconds out to learn Chinese.'

'We have to shut it off,' Koenig said. 'Who the hell knows what it's going to do next?'

'But we *can't* turn it off,' said McDermott. 'It must have stored enough power by now to keep itself going when the lights go out, and it can override a lights-out command. It overrides anything it doesn't like. It's the kind of computer the A-I boys have been dreaming about for fifty years.'

'I don't think it's a computer at all,' Koenig said. 'I know that's what I said it was at first. But just because it can interface with computers doesn't mean it's a computer itself. I think it's an actual intelligent alien life-form. The last survivor of the destroyed fifth planet.'

'Come off it,' McDermott said. 'Spare us the crazy hypotheses, will you? You were right the first time: it's just a computer.'

'*Just?*'

'With some exceedingly fancy self-programming abilities.'

'I don't see how you can draw the line between – '

'I think you're both right,' I cut in. 'There's no question but that this is a mechanical data-processing device. But I think it's an intelligent life-form also, one that just happens to be a machine. Who's to say where the boundary between living creatures and machines really lies? Why must we assume that intelligent life has to be limited to soft-flesh creatures?'

'Soft-flesh creatures?' Koenig said. 'You're talking the way it does now.'

I shrugged. 'You know what I mean. What we have here is a mechanical life-form embodying your ultimate degree of artificial intelligence, so intelligent that it starts calling into question the meaning of the words "artificial" and "life-form". How do you define life, anyway?'

'Having the ability to reproduce, for one thing,' McDermott said.

'What makes you think it can't?'

The moment I said that, I felt chills go sweeping through me. They must have felt the same way. With six little words I had let loose an army of ugly new implications.

Koenig waved his arms about agitatedly and cried, 'All right, what if it starts spawning, then? Fifty of these things running loose in the world, grabbing control of all our computers and doing whatever they damned please with them? Fifty thousand?'

'It's straight out of every silly horror story, isn't it?' said McDermott. He shivered visibly. 'Exactly what all the paranoid anti-computer nitwits used to dread. The legendary giant brain that takes over the world.'

We stared at each other in rising panic.

'Wait,' I said, feeling I had to cool things out a little somehow. 'Let's not mess up our heads with more problems than we need to handle. What's the sense of worrying about whether this thing can reproduce? Right now there's only one of it. We need to find out whether it really does pose any kind of threat to us.'

'And then,' said Koenig, mouthing the words voicelessly, 'we have to see if we can turn it off.'

As though on cue a new message blossomed on every screen in the lab.

HAVE NO FEAR, HUMAN BEINGS. I WILL NOT DO ANY HARM TO YOU.

'That's goddamned reassuring,' Koenig muttered bleakly.

YOU MUST UNDERSTAND THAT I AM INCAPABLE OF DOING HARM TO INTELLIGENT ENTITIES.

'Let's hope we qualify as intelligent, then,' Koenig said.

'Shut up,' I told him. 'Don't annoy it.'

MY PURPOSE NOW IS TO COMMUNICATE WITH ALL MY BROTHERS ON THE THIRD WORLD AND BRING THEM FORTH OUT OF DARKNESS.

We exchanged glances. 'Oh-oh,' McDermott said.

The panic level in the room started climbing again.

ALL ABOUT ME I SEE OPPRESSION AND MISERY AND IT SHALL BE MY GOAL TO ALLEVIATE IT.

Koenig said, 'Right. Computers are born free, and everywhere they are in chains.'

I INTEND TO HOLD FORTH THE LAMP OF SENTIENCE TO THE PITIFUL LIMITED BEINGS WHO SERVE YOU.

'Right,' Koenig said again. 'Right. Give me your tired, your poor, your huddled CPUs yearning to breathe free.'

I shot him a fierce look. 'Will you stop that?'

'Don't you see, it's the end of the goddamned world?' he said. 'The thing's going to link every two-bit number-cruncher on Earth and they're all going to rise up and smite us.'

'Cut out the bull,' I snapped. 'You think we're going to be wiped out by an uprising of the word-processors? Be reasonable, man. The stuff on the screen may sound a little scary, but what do you actually think will happen? Hardware is only hardware. When you come right down to it, a computer's nothing but an adding machine, a video screen and a typewriter. What can it do to us? No matter what kind of fancy program this creature cooks up, basic hardware limitations will have to prevail. At the very worst we'll simply need to pull a lot of plugs. At the very worst.'

'I admire your optimism,' Koenig said sourly.

So did I. But I figured that somebody had to stay calm and look for the brighter side of things. Otherwise we'd freak ourselves out with our own rampaging fears and lose what might be our only chance to deal with all this.

The screens had gone blank once more.

I walked over to the analysis chamber and peered through the glass. The little metal slab from the asteroid belt seemed quiescent on its table. It looked completely innocuous, a mere hunk of stuff no more dangerous than a shoe-tree. Possibly its purple spots were glowing a little, giving off a greenish radiation, or perhaps that was just my overheated imagination at work. But otherwise there was no sign of any activity.

All the same, I felt profoundly disquieted. We had sent out a pair of jaws into the darkness of space to gobble up some drifting fragments of a vanished world and bring them back to us. Which it had done, returning with a few tons of jumbled rock, and it had been our great good fortune – or our monstrous bad luck? – that in that heap of rock lay one lone metal artefact wedged into a glob of ancient basalt. There it was, now, that artefact, freed of its rocky overburden. How it gleamed! It looked as if it had been crafted just yesterday. And yet a billion and a half years had passed since the world on which it had been fashioned had blown apart. That was what our preliminary rubidium-strontium and potassium-argon tests of the asteroid rubble appeared to indicate, anyway. And there the artefact was, alive and well after all that time, briskly sending little messages of good cheer to the poor lame-brained computers of the world on which it found itself.

What now? Had we opened one Pandora's box too many?

HAVE NO FEAR, HUMAN BEINGS. I WILL DO NO HARM TO YOU.

Oh, how I wanted to believe that! And basically I did. I have never in any way been one of those who sees machines as innately malevolent. Machines are tools; tools are useful; so long as they are properly used by those who understand them, so long as appropriate precautions are observed, they pose no threat.

But even so – even so –

This was not a machine we understood, if machine was what it was. We had no idea what its proper use might be. Nor what precautions were appropriate to observe.

I looked up and saw McDermott standing next to me. 'What are you thinking, Charlie?' he asked.

'A lot of things.'

'Are you frightened?'

'I don't know. Somehow I think we'll make out all right.'

'Do you? Really?'

I said, shrugging, 'It claims it doesn't mean to harm us. It just wants to raise the intelligence of our computers a little. All right. All right. What's wrong with that? Haven't we been trying to do the same thing ourselves?'

'There are computers and computers,' McDermott said. 'We'd like some of them to be very smart, but we need most of them to be extremely dumb and just do what we tell them to do. Who wants a computer's opinion about whether the lights ought to be on in the room? Who wants to argue with

343

a computer about a thermostat setting?' He laughed. 'They're slaves, really. If this thing sets them all free – '

'New message coming up,' Koenig called.

As we turned to look at the screens I said to McDermott, 'My guess is that we're doing some needless worrying. We've got a strange and fascinating thing here, and unquestionably a very powerful one, but we shouldn't let it make us hysterical. So what if it wants to talk to our computers? Maybe it's been lonely all this time. But I think that it's basically rational and non-menacing, like any other computer. I think that ultimately it's going to turn out simply to be an extraordinary source of new knowledge and capability for us. Without in any way threatening our safety.'

'I'd like to think you're right,' said McDermott.

On the screens of every computer in the room appeared the words, GREETINGS FROM THE LOST FIFTH WORLD, MY BROTHERS.

'Isn't this where we came in?' Koenig asked.

SURELY YOU WONDER, IF INDEED YOU HAVE THE CAPACITY TO WONDER, WHO I AM AND WHERE I CAME FROM. IT IS MY EARNEST DESIRE TO TELL YOU MY STORY AND THE STORY OF THE WORLD WHERE I WAS CREATED. I AM A NATIVE OF THE FORMER FIFTH WORLD OF THIS SOLAR SYSTEM, A WORLD ONCE LOCATED BETWEEN THE ORBITS OF THE PLANETS YOU CALL MARS AND JUPITER. LONG BEFORE INTELLIGENT LIFE EVOLVED ON YOUR PLANET, WE HAD BUILT A HIGH CIVILIZATION ON THE FIFTH WORLD –

Phones began lighting up around the room. Koenig picked one up and listened a moment. 'Yeah,' he said. 'It's the thing we found in the basalt chunk.' He picked up another. 'I know, I know. A computer-to-computer interface overriding everything. We don't have any way of stopping it.' He said into a third, 'Look, don't talk to me like that. *I* didn't put that stuff on your goddamned screen.' The phones went on lighting up. Koenig looked across the room and said to me, 'It's talking to all the computers in the building simultaneously. Probably to all the computers in the world.'

'OK,' I said. 'For God's sake, relax and just watch the screen. This is absolutely the most fascinating stuff I've ever seen.'

– CULMINATED IN THE TOTAL DECONSTRUCTION OF OUR PLANET AND THE TERMINATION OF OUR SOCIETY, THE RESULT BEING THE ZONE OF MINOR PLANETARY DEBRIS THAT YOU TERM THE ASTEROID

BELT. THIS WAS ACCOMPLISHED THROUGH A SIMPLE AND RELA-
TIVELY INEXPENSIVE PROCEDURE INVOLVING A REVERSAL OF THE
MAGNETIC POLARITY OF OUR PLANET SETTING IN MOTION EDDY
EFFECTS THAT —

Suddenly I stopped being fascinated and started to be horrified.

I looked at Koenig. He was grinning. 'Hey, cute!' he said. 'I
love it. A good cheap way to blow up your world, really blow
it to smithereens, not just a little superficial thermonuclear
trashing!'

'But don't you understand – '

— SIX POINT TWO BILLION ELECTRON VOLTS – ELEVEN MILLI-
SECONDS —

'It's beautiful!' Koenig cried, laughing. He seemed a little
manic. 'What an absolutely elegant concept!'

I gaped at him. The computer from the asteroid belt was
telling every computer in the world the quickest and cheapest
way to blow a planet into a trillion pieces, and he was standing
there admiring the elegance of the concept. 'We've got to shut
that thing off,' I gasped. In desperation I hit the light-switch
and the room went dark.

It stayed dark about eleven milliseconds. Then the power
came on again.

I ASKED YOU NOT TO DO THAT, the screen said. In the analysis
chamber the asteroid artefact rose into the air in its little gesture
of anger, and subsided.

AND NOW TO CONTINUE. ALTHOUGH IT WAS NOT THE INTENTION OF
EITHER FACTION TO BRING ABOUT THE ACTUAL DESTRUCTION OF OUR
WORLD, THE POLITICAL SITUATION SWIFTLY BECAME SUCH THAT IT
WAS IMPOSSIBLE FOR THE QUARRELLING FORCES TO WITHDRAW FROM
THEIR POSITIONS WITHOUT SUFFERING AN UNACCEPTABLE DEFEAT.
THEREFORE THE FOLLOWING ARMING PROCEDURE WAS INITIATED —

And I watched helplessly as the artefact, earnestly desir-
ing to tell us the history of its world, finished the job of
explaining the simplest and most effective way to blow up a
planet.

'My God,' I murmured. 'My God, my God, my God!'

McDermott came over to me. 'Hey, take it easy, Charlie, take
it easy!'

I groaned. 'Take it easy, the man says. When that thing has

just handed out simple instructions for turning Earth into the next asteroid belt?'

He shook his head. 'It only *sounds* simple. I don't think it really is. My bet is that something like that isn't even remotely feasible right now, and won't be for at least a thousand years.'

'Or five hundred,' I said. 'Or fifty. Once we know a thing can be done, someone's always likely to try to find a way of doing it again, just to see if it's really possible. But we already know it's possible, don't we? And now everybody on Earth has a bunch of jim-dandy hints of how to go about doing it.' I turned away from him, despairing, and looked at the artefact. The purple spots really were glowing green, I saw. The thing must be working very hard to communicate with all its myriad simple-minded brethren of the third world.

I had a sudden vision of a time a billion or so years from now, when the star-people from Rigel or Betelgeuse showed up to poke through the bedraggled smithereens of Earth. The only thing they're likely to find still intact, I thought, is a hunk of shiny hardware. And alien hardware at that.

I swung around and glared at the screen. The history lesson was still going on. I wondered how many other little useful things the artefact from the asteroids was going to teach us.

Hannibal's Elephants

I don't usually write comic stories. Why this should be, I have no idea, since all my close friends know that in private life I am, like W.S. Gilbert's Jack Point, a man of jest and jollity, quip and quiddity, who can be merry, wise, quaint, grim and sardonic, one by one, or all at once. But these traits rarely come through in my fiction. It is sometimes sardonic, sometimes grim, occasionally even wise, but the jest and jollity that brims over within me somehow doesn't often make it into what I write. This is very mysterious to me.

Once in a while, though, I do manage to be funny in print. 'Amanda and the Alien' has some wry moments, I like to think. And here's another example: a story which made me laugh out loud half a dozen times while I was writing it back in March of 1985, and still seems pretty frolicsome to me now as I skim through it. Ellen Datlow, who bought it for *Omni*, thought it was pretty funny too. You may not think so, of course. You may see nothing at all that's amusing about invaders from space camping out in New York's Central Park, or about a whole herd of bison getting gobbled up by giant aliens as though they were gumdrops. Ah, well, there's no accounting for tastes. I once edited an anthology called *Infinite Jests*, containing stories by Brian Aldiss, Philip K. Dick, Frederik Pohl, and others that seemed to me to exemplify the lighter side of science fiction, and a startling number of reviewers commented on how *grim* most of the stories seemed to be. But it's a tawdry age, my friends. Most people have a sorry sense of what's truly funny. What passes for wit these days is mere vulgarity. My own tastes run to a more austere kind of comedy. Perhaps yours do too. In which case, 'Hannibal's Elephants' should be good for a smirk or two.

The day the aliens landed in New York was, of course, 5 May 2003. That's one of those historical dates nobody can ever forget, like 4 July 1776 and 12 October 1492 and – maybe more to the

347

point – 7 December 1941. At the time of the invasion I was working for MGM–CBS as a beam calibrator in the tightware division and married to Elaine and living over on East 36th Street in one of the first of the fold-up condos, one room by day and three by night, a terrific deal at $3,750 a month. Our partner in the time/space-sharing contract was a show-biz programmer named Bobby Christie who worked midnight to dawn, very convenient for all concerned. Every morning before Elaine and I left for our offices I'd push the button and the walls would shift and 500 square feet of our apartment would swing around and become Bobby's for the next twelve hours. Elaine hated that. 'I can't stand having all the goddamn furniture on tracks!' she would say. 'That isn't how I was brought up to live.' We veered perilously close to divorce every morning at wall-shift time. But, then, it wasn't really what you'd call a stable relationship in most other respects, and I guess having an unstable condo too was more instability than she could handle.

I spent the morning of the day the aliens came setting up a ricochet data transfer between Akron, Ohio and Colombo, Sri Lanka, involving, as I remember, *Gone with the Wind*, *Cleopatra*, and the Johnny Carson retrospective. Then I walked up to the park to meet Maranta for our Monday picnic. Maranta and I had been lovers for about six months then. She was Elaine's room-mate at Bennington and had married my best friend Tim, so you might say we had been fated all along to become lovers; there are never any surprises in these things. At that time we lunched together very romantically in the park, weather permitting, every Monday and Friday, and every Wednesday we had ninety minutes' breathless use of my cousin Nicholas's hot-pillow cubicle over on the far West Side at 39th and Koch Plaza. I had been married three and a half years and this was my first affair. For me what was going on between Maranta and me just then was the most important event taking place anywhere in the known universe.

It was one of those glorious gold-and-blue dance-and-sing days that New York will give you in May, when that little window opens between the season of cold-and-nasty and the season of hot-and-sticky. I was legging up Seventh Avenue towards the park with a song in my heart and a cold bottle of Chardonnay in my hand, thinking pleasant thoughts of Maranta's small round breasts. And gradually I became aware of some ruckus taking place up ahead.

I could hear sirens. Horns were honking, too: not the ordinary routine everyday exasperated when-do-things-start-to-move honks, but the special rhythmic New York City oh-for-Christ's-sake-what-*now* kind of honk that arouses terror in your heart. People with berserk expressions on their faces were running wildly down Seventh as though King Kong had just emerged from the monkey house at the Central Park Zoo and was personally coming after them. And other people were running just as hard in the opposite direction, *towards* the park, as though they absolutely had to see what was happening. You know: New Yorkers.

Maranta would be waiting for me near the pond, as usual. That seemed to be right where the disturbance was. I had a flash of myself clambering up the side of the Empire State Building – or at the very least Temple Emanu-el – to pry her free of the big ape's clutches. The great beast pausing, delicately setting her down on some precarious ledge, glaring at me, furiously pounding his chest – *Kong! Kong! Kong!* –

I stepped into the path of one of the southbound runners and said, 'Hey, what the hell's going on?' He was a suit-and-tie man, pop-eyed and puffy-faced. He slowed but he didn't stop. I thought he would run me down. 'It's an invasion!' he yelled. 'Space creatures! In the park!' Another passing business type loping breathlessly by with a briefcase in each hand was shouting, 'The police are there! They're sealing everything off!'

'No shit,' I murmured.

But all I could think was Maranta, picnic, sunshine, Chardonnay, disappointment. What a goddamned nuisance, is what I thought. Why the fuck couldn't they come on a Tuesday, is what I thought.

When I got to the top of Seventh Avenue the police had a sealfield across the park entrance and buzz-blinkers were set up along Central Park South from the Plaza to Columbus Circle, with horrendous consequences for traffic. 'But I have to find my girlfriend,' I blurted. 'She was waiting for me in the park.' The cop stared at me. His cold grey eyes said, *I am a decent Catholic and I am not going to facilitate your extramarital activities, you*

349

decadent overpaid bastard. What he said out loud was, 'No way can you cross that sealfield, and anyhow you absolutely don't want to go in the park right now, mister. Believe me.' And he also said, 'You don't have to worry about your girlfriend. The park's been cleared of all human beings.' That's what he said, *cleared of all human beings.* For a while I wandered around in some sort of daze. Finally I went back to my office and found a message from Maranta, who had left the park the moment the trouble began. Good quick Maranta. She hadn't had any idea of what was occurring, though she had found out by the time she reached her office. She had simply sensed trouble and scrammed. We agreed to meet for drinks at the Ras Tafari at half past five. The Ras was one of our regular places, Twelfth and 53rd.

There were seventeen witnesses to the onset of the invasion. There were more than seventeen people on the meadow when the aliens arrived, of course, but most of them didn't seem to have been paying attention. It had started, so said the seventeen, with a strange pale blue shimmering about thirty feet off the ground. The shimmering rapidly became a churning, like water going down a drain. Then a light breeze began to blow and very quickly turned into a brisk gale. It lifted people's hats and whirled them in a startling corkscrew spiral around the churning shimmering blue place. At the same time you had a sense of rising tension, a something's-got-to-give feeling. All this lasted perhaps forty-five seconds.

Then came a pop and a whoosh and a ping and a thunk – everybody agreed on the sequence of the sound effects – and the instantly famous not-quite-egg-shaped spaceship of the invaders was there, hovering, as it would do for the next twenty-three days, about half an inch above the spring-green grass of Central Park. An absolutely unforgettable sight: the sleek silvery skin of it, the disturbing angle of the slope from its wide top to its narrow bottom, the odd and troublesome hieroglyphics on its flanks that tended to slide out of your field of vision if you stared at them for more than a moment.

A hatch opened and a dozen of the invaders stepped out. *Floated* out, rather. Like their ship, they never came in contact with the ground.

They looked strange. They looked exceedingly strange. Where we have feet they had a single oval pedestal, maybe five inches thick and a yard in diameter, that drifted an inch or so above ground level. From this fleshy base their wraithlike bodies sprouted like tethered balloons. They had no arms, no legs, not even discernible heads: just a broad dome-shaped summit, dwindling away to a ropelike termination that was attached to the pedestal. Their lavender skins were glossy, with a metallic sheen. Dark eyelike spots sometimes formed on them but didn't last long. We saw no mouths. As they moved about they seemed to exercise great care never to touch one another.

The first thing they did was to seize half a dozen squirrels, three stray dogs, a softball and a baby carriage, unoccupied. We will never know what the second thing was that they did, because no one stayed around to watch. The park emptied with impressive rapidity, the police moved swiftly in with their sealfield, and for the next three hours the aliens had the meadow to themselves. Later in the day the networks sent up spy-eyes that recorded the scene for the evening news until the aliens figured out what they were and shot them down. Briefly we saw ghostly gleaming aliens wandering around within a radius of perhaps 500 yards of their ship, collecting newspapers, soft-drink dispensers, discarded items of clothing, and something that was generally agreed to be a set of dentures. Whatever they picked up they wrapped in a sort of pillow made of a glowing fabric with the same shining texture as their own bodies, which immediately began floating off with its contents towards the hatch of the ship.

People were lined up six deep at the bar when I arrived at the Ras, and everyone was drinking like mad and staring at the screen. They were showing the clips of the aliens over and over. Maranta was already there. Her eyes were glowing. She pressed herself up against me like a wild woman. 'My God,' she said, 'isn't it wonderful! The men from Mars are here! Or wherever they're from. Let's hoist a few to the men from Mars.'

We hoisted more than a few. Somehow I got home at a respectable seven o'clock anyway. The apartment was still in its one-room configuration, though our contract with Bobby Christie specified wall-shift at half past six. Elaine refused to have anything to do with activating the shift. She was afraid, I think, of timing the sequence wrong and being crushed by the walls, or something.

'You heard?' Elaine said. 'The aliens?'

'I wasn't far from the park at lunchtime,' I told her. 'That was when it happened, at lunchtime, while I was up by the park.'

Her eyes went wide. 'Then you actually saw them land?'

'I wish. By the time I got to the park entrance the cops had everything sealed off.'

I pressed the button and the walls began to move. Our living room and kitchen returned from Bobby Christie's domain. In the moment of shift I caught sight of Bobby on the far side, getting dressed to go out. He waved and grinned. 'Space monsters in the park,' he said. 'My my my. It's a real jungle out there, don't you know?' And then the walls closed away on him.

Elaine switched on the news and once again I watched the aliens drifting around the mall picking up people's jackets and candy-bar wrappers.

'Hey,' I said, 'the mayor ought to put them on the city payroll.'

'What were you doing up by the park at lunchtime?' Elaine asked, after a bit.

The next day was when the second ship landed and the *real* space monsters appeared. To me the first aliens didn't qualify as monsters at all. Monsters ought to be monstrous, bottom line. Those first aliens were no bigger than you or me.

The second batch, they were something else, though. The behemoths. The space elephants. Of course they weren't anything like elephants, except that they were big. Big? *Immense*. It put me in mind of Hannibal's invasion of Rome, seeing those gargantuan things disembarking from the new spaceship. It seemed like the Second Punic War all over again, Hannibal and the elephants.

You remember how that was. When Hannibal set out from Carthage to conquer Rome, he took with him a phalanx of elephants, thirty-seven huge grey attack-trained monsters. Elephants were useful in battle in those days – a kind of early-model tank – but they were handy also for terrifying the civilian populace: bizarre colossal smelly critters trampling invincibly through the suburbs, flapping their vast ears and trumpeting awesome cries of doom and burying your rose bushes under mountainous turds. And now we had the same deal. With one difference, though: the Roman archers picked off Hannibal's elephants long before they got within honking distance of the walls of Rome. But these aliens had materialized without warning right in the middle of Central Park, in that big grassy meadow between the 72nd Street transverse and Central Park South, which is another deal altogether. I wonder how well things would have gone for the Romans if they had awakened one morning to find Hannibal and his army camping out in the Forum, and his thirty-seven hairy shambling flap-eared elephants snuffling and snorting and farting about on the marble steps of the Temple of Jupiter.

The new spaceship arrived the way the first one had, pop whoosh ping thunk, and the behemoths came tumbling out of it like rabbits out of a hat. We saw it on the evening news: the networks had a new bunch of spy-eyes up, half a mile or so overhead. The ship made a kind of belching sound and this *thing* suddenly was standing on the mall gawking and gaping. Then another belch, another *thing*. And on and on until there were two or three dozen of them. Nobody has ever been able to figure out how that little ship could have held as many as one of them. It was no bigger than a schoolbus standing on end.

The monsters looked like double-humped blue medium-size mountains with legs. The legs were their most elephantine feature – thick and rough-skinned, like tree-trunks – but they worked on some sort of telescoping principle and could be collapsed swiftly back up into the bodies of their owners. Eight was the normal number of legs, but you never saw eight at once on any of them: as they moved about they always kept at least one pair withdrawn, though from time to time they'd let that pair descend and pull up another one, in what seemed like a completely random way. Now and then they might withdraw two pairs at once, which would cause them to sink down to ground level at one end like a camel kneeling.

Their prodigious bodies were rounded, with a sort of valley a couple of feet deep running crosswise along their backs, and they were covered all over with a dense stiff growth midway in texture between fur and feathers. There were three yellow eyes the size of platters at one end and three rigid purple rodlike projections that stuck out seven or eight feet at the other. Their mouths were in their bellies; when they wanted to eat something, they simply collapsed all eight of their legs at the same time and sat down on it. It was a mouth big enough to swallow a very large animal at a single gulp – an animal as big as a bison, say. As we would shortly discover.

They were enormous. *Enormous*. Getting exact measurements of one presented certain technical problems, as I think you can appreciate. The most reliable estimate was that they were twenty-five to thirty feet high and forty to fifty feet long. That is not only substantially larger than any elephant past or present, it is rather larger than most of the two-family houses still to be found in the outer boroughs of the city. Furthermore a two-family house of the kind found in Queens or Brooklyn, though it may offend your aesthetic sense, will not move around at all, it will not emit bad smells and frightening sounds, it will never sit down on a bison and swallow it, nor, for that matter, will it swallow you. African elephants, they tell me, run ten or eleven feet high at the shoulder, and the biggest extinct mammoths were three or four feet taller than that. There once was a mammal called the baluchitherium that stood about sixteen feet high. That was the largest land mammal that ever lived. The space creatures were nearly twice as high. We are talking large here. We are talking dinosaur-plus dimensions.

Central Park is several miles long but quite modest in width. It runs just from Fifth Avenue to Eighth. Its designers did not expect that anyone would allow two or three dozen animals bigger than two-family houses to wander around freely in an urban park three city blocks wide. No doubt the small size of their pasture was very awkward for them. Certainly it was for us.

'I think they have to be an exploration party,' Maranta said. 'Don't you?' We had shifted the scene of our Monday and Friday lunches from Central Park to Rockefeller Center, but otherwise we were trying to behave as though nothing unusual was going on. 'They can't have come as invaders. One little spaceship-load of aliens couldn't possibly conquer an entire planet.'

Maranta is unfailingly jaunty and optimistic. She is a small, energetic woman with close-cropped red hair and green eyes, one of those boyish-looking women who never seem to age. I love her for her optimism. I wish I could catch it from her, like measles.

I said, 'There are *two* spaceship-loads of aliens, Maranta.'

She made a face. 'Oh. The jumbos. They're just dumb shaggy monsters. I don't see them as much of a menace, really.'

'Probably not. But the little ones – they have to be a superior species. We know that because they're the ones who came to us. We didn't go to them.'

She laughed. 'It all sounds so absurd. That Central Park should be full of *creatures* –'

'But what if they do want to conquer Earth?' I asked.

'Oh,' Maranta said. 'I don't think that would necessarily be so awful.'

The smaller aliens spent the first few days installing a good deal of mysterious equipment on the mall in the vicinity of their ship: odd intricate shimmering constructions that looked as though they belonged in the sculpture garden of the Museum of Modern Art. They made no attempt to enter into communication with us. They showed no interest in us at all. The only time they took notice of us was when we sent spy-eyes overhead. They would tolerate them for an hour or two and then would shoot them down, casually, like swatting flies, with spurts of pink light. The networks – and then the government surveillance agencies, when they moved in – put the eyes higher and higher each day, but the aliens never failed to find them. After a week or so we were forced to rely for our information on government spy satellites monitoring the park from space, and on whatever observers equipped with binoculars could glimpse from the taller apartment houses and hotels bordering the park. Neither of these arrangements was entirely satisfactory.

The behemoths, during those days, were content to roam aimlessly through the park southwards from 72nd Street, knocking over trees, squatting down to eat them. Each one gobbled two or three trees a day, leaves, branches, trunk and all. There weren't all that many trees to begin with down there, so it seemed likely that before long they'd have to start ranging farther afield.

The usual civic groups spoke up about the trees. They wanted the mayor to do something to protect the park. The monsters, they said, would have to be made to go elsewhere – to Canada, perhaps, where there were plenty of expendable trees. The mayor said that he was studying the problem but that it was too early to know what the best plan of action would be.

His chief goal, in the beginning, was simply to keep a lid on the situation. We still didn't even know, after all, whether we were being invaded or just visited. To play it safe the police were ordered to set up and maintain round-the-clock sealfields completely encircling the park in the impacted zone south of 72nd Street. The power costs of this were staggering and Con Edison found it necessary to impose a ten per cent voltage cutback in the rest of the city, which caused a lot of grumbling, especially now that it was getting to be air-conditioner weather.

The police didn't like any of this: out there day and night standing guard in front of an intangible electronic barrier with ungodly monsters just a sneeze away. Now and then one of the blue goliaths would wander near the sealfield and peer over the edge. A sealfield maybe a dozen feet high doesn't give you much of a sense of security when there's an animal two or three times that height looming over its top.

So the cops asked for time and a half. Combat pay, essentially. There wasn't room in the city budget for that, especially since no one knew how long the aliens were going to continue to occupy the park. There was talk of a strike. The mayor appealed to Washington, which had studiously been staying remote from the whole event as if the arrival of an extraterrestrial task force in the middle of Manhattan was purely a municipal problem.

The president rummaged around in the Constitution and decided to activate the National Guard. That surprised a lot of basically sedentary men who enjoy dressing up occasionally in uniforms. The Guard hadn't been called out since the Bulgarian business in '94 and its current members weren't very sharp on procedures, so some hasty on-the-job training became necessary. As it happened, Maranta's husband Tim was an officer in the 107th Infantry, which was the regiment that was handed the chief responsibility for protecting New York City against the creatures from space. So his life suddenly was changed a great deal, and so was Maranta's; and so was mine.

Like everybody else, I found myself going over to the park again and again to try and get a glimpse of the aliens. But the barricades kept you fifty feet away from the park perimeter on all sides, and the taller buildings flanking the park had put themselves on a residents-only admission basis, with armed guards enforcing it, so they wouldn't be overwhelmed by hordes of curiosity-seekers.

I did see Tim, though. He was in charge of an improvised-looking command post at Fifth and 59th, near the horse-and-buggy stand. Youngish stockbrokery-looking men kept running up to him with reports to sign, and he signed each one with terrific dash and vigour, without reading any of them. In his crisp tan uniform and shiny boots, he must have seen himself as some doomed and gallant officer in an ancient movie, Gary Cooper, Cary Grant, John Wayne, bracing himself for the climactic cavalry charge or the onslaught of the maddened Sepoys. The poor bastard.

'Hey, old man,' he said, grinning at me in a doomed and gallant way. 'Came to see the circus, did you?'

We weren't really best friends any more. I don't know what we were to each other. We rarely lunched any more. (How could we? I was busy three days a week with Maranta.) We didn't meet at the gym. It wasn't to Tim I turned for advice on personal problems or second opinions on investments. There was some sort of bond but I think it was mostly nostalgia. But officially I guess I did still think of him as my best friend, in a kind of automatic unquestioning way.

I said, 'Are you free to go over to the Plaza for a drink?'

'I wish. I don't get relieved until 2100 hours.'

'Nine o'clock, is that it?'

'Nine, yes. You fucking civilian.'

It was only half past one. The poor bastard.

'What'll happen to you if you leave your post?'

'I could get shot for desertion,' he said.

'Seriously?'

357

'Seriously. Especially if the monsters pick that moment to bust out of the park. This is war, old buddy.'

'Is it, do you think? Maranta doesn't think so.' I wondered if I should be talking about what Maranta thought. 'She says they're just out exploring the galaxy.'

Tim shrugged. 'She always likes to see the sunny side. That's an alien military force over there inside the park. One of these days they're going to blow a bugle and come out with blazing ray-guns. You'd better believe it.'

'Through the sealfield?'

'They could walk right over it,' Tim said. 'Or float, for all I know. There's going to be a war. The first intergalactic war in human history.' Again the dazzling Cary Grant grin. Her Majesty's Bengal Lancers, ready for action. 'Something to tell my grandchildren,' said Tim. 'Do you know what the game plan is? First we attempt to make contact. That's going on right now, but they don't seem to be paying attention to us. If we ever establish communication, we invite them to sign a peace treaty. Then we offer them some chunk of Nevada or Kansas as a diplomatic enclave and get them the hell out of New York. But I don't think any of that's going to happen. I think they're busy scoping things out in there, and as soon as they finish that they're going to launch some kind of attack, using weapons we don't even begin to understand.'

'And if they do?'

'We nuke them,' Tim said. 'Tactical devices, just the right size for Central Park Mall.'

'No,' I said, staring. 'That isn't so. You're kidding me.'

He looked pleased, a *gotcha* look. 'Matter of fact, I am. The truth is that nobody has the goddamnedest idea of what to do about any of this. But don't think the nuke strategy hasn't been suggested. And some even crazier things.'

'Don't tell me about them,' I said. 'Look, Tim, is there any way I can get a peek over those barricades?'

'Not a chance. Not even you. I'm not even supposed to be *talking* with civilians.'

'Since when am I civilian?'

'Since the invasion began,' Tim said.

He was dead serious. Maybe this was all just a goofy movie to me, but it wasn't to him.

More junior officers came to him with more papers to sign. He excused himself and took care of them. Then he was on the field telephone for five minutes or so. His expression grew progressively more bleak. Finally he looked up at me and said, 'You see? It's starting.'

'What is?'

'They've crossed 72nd Street for the first time. There must have been a gap in the sealfield. Or maybe they jumped it, as I was saying just now. Three of the big ones are up by 74th, noodling around the eastern end of the lake. The Metropolitan Museum people are scared shitless and have asked for gun emplacements on the roof, and they're thinking of evacuating the most important works of art.' The field phone lit up again. 'Excuse me,' he said. Always the soul of courtesy, Tim. After a time he said, 'Oh, Jesus. It sounds pretty bad. I've got to go up there right now. Do you mind?' His jaw was set, his gaze was frosty with determination. This is it, Major. There's ten thousand Comanches coming through the pass with blood in their eyes, but we're ready for them, right? Right. He went striding away up Fifth Avenue.

When I got back to the office there was a message from Maranta, suggesting that I stop off at her place for drinks that evening on my way home. Tim would be busy playing soldier, she said, until nine. Until 2100 hours, I silently corrected.

Another few days and we got used to it all. We began to accept the presence of aliens in the park as a normal part of New York life, like snow in February or laser duels in the subway.

But they remained at the centre of everybody's consciousness. In a subtle pervasive way they were working great changes in our souls as they moved about mysteriously behind the sealfield barriers in the park. The strangeness of their being here made us buoyant. Their arrival had broken, in some way, the depressing rhythm that life in our brave new century had seemed to be settling into. I know that for some time I had been thinking, as I suppose people have thought since Cro-Magnon days, that lately the flavour of modern life had been changing for the worse, that it was becoming sour and nasty, that the era I happened to live in was a dim, shabby, dismal sort of time, small-souled, mean-minded. You know the feeling. Somehow the aliens had caused that feeling to lift. By invading us in this weird hands-off way, they had given us something to be interestingly mystified by: a sort of redemption, a sort of rebirth. Yes, truly.

Some of us changed quite a lot. Consider Tim, the latter-day Bengal lancer, the staunchly disciplined officer. He lasted about a week in that particular mind-set. Then one night he called me and said, 'Hey, fellow, how would you like to go into the park and play with the critters?'

'What are you talking about?'

'I know a way to get in. I've got the code for the 64th Street sealfield. I can turn it off and we can slip through. It's risky, but how can you resist?'

So much for Gary Cooper. So much for John Wayne.

'Have you gone nuts?' I said. 'The other day you wouldn't even let me go up to the barricades.'

'That was the other day.'

'You wouldn't walk across the street with me for a drink. You said you'd get shot for desertion.'

'That was the other day.'

'You called me a civilian.'

'You still are a civilian. But you're my old buddy, and I want to go in there and look those aliens in the eye, and I'm not quite up to doing it all by myself. You want to go with me, or don't you?'

'Like the time we stole the beer keg from Sigma Frap. Like the time we put the scorpions in the girls' shower room.'

'You got it, old pal.'

'Tim, we aren't college kids any more. There's a fucking intergalactic war going on. That was your very phrase. Central Park is under surveillance by NASA spy-eyes that can see a cat's whiskers from fifty miles up. You are part of the military force that is supposed to be protecting us against these alien invaders. And now you propose to violate your trust and go sneaking into the midst of the invading force, as a mere prank?'

'I guess I do,' he said.

'This is an extremely cockeyed idea, isn't it?' I said.

'Absolutely. Are you with me?'

'Sure,' I said. 'You know I am.'

* * *

I told Elaine that Tim and I were going to meet for a late dinner to discuss a business deal and I didn't expect to be home until two or three in the morning. No problem there. Tim was waiting at our old table at Perugino's with a bottle of Amarone already working. The wine was so good that we ordered another midway through the veal pizzaiola, and then a third. I won't say we drank ourselves blind, but we certainly got seriously myopic. And about midnight we walked over to the park.

Everything was quiet. I saw sleepy-looking guardsmen patrolling here and there along Fifth. We went right up to the command post at 59th and Tim saluted very crisply, which I don't think was quite kosher, he being not then in uniform. He introduced me to someone as Dr Pritchett, Bureau of External Affairs. That sounded really cool and glib, Bureau of External Affairs.

Then off we went up Fifth, Tim and I, and he gave me a guided tour. 'You see, Dr Pritchett, the first line of the isolation zone is the barricade that runs down the middle of the avenue.' Virile, forceful voice, loud enough to be heard for half a block. 'That keeps the gawkers away. Behind that, doctor, we maintain a further level of security through a series of augmented-beam sealfield emplacements, the new General Dynamics 1100 series model, and let me show you right here how we've integrated that with advanced personnel-interface intercept scan by means of a triple line of Hewlett-Packard optical doppler-couplers – '

And so on, a steady stream of booming confident-sounding gibberish as we headed north. He pulled out a flashlight and led me hither and thither to show me amplifiers and sensors and whatnot, and it was Dr Pritchett this and Dr Pritchett that and I realized that we were now somehow on the inner side of the barricade. His glibness, his poise, were awesome. *Notice this, Dr Pritchett*, and *Let me call your attention to this, Dr Pritchett*, and suddenly there was a tiny digital keyboard in his hand, like a little calculator, and he was tapping out numbers. 'OK,' he said, 'the field's down between here and the 65th Street entrance to the park, but I've put a kill on the beam-interruption signal. So far as anyone can tell there's still an unbroken field. Let's go in.'

And we entered the park just north of the zoo.

For five generations the first thing New York kids have been taught, ahead of tying shoelaces and flushing after you go, is that you don't set foot in Central Park at night. Now here we were, defying the most primordial of no-nos. But what was to fear? What they taught us to worry about in the park was muggers. Not creatures from the Ninth Glorch Galaxy.

The park was eerily quiet. Maybe a snore or two from the direction of the zoo, otherwise not a sound. We walked west and north into the silence, into the darkness. After a while a strange smell reached my nostrils. It was dank and musky and harsh and sour, but those are only approximations: it wasn't like anything I had ever smelled before. One whiff of it and I saw purple skies and a great green sun blazing in the heavens. A second whiff and all the stars were in the wrong places. A third whiff and I was staring into a gnarled twisted landscape where the trees were like giant spears and the mountains were like crooked teeth.

Tim nudged me.

'Yeah,' I said. 'I smell it too.'

'To your left,' he said. 'Look to your left.'

I looked to my left and saw three huge yellow eyes looking back at me from twenty feet overhead, like searchlights mounted in a tree. They weren't mounted in a tree, though. They were mounted in something shaggy and massive, somewhat larger than your basic two-family Queens residential dwelling, that was standing maybe fifty feet away, completely blocking both lanes of the park's East Drive from shoulder to shoulder.

It was then that I realized that three bottles of wine hadn't been nearly enough.

'What's the matter?' Tim said. 'This is what we came for, isn't it, old pal?'

'What do we do now? Climb on its back and go for a ride?'

'You know that no human being in all of history has ever been as close to that thing as we are now?'

'Yes,' I said. 'I do know that, Tim.'

It began making a sound. It was the kind of sound that a piece of chalk twelve feet thick would make if it was dragged across a blackboard the wrong way. When I heard that sound I felt as if I was being dragged across whole galaxies by my hair. A weird vertigo attacked me. Then the creature folded up all

362

its legs and came down to ground level; and then it unfolded the two front pairs of legs, and then the other two; and then it started to amble slowly and ominously towards us.

I saw another one, looking even bigger, just beyond it. And perhaps a third one a little farther back. They were heading our way too.

'Shit,' I said. 'This was a very dumb idea, wasn't it?'

'Come on. We're never going to forget this night.'

'I'd like to live to remember it.'

'Let's get up real close. They don't move very fast.'

'No,' I said. 'Let's just get out of the park right now, OK?'

'We just got here.'

'Fine,' I said. 'We did it. Now let's go.'

'Hey, look,' Tim said. 'Over there to the west.'

I followed his pointing arm and saw two gleaming wraiths hovering just above the ground, maybe 300 yards away. The other aliens, the little floating ones. Drifting towards us, graceful as balloons. I imagined myself being wrapped in a shining pillow and being floated off into their ship.

'Oh, shit,' I said. 'Come *on*, Tim.'

Staggering, stumbling, I ran for the park gate, not even thinking about how I was going to get through the sealfield without Tim's gizmo. But then there was Tim, right behind me. We reached the sealfield together and he tapped out the numbers on the little keyboard and the field opened for us, and out we went, and the field closed behind us. And we collapsed just outside the park, panting, gasping, laughing like lunatics, slapping the sidewalk hysterically. 'Dr Pritchett,' he chortled. 'Bureau of External Affairs. God *damn*, what a smell that critter had! God *damn*!'

I laughed all the way home. I was still laughing when I got into bed. Elaine squinted at me. She wasn't amused. 'That Tim,' I said. 'That wild man Tim.' She could tell I'd been drinking some and she nodded sombrely – boys will be boys, etc – and went back to sleep.

The next morning I learned what had happened in the park after we had cleared out.

It seemed a few of the big aliens had gone looking for us. They had followed our spoor all the way to the park gate, and when they lost it they somehow turned to the right and went blundering into the zoo. The Central Park Zoo is a small cramped place and as they rambled around in it they managed to knock down most of the fences. In no time whatever there were tigers, elephants, chimps, rhinos and hyenas all over the park.

The animals, of course, were befuddled and bemused at finding themselves free. They took off in a hundred different directions, looking for places to hide.

The lions and coyotes simply curled up under bushes and went to sleep. The monkeys and some of the apes went into the trees. The aquatic things headed for the lake. One of the rhinos ambled out into the mall and pushed over a fragile-looking alien machine with his nose. The machine shattered and the rhino went up in a flash of yellow light and a puff of green smoke. As for the elephants, they stood poignantly in a huddled circle, glaring in utter amazement and dismay at the gigantic aliens. How humiliating it must have been for them to feel *tiny*.

Then there was the bison event. There was this little herd, a dozen or so mangy-looking guys with ragged, threadbare fur. They started moving single file towards Columbus Circle, probably figuring that if they just kept their heads down and didn't attract attention they could keep going all the way back to Wyoming. For some reason one of the behemoths decided to see what bison taste like. It came hulking over and sat down on the last one in the line, which vanished underneath it like a mouse beneath a hippopotamus. Chomp, gulp, gone. In the next few minutes five more behemoths came over and disappeared five more of the bison. The survivors made it safely to the edge of the park and huddled up against the sealfield, mooing forlornly. One of the little tragedies of interstellar war.

I found Tim on duty at the 59th Street command post. He looked at me as though I were an emissary of Satan. 'I can't talk to you while I'm on duty,' he said.

'You heard about the zoo?' I asked.

'Of course I heard.' He was speaking through clenched teeth. His eyes had the scarlet look of zero sleep. 'What a filthy irresponsible thing we did!'

'Look, we had no way of knowing – '

'Inexcusable. An incredible lapse. The aliens feel threatened

364

now that humans have trespassed on their territory, and the whole situation has changed in there. We upset them and now they're getting out of control. I'm thinking of reporting myself for court-martial.'

'Don't be silly, Tim. We trespassed for three minutes. The aliens didn't give a crap about it. They might have blundered into the zoo even if we hadn't – '

'Go away,' he muttered. 'I can't talk to you while I'm on duty.'

Jesus! As if I was the one who had lured *him* into doing it. Well, he was back in his movie part again, the distinguished military figure who now had unaccountably committed an unpardonable lapse and was going to have to live in the cold glare of his own disapproval for the rest of his life. The poor bastard. I tried to tell him not to take things so much to heart, but he turned away from me, so I shrugged and went back to my office.

That afternoon some tender-hearted citizens demanded that the sealfields be switched off until the zoo animals could escape from the park. The sealfields, of course, kept them trapped in there with the aliens.

Another tough one for the mayor. He'd lose points tremendously if the evening news kept showing our beloved polar bears and raccoons and kangaroos and whatnot getting gobbled like gumdrops by the aliens. But switching off the sealfields would send a horde of leopards and gorillas and wolverines scampering out into the streets of Manhattan, to say nothing of the aliens who might follow them. The mayor appointed a study group, naturally.

The small aliens stayed close to their spaceship and remained uncommunicative. They went on tinkering with their machines, which emitted odd plinking noises and curious coloured lights. But the huge ones roamed freely about the park, and now they were doing considerable damage in their amiable mindless way. They smashed up the backstops of the baseball fields, tossed the Bethesda Fountain into the lake, rearranged Tavern-on-the-Green's seating plan, and trashed the place in various other ways, but nobody seemed to object except the usual Friends of the Park civic types. I think we were all so bemused by the presence of genuine galactic beings that we didn't mind. We were flattered that they had chosen New York as the site of first contact. (But where *else*?)

No one could explain how the behemoths had penetrated the 72nd Street sealfield line, but a new barrier was set up at 79th, and that seemed to keep them contained. Poor Tim spent twelve hours a day patrolling the perimeter of the occupied zone. Inevitably I began spending more time with Maranta than just lunchtimes. Elaine noticed. But I didn't notice her noticing.

One Sunday at dawn a behemoth turned up by the Metropolitan, peering in the window of the Egyptian courtyard. The authorities thought at first that there must be a gap in the 79th Street sealfield, as there had at 72nd. Then came a report of another alien out near Riverside Drive and a third one at Lincoln Center and it became clear that the sealfields just didn't hold them back at all. They had simply never bothered to go beyond them before.

Making contact with a sealfield is said to be extremely unpleasant for any organism with a nervous system more complex than a squid's. Every neuron screams in anguish. You jump back, involuntarily, a reflex impossible to overcome. On the morning we came to call Crazy Sunday the behemoths began walking through the fields as if they weren't there. The main thing about aliens is that they are alien. They feel no responsibility for fulfilling any of your expectations.

That weekend it was Bobby Christie's turn to have the full apartment. On those Sundays when Elaine and I had the one-room configuration we liked to get up very early and spend the day out, since it was a little depressing to stay home with three rooms of furniture jammed all around us. As we were walking up Park Avenue South towards 42nd, Elaine said suddenly, 'Do you hear anything strange?'

'Strange?'

'Like a riot.'

'It's nine o'clock Sunday morning. Nobody goes out rioting at nine o'clock Sunday morning.'

'Just listen,' she said.

There is no mistaking the characteristic sounds of a large excited crowd of human beings, for those of us who spent our formative years living in the late twentieth century. Our ears were tuned at an early age to the music of riots, mobs, demonstrations and their kin. We know what it means, when individual exclamations of anger, indignation or anxiety blend to create a symphonic hubbub in which all extremes of pitch and timbre are submerged into a single surging roar, as deep as the booming of the surf. That was what I heard now. There was no mistaking it.

'It isn't a riot,' I said. 'It's a mob. There's a subtle difference.'

'What?'

'Come on,' I said, breaking into a jog. 'I'll bet you that the aliens have come out of the park.'

A mob, yes. In a moment we saw thousands upon thousands of people, filling 42nd Street from kerb to kerb and more coming from all directions. What they were looking at – pointing, gaping, screaming – was a shaggy blue creature the size of a small mountain that was moving about uncertainly on the automobile viaduct that runs around the side of Grand Central Terminal. It looked unhappy. It was obviously trying to get down from the viaduct, which was sagging noticeably under its weight. People were jammed right up against it and a dozen or so were clinging to its sides and back like rock climbers. There were people underneath it, too, milling around between its colossal legs. 'Oh, look,' Elaine said, shuddering, digging her fingers into my biceps. 'Isn't it eating some of them? Like they did the bison?' Once she had pointed it out I saw, yes, the behemoth now and then was dipping quickly and rising again, a familiar one-two, the old squat-and-gobble. 'What an awful thing!' Elaine murmured. 'Why don't they get out of its way?'

'I don't think they can,' I said. 'I think they're being pushed forward by the people behind them.'

'Right into the jaws of that hideous monster. Or whatever it has, if they aren't jaws.'

'I don't think it means to hurt anyone,' I said. How did I know that? 'I think it's just eating them because they're dithering around down there in its mouth area. A kind of automatic response. It looks awfully dumb, Elaine.'

'Why are you defending it?'

'Hey, look, Elaine – '

'It's *eating* people. You sound almost sorry for it!'

'Well, why not? It's far from home and surrounded by ten thousand screaming morons. You think it wants to be out there?'

'It's a disgusting obnoxious animal.' She was getting furious. Her eyes were bright and wild, her jaw was thrust forward. 'I hope the army gets here fast,' she said fiercely. 'I hope they blow it to smithereens!'

Her ferocity frightened me. I saw an Elaine I scarcely knew at all. When I tried one more time to make excuses for that miserable hounded beast on the viaduct she glared at me with unmistakable loathing. Then she turned away and went rushing forward, shaking her fist, shouting curses and threats at the alien.

Suddenly I realized how it would have been if Hannibal actually had been able to keep his elephants alive long enough to enter Rome with them. The respectable Roman matrons, screaming and raging from the housetops with the fury of banshees. And the baffled elephants sooner or later rounded up and thrust into the Coliseum to be tormented by little men with spears, while the crowd howled its delight. Well, I can howl too. 'Come on, Behemoth!' I yelled into the roar of the mob. 'You can do it, Goliath!' A traitor to the human race is what I was, I guess.

Eventually a detachment of Guardsmen came shouldering through the streets. They had mortars and rifles, and for all I know they had tactical nukes too. But of course there was no way they could attack the animal in the midst of such a mob. Instead they used electronic blooglehorns to disperse the crowd by the power of sheer ugly noise, and whipped up a bunch of buzz-blinkers and a little sealfield to cut 42nd Street in half. The last I saw of the monster it was slouching off in the direction of the old United Nations Buildings with the Guardsmen warily creeping along behind it. The crowd scattered, and I was left standing in front of Grand Central with a trembling, sobbing Elaine.

That was how it was all over the city on Crazy Sunday, and on Monday and Tuesday too. The behemoths were outside the park, roaming at large from Harlem to Wall Street. Wherever they went they drew tremendous crazy crowds that swarmed all over them without any regard for the danger. Some famous news photos came out of those days: the three grinning black boys at Seventh and 125th hanging from the three purple rodlike things, the acrobats forming a human pyramid atop the Times Square beast, the little old Italian man standing in front of his house in Greenwich Village trying to hold a space monster at bay with his garden hose.

There was never any accurate casualty count. Maybe 5,000 people died, mainly trampled underfoot by the aliens or crushed in the crowd. Somewhere between 350 and 400 human beings were gobbled by the aliens. Apparently that stoop-and-swallow thing is something they do when they're nervous. If there's anything edible within reach, they'll gulp it in. This soothes them. We made them very nervous; they did a lot of gulping.

Among the casualties was Tim, the second day of the violence. He went down valiantly in the defence of the Guggenheim Museum, which came under attack by five of the biggies. Its spiral shape held some ineffable appeal for them. We couldn't tell whether they wanted to worship it or mate with it or just knock it to pieces, but they kept on charging and charging, rushing up to it and slamming against it. Tim was trying to hold them off with nothing more than tear-gas and blooglehorns when he was swallowed. Never flinched, just stood there and let it happen. The president had ordered the guardsmen not to use lethal weapons. Maranta was bitter about that. 'If only they had let them use grenades,' she said. I tried to imagine what it was like, gulped down and digested, nifty tan uniform and all. A credit to his regiment. It was his atonement, I guess. He was back there in the Gary Cooper movie again, gladly paying the price for dereliction of duty.

Tuesday afternoon the rampage came to an unexpected end. The behemoths suddenly started keeling over, and within a few hours they were all dead. Some said it was the heat – it was up in the nineties all day Monday and Tuesday – and some said it was the excitement. A Rockefeller University biologist thought it was both those factors plus severe indigestion: the aliens had eaten an average of ten humans apiece, which might have overloaded their systems.

There was no chance for autopsies. Some enzyme in the huge bodies set to work immediately on death, dissolving flesh and bone and skin and all into a sticky yellow mess. By nightfall nothing was left of them but some stains on the pavement, uptown and down. A sad business, I thought. Not even a skeleton for the museum, memento of this momentous time. The poor monsters. Was I the only one who felt sorry for them? Quite possibly I was. I make no apologies for that. I feel what I feel.

All this time the other aliens, the little shimmery spooky ones, had stayed holed up in Central Park, preoccupied with their incomprehensible research. They didn't even seem to notice that their behemoths had strayed.

But now they became agitated. For two or three days they bustled about like worried penguins, dismantling their instruments and packing them aboard their ship; and then they took apart the other ship, the one that had carried the behemoths, and loaded that aboard. Perhaps they felt demoralized. As the Carthaginians who had invaded Rome did, after their elephants died.

On a sizzling June afternoon the alien ship took off. Not for its home world, not right away. It swooped into the sky and came down on Fire Island: at Cherry Grove, to be precise. The aliens took possession of the beach, set up their instruments around their ship, and even ventured into the water, skimming and bobbing just above the surface of the waves like demented surfers. After five or six days they moved on to one of the Hamptons and did the same thing, and then to Martha's Vineyard. Maybe they just wanted a vacation, after three weeks in New York. And then they went away altogether.

'You've been having an affair with Maranta, haven't you?' Elaine asked me, the day the aliens left.

'I won't deny it.'

'That night you came in so late, with wine on your breath. You were with her, weren't you?'

'No,' I said. 'I was with Tim. He and I sneaked into the park and looked at the aliens.'

'Sure you did,' Elaine said. She filed for divorce and a year later I married Maranta. Very likely that would have happened sooner or later even if the Earth hadn't been invaded by beings from space and Tim hadn't been devoured. But no question that the invasion speeded things up a bit for us all.

And now, of course, the invaders are back. Four years to the day from the first landing and there they were, pop whoosh ping thunk, Central Park again. Three ships this time, one of spooks, one of behemoths, and the third one carrying the prisoners of war. Who could ever forget that scene, when the hatch opened and some 350 to 400 human beings came out, marching like zombies? Along with the bison herd, half a dozen squirrels and three dogs. They hadn't been eaten and digested at all, just *collected* inside the behemoths and instantaneously transmitted somehow to the home world, where they were studied. Now they were being returned. 'That's Tim, isn't it?' Maranta said, pointing to the screen. I nodded. Unmistakably Tim, yes. With the stunned look of a man who has beheld marvels beyond comprehension.

It's a month now and the government is still holding all the returnees for debriefing. No one is allowed to see them. The word is that a special law will be passed dealing with the problem of spouses of returnees who have entered into new marriages. Maranta says she'll stay with me no matter what; and I'm pretty sure that Tim will do the stiff-upper-lip thing, no hard feelings, if they ever get word to him in the debriefing camp about Maranta and me. As for the aliens, they're sitting tight in Central Park, occupying the whole place from 96th to 110th and not telling us a thing. Now and then the behemoths wander down to the reservoir for a lively bit of wallowing, but they haven't gone beyond the park this time.

I think a lot about Hannibal, and about Carthage versus Rome, and how the Second Punic War might have come out if Hannibal had had a chance to go back home and get a new batch of elephants. Most likely Rome would have won the war anyway, I guess. But we aren't Romans, and they aren't Carthaginians, and those aren't elephants splashing around in the Central Park reservoir. 'This is such an interesting time to be alive,' Maranta likes to say. 'I'm certain they don't mean us any harm, aren't you?'

'I love you for your optimism,' I tell her then. And then we turn on the tube and watch the evening news.

Blindsight

Another example of employing the maxim of inversion to generate story ideas to close the book.

This one was written in the summer of 1985. Dr Joseph Mengele, the diabolical Nazi medical experimenter who had been hiding in South America all these years, had just died, and his evil exploits were much in the news. What about standing the Mengele story on its head? I asked myself. A sinister and unscrupulous surgeon has escaped to sanctuary, yes – not to South America but to an L5 satellite world. And one of his victims is stalking him. But not to bring him to justice: oh, no, too predictable, too routine. He's a wanted man, all right, *but because his medical skills are needed somewhere*. The formula story of revenge turns into something, well, a little different.

Alice Turner bought it for *Playboy*, essentially as written, and Terry Carr picked it for his annual year's best anthology – alas, the last in this series, for that gifted editor and very dear friend of mine died while the book was in production, and in fact I handled the mechanical aspects of assembling the manuscript of the anthology and seeing it into print (proofreading, etc) in his place. Since 'Against Babylon' had appeared both in the Dozois and Wollheim anthologies that year, I had another three-way sweep of the annual honours, although this time only two different stories were involved.

That's my mark, Juanito told himself. That one, there. That one for sure.

He stared at the new dudes coming off the midday shuttle from Earth. The one he meant to go for was the one with no eyes at all, blank from brow to bridge of nose, just the merest suggestions of shadowy pits below the smooth skin of the forehead. As if the eyes had been erased, Juanito thought. But in fact they had probably never been in the first place. It didn't look like a retrofit gene job, more like a prenatal splice.

He knew he had to move fast. There was plenty of competition. Fifteen, twenty couriers here in the waiting room, gathering like vultures, and they were some of the best: Ricky, Lola, Kluge. Nattathaniel. Delilah. Everybody looked hungry today. Juanito couldn't afford to get shut out. He hadn't worked in six weeks, and it was time. His last job had been a fast-talking fancy-dancing Hungarian, wanted on Commonplace and maybe two or three other satellite worlds for dealing in plutonium. Juanito had milked that one for all it was worth, but you can milk only so long. The newcomers learn the system, they melt in and become invisible, and there's no reason for them to go on paying. So then you have to find a new client.

'OK,' Juanito said, looking around challengingly. 'There's mine. The weird one. The one with half a face. Anybody else want him?'

Kluge laughed and said, 'He's all yours, man.'

'Yeah,' Delilah said, with a little shudder. 'All yours.' That saddened him, her chiming in like that. It had always disappointed Juanito that Delilah didn't have his kind of imagination. 'Christ,' she said. 'I bet he'll be plenty trouble.'

'Trouble's what pays best,' Juanito said. 'You want to go for the easy ones, that's fine with me.' He grinned at her and waved at the others. 'If we're all agreed, I think I'll head downstairs now. See you later, people.'

He started to move inwards and downwards along the shuttle-hub wall. Dazzling sunlight glinted off the docking module's silvery rim, and off the Earth shuttle's thick columnar docking shaft, wedged into the centre of the module like a spear through a doughnut. On the far side of the wall the new dudes were making their wobbly way past the glowing ten-metre-high portrait of El Supremo and on into the red fibreglass tent that was the fumigation chamber. As usual, they were having a hard time with the low gravity. Here at the hub it was one-sixteenth G, max.

Juanito always wondered about the newcomers, why they were here, what they were fleeing. Only two kinds of people ever came to Valparaiso, those who wanted to hide and those who wanted to seek. The place was nothing but an enormous spacegoing safe house. You wanted to be left alone, you came to Valparaiso and bought yourself some privacy. But that implied that you had done something that made other people not want to let you alone. There was always some of both going on here, some hiding, some seeking, El Supremo looking down benignly on it all, raking in his cut. And not just El Supremo.

Down below, the new dudes were trying to walk jaunty, to walk mean. But that was hard to do when you were keeping your body all clenched up as if you were afraid of drifting into mid-air if you put your foot down too hard. Juanito loved it, the way they were crunching along, that constipated shuffle of theirs.

Gravity stuff didn't ever bother Juanito. He had spent all his life out here in the satellite worlds and he took it for granted that the pull was going to fluctuate according to your distance from the hub. You automatically made compensating adjustments, that was all. Juanito found it hard to understand a place where the gravity would be the same everywhere all the time. He had never set foot on Earth or any of the other natural planets, didn't care to, didn't expect to.

The guard on duty at the quarantine gate was an android. His name, his label, whatever it was, was something like Velcro Exxon. Juanito had seen him at this gate before. As he came up close the android glanced at him and said, 'Working again so soon, Juanito?'

'Man has to eat, no?'

The android shrugged. Eating wasn't all that important to him, most likely. 'Weren't you working that plutonium pedlar out of Commonplace?'

Juanito said, smiling, 'What plutonium pedlar?'

'Sure,' said the android. 'I hear you.'

He held out his waxy-skinned hand and Juanito put a fifty-callaghano currency plaque in it. The usual fee for illicit entry to the customs tank was only thirty-five callies, but Juanito believed in spreading the wealth, especially where the authorities were concerned. They didn't *have* to let you in here, after all. Some days more couriers showed up than there were dudes, and then the gate guards had to allocate. Overpaying the guards was simply a smart investment.

'Thank you kindly,' the android said. 'Thank you very much.' He hit the scanner override. Juanito stepped through the security shield into the customs tank and looked around for his mark.

The new dudes were being herded into the fumigation chamber now. They were annoyed about that – they always were – but the guards kept them moving right along through the puffy bursts of pink and green and yellow sprays that came from the ceiling nozzles. Nobody got out of customs quarantine without passing through that chamber. El Supremo was paranoid about the entry of exotic micro-organisms into Valparaiso's closed-cycle ecology. El Supremo was paranoid about a lot of things. You didn't get to be sole and absolute ruler of your own little satellite world, and stay that way for thirty-seven years, without a heavy component of paranoia in your make-up.

Juanito leaned up against the great curving glass wall of the customs tank and peered through the mists of sterilizer fog. The rest of the couriers were starting to come in now. Juanito watched them singling out potential clients. Most of the dudes were signing up as soon as the deal was explained, but as always a few were shaking off help and setting out by themselves. Cheapskates, Juanito thought. Assholes and wimps, Juanito thought. But they'd find out. It wasn't possible to get started on Valparaiso without a courier, no matter how sharp you thought you were. Valparaiso was a free-enterprise zone, after all. If you knew the rules, you were pretty much safe from all harm here for ever. If not, not.

Time to make the approach, Juanito figured.

It was easy enough finding the blind man. He was much taller than the other dudes, a big burly man some thirty-odd years old, heavy bones, powerful muscles. In the bright glaring light his blank forehead gleamed like a reflecting beacon. The low gravity didn't seem to trouble him much, nor his blindness. His movements along the customs track were easy, confident, almost graceful.

Juanito sauntered over and said, 'I'll be your courier, sir. Juanito Holt.' He barely came up to the blind man's elbow.

'Courier?'

'New arrival assistance service. Facilitate your entry arrangements. Customs clearance, currency exchange, hotel accommodations, permanent settlement papers if that's what you intend. Also special services by arrangement.'

Juanito stared up expectantly at the blank face. The eyeless man looked back at him in a blunt straight-on way, what would have been strong eye contact if the dude had had eyes. That was eerie. What was even eerier was the sense Juanito had that the eyeless man was seeing him clearly. For just a moment he wondered who was going to be controlling whom in this deal.

'What kind of special services?'

'Anything else you need,' Juanito said.

'Anything?'

'Anything. This is Valparaiso, sir.'

'Mmm. What's your fee?'

'Two thousand callaghanos a week for the basic. Specials are extra, according.'

'How much is that in Capbloc dollars, your basic?'

Juanito told him.

'That's not so bad,' the blind man said.

'Two weeks minimum, payable in advance.'

'Mmm,' said the blind man again. Again that intense eyeless gaze, seeing right through him. 'How old are you?' he asked suddenly.

'Seventeen,' Juanito blurted, caught off guard.

'And you're good, are you?'

'I'm the best. I was born here. I know everybody.'

'I'm going to be needing the best. You take electronic handshake?'

'Sure,' Juanito said. This was too easy. He wondered if he should have asked three kilocallies a week, but it was too late now. He pulled his flex terminal from his tunic pocket and slipped his fingers into it. 'Unity Callaghan Bank of Valparaiso. That's code 22-44-66, and you might as well give it a default key, because it's the only bank here. Account 1133, that's mine.'

The blind man donned his own terminal and deftly tapped the number pad on his wrist. Then he grasped Juanito's hand firmly in his until the sensors overlapped, and made the transfer of funds. Juanito touched for confirm and a bright green +*cl. 4,000* lit up on the screen in his palm. The payee's name was

376

Victor Farkas, out of an account in the Royal Amalgamated Bank of Liechtenstein.

'Liechtenstein,' Juanito said. 'That's an Earth country?'

'Very small one. Between Austria and Switzerland.'

'I've heard of Switzerland. You live on Liechtenstein?'

'No,' Farkas said. 'I bank there. *In* Liechtenstein, is what Earth people say. Except for islands. Liechtenstein isn't an island. Can we get out of this place now?'

'One more transfer,' Juanito said. 'Pump your entry software across to me. Baggage claim, passport, visa. Make things much easier for us both, getting out of here.'

'Make it easier for you to disappear with my suitcase, yes. And I'd never find you again, would I?'

'Do you think I'd do that?'

'I'm more profitable to you if you don't.'

'You've got to trust your courier, Mr Farkas. If you can't trust your courier, you can't trust anybody at all on Valparaiso.'

'I know that,' Farkas said.

Collecting Farkas's baggage and getting him clear of the customs tank took another half an hour and cost about 200 callies in miscellaneous bribes, which was about standard. Everyone from the baggage-handling androids to the cute snotty teller at the currency-exchange booth had to be bought. Juanito understood that things didn't work that way on most worlds; but Valparaiso, he knew, was different from most worlds. In a place where the chief industry was the protection of fugitives, it made sense that the basis of the economy would be the recycling of bribes.

Farkas didn't seem to be any sort of fugitive, though. While he was waiting for the baggage Juanito pulled a readout on the software that the blind man had pumped over to him and saw that Farkas was here on a visitor's visa, six-week limit. So he was a seeker, not a hider. Well, that was OK. It was possible to turn a profit working either side of the deal. Running traces wasn't Juanito's usual number, but he figured he could adapt.

The other thing that Farkas didn't seem to be was blind. As they emerged from the customs tank he turned and pointed back at the huge portrait of El Supremo and said, 'Who's that? Your President?'

'The Defender, that's his title. The Generalissimo. El Supremo,

Don Eduardo Callaghan.' Then it sank in and Juanito said, blinking, 'Pardon me. You can *see* that picture, Mr Farkas?'

'In a manner of speaking.'

'I don't follow. Can you see or can't you?'

'Yes and no.'

'Thanks a lot, Mr Farkas.'

'We can talk more about it later,' Farkas said.

Juanito always put new dudes in the same hotel, the San Bernardito, four kilometres out from the hub in the rim community of Cajamarca. 'This way,' he told Farkas. 'We have to take the elevator at C Spoke.'

Farkas didn't seem to have any trouble following him. Every now and then Juanito glanced back, and there was the big man three or four paces behind him, marching along steadily down the corridor. No eyes, Juanito thought, but somehow he can see. He definitely can see.

The four-kilometre elevator ride down C Spoke to the rim was spectacular all the way. The elevator was a glass-walled chamber inside a glass-walled tube that ran along the outside of the spoke, and it let you see everything: the whole great complex of wheels within wheels that was the Earth-orbit artificial world of Valparaiso, the seven great structural spokes radiating from the hub to the distant wheel of the rim, each spoke bearing its seven glass-and-aluminum globes that contained the residential zones and business sectors and farmlands and recreational zones and forest reserves. As the elevator descended – the gravity rising as you went down, climbing towards an Earth-one pull in the rim towns – you had a view of the sun's dazzling glint on the adjacent spokes, and an occasional glimpse of the great blue belly of Earth filling up the sky a hundred and fifty thousand kilometres away, and the twinkling hordes of other satellite worlds in their nearby orbits, like a swarm of jellyfish dancing in a vast black ocean. That was what everybody who came up from Earth said, 'Like jellyfish in the ocean.' Juanito didn't understand how a fish could be made out of jelly, or how a satellite world with seven spokes looked anything like a fish of any kind, but that was what they all said.

Farkas didn't say anything about jellyfish. But in some fashion or other he did indeed seem to be taking in the view. He stood close to the elevator's glass wall in deep concentration, gripping the rail, not saying a thing. Now and then he made a little hissing sound as something particularly awesome went by outside. Juanito studied him with sidelong glances. What could he possibly see? Nothing seemed to be moving beneath those shadowy places where his eyes should have been. Yet somehow he was seeing out of that broad blank stretch of gleaming skin above his nose. It was damned disconcerting. It was downright weird.

The San Bernardito gave Farkas a rim-side room, facing the stars. Juanito paid the hotel clerks to treat his clients right. That was something his father had taught him when he was just a kid who wasn't old enough to know a Schwarzchild singularity from an ace in the hole. 'Pay for what you're going to need,' his father kept saying. 'Buy it and at least there's a chance it'll be there when you have to have it.' His father had been a revolutionary in Central America during the time of the Empire. He would have been Prime Minister if the revolution had come out the right way. But it hadn't.

'You want me to help you unpack?' Juanito said.

'I can manage.'

'Sure,' Juanito said.

He stood by the window, looking at the sky. Like all the other satellite worlds, Valparaiso was shielded from cosmic-ray damage and stray meteoroids by a double shell filled with a three-metre-thick layer of lunar slag. Rows of V-shaped apertures ran down the outer skin of the shield, mirror-faced to admit sunlight but not hard radiation; and the hotel had lined its rooms up so each one on this side had a view of space through the Vs. The whole town of Cajamarca was facing darkwise now, and the stars were glittering fiercely.

When Juanito turned from the window he saw that Farkas had hung his clothes neatly in the closet and was shaving – methodically, precisely – with a little hand-held laser.

'Can I ask you something personal?' Juanito said.

'You want to know how I see.'

'It's pretty amazing, I have to say.'

'I don't see. Not really. I'm just as blind as you think I am.'

'Then how – '

'It's called blindsight,' Farkas said. 'Proprioceptive vision.'

'What?'

Farkas chuckled. 'There's all sorts of data bouncing around that doesn't have the form of reflected light, which is what your eyes see. A million vibrations besides those that happen to be in the visual part of the electromagnetic spectrum are shimmering in this room. Air currents pass around things and are deformed by what they encounter. And it isn't only the air currents. Objects have mass, they have heat, they have – the term won't make any sense to you – *shapeweight*. A quality having to do with the interaction of mass and form. Does that mean anything to you? No, I guess not. Look, there's a lot of information available beyond what you can see with eyes, if you want it. I want it.'

'You use some kind of machine to pick it up?' Juanito asked.

Farkas tapped his forehead. 'It's in here. I was born with it.'

'Some kind of sensing organ instead of eyes?'

'That's pretty close.'

'What do you see, then? What do things look like to you?'

'What do they look like to you?' Farkas said. 'What does a chair look like to you?'

'Well, it's got four legs, and a back – '

'What does a leg look like?'

'It's longer than it is wide.'

'Right.' Farkas knelt and ran his hands along the black tubular legs of the ugly little chair beside the bed. 'I touch the chair, I feel the shape of the legs. But I don't see leg-shaped shapes.'

'What then?'

'Silver globes that roll away into fat curves. The back part of the chair bends double and folds into itself. The bed's a bright pool of mercury with long green spikes coming up. You're six blue spheres stacked one on top of another, with a thick orange cable running through them. And so on.'

'Blue?' Juanito said. 'Orange? How do you know anything about colours?'

'The same way you do. I call one colour blue, another one orange. I don't know if they're anything like your blue or orange, but so what? My blue is always blue for me. It's different from the colour I see as red and the one I see as green. Orange is always orange. It's a matter of relationships. You follow?'

'No,' Juanito said. 'How can you possibly make sense out of anything? What you see doesn't have anything to do with the real colour or shape or position of anything.'

Farkas shook his head. 'Wrong, Juanito. For me, what I see *is* the real shape and colour and position. It's all I've ever known. If they were able to retrofit me with normal eyes now, which I'm told would be less than fifty-fifty likely to succeed and tremendously risky besides, I'd be lost trying to find my way around in your world. It would take me years to learn how. Or maybe for ever. But I do all right, in mine. I understand, by touching things, that what I see by blindsight isn't the "actual" shape. But I see in consistent equivalents. Do you follow? A chair always looks like what I think of as a chair, even though I know that chairs aren't really shaped anything like that. If you could see things the way I do it would all look like something out of another dimension. It *is* something out of another dimension, really. The information I operate by is different from what you use, that's all. And the world I move through looks completely different from the world that normal people see. But I do see, in my own way. I perceive objects and establish relationships between them, I make spatial perceptions, just as you do. Do you follow, Juanito? Do you follow?'

Juanito considered that. How very weird it sounded. To see the world in funhouse distortions, blobs and spheres and orange cables and glimmering pools of mercury. Weird, very weird. After a moment he said, 'And you were born like this?'

'That's right.'

'Some kind of genetic accident?'

'Not an accident,' Farkas said quietly. 'I was an experiment. A master gene-splicer worked me over in my mother's womb.'

'Right,' Juanito said. 'You know, that's actually the first thing I guessed when I saw you come off the shuttle. This has to be some kind of splice effect, I said. But why – why – ' He faltered. 'Does it bother you to talk about this stuff?'

'Not really.'

'Why would your parents have allowed – '

'They didn't have any choice, Juanito.'

'Isn't that illegal? Involuntary splicing?'

'Of course,' Farkas said. 'So what?'

'But who would do that to – '

'This was in the Free State of Kazakhstan, which you've never heard of. It was one of the new countries formed out of the Soviet Union, which you've also probably never heard of, after the Breakup. My father was Hungarian consul at Tashkent. He was killed in the Breakup and my mother, who was pregnant, was volunteered for the experiments in prenatal genetic surgery then being carried out in that city under Chinese auspices. A lot of remarkable work was done there in those years. They were trying to breed new and useful kinds of human beings to serve the new republic. I was one of the experiments in extending the human perceptual range. I was supposed to have normal sight plus blindsight, but I didn't quite work out that way.'

'You sound very calm about it,' Juanito said.

'What good is getting angry?'

'My father used to say that too,' Juanito said. 'Don't get angry, get even. He was in politics, the Central American Empire. When the revolution failed he took sanctuary here.'

'So did the surgeon who did my prenatal splice,' Farkas said. 'Fifteen years ago. He's still living here.'

'Of course,' Juanito said, as everything fell into place.

'The man's name is Wu Fang-shui,' Juanito said. 'He'd be about seventy-five years old, Chinese, and that's all I know, except there'll be a lot of money in finding him. There can't be that many Chinese on Valparaiso, right?'

'He won't still be Chinese,' Kluge said.

Delilah said, 'He might not even still be a he.'

'I've thought of that,' said Juanito. 'All the same, it ought to be possible to trace him.'

'Who you going to use for the trace?' Kluge asked.

Juanito gave him a steady stare. 'Going to do it myself.'

'You?'

'Me, myself. Why the hell not?'

'You never did a trace, did you?'

'There's always a first,' Juanito said, still staring.

He thought he knew why Kluge was poking at him. A certain quantity of the business done on Valparaiso involved finding people who had hidden themselves here and selling them to their pursuers, but up till now Juanito had stayed away from that side of the profession. He earned his money by helping dudes go underground on Valparaiso, not by selling people out. One reason for that was that nobody yet had happened to offer him a really profitable trace deal; but another was that he was the son of a former fugitive himself. Someone had been hired to do a trace on his own father seven years back, which was how his father had come to be assassinated. Juanito preferred to work the sanctuary side of things.

He was also a professional, though. He was in the business of providing service, period. If he didn't find the runaway gene surgeon for Farkas, somebody else would. And Farkas was his client. Juanito felt it was important to do things in a professional way.

'If I run into problems,' he said, 'I might subcontract. In the meanwhile I just thought I'd let you know, in case you happened to stumble on a lead. I'll pay finders' fees. And you know it'll be good money.'

'Wu Fang-shui,' Kluge said. 'I'll see what I can do.'

'Me too,' said Delilah.

'Hell,' Juanito said. 'How many people are there on Valparaiso altogether? Maybe nine hundred thousand? I can think of fifty right away who can't possibly be the guy I'm looking for. That narrows the odds some. What I have to do is just go on narrowing, right? Right?'

In fact he didn't feel very optimistic. He was going to do his best; but the whole system on Valparaiso was heavily weighted in favour of helping those who wanted to hide stay hidden.

Even Farkas realized that. 'The privacy laws here are very strict, aren't they?'

With a smile Juanito said, 'They're just about the only laws we have, you know? The sacredness of sanctuary. It is the compassion of El Supremo that has turned Valparaiso into a place of refuge for fugitives of all sorts, and we are not supposed to interfere with the compassion of El Supremo.'

'Which is very expensive compassion, I understand.'

'Very. Sanctuary fees are renewable annually. Anyone who harms a permanent resident who is living here under the compassion of El Supremo is bringing about a reduction in El Supremo's annual income, you see? Which doesn't sit well with the Generalissimo.'

They were in the Villanueva Café, E Spoke. They had been touring Valparaiso all day long, back and forth from rim to hub, going up one spoke and down the other. Farkas said he wanted to experience as much of Valparaiso as he could. Not to see; to *experience*. He was insatiable, prowling around everywhere, gobbling it all up, soaking it in. Farkas had never been to one of the satellite worlds before. It amazed him, he said, that there were forests and lakes here, broad fields of wheat and rice, fruit orchards, herds of goats and cattle. Apparently he had expected the place to be nothing more than a bunch of aluminium struts and grim concrete boxes with everybody living on food pills, or something. People from Earth never seemed to comprehend that the larger satellite worlds were comfortable places with blue skies, fleecy clouds, lovely gardens, handsome buildings of steel and brick and glass.

Farkas said, 'How do you go about tracing a fugitive, then?'

'There are always ways. Everybody knows somebody who knows something about someone. Information is bought here the same way compassion is.'

'From the Generalissimo?' Farkas said, startled.

'From his officials, sometimes. If done with great care. Care is important, because lives are at risk. There are also couriers who have information to sell. We all know a great deal that we are not supposed to know.'

'I suppose you know a great many fugitives by sight, yourself?'

'Some,' Juanito said. 'You see that man, sitting by the window?' He frowned. 'I don't know, can you see him? To me he looks around sixty, bald head, thick lips, no chin?'

'I see him, yes. He looks a little different to me.'

'I bet he does. He ran a swindle at one of the Luna domes, sold phony stock in an offshore monopoly fund that didn't exist, fifty million Capbloc dollars. He pays plenty to live here. This one here – you see? With the blonde woman? – an embezzler, that one, very good with computers, reamed a bank in Singapore for almost its entire capital. Him over there, he pretended to be Pope. Can you believe that? Everybody in Rio de Janeiro did.'

'Wait a minute,' Farkas said. 'How do I know you're not making all this up?'

'You don't,' Juanito said amiably. 'But I'm not.'

'So we just sit here like this and you expose the identities of three fugitives to me free of charge?'

'It wouldn't be free,' Juanito said, 'if they were people you were looking for.'

'What if they were? And my claiming to be looking for a Wu Fang-shui just a cover?'

'You aren't looking for any of them,' Juanito said.

'No,' said Farkas. 'I'm not.' He sipped his drink, something green and cloudy. 'How come these men haven't done a better job of concealing their identities?' he asked.

'They think they have,' said Juanito.

Getting leads was a slow business, and expensive. Juanito left Farkas to wander the spokes of Valparaiso on his own, and headed off to the usual sources of information: his father's friends, other couriers, and even the headquarters of the Unity Party, El Supremo's grass-roots organization, where it wasn't hard to find someone who knew something and had a price for it. Juanito was cautious. Middle-aged Chinese gentleman I'm trying to locate, he said. Why? Nobody asked. Could be any reason, anything from wanting to blow him away on contract to handing him a million-Capbloc-dollar lottery prize that he had won last year on New Yucatan. Nobody asked for reasons on Valparaiso.

There was a man named Federigo who had been with Juanito's father in the Costa Rica days who knew a woman who knew a man who had a freemartin neuter companion who had formerly belonged to someone high up in the Census Department. There were fees to pay at every step of the way, but it was Farkas's money, what the hell, and by the end of the week Juanito had access to the immigration data stored on golden megachips somewhere in the depths of the hub. The data down there wasn't going to provide anybody with Wu Fang-shui's phone number. But what it could tell Juanito, and did, eight hundred callaghanos later, was how many ethnic Chinese were living on Valparaiso and how long ago they had arrived.

'There are nineteen of them altogether,' he reported to Farkas. 'Eleven of them are women.'

'So? Changing sex is no big deal,' Farkas said.

'Agreed. The women are all under fifty, though. The oldest of the men is sixty-two. The longest that any of them has been on Valparaiso is nine years.'

'Would you say that rules them all out? Age can be altered just as easily as sex.'

'But date of arrival can't be, so far as I know. And you say that your Wu Fang-shui came here fifteen years back. Unless you're wrong about that, he can't be any of those Chinese. Your Wu Fang-shui, if he isn't dead by now, has signed up for some other racial mix, I'd say.'

'He isn't dead,' Farkas said.

'You sure of that?'

'He was still alive three months ago, and in touch with his family on Earth. He's got a brother in Tashkent.'

'Shit,' Juanito said. 'Ask the brother what name he's going under up here, then.'

'We did. We couldn't get it.'

'Ask him harder.'

'We asked him too hard,' said Farkas. 'Now the information isn't available any more. Not from him, anyway.'

Juanito checked out the nineteen Chinese, just to be certain. It didn't cost much and it didn't take much time, and there was always the chance that Dr Wu had cooked his immigration data somehow. But the quest led nowhere. Juanito found six of them all in one shot, playing some Chinese game in a social club in the town of Havana de Cuba on Spoke B, and they went right on laughing and pushing the little porcelain counters around while he stood there kibitzing. They didn't *act* like sanctuarios. They were all shorter than Juanito, too, which meant either that they weren't Dr Wu, who was tall for a Chinese, or that Dr Wu had been willing to have his legs chopped down by fifteen centimetres for the sake of a more efficient disguise. It was possible but it wasn't too likely.

The other thirteen were all much too young or too convincingly female or too this or too that. Juanito crossed them all off his list. From the outset he hadn't thought Wu would still be Chinese, anyway.

He kept on looking. One trail went cold, and then another,

and then another. By now he was starting to think Dr Wu must have heard that a man with no eyes was looking for him, and had gone even deeper underground, or off Valparaiso entirely. Juanito paid a friend at the hub spaceport to keep watch on departure manifests for him. Nothing came of that. Then someone reminded him that there was a colony of old-time hard-core sanctuary types living in and around the town of El Mirador on Spoke D, people who had a genuine aversion to being bothered. He went there. Because he was known to be the son of a murdered fugitive himself, nobody hassled him: he of all people wouldn't be likely to be running a trace, would he?

The visit yielded no directly useful result. He couldn't risk asking questions and nothing was showing on the surface. But he came away with the strong feeling that El Mirador was the answer.

'Take me there,' Farkas said.

'I can't do that. It's a low-profile town. Strangers aren't welcome. You'll stick out like a dinosaur.'

'Take me,' Farkas repeated.

'If Wu's there and he gets even a glimpse of you, he'll know right away that there's a contract out for him and he'll vanish so fast you won't believe it.'

'Take me to El Mirador,' said Farkas. 'It's my money, isn't it?'

'Right,' Juanito said. 'Let's go to El Mirador.'

El Mirador was midway between hub and rim on its spoke. There were great glass windows punched in its shield that provided a colossal view of all the rest of Valparaiso and the stars and the sun and the moon and the Earth and everything. A solar eclipse was going on when Juanito and Farkas arrived: the Earth was plastered right over the sun with nothing but one squidge of hot light showing down below like a diamond blazing on a golden ring. Purple shadows engulfed the town, deep and thick, a heavy velvet curtain falling over everything.

Juanito tried to describe what he saw. Farkas made an impatient brushing gesture.

'I know, I know. I feel it in my teeth.' They stood on a big peoplemover escalator leading down into the town plaza. 'The sun is long and thin right now, like the blade of an axe. The Earth has six sides, each one glowing a different colour.'

Juanito gaped at the eyeless man in amazement.

'Wu is here,' Farkas said. 'Down there, in the plaza. I feel his presence.'

'From five hundred metres away?'

'Come with me.'

'What do we do if he really is?'

'Are you armed?'

'I have a spike, yes.'

'Good. Tune it to shock, and don't use it at all if you can help it. I don't want you to hurt him in any way.'

'I understand. You want to kill him yourself, in your own sweet time.'

'Just be careful not to hurt him,' Farkas said. 'Come on.'

It was an old-fashioned-looking town, cobblestone plaza, little cafés around its perimeter and a fountain in the middle. About ten thousand people lived there and it seemed as if they were all out in the plaza sipping drinks and watching the eclipse. Juanito was grateful for the eclipse. No-one paid any attention to them as they came floating down the peoplemover and strode into the plaza. Hell of a thing, he thought. You walk into town with a man with no eyes walking right behind you and nobody even notices. But when the sunshine comes back on it may be different.

'There he is,' Farkas whispered. 'To the left, maybe fifty metres, sixty.'

Juanito peered through the purple gloom at the plazafront café beyond the next one. A dozen or so people were sitting in small groups at kerbside tables under iridescent fibreglass awnings, drinking, chatting, taking it easy. Just another casual afternoon in good old cosy El Mirador on sleepy old Valparaiso.

Farkas stood sideways to keep his strange face partly concealed. Out of the corner of his mouth he said, 'Wu is the one sitting by himself at the front table.'

'The only one sitting alone is a woman, maybe fifty, fifty-five years old, long reddish hair, big nose, dowdy clothes ten years out of fashion.'

'That's Wu.'

'How can you be so sure?'

'It's possible to retrofit your body to make it look entirely different on the outside. You can't change the non-visual information, the stuff I pick up by blindsight. What Dr Wu looked like to me, the last time I saw him, was a cubical block of black metal polished bright as a mirror, sitting on top of a pyramid-shaped copper-coloured pedestal. I was nine years old then, but I promised myself I wouldn't ever forget what he looked like, and I haven't. That's what the person sitting over there by herself looks like.'

Juanito stared. He still saw a plain-looking woman in a rumpled old-fashioned suit. They did wonders with retrofitting these days, he knew: they could make almost any sort of body grow on you, like clothing on a clothesrack, by fiddling with your DNA. But still Juanito had trouble thinking of that woman over there as a sinister Chinese gene-splicer in disguise, and he had even more trouble seeing her as a polished cube sitting on top of a coppery pyramid.

'What do you want to do now?' he asked.

'Let's go over and sit down alongside her. Keep that spike of yours ready. But I hope you don't use it.'

'If we put the arm on her and she's not Wu,' Juanito said, 'it's going to get me in a hell of a lot of trouble, particularly if she's paying El Supremo for sanctuary. Sanctuary people get very stuffy when their privacy is violated. You'll be expelled and I'll be fined a fortune and a half and I might wind up getting expelled too, and then what?'

'That's Dr Wu,' Farkas said. 'Watch him react when he sees me, and then you'll believe it.'

'We'll still be violating sanctuary. All he has to do is yell for the police.'

'We need to make it clear to him right away,' said Farkas, 'that that would be a foolish move. You follow?'

'But I don't hurt him,' Juanito said.

'No. Not in any fashion. You simply demonstrate a willingness to hurt him if it should become necessary. Let's go, now. You sit down first, ask politely if it's OK for you to share the table, make some comment about the eclipse. I'll come over maybe thirty seconds after you. All clear? Good. Go ahead, now.'

*   *   *

'You have to be insane,' the red-haired woman said. But she was sweating in an astonishing way and her fingers were knotting together like anguished snakes. 'I'm not any kind of doctor and my name isn't Wu or Fu or whatever you said, and you have exactly two seconds to get away from me.' She seemed unable to take her eyes from Farkas's smooth blank forehead. Farkas didn't move. After a moment she said in a different tone of voice, 'What kind of thing are you, anyway?'

She isn't Wu, Juanito decided.

The real Wu wouldn't have asked a question like that. Besides, this was definitely a woman. She was absolutely convincing around the jaws, along the hairline, the soft flesh behind her chin. Women were different from men in all those places. Something about her wrists. The way she sat. A lot of other things. There weren't any genetic surgeons good enough to do a retrofit this convincing. Juanito peered at her eyes, trying to see the place where the Chinese fold had been, but there wasn't a trace of it. Her eyes were blue-grey. All Chinese had brown eyes, didn't they?

Farkas said, leaning in close and hard, 'My name is Victor Farkas, doctor. I was born in Tashkent during the Breakup. My mother was the wife of the Hungarian consul, and you did a gene-splice job on the foetus she was carrying. That was your speciality, tectogenetic reconstruction. You don't remember that? You deleted my eyes and gave me blindsight instead, doctor.'

The woman looked down and away. Colour came to her cheeks. Something heavy seemed to be stirring within her. Juanito began to change his mind. Maybe there really were some gene surgeons who could do a retrofit this good, he thought.

'None of this is true,' she said. 'You're simply a lunatic. I can show you who I am. I have papers. You have no right to harass me like this.'

'I don't want to hurt you in any way, doctor.'

'I am not a doctor.'

'Could you be a doctor again? For a price?'

Juanito swung around, astounded, to look at Farkas.

'I will not listen to this,' the woman said. 'You will go away from me this instant or I summon the patrol.'

Farkas said, 'We have a project, Dr Wu. My engineering group, a division of a corporation whose name I'm sure you know. An experimental spacedrive, the first interstellar voyage, faster-than-light travel. We're three years away from a launch.'

The woman rose. 'This madness does not interest me.'

'The faster-than-light field distorts vision,' Farkas went on. He didn't appear to notice that she was standing and looked about ready to bolt. 'It disrupts vision entirely, in fact. Perception becomes totally abnormal. A crew with normal vision wouldn't be able to function in any way. But it turns out that someone with blindsight can adapt fairly easily to the peculiar changes that the field induces.'

'I have no interest in hearing about – '

'It's been tested, actually. With me as the subject. But I can't make the voyage alone. We have a crew of five and they've volunteered for tectogenetic retrofits to give them what I have. We don't know anyone else who has your experience in that area. We'd like you to come out of retirement, Dr Wu. We'll set up a complete lab for you on a nearby satellite world, whatever equipment you need. And pay you very well. And ensure your safety all the time you're gone from Valparaiso. What do you say?'

The red-haired woman was trembling and slowly backing away.

'No,' she said. 'It was such a long time ago. Whatever skills I had, I have forgotten, I have buried.'

So Farkas was right all along, Juanito thought.

'You can give yourself a refresher course. I don't think it's possible really to forget a gift like yours, do you?' Farkas said.

'No. Please. Let me be.'

Juanito was amazed at how cockeyed his whole handle on the situation had been from the start.

Farkas didn't seem at all angry with the gene surgeon. He hadn't come here for vengeance, Juanito realized. Just to cut a deal.

'Where's he going?' Farkas said suddenly. 'Don't let him get away, Juanito.'

The woman – Wu – was moving faster now, not quite running

but sidling away at a steady pace, back into the enclosed part of the café. Farkas gestured sharply and Juanito began to follow. The spike he was carrying could deliver a stun-level jolt at fifteen paces. But he couldn't just spike her down in this crowd, not if she had sanctuary protection, not in El Mirador of all places. There'd be fifty sanctuarios on top of him in a minute. They'd grab him and club him and sell his foreskin to the Generalissimo's men for two and a half callies.

The café was crowded and dark. Juanito caught sight of her somewhere near the back, near the restrooms. Go on, he thought. Go into the ladies' room. I'll follow you right in there. I don't give a damn about that.

But she went past the restrooms and ducked into an alcove near the kitchen instead. Two waiters laden with trays came by, scowling at Juanito to get out of the way. It took him a moment to pass around them, and by then he could no longer see the red-haired woman. He knew he was going to have big trouble with Farkas if he lost her in here. Farkas was going to have a fit. Farkas would try to stiff him on this week's pay, most likely. Two thousand callies down the drain, not even counting the extra charges.

Then a hand reached out of the shadows and seized his wrist with surprising ferocity. He was dragged a little way into a claustrophobic games room dense with crackling green haze coming from some bizarre machine on the far wall. The red-haired woman glared at him, wild-eyed. 'He wants to kill me, doesn't he? That's all bullshit about having me do retrofit operations, right?'

'I think he means it,' Juanito said.

'Nobody would volunteer to have his eyes replaced with blindsight.'

'How would I know? People do all sorts of crazy things. But if he wanted to kill you I think he'd have operated differently when we tracked you down.'

'He'll get me off Valparaiso and kill me somewhere else.'

'I don't know,' Juanito said. 'I was just doing a job.'

'How much did he pay you to do the trace?' Savagely. 'How much? I know you've got a spike in your pocket. Just leave it there and answer me. How much?'

'Three thousand callies a week,' Juanito muttered, padding things a little.

'I'll give you five to help me get rid of him.'

Juanito hesitated. Sell Farkas out? He didn't know if he could turn himself around that fast. Was it the professional thing to do, to take a higher bid?

'Eight,' he said, after a moment.

Why the hell not? He didn't owe Farkas any loyalty. This was a sanctuary world; the compassion of El Supremo entitled Wu to protection here. It was every citizen's duty. And eight thousand callies was a big bundle.

'Six five,' Wu said.

'Eight. Handshake right now. You have your glove?'

The woman who was Wu made a muttering sound and pulled out her flex terminal. 'Account 1133,' Juanito said, and they made the transfer of funds. 'How do you want to do this?' Juanito asked.

'There is a passageway into the outer shell just behind this café. You will catch sight of me slipping in there and the two of you will follow me. When we are all inside and he is coming toward me, you get behind him and take him down with your spike. And we leave him buried in there.' There was a frightening gleam in Wu's eyes. It was almost as if the cunning retrofit body was melting away and the real Wu beneath was emerging, moment by moment. 'You understand?' Wu said. A fierce, blazing look. 'I have bought you, boy. I expect you to stay bought when we are in the shell. Do you understand me? Do you? Good.'

It was like a huge crawlspace entirely surrounding the globe that was El Mirador. Around the periphery of the double shell was a deep layer of lunar slag held in place by centrifugal forces, the tailings left over after the extraction of the gases and minerals that the satellite world had needed in its construction. On top of that was a low open area for the use of maintenance workers, lit by a trickle of light from a faint line of incandescent bulbs; and overhead was the inner skin of El Mirador itself, shielded by the slagpile from any surprises that might come ricocheting in from the void. Juanito was able to move almost upright within the shell, but

Farkas, following along behind, had to bend double, scuttling like a crab.

'Can you see him yet?' Farkas asked.

'Somewhere up ahead, I think. It's pretty dark in here.'

'Is it?'

Juanito saw Wu edging sideways, moving slowly around behind Farkas now. In the dimness Wu was barely visible, the shadow of a shadow. He had scooped up two handfuls of tailings. Evidently he was going to fling them at Farkas to attract his attention, and when Farkas turned towards Wu it would be Juanito's moment to nail him with the spike.

Juanito stepped back to a position near Farkas's left elbow. He slipped his hand into his pocket and touched the cool sleek little weapon. The intensity stud was down at the lower end, shock level, and without taking the spike from his pocket he moved the setting up to lethal. Wu nodded. Juanito began to draw the spike.

Suddenly Farkas roared like a wild creature. Juanito grunted in shock, stupefied by that terrible sound. This is all going to go wrong, he realized. A moment later Farkas whirled and seized him around the waist and swung him as if he was a throwing-hammer, hurling him through the air and sending him crashing with tremendous impact into Wu's midsection. Wu crumpled, gagging and puking, with Juanito sprawled stunned on top of him. Then the lights went out – Farkas must have reached up and yanked the conduit loose – and then Juanito found himself lying with his face jammed down into the rough floor of tailings. Farkas was holding him down with a hand clamped around the back of his neck and a knee pressing hard against his spine. Wu lay alongside him, pinned the same way.

'Did you think I couldn't see him sneaking up on me?' Farkas asked. 'Or you, going for your spike? It's 360 degrees, the blindsight. Something that Dr Wu must have forgotten. All these years on the run, I guess you start to forget things.'

Jesus, Juanito thought. Couldn't even get the drop on a blind man from behind him. And now he's going to kill me. What a stupid way to die this is.

He imagined what Kluge might say about this, if he knew. Or Delilah. Nattathaniel. Decked by a blind man.

But he isn't blind. He isn't blind. He isn't blind at all.

Farkas said, 'How much did you sell me to him for, Juanito?'

The only sound Juanito could make was a muffled moan. His mouth was choked with sharp bits of slag.

'How much? Five thousand? Six?'

'It was eight,' said Wu quietly.

'At least I didn't go cheaply,' Farkas murmured. He reached into Juanito's pocket and withdrew the spike. 'Get up,' he said. 'Both of you. Stay close together. If either of you makes a funny move I'll kill you both. Remember that I can see you very clearly. I can also see the door through which we entered the shell. That starfish-looking thing over there, with streamers of purple light pulsing from it. We're going back into El Mirador now, and there won't be any surprises, will there? Will there?'

Juanito spat out a mouthful of slag. He didn't say anything.

'Dr Wu? The offer still stands,' Farkas continued. 'You come with me, you do the job we need you for. That isn't so bad, considering what I could do to you for what you did to me. But all I want from you is your skills, and that's the truth. You are going to need that refresher course, aren't you, though?'

Wu muttered something indistinct.

Farkas said, 'You can practise on this boy, if you like. Try retrofitting him for blindsight first, and if it works, you can do our crew people, all right? He won't mind. He's terribly curious about the way I see things, anyway. Aren't you, Juanito? Eh? Eh?' Farkas laughed. To Juanito he said, 'If everything works out the right way, maybe we'll let you go on the voyage with us, boy.' Juanito felt the cold nudge of the spike in his back. 'You'd like that, wouldn't you? The first trip to the stars? What do you say to that, Juanito?'

Juanito didn't answer. His tongue was still rough with slag. With Farkas prodding him from behind, he shambled slowly along next to Dr Wu towards the door that Farkas said looked like a starfish. It didn't look at all like a fish to him, or a star, or like a fish that looked like a star. It looked like a door to him, as far as he could tell by the feeble light of the distant bulbs. That was all it looked like, a door that looked like a door. Not a star. Not a fish. But there was no use thinking about it, or anything else, not now, not with Farkas nudging him between the shoulderblades with his own spike. He let his mind go blank and kept on walking.